Of Time and Magic

Of Time and Magic

By Laurie Graves

The Great Library Series

Maya and the Book of Everything (Book One)

Library Lost (Book Two)

Out of Time (Book Three)

Also by Laurie Graves

The Dog Angel

Tales from the Other Green Door (Limited Podcast
available at Hinterlandspress.com/podcast.)

THE ISLE OF SAMARAS
GROVE OF THE ANCIENT OAK
THE GREAT LIBRARY
KIP & ISIK'S HOUSE
SAMLAREN VILLAGE
WATERTOWN

Published by Hinterlands Press

Copyright©2022 by Laurie Graves All rights reserved.

ISBN: 987-0-9978453-8-9

No part of this publication may be reproduced, distributed, or transmitted in any form or by any means, including photocopying, recording, or other electronic or mechanical methods, without the prior written permission of the publisher, except in the case of brief quotations embodied in critical reviews and certain other noncommercial uses permitted by copyright law.

This is a work of fiction. Names, characters, businesses, places, events, and incidents are either the products of the author's imagination or used in a fictitious manner. Any resemblance to actual persons, living or dead, or actual events is purely coincidental.

Book design by Clif Graves
Hinterlandspress.com

Of Time and Magic
is dedicated to my wonderful blogging friends.

Because of your support and encouragement, my
Great Library novels have traveled all around the world.
No small feat for an indie series.

1: IN THE DARK

Jay and Lexie pulled Will through the portal. They stumbled into a room, dark except for the shimmering outline of the portal, which soon faded. Will crashed into something large and plastic. Tripping, he dragged Lexie and Jay down with him, and they yelled as they fell onto a hard floor. Jay and Lexie had let go of Will, and for a moment nobody said anything. The darkness was complete, and reaching out, Will found what he had tripped over. It had wheels and a metal handle and was hollow with tall sides.

Jay came up with the answer. "It's a bucket. A really big one."

"We're in a closet with cleaning supplies," Lexie said. "Maybe even a janitor's closet. There must be a light switch somewhere."

Will heard her stand up and knock something over. A long handle grazed his cheek, but Will hardly flinched. All he could feel was his own anger. And grief. Maya was alone with the ogres, and Jay and Lexie had hauled him through the portal, leaving Maya to fend for herself.

As Lexie found the switch, the light came on, and blinking, they looked around. Lexie was right. They were in a janitor's closet, small but big enough for the three of them and lots of cleaning supplies. Will had tripped over one of the buckets, and Lexie had knocked over a mop. Nobody said anything. Lexie kept her hand on the light switch, and Will could see she was crying. Will and Jay slowly stood, and Jay gave Will a searching look but then turned away.

Will could tell that both Lexie and Jay were in as much pain as he was, but he didn't care. His own emotions, hard and intense, nearly choked him, and there was a sour taste in his mouth that made him feel like gagging. Will desperately wanted to go back to Darkwood Forest, back to the cliff, to find and help Maya. She was alive. Will knew she was. He could feel it deep inside. However, the portal, which had been on the wall by the door, was gone. Without a doubt, Will knew it wouldn't come back for him, no matter how much he begged. Hanss had given the portal instructions, and it would listen to a cat from Elferterre, not a human boy from the Other Side.

Furious, Will kicked the wall again and again. There was a slight glimmer, as though the portal was rebuking him, but nothing more. Then Will turned on Lexie and Jay. "How could you leave Maya there all by herself? How could you bring me here when I didn't want to come? I'll never forgive either of you. Never. You're traitors. And cowards. You deserted her." Will's breath came out in ragged gasps, and he stopped, unable to go on.

Sobbing, Lexie crumpled to the floor, and Jay staggered back against some shelves. But with his chin up, Jay faced Will, who had pulled his arm back and had clenched his hand into a fist, ready to punch Jay in the face.

"Go ahead," Jay urged. "Hit me." Will's fist trembled but stayed where it was. "What are you waiting for, Will? Go ahead! Do it. Punch me as hard as you can. You're right. I deserve it. Hit me!"

Jay's sharp words broke through Will's grief, and finally he could see how devastated both Lexie and Jay were. He remembered what Maya had told him—once you could really see how other people felt, it was harder to be angry with them. That's how she had been able to forgive Sir John and Andy, even though their betrayal had been terrible.

Will's fist unclenched, and his arm slowly came down to his side. Jay's breathing was as ragged as Will's, and his dark eyes glittered wildly. "We promised her we would go on without her if we had to," Jay managed to say, his voice tight and intense. "I did. Lexie did. And you did."

Will swallowed. "You're right." His voice sounded far away, and he felt lightheaded. Will pitched forward, and Jay caught him.

"But I didn't mean it," Will whispered. "I could never leave her by herself."

Jay hugged him. "I know."

Will bowed his head in sorrow but did not pull away.

Lexie had stopped crying. Standing slowly, she reached into her pocket, pulling out the velvet pouch with the key and the lock they had stolen from Galli's workshop in Elferterre.

"Yeah." Jay let go of Will. "Now we have to see where we are and then get the pouch to Pawel."

"Could we be in New York City?" Will asked. A plan was starting to form, and New York City was exactly where he wanted to be.

The three stood quietly and listened. Outside the door, they could hear the hubbub of people moving around and talking.

"Maybe," Lexie said.

"Only one way to find out," Jay replied. "Let's open the door and see."

"Right." Lexie's voice was brisk. "Ready?"

"Ready," Will and Jay answered together.

Lexie cautiously cracked the door open, and the three peeked out into a hall with people going back and forth. No one glanced in their direction, but the door wasn't open enough for anyone to notice them.

"Okay," Lexie said. "We can't all pop out at the same time. It would be weird if the three of us came out together."

Jay smiled a little. "What would people think?"

"You know what they'd think," Lexie shot back, and Will was relieved to hear that some of the spunk had returned to her voice.

Will smiled, too. "Lexie's right. When it looks as though nobody's going by, Lexie can go out. And then Jay. And then me."

This took a while, but there were breaks in the people going back and forth, and finally all three were out in a hallway that had openings to two restrooms as well as the door to the janitor's closet. The teenagers looked at each other.

Lexie said, "I need to go."

"Me, too," Jay said.

Will didn't say anything as he headed toward the men's room.

When they were done, the teenagers met back in the hallway. They had all splashed water on their faces and had patted down their hair as best they could. When Will had looked in the mirror, he saw that his brown hair was sticking up straight in places, and Jay's thick black hair was fluffed in a tangle around his head. Without combs or brushes, there was a limit to what they could do, but at least they didn't look quite as wild as they had when they had come out of the closet. Lexie's blonde hair was pulled back into a pony tail, and she looked the best of the three of them.

Will thought, *As usual.*

Lexie grinned then frowned as she looked down at her clothes and then at Will's and Jay's. "We look like freaks all dressed the same in these tunics, vests, and pants."

"Like escapees from a fantasy game," Jay said with some of his old puckishness.

Will stared at Jay and Lexie. "In a way that's just what we're in. A game between Time and Magic and Chaos. Right now we can't help the way we look. But let's find out where we are and what time we're in."

The hall led to a food court that sold pizzas and burgers and soft pretzels. When the teenagers looked out large glass doors, they saw a big parking lot not far from a busy highway.

"We're in a travel plaza," Jay said.

Lexie frowned. "But where?"

"I don't know," Jay answered. "But it sure doesn't look like New York."

"I bet we're in Maine," Will said, pointing to a big sign behind them that advertised live Maine lobsters.

"What is it about Maine?" Lexie asked plaintively. "Why would the portal take us here?"

"But more important, what year are we in?" Turning, Will saw a small convenience store on one side of the food court. "Maybe we can find out in there."

The store was busy, and while a few people glanced at them, nobody said anything. Finding a local newspaper, the teenagers stood still for a while, gazing at the date.

Lexie cleared her throat. "Let's go find a place to sit in the food court."

"Good idea," Jay said.

Will didn't say anything. Taking a deep breath as he followed Jay and Lexie to the food court, Will's thoughts scrabbled frantically as he tried to readjust his plans.

Finding an empty table, they all sat down and looked at each other.

Lexie drummed her fingers on the table. "We knew this would happen. We were warned. But we didn't have a choice. We had to go through the portal."

"I was hoping we'd at least be in the right place," Will replied.

"Me, too." Jay leaned forward, and Will and Lexie followed his example. "But here we are. Ten years in the future. In Maine. How in the hell are we supposed to get to New York City from here?"

Sitting up straight, Will looked around. The food court was loud and busy, and their table was off to one side. Nobody would be able to hear what they said. Will leaned back toward Jay and Lexie. "And is Pawel still waiting for us? Or did he send somebody else to get another key somewhere else? Did that person get it? Did Pawel and his family go back to Elferterre? And what about Alani and Alexander? Are they still in Brooklyn?"

"Ten years is a long time to wait for us," Jay said. Then he hesitated before asking, "And what about our parents?"

They stared at each other in shocked silence. "They must think we're dead," Lexie replied in a low voice.

Again there was silence as they thought about the implications of this.

Will finally said, "All right. Pawel might be gone, and so might Alani and Alexander. And we can't go back to our parents after being missing for ten years. Especially when we look exactly the way we did when we left."

"What do we do?" Jay asked, and there was a note of panic in his voice.

Will understood. He felt panicked, too, but he pushed it down, the way he had pushed down his loneliness and grief when his mother had died. In the janitor's closet, he'd had the glimmer of a plan, and he was resolved to stick with the plan, even though too much time might have passed. *No*, Will thought firmly. *No. It's not too late.* As if in response, a flash came to Will of Pawel and his family—they were still at The Other Green Door, and they were waiting for the key to unlock their chains.

As the flash faded, Will sighed in relief. "Pawel isn't gone."

"How do you know?" Lexie asked.

"It just came to me," Will told her. "In my mind, I saw Pawel and his family, and right now they are in Brooklyn at The Other Green Door."

Lexie frowned. "What if you're wrong?"

But it was Jay who replied, "We've had our eyes peeled, and Will's the best of the three of us. Stuff like that used to happen to Maya all the time. Remember?"

"I sure do," Lexie said in both a grudging and admiring way. "At times I thought Maya was crazy, but she was always right, wasn't she?"

"Yeah." Will thought of the pouch in Lexie's pocket. "Maya knew something might happen to her in Darkwood Forest." His voice was quiet, and Jay and Lexie had to lean even closer to hear what he said. "The night before we left Elferterre, when we were at Ehren and Tagen's cottage, Maya started crying. I tried to find out what was wrong, but she wouldn't tell me. Then Maya went on about how she wasn't the only one."

Jay's voice was even lower than Will's. "I knew Maya was keeping something from us."

"Yeah," Lexie said. Then licking her lips, she glanced around. "You two thirsty?"

Will felt as though his throat had never been drier. "Yeah, really thirsty."

"Same," Jay added.

"I'll be right back," Lexie told them.

Will and Jay watched as Lexie went to the burger place and came back carrying three large cups.

Lexie set them on the table. "Don't get too excited. It's only water."

Jay reached for a cup. "Water's great."

Will took another cup. "Sure is."

Lexie grabbed the last cup. "Cheers."

After they had gulped down the water, Lexie asked, "You boys hungry?"

"Yeah," Jay answered. "Amazingly, I am."

"Me, too." Will's tone was sheepish. With Maya being trapped in Elferterre, the last thing he should be thinking about was food, but his traitor stomach rumbled in disagreement.

Lexie smiled. From her pocket, she took out three Snickers candy bars.

"Lexie!" Jay remonstrated, but he couldn't stop himself from grinning as he took a candy bar.

Will stared sternly at Lexie. "You shouldn't have stolen those."

But Lexie waved her hand at him. "Don't give me one of your looks. Here we are, trying to save Earth and the whole freaking universe. I think that's worth a few candy bars, don't you?"

Will secretly agreed with her, but he shook his head. There was something about Lexie's personality that always grated on his nerves. Will could never give in to Lexie the way he could with Maya, who managed to be both strong-minded and endearing at the same time. Will realized it was Maya's generous nature, which made her willing to give almost anyone a second chance. When Will thought of whom Maya had forgiven, he felt humbled, knowing he could never forgive as easily.

Lexie, on the other hand, was brash and arrogant, and even her stunning good looks could not make up for these flaws. At the end of their junior year, he had known it was a mistake to go off with her at the party. But Will had had too much to drink and had let his guard down. And Lexie was so very beautiful. Shaking his head, Will thought about how this had all happened only two short months ago. Instead, it seemed like years.

Lexie's eyes were narrow as she considered Will. "Okay, Mr. Stuffy Pants, if you don't want the candy bar, then Jay and I will split it."

Grabbing the candy bar, Jay shoved it toward Will. "For God's sake, Will, take it. Who knows when we'll get something else to eat?"

Will took the candy bar and tried not to gulp it down.

"Lexie, when did you swipe those candy bars?" Jay asked. "We never even saw you do it."

Lexie answered, "That's the point, isn't it?"

Will frowned. "How did you learn to steal without anyone catching you?"

"I've lived a life of crime," Lexie replied. "From the time I was little, I had to steal to survive."

Even Will had to laugh. Grinning, Lexie winked at him, and the tension between them went away.

"Lexie," Jay said in admiration, "you're something else."

Lexie turned to Jay. "I told you I had many talents." Then she relented and explained, "About a year ago, my brother Charlie was obsessed with magic tricks. He practiced a lot. I've got to admit—the kid is really good. Anyway, he always bugged me to help him practice. Sometimes I did, and I learned right along with him. But I never thought I'd be stealing candy bars with magic tricks I learned from Charlie."

Jay looked down at the table. "We've all done a lot of things we'd never thought we'd do."

"Like desert Maya." Will winced as he pictured her surrounded by ogres who wanted to eat her.

Biting her lip, Lexie put her hand over her eyes, and Jay sighed deeply.

Again, Will could feel Lexie's and Jay's deep sorrow. "I know." He took Lexie's free hand and then one of Jay's. "We'll fix this. I have a plan."

But before Will could say anything else, a voice asked, "Are you kids all right?"

Startled, they looked up. Standing by their table was a tall middle-aged woman with white shoulder-length hair and bright red lipstick.

"We've been better," Jay answered.

Will wished Jay hadn't even said that much. He didn't trust this woman.

Then the woman smiled, and even though he knew he shouldn't, Will felt pulled in by her charm. He could tell Jay felt the same way, and that he, too, was trying to resist the woman's bright charisma.

"My name's Lillian Rourke," the woman said. "Need a ride someplace south? If so, maybe I can help you. I'm heading to New York City."

Lexie, on the other hand, looked skeptical. Her fingers tapped the table, but she didn't say anything.

2: LILLIAN AND JEFF

Sitting in the back row of Lillian's green SUV, Will stared out the side window as they headed toward the big bridge that led from Maine to New Hampshire. Even though Lillian had been dazzlingly nice and had bought them veggie burgers, fries, and drinks, Will knew that accepting her offer of a ride was a bad idea, and no matter how hard he tried to ignore the feeling, it wouldn't go away. Jay and Lexie sat in front of him, and by the way their shoulders were twitching, Will could tell they were having similar thoughts. None of them wanted to be in this SUV with Lillian.

But what choice did they have? How else were they supposed to get to New York City, to Pawel and The Other Green Door? They had no money and no phones. Will supposed they could have gone around the food court, asking various people for a ride south. He shook his head as he pictured how weird the three of them looked in their tunics, vests, and trousers. Although Lexie was with them, Will was certain that their chance of success would have been small. The way they were dressed trumped even Lexie's beauty and powers of persuasion.

There was a man in the passenger seat next to Lillian. His hair was as white as hers, and at first Will had wondered if they were related. When they had climbed into the SUV, the man had hardly moved, only glancing at them briefly before slumping back into the seat. But when Lillian introduced the man, it was clear that there was no family connection between the two.

9

"This is Jeff Perry," Lillian had said brightly as she started the SUV. "And Jeff, this is Will, Jay, and Lexie. They need a ride to New York City, which is exactly where we happen to be going."

"Quite a coincidence," Jeff had muttered.

"Indeed," Lillian had replied, but this time there was a slight edge to her voice.

Staring at the two in front, Will wondered if Nemesis had had anything to do with Lillian coming over to their table.

As they crossed the bridge into New Hampshire, Jeff sadly lifted his head. "Farewell, sweet Maine."

"Jeff, are you from Maine?" Lexie asked.

Sitting up a little straighter, Jeff peered back at her. "I am. From Waterville. Ever heard of it?"

"Isn't that where the president is from?" Lexie asked, and Will marveled at her quick thinking. Of course Andy was president now. This was Maya's present.

"He sure is," Jeff replied, frowning. "President Drew Murphy. When he was young, he used to come to my library. I've been told he was quite a reader."

Jay leaned forward. "Your library?"

"I'm a librarian at the Waterville Public Library. Or at least I was."

"But now you're starting a new life in New York City, aren't you?" Lillian asked. "Time to get out of poky Waterville, Maine, and go to the big city. You've wanted to leave for quite a while. Admit it."

"I have," Jeff answered. "But now that I'm leaving..." His voice trailed off, and he blinked rapidly as though he was trying to hold back tears. Jeff exchanged looks with Lillian, quickly turned away, and slouched into his seat.

"Well," Lillian said, smiling a little, "nothing ever goes exactly the way we plan, does it?"

"No, it doesn't," Jeff replied in a faint voice.

"Take a nap," Lillian suggested. "Your system hasn't quite recovered." She looked into the rearview mirror, fixing Lexie, Jay, and Will with her formidable gaze. "Jeff had quite the going-away party. It ended with a real bang, didn't it?" Jeff flinched but didn't say anything as Lillian turned her attention back to the road. Leaning his head against the seat, Jeff closed his eyes.

Will thought, *Too much to drink?* But this was no ordinary hangover. Will had caught fear and sorrow coming from Jeff.

For the first time since leaving Elferterre, Will tried to communicate directly with his thoughts to Jay and Lexie: *Hey, guys. This isn't good. We've got to get away from Lillian.*

Although Lexie and Jay looked over their shoulders at Will, there were no responding thoughts, and Will realized that on Earth it wasn't as easy to converse with thoughts as it had been in Elferterre. Because they had had their eyes peeled and had become close friends, Jay and Lexie sensed that Will wanted to tell them something, but they didn't know what. Shrugging, Will decided it was Magic that had let them communicate with their thoughts with such ease in Elferterre. But on Earth, with Time in charge, the rules were different.

Lillian's sharp gaze flickered in the rearview mirror as she considered them. "Are you three from New York City?"

"We are," Lexie answered, meeting Lillian's gaze in the mirror. "And we all go to the same school."

It was Lillian who looked away first. She was driving and had to concentrate on the traffic and the road. But Will got the feeling that if Lillian hadn't been driving, there would have been a staring contest, and he wondered who would have turned away first: Lillian or Lexie? It probably would have been Lexie. Even so, Will had to admit that at times Lexie's bold confidence was an asset. He had seen this in Elferterre, and he was seeing it now.

Lillian sat stiffly as she drove, and Will thought, *No adult likes to cave to a teenager.* Then another thought, unbidden, came to him: *Lillian's an elf.*

An elf? Really? In Maine? Will shook his head, trying to clear it of this ridiculous thought, but the idea wouldn't go away, and it continued to nag at him. Well, why not in Maine? After all, weirdly enough, there was an Elferterre portal in the Maine travel plaza in the janitor's closet. And hadn't Khirra, Pawel's wife, explained that many elves crossed over from Elferterre to Earth? She had said it was easier for low-born but ambitious elves to get ahead on Earth than it was in Elferterre. Perhaps even more important, Lillian radiated a certain essence. Will had felt it as soon as he met her, and at first he hadn't been able to place what it was. But Will now understood that essence was magic, something he had felt all the time in Elferterre.

11

Was Jeff Perry an elf, too, even though he and Lillian were not related? No, Will decided, Jeff Perry wasn't an elf. He didn't radiate a magical essence, the way Lillian did. Instead, Jeff was Lillian's prisoner. But why? Will remembered something else Khirra had told them—that the head of APO, the Association for the Preservation of Order, was an elf. Will couldn't remember the elf's name, but it didn't really matter. Was Lillian connected with APO? Will was certain she was, and he knew something else: Lillian and Jeff Perry were linked to Chet and to Maya and to Earth's Book of Everything.

Thinking about all this, Will sat still. Then he felt that Lillian's attention had passed from Lexie to him. In the rearview mirror, Lillian was staring at him, and Will sensed that if Lillian hadn't been driving, she would have been probing and pushing as she tried to discover what these three teenagers who were dressed in clothes from Elferterre were doing at a travel plaza in Maine. Then Will realized this would all come later, probably at APO's headquarters in Brooklyn, and it wouldn't be pleasant.

Despite his inner turmoil, Will smiled coolly at Lillian's reflection, and her eyes narrowed before she turned her focus back to the road. From the time he was little, Will had been able to look calm on the outside no matter how he felt on the inside. He had gotten this ability from his father, and it was one of the many reasons why they didn't get along. Neither Will nor his father was willing to give in and express what they were really feeling. Because of this, there was an uncomfortable silence when Will and his father were together as they worked hard to keep their true emotions hidden from each other. Will thought about Maya, who was as fearless and openhearted about revealing her emotions as she was about everything else. Yet another reason why he was drawn to her.

"Where are you from?" Jay asked Lillian.

"I'm from all over," came the breezy reply. "But I live in New York City right now. Same as you three."

There was something in Lillian's tone that suggested she didn't want to discuss where she was from, and Jay didn't push it. He glanced back at Will, who nodded slightly.

Lillian asked, "How did you three wind up stranded in Maine?"

Again, with her quick thinking, Lexie came to the rescue. "The three of us got into a little trouble at school." Lexie shrugged. "Nothing much. Just some vandalism. The principal agreed not to suspend us if our parents would send us to this Outward Bound kind of camp in Maine this summer. Where they drop you off in the wilderness to survive all by yourself for days and days." She rolled her eyes. "Yeah. Right. Not us. We got out of camp as fast as we could and hitchhiked to the travel plaza."

The three teenagers kept their minds and their faces completely neutral, even Jay, who was normally expressive.

"Uh-huh." Lillian's tone indicated she didn't believe a word of Lexie's story. "Your clothes are a little unusual for an Outward Bound kind of summer camp."

Lexie looked down at her vest, tunic, and trousers. "This is what they make us wear when we aren't trekking to some God-awful place in the wilderness. It's a kind of uniform to remind us campers we are all in the same boat. Prisoners, under the command of those who are in charge." Lexie's expression was steely as she regarded Lillian. "And those who were in charge never let us forget for one minute that we were beneath them. No matter what we did, it's not right how they treated us. That's another reason why we left."

Lillian's mouth was a straight line as she drove down the turnpike, and Will felt that in some strange way, Lexie had scored a point over Lillian. Then Will thought about how in school, Lexie had been the leader of a large group of girls, and she always knew what to say to keep them in line. Even before having her eyes peeled, Lexie had had a sense of what a person's weakness was and how to exploit it. Will wondered if this quality helped make her more resistant to Lillian's charisma.

When they stopped in Connecticut for gas, Lillian had regained her composure. Looking back at them, Lillian was at her brightest. Will began to feel a little foolish for thinking she might be part of APO even as a part of him understood that much of Lillian's power was in her gaze and smile.

"You kids hungry?" Lillian asked as she drove into the parking lot.

"Yeah," Will and Jay said together, and Lexie shrugged.

"Let's grab a snack."

"All right," Jay replied.

Lillian considered Jeff, who still seemed to be sleeping. "We'll let him rest. But let's bring the food back to the car. We can wake him up then. Come with me and pick out what you want."

However, when they came back to the SUV, Jeff was gone.

"Where could he be?" Lillian asked in surprise.

The teenagers shook their heads. They, too, were surprised. To them it seemed that Jeff barely had enough energy to hold his head up, much less get out of the SUV.

Will and Jay had the bags of food, and Lillian said, "Get in. I'll go look for Jeff. He must have gone to the restroom. But he's so shaky that something might have happened."

Nodding, the teenagers climbed into the SUV as Lillian hurried back to the food court. But Lexie stepped on something as she sat down, and she picked up a note wrapped around a wad of cash.

Lexie read the note: "Run! Now, while you can."

For a moment, Lexie, Jay, and Will stared at each other, then they scrambled into action as Will said, "Right. Let's go to where the trucks are parked. Even though we look weird, maybe we can find a ride to New York. We should have done this in Maine."

Lexie stuffed the money and note into one of her pockets. Leaving the food behind, the teenagers raced to the far side of the parking lot where there was a long line of trucks. The engines were all idling, but most of the drivers were gone, taking a break in the food court. But there were a few drivers who were in their cabs, and as the teenagers raced by they got a flash from each driver.

No, no, no. Then when they were nearly at the end of the line: him.

They stopped by a truck where a man with short sandy blond hair was getting ready to go back on the highway. Glancing down at their upturned faces, he blinked in surprise at them.

He put down the window. "You kids all right?" They shook their heads, and he didn't ask questions. "Get in."

Running to the other side, they climbed into the truck. There was only one seat beside the driver, but he motioned behind him. "You can ride back there. Nobody will see you."

"Wow!" Lexie said as they slid between the two seats and made their way into a narrow little room that had everything a person would need to be comfortable on the road: a couch, a microwave, a television, a small refrigerator.

"Nice!" Jay said.

"Sure is," Will agreed.

The driver grinned. "My home away from home. There are drinks in the refrig. Help yourself. There's some food, too. Take what you want."

Will, Jay, and Lexie looked at each other. Here was someone else who had a generous nature, who was willing to help, and, even more important, who could see. Not as much as Jay and Will, but a little more than Lexie. Will knew it the moment he had considered this driver, and he was beginning to understand how seeing was on a continuum, with a few people being able to see a lot and most others not so much. Now that Will's eyes were peeled, it was obvious to him who could see and who could be trusted. It just came to him with a startling clarity.

Good, Will said to himself, realizing what an asset it was to be able to tell with a quick glance how people were inside, despite the image they wanted to project.

As the truck driver drove onto the highway, Jay took out pickles, cheese, mayonnaise, and soda from the small refrigerator while Lexie found bread, plates, and silverware. Soon there were sandwiches. As they ate and drank, the three teenagers sat side by side on the couch.

Knowing the truck driver couldn't hear them over the noise of the road, Will said, "Lillian's an elf. I'm sure of it."

Jay swallowed a bite of sandwich. "I thought so, too. Lillian's got quite the stare, doesn't she? If she told me to jump off a cliff, I'd have a hard time not doing it."

"Same," Will agreed.

"Not me," Lexie said. "Lillian didn't impress me at all, even if she is an elf."

Jay grinned. "Another one of your talents. You're impervious to elf magic."

Lexie swatted his arm. "Not all elf magic. Only the kind Lillian has."

Will stared steadily at Lexie. "It's a good talent to have."

"What?" Lexie asked in mock surprise. "A compliment from you?"

Smiling a little, Will shrugged at her. "A compliment from me."

Lexie shook her head. "You hardly ever said anything nice like that even when we were going out. You're a cool customer, aren't you?"

"Yeah," Will said, and a part of him wished that he wasn't such a cool customer, that he could be more like Maya, Jay, and even Lexie, who never hesitated to express how she felt.

Jay put his hand on Will's shoulder. "We are who we are, young Skywalker."

Will laughed. "Does this mean you're Yoda?"

"God, I hope I'm better looking than Yoda."

Lexie regarded Jay affectionately. "You are."

Blushing a little, Jay changed the subject. "Do you think Lillian's with APO?"

"I do," Will answered.

Lexie asked, "What about Jeff Perry?"

"Yeah, him, too, but he's not an elf," Will replied. "But both Lillian and Jeff are connected to Chet and to Earth's Book of Everything."

"And APO's headquarters are not far from The Other Green Door," Jay said.

"They are?" Lexie asked in surprise.

Jay nodded. "On the day we left Brooklyn to go to Elferterre, Thirret, Pawel's son, took us to the subway where the portal was. On the way, Maya saw Chet, but he didn't recognize her. And Thirret told us APO's headquarters were close by, underneath a hardware store."

"Well, that's a surprise," Lexie said. "Who would think an evil organization would be underneath a hardware store?"

Having finished his sandwich and drink, Jay stretched his legs. "That's the point, isn't it? They don't want to be noticed. It would be a little too obvious if their headquarters were in Trump Tower."

Lexie smirked. "Sure would."

Will stood. "I'm going to talk to the driver. He deserves to know a little bit about us. I'll be as honest as I can without telling everything."

"Good idea," Lexie said.

"If you need any help..." Jay added.

Will smiled at his friend. "I'll be fine. But thanks."

Jay smiled back. "Of course you will. When did you ever need help?"

Will didn't say anything, but as he went to the front of the truck, he thought, *More than you'll ever know.*

However, this part of him was hidden so deep that even Jay, his best friend, couldn't see it. There was only one person who had caught a glimpse of his extreme loneliness, and that was Maya. But then again, she could see better than any of them.

3: TO THE OTHER GREEN DOOR

Not wanting to be seen, Will crouched beside the truck driver. "Thanks for letting us ride with you."

The truck driver nodded. "My name is Cal Thompson."

"I'm Will Henley, and back there are Lexie Norton and Jay Valdez."

"Can you tell me what's going on?"

"Some, but not all."

"Go ahead."

"We were stranded in Maine, and we got a ride with a woman named Lillian Rourke. We didn't trust her and knew we shouldn't have gone with her, but we didn't think we had a choice. Not just anyone would give us a ride. We look kind of weird in these clothes."

"You sure do. Running away?" Cal asked with a frown.

"Not really," Will said. "More like running to someplace." He studied Cal and felt the man's decency, which was as solid as Ehren's and Tagen's had been. "We're on a mission. I can't explain any more than that. But we need to get to New York City."

"Kind of young to be on a mission, aren't you?" Cal stared straight ahead, not turning his head. Nevertheless, as Will looked at the truck driver's profile, he could see Cal wasn't sure whether or not he should believe Will's story.

"You're right," Will agreed. "We are young to be on a mission. But I'm telling the truth. Really."

Please trust me, Will thought as Cal glanced at him.

"Okay." Cal turned back to the road. "Is Lillian connected with your mission?"

"She is," Will said.

"What's Lillian driving?"

"A green SUV with New York license plates."

"Like the one passing us now? There's a white-haired man on the passenger's side."

"Jeff Perry." Will crouched lower even though he knew he was probably well out of sight.

"I'm guessing Jeff Perry is with Lillian."

"Yeah. Jeff Perry helped us escape, but Lillian is smart. And dangerous," Will said. "Sorry to get you involved in all this."

Cal shrugged. "Did you have a choice?"

"No, not really. If we hadn't gotten a ride, Lilian would have caught us. And she would have stopped us from completing our mission."

"Okay, then. Why did you pick me?"

"You seemed like someone we could trust."

Cal laughed shortly. "I've been told that before, and sometimes I get involved in things I shouldn't."

"Do you feel that way right now?"

"No," Cal answered. "I had the strongest feeling I should help you three. That if I didn't, it wouldn't be good."

"It wouldn't be good at all," Will said. "We have to bring something to someone. It's very important that he get it."

"Not drugs, I hope."

"No, not drugs."

"Didn't think so. Still, I'm glad to hear you say it. I would have known if you were lying. Somehow, I can always tell whether or not someone's telling the truth. But you already knew that, didn't you?"

"I did."

"You look wiped. Why don't you go back there and take a nap with your friends? I'll wake you up when we get near New York City."

Until Cal had suggested a nap, Will hadn't realized how exhausted he was, and he drooped with fatigue. "Yeah. And thanks again, Cal. We really do appreciate this."

Smiling, Cal motioned with his head toward the back. "Go get some sleep."

Will stumbled to the couch, where Jay and Lexie were already sleeping. They were cuddled together, and Lexie's head was on Jay's shoulder. Smiling, Will sat beside them, leaned back, closed his eyes, and fell asleep.

When Will woke up, the truck had stopped. Jay and Lexie were also stirring, and they all looked toward Cal. Standing and stretching, Will went to the front.

"Traffic," Cal said. "An accident. We've been here for quite a while. We're still in Connecticut."

"Any sign of the green SUV?" Will asked.

"Nope, haven't seen it."

"Have we gone by Stamford?"

"We have not."

"If you drop us off somewhere near the train station, we could ride into the city."

"Sounds good," Cal replied. "Do you have money? If not, I can give you some."

"We do, but thanks."

Slowly, the traffic started moving, and Cal said, "I'll drop you off at the train station. It shouldn't be long now."

A half hour later, the truck pulled into the train station, and one by one, the teenagers filed past Cal as they left.

Will, in the lead, inclined his head toward the truck driver. "We can never thank you enough. We wouldn't have gotten this far without you."

"My pleasure," Cal said, smiling a little.

Jay clapped Cal on the shoulder. "Yeah, many thanks! You're the best."

Lexie didn't say anything. Instead, she kissed Cal on the cheek before following Jay.

"You kids be careful," Cal called as Jay shut the door.

"We will," they called back.

The teenagers had enough money to buy tickets. Not much was left over, but Will figured there was enough for subway tickets to Brooklyn, to The Other Green Door. Because it was midday, there weren't many passengers on the train, and Will, Lexie, and Jay were able to find three empty seats side by side. They didn't have to wait long for the train to leave, and as it slowly began to move, Lexie said, "Guess who found us."

Lexie was staring out the window, and Will and Jay looked, too. There was Lillian standing on the platform. Her face was expressionless, but Will could feel the elf's anger come at them in a wave.

"Wow," Jay said, shivering a little.

"No kidding," Will replied.

Lexie, on the other hand, smiled and blew Lillian a kiss. "So long, sucker."

Clenching her fists, the elf glared at them.

"Lexie!" Will and Jay said together as the train pulled out of the station, leaving the enraged Lillian behind.

"Oh, relax," Lexie said. "On Earth, Lillian's magic isn't strong enough to stop a train."

"How can you be so sure?" Jay asked.

"I can just tell. Can't you?"

As Jay shrugged, Will stared out the window at the receding station. "Yes, Lexie's right."

Lexie settled comfortably back into her seat. "We'll be at The Other Green Door way before Lillian and Jeff even reach the outskirts of the city. And I doubt she would dare go up against Pawel."

As it turned out, Lexie was right. They went from Manhattan to Brooklyn without catching a glimpse of Lillian trailing them.

"Just because we can't see her doesn't mean she isn't there," Jay said, glancing over his shoulder as they left the subway station and headed to The Other Green Door.

Will shook his head. "No, she's not near us. I would be able to tell. And so would the two of you."

Lexie twined her arm through Jay's. "We skunked her."

"Yeah, but for how long?"

"Long enough. Stop worrying."

Jay and Lexie grinned at each other, and Will had the strange feeling of being the odd one out instead of being at the center, the way he had been when he and Lexie were together. Then Will's thoughts turned to Maya, and he sighed. When would they be together again?

Long, low, green, and with a kind of shimmer, The Other Green Door looked exactly the same as it did when they had left it ten years ago. But a watchfulness hovered over the café as though it were waiting for them.

I suppose in a way it is, Will thought, following Jay and Lexie into The Other Green Door. Will had no doubt that magic from the elves and the relics had seeped into the café, and while it would never be as animated on Earth as it would have been in Elferterre, it had a presence most buildings didn't have in New York City. Will had felt it the first time he had gone to The Other Green Door, and even though he hadn't yet had his eyes peeled, Will had been drawn to the place.

When Jay, Lexie, and Will walked into the café, it seemed as though Time paused. Thirret and two elven servers froze in midaction, Thirret with a mug in his hand and the other two with plates of steaming food. The patrons, sensing something big had happened, stopped talking and turned to gape at the three teenagers.

Jay broke the spell. "Hey, Thirret! We're back."

The mug slipped from Thirret's hand. Crashing to the floor, it exploded into pieces as it splattered hot chamomile tea everywhere.

"Sorry, sorry, sorry!" Thirret exclaimed as the other servers carefully put their plates down on the tables in front of the customers and rushed to help him. Khirra hurried out from the kitchen, gave each of the teenagers a quick hug, and hustled Will, Jay, and Lexie out of the dining area. They passed Pawel, who was standing perfectly still with a spatula in one hand while black bean burgers began to smoke on the grill. He stared at the teenagers.

"Do you have it?" he finally asked, even though Will suspected the elf knew the answer.

"Yes," they answered together.

Closing his eyes, Pawel put the spatula down on the counter by the grill.

"Uncle Pawel!" his niece Jace called. "The bean burgers are burning."

Pawel took a deep breath. "Let them, Jace. We have more burgers. And this afternoon, everyone who is here gets a free meal." His face was lit up by an intense joy, which illuminated the kitchen and filled every corner. Some of the joy flowed into the dining room. Soon the whole building was aglow with it, giving diners the feeling that they had never eaten such good food and that this café was an underappreciated gem in a part of Brooklyn that wasn't considered as hip as other parts were.

Khirra brought Will, Jay, and Lexie to the break room. With its moss-colored carpeting, the room was as green as ever, and potted trees lined one of the walls.

21

Khirra motioned to the chairs grouped around the wooden table. "Sit down, sit down! May I bring you some chamomile tea? Some sweet potato fries? Or anything else you might want?"

"Sure," Will and Jay said together as Lexie rolled her eyes.

"Do you still make that walnut pâté?" Jay asked.

Khirra smiled. "We do. I'll include plenty of fresh bread to go along with it."

Along with the pâté, Khirra brought hummus, grapes, flatbread, and a platter of cookies, which looked so delectable that Will wondered whether he should skip the savory food and dig right into dessert.

Lexie gave him a look. "Real food first, dessert later."

This reminded him of what his nanny would have said, and Will grinned. "Okay, okay."

Khirra said, "We'll be closing soon, but we have to wait until our customers have finished eating." She smiled. "However, today with a little nudge from us, nobody will be lingering over a second cup of tea or coffee. Despite the jolly mood, our customers will leave as soon as they're done eating even though they won't know exactly why. I'll be back as soon as I can with the others."

After Khirra left, Will and Jay heaped their plates with food, and they soberly recapped all that had happened when they were in Elferterre. They really hadn't had a chance to talk about it in detail until now.

"But I bet Pawel knows a lot of what went on," Jay said. "I remember he said he had ways of staying informed."

Will spread some hummus on a piece of flatbread. "Pawel must have elves who can come and go and keep him up-to-date."

While Will and Jay talked, Lexie chewed the side of her lip as she ran her finger around the rim of her empty plate. After a while, Will and Jay noticed her silence and gave her questioning looks. Lexie sighed and looked sadder than she had since they left the janitor's closet. Will knew exactly what was wrong, and Jay did, too.

Jay cleared his throat. "Lexie..."

"No," Lexie said. "Don't try to make me feel better. No matter how you look at the situation we're in, it always comes down to the same thing. Because of me, Maya was left behind with those ogres."

"That's not true," Jay protested, but he said it without conviction.

Will remained silent, looking down at the food on his plate. All the time they had been talking, Maya had hovered over the conversation. Of course she had. Maya was central to all that had happened, and now that she was gone, it felt as though the heart had been ripped out of their mission. But they had to go on. They had to trap Cinnial and remove him from the Great Library. At least Jay and Lexie did. Will, on the other hand, had different plans.

Lexie's voice caught. "It's my fault the ogres were after us. If I hadn't gone to the stream to wash up, Novok wouldn't have caught me, and you wouldn't have had to rescue me. Then, the ogres wouldn't have been waiting for us in the forest, and they wouldn't have chased us to the wrong portal. Maya wouldn't have had to stay behind so we could escape. I should have listened to Hanss and stayed in the den until morning instead of going off on my own." Lexie put her hand over her eyes, and her shoulders shook.

Jay put his arm around Lexie as she cried, and the blonde girl leaned against him.

Will's throat felt tight as Lexie's grief washed over him, and he almost felt it as his own. This, too, was part of seeing, and Will was beginning to realize how draining it could be.

Khirra had come into the room, and she sat on the other side of Lexie. Murmuring, the elf put a hand on Lexie's arm. Taking deep breaths, Lexie gradually stopped crying, and Khirra passed a napkin to her so that she could wipe her face and blow her nose.

Khirra's voice was soft and soothing. "Lexie, I heard most of what you said. Yes, it is true that your carelessness got you caught. But if we hadn't imprisoned the ogres in the forest, then there wouldn't have been any nearby to find you. Therefore, in a way it's our fault this all happened."

Pawel, followed by Thirret, Jace, and her brother, Dagan, came into the room. Pawel said, "We act, and even those of us who can really see don't know what all the ramifications will be. Imprisoning those ogres in the forest was the right thing to do. They were ripping through the countryside, killing any humans they could find. But trapping the ogres in the Dark Forest endangers any human who might be there." Pawel sat down as did Thirret, Jace, and Dagan. Pawel continued, "The ogres have even managed to get a couple of elves who collect information for me." Pawel sighed. "Those ogres are relentless."

23

Khirra said, "The ogres are skilled hunters. We had hoped that as soon as you had recovered from the magic, Hanss would be able to whisk you out of the forest without the ogres being any the wiser."

"But they couldn't because of me," Lexie said in the smallest voice Will had ever heard come from this confident girl. "It took me longer to recover, and we had to leave the next day. And then I was caught." Again, Khirra put her hand on Lexie's arm, and while there were a few ragged breaths, there was no crying.

"Yes, we heard all about it." Pawel's normally stern voice was sympathetic. "Hanss made a report that was delivered to us, and he related everything that happened. We also learned you had stolen the key and lock. Something no elf has managed to do." He inclined his head toward Will, Jay, and Lexie as did the other elves, and their smiles were so brilliant that Will felt a little dazed. "We knew you had gone through the wrong portal into a time different from your own."

"And that you would come to us this summer," Khirra told the teenagers.

"On this day," Dagan said.

"But still," Jace put in. "It certainly was good to see you three walk into the diner as predicted."

"Because with Chaos and Nemesis working against Time and Magic, you never really know what might happen between here and there," Thirret said.

"How did you know we would come now?" Will asked in astonishment.

"Hanss told us that, too," Pawel answered.

Jay frowned. "How would Hanss know?"

"He found out from the portal where you went through. Because of what Hanss told us, we had someone at the rest area in Maine watching out and waiting for you. His name is Gred Oakleaf. Did he find and help you?"

"No," Will answered, knowing that in all likelihood Lillian had something to do with this.

Pawel said, "We'll have to look into what happened to Gred." Then he asked eagerly. "The key?"

From her pocket, Lexie pulled the pouch with the web-encased key and lock and handed it to Khirra. Blinking back tears, the elf stared down at the cocoon in her hand and closed her fingers around it.

"At last," Khirra murmured. "After all these long years."

Pawel, Thirret, Jace, and Dagan gazed at Khirra, and the air around them thrummed with anticipation.

There was still one missing piece. "What about Maya?" Will asked, his heart beating fast and hard. "Does Hanss know what happened to her?"

On a nearby shelf, Khirra found some small scissors and began to cut through the cocoon. "Yes. But that, I'm afraid, is complicated."

4: IN THE JAWS OF THE BEAST

Maya closed her eyes as she plummeted down with Novok into the deep ravine. *This is it*, she thought, strangely detached. *It's over for me.*

Then two things happened. Aiken flew to where Novok's hand gripped Maya's arm. The ogre was nearly dead, choking and gasping for air, and was unable to resist as the little dragon quickly burned through his wrist. Within seconds, the hand dropped away from Maya's arm and fell on its own, separate from Novok.

While Aiken was burning through Novok's wrist, Orlaith sprang into action. Moving so fast that she was a blur, the spider spun a tight cocoon around Maya.

This will never work, Maya thought as she felt herself being wrapped in tight but protective threads. *I'll hit the ground before Orlaith is done.*

But it did work. Orlaith spun faster than Maya could have imagined, and the little spider blinked in and out of time as she finished weaving. When Maya hit the bottom of the ravine, the cocoon was done, and exhausted, Orlaith huddled on Maya's shoulder. Aiken was beside the spider, his tiny claws gripping Maya's vest as the cocoon bounced over rocks and sticks. Although the breath was knocked out of Maya, the cocoon protected her not only from the impact but also from the jagged edges of everything it went over. With a final bounce, the cocoon landed in the wide river that rushed through the ravine.

With a gurgling laugh, the river gathered the cocoon and hurried it toward the ocean. It played with the cocoon the way a dolphin might play with a piece of seaweed, and by the time the river had catapulted the cocoon into the ocean, Maya lay in a swoon, knocked nearly senseless by the constant bouncing. But the cocoon held fast, and although Maya was dazed, she was alive and in one piece, cushioned by a web that somehow managed to keep her dry while at the same time allowing her to breathe.

"Well done," Aiken said to Orlaith who was too tired to make a reply. All she could do was blink her eight tiny eyes.

Grateful to be alive, Maya lost consciousness, and when she woke up, she heard Aiken say in alarm, "The tide is moving fast, and it has taken us out really far. How are we ever going to make it back to land?"

"I don't know," Orlaith answered. "I didn't think about the river. All I could focus on was saving Maya."

"And that river was in quite a mood," Aiken said. "Oh, I hate water."

"Are we in the middle of the ocean?" Maya asked, barely able to move in the tight cocoon.

"Yes, we are," Aiken told her. "I burnt a small hole through the top of the cocoon so that I could go out and take a look. No land in sight."

"What are we going to do?" Maya was unable to keep the panic out of her voice. In only a few minutes, she had gone from feeling safe to feeling trapped.

Aiken said, "I don't know."

As the rushing tide brought them farther and farther out to sea, Maya began to cry, wishing that Will, Jay, and Lexie were there to help her figure things out. The cocoon now felt like a coffin, tight and unyielding. Orlaith stroked Maya's blonde curls, and Aiken blew a warm gentle breath on Maya's cheeks to dry her tears. Trying to calm herself down, Maya rubbed her hands along the tight weave of the cocoon, and despite their desperate situation, she marveled at how strong the fiber was; there wasn't even a hint of dampness from the sea. And the cocoon was buoyant like a little boat, floating rather than sinking. A flash of an idea came to Maya. Would it be enough to save them? Maya didn't know, but at least they would be doing something. They wouldn't be imprisoned in the cocoon, unable to see what was around them or where they were going.

Maya asked, "Orlaith, do you have enough energy to spin some more, to add to the cocoon?"

"I do," Orlaith answered. "I've regained most of my energy while we've been at sea. What do you have in mind?"

"Could you build the cocoon into a small boat? That way we could at least see where we are going."

Orlaith was silent, rubbing her two front legs together as her eyes blinked thoughtfully.

Aiken said, "Orlaith, you wouldn't have to move as fast as you did when you made the cocoon. You can take your time, and that would make it easier for you."

"You can rest whenever you want," Maya added. "Because here we are. At sea."

"It's possible." Orlaith poked the roof of the cocoon with one of her sharp legs. "But in the end, will it do any good to make a boat?"

"I don't know," Maya answered. "But we have to try something. If we're in a boat, we can flag a passing ship if one goes by. The way we are now, nobody's going to notice us. We're too small."

"Maya is right," Aiken said. "Orlaith, build us a boat."

"Okay then," Orlaith replied. "I will."

And she did. The spider squeezed through the little hole Aiken had made at the top. She expanded the cocoon in width and length until it was the size of a small lifeboat whose sides went up, and they were all protected from the water.

Maya sat up, grateful to feel the salt air on her face. For as far as she could see, there was the rolling ocean, gentle and calm. But Maya felt the presence of an immense power, waiting to be released if the conditions were right. Pushing down her fear, Maya watched in admiration as Orlaith finished constructing their boat. It was as tight and cleverly made as anything Maya had ever seen. The spider made a good-sized canopy with sides that fit over half the boat, and it had an opening with a flap. There were even fasteners for the flap, which could be closed if the weather was bad. There was also a short mast with a sail that could be lowered and raised.

Tired, Orlaith settled beside Maya, who stroked the spider's back. "Orlaith, you are a wonder," Maya said. "And so are you, Aiken."

Orlaith's eyes winked with pleasure, and Aiken replied, "We were made from the same metal, at around the same time. Outside, we might look different, but inside we are kin." With his claw, Aiken reached for one of Orlaith's front legs and held it tenderly.

Maya smiled at the two creatures who had such affection for each other.

Orlaith said, "After I've rested, I'll make a blanket for Maya and buckets for catching rain water."

Aiken's voice was gentle. "You rest. I'll see what I can find for Maya to eat."

While Aiken was gone, Maya felt something wiggle in her pocket, and squealing, she jumped.

"What?" Orlaith jumped, too, raising her front legs in alarm.

"Something moved," Maya whispered. "In my pocket."

"What could it be?" Orlaith whispered back, clicking her legs together.

"I have no idea." But then it came to Maya: It was the tawny lioness Will had given her in what seemed like ages ago but had really only been that morning, at Tagen and Ehren's cottage. Reaching into her pocket, Maya pulled out the velvet pouch and removed the lioness.

The elegant creature blinked at Maya. "Finally you let me out."

"Sorry!" Maya replied, using a finger to stroke the smooth head, and the response was a soft purr. "It's been a little hectic. Do you have a name?"

"I do. It's Eloise."

"Beautiful. Like you." Again, there was a purr. "Eloise, this is Orlaith."

The spider bowed a little, and Eloise nodded regally. "Pleased to meet you, Orlaith."

"The pleasure is mine," Orlaith replied. Then she told Maya, "Eloise is made from the heartwood of a golden oak, which is rare and precious. If you look closely, you might be able to see a shimmer in the wood."

As Maya stared at the lioness, she saw a faint glow radiating throughout the little creature's whole body.

Maya set Eloise on her lap, and the lioness said, "The boy gave five whole bags of chamomile tea for me."

"Wow," Maya replied. "I had no idea Will had spent that much."

Eloise smiled. "When you need me most, my light will be there for you."

When Aiken came back with a small fish, Maya introduced him to Eloise, and like Orlaith, he was impressed that the lioness was made with heartwood from a golden oak. Before giving the fish to Maya, Aiken scaled and gutted it with his sharp claws. Then, he flame broiled it with his fire. Maya took the fish, but she hesitated, looking at the charred flesh in her hand.

Aiken shrugged. "I know. It was once alive. But Maya, what choice do you have? Who knows how long you'll be in this boat? You have to eat something."

"Eat the fish," Eloise said. "When you are no longer at sea in this little boat, you can stop eating flesh."

"All right." Maya bit into the fish, which she had to admit tasted sweet and good. Now, if she could only have a drink of water, and she licked her parched lips.

But Chance, or Magic, was with Maya. Before going to sleep, Maya attached Orlaith's buckets to hooks on the side of the canopy. That night there was a gentle rain, and when the buckets were filled, Orlaith and Aiken covered them with tight-fitting lids. When Maya woke up, there was fresh water, and she drank gratefully as Aiken flew away to find another fish for her breakfast.

For two days, they bobbed on top of the dark sea. At night it was cool, and Maya gratefully wrapped herself in the soft blanket Orlaith had made. From time to time, various creatures, some big, some small, swam by, but none of them gave the little boat more than a passing glance. During the afternoon of the second day, purple dolphin-like creatures leaped and shimmered by the boat.

"How close are we to land?" Maya called out.

"Oh, my fin," answered one of the largest purple creatures, clearly the leader. "You are far out to sea. No land for days and days even if you can swim the way we do, which you can't." The others clicked in response. "But if you hoist your sail and head toward where the sun rises, you should eventually reach land, a big island with a port where boats come and go. The elves call it Port Isleros."

"Thanks," Maya called as they sped away.

Maya did as the purple creature advised. She hoisted the sail and steered the boat toward where the sun rose each morning.

To distract herself from the vast ocean and the unrelenting blue sky, Maya looked at Aiken, Orlaith, and Eloise, who were all on her lap. "Tell me something about yourselves."

Aiken squinted as he remembered. "As you know, Orlaith and I were made by Duca, the elf you met at Summer Gathering. Duca is a true artist when it comes to metal. Unlike her dud of a partner Balric, who fancies himself an artisan but really isn't."

Orlaith sniffed. "Balric lacks talent. And there's nothing he can do about it, no matter how hard he tries. Unlike Duca, Balric can only make ornaments and not very good ones."

Aiken blew two puffs of dark smoke. "Because of her skills with magic and metal, Duca creates relics, even though they are classified as ornaments. The Board of Relics refuses to certify her."

"But why?" Maya asked.

"Because Duca is a working-class elf who lacks education and connections," Aiken answered.

"That's just wrong!" As always, Maya was rankled by unfairness, whether she was on Earth or in Elferterre.

"It certainly is," Aiken said. "And anyone with any sense can tell right away that Orlaith and I are relics."

There was silence in the little boat as they all brooded about injustice.

When her anger had calmed down, Maya sheepishly realized she didn't understand the distinction between a relic and an ornament. "But what's the difference between a relic and an ornament?"

Aiken gave her a pitying look, Orlaith blinked, and Eloise patted Maya's leg.

"Sorry!" Maya said, stung by their reactions. "I'm from the Other Side. I'm still learning about Elferterre."

"Of course you are," Orlaith replied kindly. "You seem to be such a part of Elferterre that sometimes we forget. Ornaments are not imbued with magic, the way relics are. Ornaments get their power indirectly, from the magic that swirls around Elferterre. This means ornaments are very limited. In both thoughts and actions."

Maya thought of the wooden figures Ehren and Tagen had carved. "And relics?"

Aiken said, "Relics are creations filled with magic by their makers. In our case, Duca. We are relics, no matter how we are certified. And along with the magic, Duca also gave us the gift of movement and speech. With no requirements."

Maya looked from Aiken to Orlaith. "Requirements?"

Aiken's eyes narrowed. "Some artisans weave restrictions and conditions into the magic. This means the relics can't move unless they agree to the conditions. Other artisans create relics that can't move at all, but maybe they can talk. Still others make relics that can neither move nor speak."

Orlaith's eight eyes stared into the distance. "Duca is too compassionate to put restrictions on any of her creations. We can all move freely on our own and decide where we want to be and what we want to do. It is quite a gift. And not without risk. Relics who can get around on their own without requirements are harder to control than those who can't."

Aiken grinned. "We're wild cards."

"I see." Then Maya frowned. "And what about those relics that can't move at all? Or talk?"

"They might not have the freedom we have," Orlaith replied. "But they think and feel as much as we do. The ones that can neither move nor talk have it the worst. Their magic is trapped inside with no means of expression except for specific tasks. I've heard of relics going crazy in those circumstances."

"And crazy relics are no joke," Aiken said. "They can be dangerous. Because even silent stationary relics plot and plan as much as they can. Usually they just want to be useful and stay with whoever bought them. But relics that have lost it can become mean and conniving, using their magic in cunning ways until they maneuver themselves to where they want to be. And usually that's not a good place."

For a while, Maya was silent as she thought about ornaments, relics, and magic. Then, "How long were you with Duca?"

"Too long," Aiken replied. "Duca didn't want to sell us. She was extremely attached to us. We felt a bond with her, too, but as soon as we met you, we knew we had to leave Duca."

"We could see that adventures awaited us," Orlaith said. "We were tired of being idle. And we were tired of Balric. He drags Duca down." Orlaith's voice was fierce. "I hope someday she gets enough strength to leave him."

As the boat rocked gently, Maya thought about love and all the various complicated ways it worked. She still loved her father even though he had left and moved far away. And once upon a time, her father had loved her mother until he met Inga Peterson and had fallen in love with her. Maya had really liked Andy, but then she had discovered how old he was in her own time, and that was definitely the end of that. And what about Will? Maya pictured the way he smiled and frowned, how his eyes crinkled at the edges, the way he smelled. She did love him. Deep inside, she could feel it. But for how long, Maya wondered, and here her ability to see failed her. All Maya knew was that right now she loved him. She wished Will were with her in the little boat, where they could hold hands and be together to face whatever was going to happen next. His presence always steadied her.

"Who created you, Eloise?" Maya asked, blinking back tears.

The lioness smiled. "An elf named Aram, who, like Duca, is an artisan. Fortunately Aram's partner isn't like Balric. He supports Aram any way he can. Unlike Aiken and Orlaith, I'm classified as a relic. All that Aram makes comes from the heartwood of golden oak, and his pieces are much in demand. The boy was lucky to have chamomile tea. Otherwise, he never would have been able to afford me."

Maya remembered how she, Will, and Jay had had to stop themselves from laughing when Pawel had given them boxes of chamomile tea and had advised them not to flash it around because the tea was valuable. Maya realized that without the chamomile tea, there would have been no Aiken or Orlaith to help her, and she wouldn't be alive right now. *Thank you, Pawel*, Maya thought.

A school of blazing neon blue fish leaped and swam by the boat as though trying to escape from something. More fish went speeding by. Maya peeked around the walls of the canopy, and what she saw made her scream. Barreling at great but silent speed toward the little boat was an immense gray wall of a creature, a sea beast, with a gigantic open mouth coming closer and closer until the boat was swept with a whoosh into the sea beast's great maw.

Inside the beast's mouth it was as dark as a starless night and as damp as an underground cave. There was a horrible stench of fish, and gripping the sides of the boat, Maya gagged. Beside her, Aiken sparked on like a flashlight, illuminating a vast cavern with spiked teeth on the top and bottom. The sea beast's wide tongue cradled the boat, and flinching, Maya waited for the sharp teeth to come crunching down on them all.

"I will burn your tongue," Aiken cried out. "Don't think I won't. I'll slice it right in two."

33

Oh, calm down, came the sea beast's booming thoughts. *I'm not going to eat you. If I had wanted to do that, you'd be down the gullet by now.*

"Then why did you catch us?" Maya asked, trembling. She had been in some scary places, but the sea beast's mouth certainly had to count as one of the scariest.

To bring you to Captain Blythewood, the beast replied.

Maya hadn't expected that answer. "Whatever for?"

I am scouring the Norlandic Sea for the captain, and if I come across anything interesting, I bring it to him. Never have I seen anything like your boat, and I knew it would fascinate the captain, who always likes to see something new.

"Where is Captain Blythewood?" Maya asked.

On the high seas, on his ship, The Resolute.

"Oh, great," Maya muttered, thinking about how they would be going even farther out into the vast sea, away from land.

Aiken's voice was fierce. "I could still burn your tongue in two."

"Do it," Orlaith urged.

Eloise shook her head.

Wouldn't matter, the beast said proudly. *I am devoted to Captain Blythewood. He saved me when I was a young beastie. With a whole tongue or a tongue cut in two, I will bring you to him.*

Maya sighed. "Do you have a name?"

Cali. My name is Cali.

"Is Captain Blythewood an elf?"

He is. And a very powerful one. Few dare cross him.

"What sort of elf is he?" Eloise asked. "Aside from being a powerful one."

Determined, came the immediate reply. *He is on a quest, and nothing will alter his course.*

Maya shook her head. "Oh, great. Now we'll be going on a quest with this Captain Ahab of an elf?"

Cali rumbled with what might have been a laugh. *I do not know who Captain Ahab is, but I'm guessing it is not a compliment to compare him to Captain Blythewood.*

Despite being in the maw of a sea beast, Maya smiled. "No, it's not. Obsessive behavior is never good." Maya pushed away the uncomfortable thought that her own quest to trap Cinnial and remove him from the Great Library was more than a little obsessive.

"How long will it take us to get to Captain Blythewood's ship?" Orlaith asked.

A while, but not a full day. I can swim very fast.

"Won't you let us go?" Maya asked. "I can't see why Captain Blythewood would care about one girl, one small metal dragon, an equally small metal spider, and a carved lioness, also little."

No. Sorry. I never know what the captain will be interested in. And besides, do you really want to bob out here in the sea, puttering around with that little sail? There are a lot of things that would like to eat you. You're lucky I came upon you first.

Maya shivered. "No, I guess not. But I wonder what the captain will think of me."

I do not think you have anything to fear from him.

"I hope so," Maya muttered, torn between feeling doubtful and reassured.

Aiken tapped Maya. "Shall I burn the beast's tongue in two?"

"No," Maya replied. "Leave Cali alone. Why hurt him when you don't have to? He's going to bring us to Captain Blythewood, no matter what. And maybe Cali is right. Maybe it's for the best."

There was an appreciative hum that came from deep inside Cali, and Maya knew that she had made the right decision by sparing the sea beast's tongue.

5: ON BOARD THE RESOLUTE

Maya was right. The great wide tongue held the boat firmly in place as Cali raced through the water with such velocity that without the support, the boat would have been thrown from side to side in the sea beast's cavern of a mouth and dashed upon the huge teeth. Gradually, Maya got used to the overwhelming smell of fish in Cali's mouth, and she wondered about Captain Blythewood and his quest. What was he after? Would the captain be as fascinated with Orlaith's boat as Cali thought he would be? Despite all the unanswered questions, a part of Maya was thrilled to be speeding toward this unknown adventure. Cali wasn't going to eat them, and he had assured Maya that the captain wouldn't hurt her. Her friends had escaped with the key and lock, and with the help of Pawel, Alani, and Alexander, they would be able to carry on with the mission.

"After all," Maya said aloud. "I'm not the only one."

Still, Maya felt guilty that she was enjoying herself. A lot could go wrong for Will, Jay, and Lexie. Their mission was dangerous. They could all be killed. Then there was Ariel, trapped in Mortmain. Maya had not forgotten about the stalwart Apprentice Book and was determined to rescue Ariel. Following her train of thought, Aiken and Orlaith regarded Maya quizzically, but purring, Eloise tapped Maya's leg and looked at her with half-opened eyes.

"There's nothing you can do right now to help Will, Jay, and Lexie," Eloise said.

Maya nodded, feeling less guilty. If there was nothing she could do, then why not enjoy the adventure? Maya knew as soon as it was possible, she would return to her own universe and help in any way she could. In the meantime, she and her small friends were zipping through the ocean in the mouth of a sea beast toward an uncertain fate with a determined elf captain on some kind of obsessive mission.

Aiken blew a puff of smoke. "What's not to like?"

In spite of herself, Maya laughed. "Right?"

Onward they raced, until finally Cali's thoughts called out, *Ahoy, Resolute! Ahoy, Chantay! Ahoy, Captain Blythewood! I've got something for you.*

Cali opened his mouth, and with his tongue, gently pushed the little boat onto the sea beside a big ship. A figurehead, a young elven woman in a blue dress, suspiciously eyed the web boat and its occupants. After some consideration, the carved elf nodded at Cali, and Maya got the impression that without the figurehead's permission, they would not have been allowed to board the ship.

In awe, Maya took in *The Resolute* with its large deck house at the stern, its long set of portholes on the side, and its three taut sails on trim masts. The sails were open and full, but *The Resolute* was not moving, unaffected by the blowing wind. The ship was made of a gleaming metal that looked like new copper, but Maya suspected it wasn't copper at all. This was Elferterre, and Maya had learned that everything was different here. Under the portholes were green panels, shimmering and pulsing with magic.

"Now to meet Captain Blythewood," Maya said as magic swirled around the boat, lifting it from the sea. Orlaith and Aiken skittered into one pocket of Maya's trousers, and Eloise made her elegant, deliberate way into the other.

As soon as the boat was set on the deck, a broad-shouldered elf came over to inspect the snug but strange little craft made of web. The elf was tall and stern, and Maya figured this must be Captain Blythewood. Looking up at him, Maya knew Cali had been right; she had nothing to fear from the captain. The captain's expression immediately softened when he saw Maya, and an image came to her of another teenager, his daughter, whom he loved dearly and was absolutely devoted to.

Captain Blythewood offered his hands to Maya to help her out of the boat, and Maya accepted gratefully. After two days of being cramped in the vessel Orlaith had made, Maya's legs were stiff. Gently but firmly, the captain hoisted her onto the deck of *The Resolute*.

Staring at Orlaith's creation, Captain Blythewood asked in wonder, "What is a young human girl doing all by herself on the sea in a tiny boat unlike any I have ever seen?"

Maya's legs were unsteady, and she gripped his arm. "It's a long story."

The captain's eyes gleamed. "I look forward to hearing it. I'm Captain Christophe Blythewood."

"And I'm Maya Hammond." She smiled tentatively at him and saw him soften even further.

"Welcome aboard *The Resolute*, Maya Hammond. Hawthorn, come here and meet our young guest. Maya, this is my first mate, Azal Hawthorn."

An elf stepped forward. She had a long diagonal scar across her face, and she was nearly as tall as the captain. The elf regarded Maya coolly, and when her expression did not change, Maya knew she would have to work on Hawthorn for a long time to get in her good graces.

Good luck with that, came Hawthorn's blunt thoughts, which seemed to be directed only at Maya. Captain Blythewood continued to smile, and it was clear he had not overheard Hawthorn. Aloud Hawthorn said, "Welcome aboard *The Resolute*." Gripping Maya's hand, she squeezed it in a hard shake, but Maya did not flinch, did not look away.

Hawthorn wrinkled her nose. "You need a shower."

"I'm sure I do," Maya replied, a little embarrassed. "I've been in the boat for two days. And then in Cali's mouth."

Captain Blythewood frowned in sympathy. "Have you had anything to eat? Or to drink?"

Before Maya could answer, Cali's immense gray head rose from the sea, and the sea beast peered onto the ship's deck.

"Wow!" Maya exclaimed, jumping back. "He really is big."

"Enormous," Captain Blythewood agreed. "Nevertheless, Cali can go much faster than *The Resolute*. Did you discover anything else?" he asked the sea beast.

"No, only the boat. I thought you would find it interesting. Do you like it?"

"Very much," the captain answered, considering the craft. "This boat is certainly unique. It seems to be made of some kind of webbing." He touched the side. "But look how secure it is."

"The little boat is amazingly strong," Cali agreed. "But I thought the girl would be safer with you than out at sea in that tiny craft."

The captain said, "Quite right."

"You should also know that the girl has three companions. They are small, and I expect they are in her pockets."

Maya frowned at Cali for revealing her secret, but the sea beast was looking eagerly at Captain Blythewood.

"Does she?" Captain Blythewood's voice was mild, and as he studied her, Maya realized he had come to the conclusion that she was not a threat. Maya kept her expression neutral. She had been underestimated many times, and this had always served her well.

Hawthorn, however, was not as easily fooled. "Let's see what you have."

Captain Blythewood waved his hand. "Leave Maya alone. She can show us later."

"Captain," Hawthorn insisted, "I think we should know sooner rather than later what the girl is carrying."

As the first mate and the captain considered each other, Maya got the impression there had been clashes like this before, and there would be clashes like this again. Hawthorn was as strong-minded as Captain Blythewood, and Maya could tell he admired this quality in his stern first mate and respected her opinions. Maya could also see that the first mate was deeply in love with the captain, who, unfortunately for Hawthorn, did not feel the same way about her.

Hawthorn pressed her case. "For the safety of the ship and her crew."

"Very well," Captain Blythewood conceded with the barest hint of a grin. "Let's see what folderol the girl is carrying."

However, Captain Blythewood's grin went away as Maya reluctantly took Aiken, Orlaith, and Eloise out of her pockets. He gave Maya the same sort of stern look her father might have given her. "How in Magic's name could you, a human, ever afford these three relics? Did you steal them?"

"No," Maya answered quickly. "I didn't." Aiken and Orlaith had scampered onto Maya's shoulder, while Eloise settled in Maya's cupped hand.

39

With a triumphant expression, Hawthorn moved toward Maya. "Shall I take them from her?"

"No!" Maya took a step back as Aiken blew two warning puffs of smoke from his nose. "They're my friends. They won't do anything to hurt this ship or anyone on it. Will you?"

"Of course not," Orlaith said. "We don't want to put ourselves or Maya in any kind of danger."

"Right," Aiken agreed, and his small dark eyes glared at Hawthorn. "But you keep your distance." More smoke came from his nose.

Eyes narrow, Hawthorn raised her hand, but Captain Blythewood commanded, "Steady, Hawthorn, steady."

Glowing slightly, Eloise addressed the captain, "You have nothing to fear from any of us. You know what I'm made of, and you know I do not lie. This girl has been through quite an ordeal. It's a wonder she's still alive. And she has done a lot for Norlander."

"Heartwood from a golden oak," Captain Blythewood said. "You see right to the essence of things, don't you?"

"Almost always," Eloise replied. "And I certainly have this time. Now let us stay with Maya. After she has washed and has had something to eat, she will tell you her story."

The captain made his decision. "Very well. Hawthorn, Maya will keep the dragon, the spider, and the lioness." Hawthorn looked as though she was going to speak, and Captain Blythewood held up his hand. "No argument!"

Hawthorn stood stiff and straight. "Aye, aye, captain."

By now most of the crew had gathered round to stare at the web boat and the newcomers.

Captain Blythewood smiled. "Maya, meet the crew of *The Resolute*." He pointed to two blond elves, large and big boned. "Hannie Snowrunner, Chief Magic Engineer, and her nephew and assistant, Larz Snowrunner." Their broad smiles and open faces welcomed Maya on board, and Maya immediately felt it would be easy to make friends with Larz, who appeared to be in his early twenties. Maya thought, *But he's an elf. Who knows how old he really is?*

Then the captain pointed to three creatures who looked like a cross between an otter and a beaver, but taller, standing on two legs and with arms and hands. They were dressed in green trousers and shirts and vests, much the way Maya was, but their webbed feet were bare.

The captain motioned to the tallest one. "This is Zeynip Lakewood. She's the bosun."

With a bright curious expression that was neither welcoming nor hostile, Zeynip nodded at Maya.

The captain gestured toward the two smaller ones. "And Takis and Proko Branch, the bosun mates. They're sisters, twins." Takis and Proko followed Zeynip's example, and Maya tried not to stare too long at these charming creatures with their sparkling eyes, black-button noses, and whiskers.

Maya wondered, *What could they be?*

Eloise thoughts answered Maya's question. *They're castors, and they come from the wooded wetlands of Norlander.*

As the captain had been introducing Maya to the crew, two more came onto the upper deck from a covered stairway. One was a woman, an elf—tall, dark, and slender like the elves who worked at The Other Green Door. Following the elf was a frog-like creature, green with an upturned mouth and large dark eyes.

"A grenog," Eloise said, answering Maya's question before she had even asked it.

Maya had seen grenogs before. There had been some at the park in Foretcour, when Jay and Lexie had sung to distract the imps, while she, Will, Hanss, Orlaith, and Aiken had stolen the key and lock from Galli's workshop.

"Ah," the captain said, "here they are! Two of the most important members of the crew. Our cook, Symi Larchgrove, and her assistant, Alie Lilywater."

Maya didn't need to be told who was the cook and who was the assistant. Symi smiled confidently at Maya, and Alie shyly bobbed her head. From Alie came a mix of conflicting emotions: self-consciousness, doubt, longing, curiosity. And to Maya's surprise, of all the crew, the timid grenog was the one who could see the deepest.

Moved, Maya thought, *Alie and I could be friends. I know we could.* Then she blinked at the thought. Friends? Really? There was that word again, flitting across her mind, first with Larz then with Alie. Was she going to be on *The Resolute* long enough to make friends with anyone?

Could be, Eloise's thoughts replied. Aiken blew a little puff of steam, and Orlaith tapped Maya on the arm.

Maya sighed, knowing Eloise was right. Sadly, she thought about Will, Jay, and Lexie and how much she missed their company.

41

And how without them, she never would have been able to steal the lock and key from Galli.

Exactly, Eloise's thoughts said. *So keep your options open.*

From the ocean, the sea beast called, "What next, captain?"

The captain said, "Keep looking until you find them."

"Aye, aye!" And then Cali was gone, diving deep and fast, leaving a wide wake of waves behind.

As the crew went back to their various jobs, the captain looked out to sea. His jaw was tight, and Maya felt his loneliness and anger. Again, Maya caught the image of a teenage elf—tall, blonde, and lively. Turning abruptly to Hawthorn, the captain said, "Bring Maya to my cabin. She'll be staying with me. Finneas can help her get settled. In the meantime, I'll be looking at maps in the wheelhouse."

Hawthorn hesitated slightly, and the captain gave her a look indicating there would be no argument about this. "Aye, aye," came the first mate's quick reply.

The captain left, and Hawthorn considered Maya. "Lucky you to be a guest of the captain."

"That is nice of him," Maya replied, not wanting to say anything that would further antagonize the first mate.

"Look," Hawthorn said. "I am never going to like you, so don't even try. Even though you are short and human, you remind the captain of his daughter. And with her foolish carelessness, she has caused us a lot of trouble."

Hurt by Hawthorn's disapproval, Maya remained silent as the first mate took her to the large deckhouse at the back of the ship and rapped sharply on the door. "Finneas," Hawthorn called. "Cali has brought us a young human and three relics. The captain wants them to stay with him."

The door was opened by a slender grenog, neatly dressed in brown trousers, a spotless white shirt with a blue tie, and a vest. Like the castors, the grenog was barefoot. He smiled pleasantly at Maya, Eloise, Aiken, and Orlaith. "Well, my goodness. What a surprise."

Hawthorn laughed shortly. "Sure is."

"Now, now," Finneas said. "It's not the girl's fault she's here, is it?"

"No, it isn't," came the curt reply. "But we still have to deal with her. Rather, you have to deal with her. I don't want anything to do with this human. Or her relics." She glared down at Maya. "Stay out of my way. And make sure those relics behave."

Chastened, Maya nodded. But Finneas smiled kindly at Maya and put a hand with three fingers and a thumb on her shoulder. "Welcome, child. What's your name?"

Instead of telling Finneas her name, Maya, exhausted and overcome by all that had happened, began to cry.

"There, there," Finneas said, drawing her into the deckhouse. "Come in, come in." He regarded Hawthorn, and his mild voice had an undercurrent of sternness. "Off you go now. I'll take care of the child."

Hawthorn sighed. Even though Maya was crying, she could feel that for a moment there was a chink in the first mate's irritation. But with a snap, Hawthorn's anger came back, and the elf stalked away without saying anything else.

"Dear, dear, dear. How very disturbing," Finneas said as he shut the door, grabbed a tissue from a side table, and handed it to Maya. "Hawthorn is an excellent first mate. Like Cali, she is completely devoted to the captain. Maybe even a little too devoted. But Hawthorn is thin skinned and holds a grudge. Unfortunately. And sometimes her grudges are misplaced."

Maya blew her nose and stopped crying. "But I haven't done anything to either her or the captain. I asked Cali to let us go before he brought us here, but he wouldn't."

"I know, I know. However, you remind Hawthorn of the captain's daughter, even though you are a human. And she thinks that because of the captain's daughter, we are neglecting our work." Finneas paused, and Maya could tell that he reluctantly agreed with Hawthorn. Shaking his head, Finneas motioned to one of the two chairs that were on either side of a sofa. All were grouped in front of a small black stove. "Sit down for a moment before you get cleaned up. Would you like some fizzy water? And some cookies?"

Maya settled on one of the soft chairs. "Yes, please."

"What is your name?"

"Maya."

Finneas regarded Eloise, Aiken, and Orlaith. "And the relics?"

Maya introduced them.

Eloise inclined her head toward Finneas. "We can trust him."

Maya smiled a little. "I know."

"Well, there," Finneas said, smiling back. "Now that's settled, I'll bring us some refreshments."

43

As Finneas went to the kitchenette at the far end of the room, Maya looked around at the captain's comfortable quarters. Between the kitchenette and sitting area, there was a large rectangular dining table and chairs. Across from where she sat, Maya could see a corridor that led from the room.

"The captain's chambers are down there," Finneas said, setting a tray with two bottles of sparkling water and a plate of chocolate cookies on a low table by the chairs and sofa. "As is my room. There is also a room for you, and a bathroom for all of us. You can take a shower after you've had your snack."

Maya grinned. Finneas was talking to her as though she were a young child rather than a teenager who had traveled across two universes. But Maya could feel care, concern, and kindness coming from the grenog, and she was not offended, the way she normally would have been if an adult at home had spoken to her that way.

Finneas gave her a shrewd look. "You've come a long way, haven't you?"

"I have," Maya answered, realizing Finneas saw more than his easy-going countenance indicated.

"The captain will want to hear all about it, and I'll wait until then to hear it, too. No need to repeat yourself."

Maya asked, "Finneas, can you tell me about the captain's daughter?"

"I can," Finneas said. "It's common knowledge that everyone aboard this ship knows, and there's no reason why you shouldn't know, too. The captain's daughter's name is Clarin. It's because of her that we are off on this mission rather than doing what the captain was hired to do. But Rhye, of course, is really to blame." The grenog frowned as much as his upturned mouth allowed.

With a cookie in one hand and a drink in the other, Maya settled back in the chair. "Tell me their story."

6: STORIES TOLD

Finneas asked, "Where to begin? I've thought about it a lot, and every time I think I've pieced the story together, I realize it goes back further, maybe even as far back as to Stella Greenwood, the captain's beloved wife. If she hadn't died so young—only 150 years old—then perhaps she could have kept Clarin out of Rhye Ashglade's clutches."

"Is Rhye related to Tamick Ashglade?" Maya asked.

"Oh, yes. Rhye is Tamick's nephew." Here Finneas hesitated, and Maya sensed he was attempting to be fair. "It's not Rhye's fault that Tamick is his uncle, but there are strong factions in Norlander, where Stella Greenwood came from. Some are on the side of the Ashglades and some on the side of the Greenwoods. Judging from your accent, I'm guessing you're from away. Do you know about Tamick Ashglade and Pawel Greenwood? How Pawel and Tamick were on Norlander's ruling council and how Tamick urged the council to exile the Greenwood family from Elferterre?"

"Even though I'm from away," Maya replied, "I do know about Tamick Ashglade and Pawel Greenwood. Was the captain's wife related to Pawel? They have the same last name."

"They were cousins. And this means the captain is dead set against the Ashglades, even though he comes from Degelis, the country on Norlander's southern border."

Maya murmured, "What's in a name?"

Orlaith replied, "In Norlander and Degelis, name and kinship count for a lot."

"For almost everything," Aiken said.

"Unfortunately," Eloise added in a low voice.

Wrinkling his smooth brow, Finneas studied Maya. "Where exactly are you from, my dear?"

Maya looked at Orlaith, Aiken, and Eloise, and they all nodded. Maya cleared her throat. "I'm from the Other Side, from a planet called Earth."

Surprised, Finneas set his bottle down with a thump on the table. "From the Other Side? And you're all the way out here on the Norlandic Sea?"

"Yes," Maya answered.

"Well, my root," Finneas said. "I didn't expect that."

Maya rubbed her face. "Yeah, I know it's common for elves to go to the Other Side, but not for humans to travel to Elferterre. At least not on their own. When the captain comes, I'll tell you both how I got here. But let's get back to Clarin and Rhye."

Finneas cleared his throat. "Clarin and Rhye. It wasn't love at first sight. Initially, they didn't like each other at all. Because of their last names, naturally. They met in Port Isleros, where the captain has a home. The captain and crew were between jobs, and Rhye had been sent to the port to prepare for his own job."

"Are the jobs secret?" Maya asked.

Finneas shook his head. "Not at all. Elferterre is vast, and the captain's job is to travel to different lands for Degelis to negotiate rights for portals, where they exist, and to install them where they don't exist. Portal rights are a great help for traveling and for transporting goods."

Maya thought about Hannie and Larz, the two magical engineers who no doubt were essential when it came to installing portals. There was a lot Maya wanted to ask about portals, but she decided this would be a subject for another day. Right now, she was interested in Clarin and Rhye.

"What about Rhye? What does he do?"

"Rhye is a young scientist, and his job is to explore the deep oceans of Elferterre to discover all the creatures that might be out there." Finneas sniffed. "Rhye has his own submarine, *The Cuttlefish*, which I'm sure was funded by his Uncle Tamick."

"Those Ashglades always stick together," Aiken said darkly.

"Yes, they do," Orlaith added.

Eloise didn't say anything.

Finneas absently scratched his cheek with a long slender finger. "Who can blame Rhye for falling in love with Clarin? She's as lively and as charming as her departed mother. Clarin has a glow about her, and everyone feels happier when they're around her. Even me, a grenog, who marches to a different croak than elves do. Clarin is the light of the captain's life, and there was no way he wanted her to wind up with an Ashglade. Plus, she's young. She just started university this year. Plenty of time for her to settle down. With the right elf, of course."

Lowering his voice, Finneas leaned forward, and Maya, Orlaith, Aiken, and Eloise instinctively leaned toward him. "It happened gradually. Clarin and Rhye would see each other here and there. At cafés, in the park, at parties. With his dark curly hair and brooding looks, Rhye is very attractive to females, both elves and humans. I've seen how they cluster around him. At first, Clarin resisted, but gradually, Rhye wormed his way into Clarin's circle of friends, and then he went everywhere with them."

"Even though he's an Ashglade?" Maya asked. "And Clarin's mother was a Greenwood?"

Finneas answered, "Yes, things are looser in Port Isleros than they are on the mainland. And Clarin and her friends are, well, artists. They tend to be more tolerant about class, race, and family names."

"That's not really a bad thing, is it?"

Finneas shook his head. "When it comes to the Ashglades, it is. They're a rotten bunch. They really are. And, in the end, Rhye Ashglade showed his true colors."

Afraid for the captain's daughter, even though she didn't know her, Maya put a hand to her face. "What did Rhye do?"

"He put a spell on Clarin," Finneas whispered, and Maya could feel the grenog's sorrow. "To make her fall in love with him and then go off with him in that dratted submarine."

Maya took a deep breath. "Wow."

Finneas sighed. "I know. Before Rhye took her, Clarin left a letter for the captain, and nothing about it was right. Not the handwriting, not the wording. Very different from our usual dear

Clarin, who is always kind and warm. This letter was curt, almost rude, and to the point. Never has Clarin communicated with her father like this. And we all knew why. Clearly, Rhye had put a spell on Clarin."

"What a terrible thing to do!" Maya said.

"It was. But the captain is going to find *The Cuttlefish* and get his daughter back. We have Cali searching the Norlandic Sea, and we also have eyes in the sky with Braird, whom you haven't met."

"Is Braird a bird?" Maya asked.

"No, Braird is a corbeau. Actually, part corbeau, on his father's side. Nevertheless, Braird can change from elf shape to bird shape whenever he wants. You haven't met him yet, but you will. Together, Cali and Braird will find that rotten pond scum of an elf, Rhye Ashglade."

"And what will happen to Rhye?" Maya asked in a hushed voice. "Will the captain kill him?"

"Of course not!" Finneas replied, clearly aghast by the suggestion. "The captain only kills under extreme circumstances." The grenog drew himself up. "Of course, putting a spell on Clarin could be considered an extreme circumstance. But unless Rhye has harmed Clarin in any way, the captain, with Hannie's help, will put a spell on Rhye, and he will be one uncomfortable elf for quite a while. Rhye might have to take an extended leave from exploring the Norlandic sea." Here Finneas actually snickered, and Maya wondered about the spell the captain planned to use on Rhye. Seeing Maya's curious expression, Finneas collected himself and continued, "Before we set out, the captain sent a strongly-worded letter to Tamick Ashglade, letting him know we are furious about what Rhye did, and we are in hot pursuit. The captain wanted to be aboveboard in dealing with Rhye, even though what he did was dastardly." The grenog smiled proudly. "Because that's how the captain is with everyone, no matter what."

Maya's eyes were wide. "What did Tamick say?"

"Nothing. Absolutely nothing."

"Is this a good thing?"

"It is not," Finneas replied. "It can only mean that Tamick is up to no good, plotting to help his nephew."

"Well," Eloise said from the table. "You living creatures certainly get yourselves into a twist about things."

"Wouldn't you, if someone put a spell on your daughter?" Finneas asked.

Eloise thought for a moment. "I suppose I would, if I could have one. But because I am a relic, I can only have brothers and sisters carved from the same piece of heartwood. From the beginning, we all know we will most likely be sold and taken in different directions."

"Ah," Finneas replied sympathetically, and they were all silent for a while. Then the grenog looked at Maya, at her dirty face and tangled hair. "You, my dear, need a shower. I will get you some clean clothes."

After showing Maya to a small but charming room that had a bed with a blue-green comforter, a white vanity, and a desk, Finneas stood in the doorway and sighed.

"This was Clarin's room, wasn't it?" Maya asked, looking at the framed pictures of sea animals and shells on the wall above the vanity and desk. "Are those her paintings?"

"Yes," came the sad answer. "Good, aren't they?"

Maya studied the delicate but vibrant work of creatures both familiar and unfamiliar. "They're beautiful."

Finneas's voice was soft. "How we miss her. Clarin always came to sea with us when she wasn't at boarding school or university. The captain and I are counting the days until she is back on *The Resolute*."

Blinking back tears, Maya thought of her own father, who had left her and her mother and then had gone to live in North Carolina, many hundreds of miles away from New York City. What a huge contrast there was between her father and Captain Blythewood, who was at sea, desperately looking for his daughter. Maya's father, on the other hand, had jumped at the offer to be chair of the Department of English at Duke University. Her father had cared more about "the chance of a lifetime" than about being near his daughter. His only child. As she had in the past, Maya felt the sharp ache of her father's betrayal.

Stepping into the room, Finneas put his hand on Maya's shoulder. "You have your own sorrows, don't you?"

Unable to speak, Maya nodded as she set Eloise, Aiken, and Orlaith on the vanity.

"So it is with all living creatures," Finneas said. "Whether we walk, fly, swim, jump, or creep."

"I thought I was over it," Maya finally said in a low voice. "Especially after all that I've seen and done."

Finneas shook his head. "Some things we never really get over. We forgive, maybe. Or maybe not. But if it's bad enough, what's been done always stays with us."

As Maya took a shower, she thought about what Finneas had said, and she knew he was right. She had forgiven her father and would forgive him again if she had to. Her love for him was too strong for it to be any other way. However, Maya sensed that what her father had done would follow her into adulthood. Most of the time it would be pushed to the back of her mind, but occasionally his desertion would come to the forefront, the way it had now. Maya realized she wasn't being fair to her father. When he had moved to North Carolina, Maya had been safe with her mother in New York City. Unlike Clarin, Maya had not been put under a spell and kidnapped. But still, the captain's obvious devotion to his daughter stood in sharp contrast to the way her own father had left easily with Inga by his side. With a deep certainty, Maya knew the captain never would have walked out on his wife and daughter to be with another woman. The captain's attachment to his family was too strong.

Filled with admiration for the captain, Maya vowed to herself, "I'm going to help Captain Blythewood any way I can. Even though he probably won't need me. After all, he's got elves and other folks to help him. But I've had my eyes peeled, and maybe I can see in a way the others can't."

After her long shower, where Maya had checked her knife wound and found it was healing well, she stood by the vanity. Finneas had given her a large bathrobe, and Maya drew it closer around her body. The aqua robe, with a swirl of silver and black fish that looked like koi, was so long that Maya had to hold it up in order not to trip over it as she walked. This was Clarin's bathrobe, and Finneas had assured Maya that Captain Blythewood wouldn't mind if Maya borrowed it. But on the bed lay new clothes: underwear, more or less like what she would wear on Earth, brown trousers, and a white tunic embroidered with red flowers.

To Maya's surprise, everything fit perfectly. Before leaving the snug room, Maya asked the relics, "Do you want to come with me?"

"Of course we do," Aiken replied.

"We like to know what's going on," Orlaith said.

"And help if needed," Eloise added.

"All right, then." Maya put both her hands down onto the vanity, where the relics had waited while Maya showered and dressed. They climbed into her hands, and Maya brought them into the living area. The table was set for three, and Finneas was bustling around, putting drinks and condiments on the table.

He motioned to a chair by the left side of the table. "Sit down, sit down. The captain should be here soon."

"May I help with anything?"

Clearly pleased by the offer, Finneas smiled broadly. "No, no. Everything's all set. Alie will bring us our supper as soon as the captain tells her he's ready." He studied Maya. "Those clothes look like a good fit."

"They are. Where do they come from?" Maya asked.

"The captain has a trunk that provides basic clothes. Nothing too fancy. That requires more magic than the trunk has. But we don't need fancy clothes out to sea, and everyone brings their own special clothes for when we reach land. I gave the trunk an estimate of your height and weight. Looks like I guessed pretty well."

Maya said, "You sure did. Pawel Greenwood has a trunk like that, and it's where my old clothes came from."

Finneas did a double take. "You know Pawel Greenwood? Personally?"

"Yeah, that's why I'm in Elferterre. I'll tell you all about it when the captain is here. Is it all right to put the relics beside my plate?"

"Yes, yes, of course. As long as they behave, which I'm sure they will." He stared at Maya in amazement. "You've come a long way for a small human, haven't you?"

Maya grinned. "I have."

It wasn't long before the captain joined them. Maya was relieved to see he was in a better mood than he had been when he went to the wheelhouse, which was on the second floor of the deckhouse. Carrying a large tray, Alie followed him, and he held open the door for her as she came into the room. Alie set the tray on the table, carefully removed steaming dishes, and gave a bow that looked like a small jump.

Captain Blythewood said, "You don't have to bow, Alie. I'm not royalty."

Alie gripped the tray. "I know, captain. Sorry. But I can't seem to help myself. At a young age, we grenogs are taught to bow to nearly every creature."

Finneas told Alie, "Stay on *The Resolute* long enough, and you'll learn not to bow whenever you greet Captain Blythewood. Then maybe you'll stop bowing to other creatures, too."

"Yes, sir." Alie's big-eyed gaze went from Finneas to Maya, who smiled reassuringly at the slender grenog. Alie tentatively smiled back and then left quickly.

Rubbing his hands together, the captain turned to the covered dishes on the table. "Let's see what the excellent Symi and Alie have prepared for us."

There was a stew that looked and tasted like curried lentils and greens along with a bowl of some kind of brown grain to go with it; a loaf of dark bread; butter; a salad made with leafy vegetables of purple, green, and red; and little berry tarts for dessert.

Smiling, Captain Blythewood sat down. As he served himself some of the stew and grain, the captain said, "All right Maya, tell us your story."

"It's a long one," Maya warned, taking the big bowl of lentil stew the captain passed to her.

"That's all right," Captain Blythewood replied. "I have nothing planned for tonight."

Maya took a deep breath. "I'm from the Other Side, and I came to Elferterre in a roundabout way."

Maya started with the train from New York to Boston, with Chet Addington, Mary Parsons, and the Book of Everything. By the time they got to dessert, Maya had reached the part about getting her eyes peeled and going to the Great Library, where she met Sydda, Elspeth, Alani, and the others.

Finneas interrupted the story. "Tea. It's time for some tea."

"Make a big pot," the captain said. "And make it strong. This is quite a story." Then he looked quizzically at Eloise.

Maya realized the captain wanted confirmation that the story was true, but she couldn't hold it against him for wondering. Even to her, the story sounded too fantastic to be believable.

"Maya's telling the truth, captain," the lioness said. "You can trust her."

"I thought so," Captain Blythewood replied. "But it's good to hear you confirm it."

By the time half of the tea had been drunk and all of the tarts were gone, Maya had taken them through Duke Owen's death, her trip with Julian to Tufrak, and her meeting with Cinnial. And Bigly, the troll. Shivering, Maya paused.

"Dear me," Finneas murmured. "Bigly has a wizened heart, doesn't he? Just like an imp."

"Yeah," Maya answered.

"Go on, child," Captain Blythewood said. "Tell us what happened."

Maya described the torture as Bigly used devices that drilled into her head to find out what she knew about Sydda, the Great Library, and other secrets she might have. With a shudder, she thought about how easy it would have been to betray the kind trolls, Jeam and Captain Creb, who had taken her in. Perhaps even more important, she didn't reveal that Tufrak's Book of Everything had not been destroyed in a fire. Instead, the Book was hidden in a compound deep inside Black Mountain.

"I didn't tell Bigly anything," Maya said. "Even though he nearly killed me." Then she told them about her escape from the Office.

Finneas's eyes were bright, and the captain looked stunned.

"How on terre did you ever escape without a Book of Everything to help you?" Captain Blythewood asked.

"Or a portal?" Finneas added.

"I did it on my own," Maya said. "I remembered a time when I went for a walk with my mother, and everything was clear and sunny. I could see the shadows of leaves on the sidewalk. And I could see a path that went from where I was in the Office to the day when I was six, on my birthday, when Mom and I went for a walk in our neighborhood in New York City. I let go and followed the path. I landed on the sidewalk not far from our home, and I saw my younger self and my mother go into the corner store." Noting the astonished expressions on the faces of Finneas and Captain Blythewood, Maya added quickly, "Actually, I wasn't exactly on my own. Mom kept calling to me, and Time helped me, too."

There was a long silence. Finneas poured himself another cup of tea and stirred some sugar into it. Sitting very still, the captain stared at Maya. The relics, too, were still, and Maya realized they had never heard her story about her adventures on the Other Side. They had only seen what she had done in Elferterre.

53

Maya continued, "Alani and Alexander, from the Great Library, were waiting for me. Sydda had sent them to Brooklyn in case I managed to escape from the Office. Alani and Alexander had their Apprentice Books with them. Of course they did. That's how they traveled from the Great Library to Brooklyn. The Books told me about someone named the Accumulator. They couldn't really see him, the way they can see most everything else. But they could sense him and knew he was nearby."

The captain blinked. "The Accumulator? In Brooklyn?"

"Yes," Maya answered.

"Do you mean Pawel, my wife's cousin, who was exiled by Tamick Ashglade?"

"The one and the same," Maya replied. "I found Pawel at a café called The Other Green Door, which he and his family own." She grinned at the captain, who was staring in astonishment at her. "They make great chamomile tea, which is common on the Other Side. Anyway, Pawel told me about the locks and chains, which bind him and his family, and how they were made by an elf named Galli, who had also made a key that would open the locks and allow the Greenwoods to return to Elferterre. Then Pawel told me Galli had a lock that would trap Cinnial. Pawel and I made a deal. I would steal the lock and key from Galli. After I returned to my universe and trapped Cinnial in the lock, Pawel would bring the lock to Elferterre, where Cinnial would never bother the Great Library again."

"Did you succeed?" Captain Blythewood asked in a low voice. "Did you get the key and lock?"

"We did."

The captain frowned. "We?"

"My companions. Will, Jay, and Lexie. They are kids my age. Humans. From the Other Side."

"Where are these kids?" the captain asked. "And where are the lock and key?"

"On the Other Side," Maya answered, missing Will, Jay, and Lexie more than ever. "They made it, but I didn't."

Briefly, Maya recounted the story of the ogres and how she had gone over the side of the ravine with Novok while her friends had escaped through a portal back to Earth. Maya told the captain and Finneas how she got away from the ogre and came to be in the little webbed boat on the vast sea.

The captain shook his head. "Maya, when we picked you up in that remarkable boat, I never thought I would hear such a story from one small human."

"Right?" Then Maya leaned toward the captain. "Finneas told me about your daughter and how she is under Rhye Ashglade's spell. I want to help you in any way I can, even though I am only a small human."

"Thank you, Maya," the captain said. "And how do you think you can help?"

An image came to Maya of a large bird. Big and strong, he soared over the sea, scouting for any sign of Rhye Ashglade's submarine. Riding on his back, Maya soared with him, casting about with her senses to find *The Cuttlefish.*

Maya told the captain about her flash.

"You were with Braird," the captain said.

Maya replied, "That's what I thought. Finneas told me about him. Braird sees with his eyes, but I can see in a different way. Together we'll have a better chance of finding the submarine, and you can rescue Clarin."

The captain considered Maya, but he didn't say anything.

"Maya's telling the truth," Eloise said. "She can help you find what you are looking for."

The captain tapped a finger on the table. "Two of you in the sky, each looking in a different way. Maya, you are small. Braird should be able to carry you on his back." Then he smiled at Maya. "I accept your offer of help. And after we find my daughter, we'll return to Port Isleros. On that island, there is the Temple of Portals, and if there is a portal where you want to go, then one at the temple will take you there."

"What if there's no portal?" Maya asked.

"There are other ways of traveling," the captain said. "But using a portal is the easiest way to cross over. However it turns out, I'll be able to help you get to the Other Side."

Maya offered her small hand. "Deal?"

The captain's firm hand grasped hers. "Deal."

On the table, Orlaith's legs tapped out a happy tune, and Aiken blew smoke rings. But Eloise remained silent, blinking thoughtfully at Finneas, the captain, and Maya.

7: ON DECK

After all she had been through, Maya should have been tired, but she couldn't sleep. Images of what had happened in Elferterre came to her, one after another, especially falling into the ravine with Novok. Maya had been sure she was going to die, but Orlaith had come to the rescue by weaving the cocoon. Right from the start, Maya had sensed Aiken and Orlaith would help her with her mission, but she had never envisioned how the two of them, in different ways, would save her life.

Finally, Maya gave up trying to fall asleep and turned on the small lamp on the vanity. Watched by the relics, she got dressed and combed her hair.

"Where are you going?" Eloise asked Maya.

"On the deck. I can't sleep." Aiken, Orlaith, and Eloise leaned toward her. "I'd like to go alone, if you don't mind. I need to think."

Aiken and Orlaith looked at Eloise, who said to Maya, "You have nothing to fear on this ship, even from the first mate, Hawthorn. She doesn't like you, but she won't hurt you."

"Well, that's good." Maya grinned. "I'd hate to think Hawthorn would throw me overboard."

"That she will not do," Eloise said. "Go look at the stars and at how they sparkle." Stopping, the lioness hesitated as though she wanted to say more.

"What?" Maya asked.

"Nothing," Eloise replied. "Enjoy the night."

On deck, Maya breathed in the cool air and tipped back her head to look at all the shimmering stars, visible despite the soft lights on the masts. She thought of Myranda, the lavender witch, who had peeled the eyes of Will, Jay, and Lexie. On the cuffs of Myranda's tunic, stars had glittered much the same way the ones in the sky did now. Walking toward the prow, Maya felt lonely as she thought about how much she missed Will, Jay, and Lexie. She wondered what they were doing. Had they made it to The Other Green Door to give Pawel and his family the key that would set them free? Then afterwards, to the Great Library to trap Cinnial? And would they succeed? There were too many questions, and while a part of Maya was eager to help the captain with his mission, another part of her longed to be with her friends.

As Maya leaned against the side of the ship, a voice asked, "A lot to think about, isn't there little human?"

Maya jumped. She scanned the deck, but nobody seemed to be around.

"Who said that?" Maya asked.

"I did. Look down."

Maya did as she was told and saw the outline of the elf figurehead, glowing softly like a small moon.

"Your Chantay, aren't you?" Maya asked. "I heard Cali call out to you when we first came here."

"I am indeed Chantay," came the figurehead's response. "And yours is Maya. I heard the introductions this afternoon when you were on the deck."

"Yes, and I'm from the Other Side." Maya gazed at Chantay. "Your name is beautiful. Like you."

"Thank you, Maya from the Other Side. But I am not merely a beautiful figurehead."

"What do you do?"

"I guide the ship while the captain and the crew sleep, and I alert them to any dangers, including storms. And with my magic, I can protect the ship from many things."

"Wow! The captain is lucky to have you."

"It's not luck at all," Chantay told Maya. "The captain paid a lot to have me created. On the sea, a strong figurehead can mean the difference between life and death. Skimp on a figurehead, and you might not make it back to land."

"It's so different here."

"No Magic on the Other Side?" Chantay asked.

"There is. A little. But mostly Time is in charge."

"Ah," Chantay said. "I'm glad I'm in Elferterre. I wouldn't be able to do very much on the Other Side."

"You'd only be a pretty face for people to admire," Maya agreed.

Chantay's voice was scornful. "Who wants to be just a pretty face?"

"Right?" Maya wrinkled her nose. "Boring. Much better to be at sea, facing storms and danger."

Chantay laughed, an enchanting rippling sound that skipped over the water. "I like the way you think, Maya from the Other Side."

Maya was about to reply, when a voice behind her boomed, "Is that you, little human, talking to Chantay?"

"Shush, Larz!" came two voices, almost in unison. "You'll wake up the captain."

Turning, Maya saw the broad figure of Larz Snowrunner, the second magic engineer. Beside Larz were the two cheerful bosun mates, the castors Takis and Proko. An elf, tall and slender, was with them, and Maya could feel his intense watchfulness. Behind them all, softly and hesitantly, came Alie, and Maya got the impression that the grenog wasn't quite sure if she belonged with these four confident figures in front of her.

Larz tried to whisper, but even that was loud. "Is that you, little human?"

Despite being repeatedly called little human, Maya grinned. "Yup, here I am."

The group settled in a circle on the deck. "Come sit with us, little human," Larz called amiably.

"Does the little human have a name?" asked the intense elf.

"Of course she does," said Takis. "Larz, stop calling her little human."

"You know I have a bad memory for names," Larz replied, stung by the rebuke.

"Then for water's sake, why don't you ask her what her name is?" Proko asked in exasperation.

Maya tried not to laugh. "My name is Maya."

"Maya, Maya, Maya," Larz repeated.

"Got it?" the intense elf asked.

"Got it, Braird," Larz replied cheerfully, and Maya got the impression there wasn't much that could keep his boisterous spirit down for very long. And here was Braird, the corbeau, who could turn into a bird whenever he wanted to, the one she was going to work with to find Clarin.

Studying Braird, who stared evenly back at her, Maya walked over to the group. Alie and Proko made room for her, and Maya sat between them.

"Little..." Larz caught himself. "Maya, what's your story?"

"It's a long one," Maya warned.

"That's all right," Larz replied. "We've got plenty to drink, and the night is still young."

Maya saw they had been carrying bottles and small cups.

Popping up with a jump, Alie said, "I'll go get a cup for Maya."

While Alie leaped across the deck and disappeared down the stairs, the others poured drinks for themselves.

Larz introduced Braird, whose eyes were bright as he considered Maya. Everything about Braird looked sharp, from his gleaming eyes, to his prominent nose, to the angular contours of his face and body. Maya got a sense of such precision and speed that when he swooped from the sky, few could see him coming until he landed.

Larz said, "Better watch out for Braird. Not only can he fly really fast and see and hear everything that goes on, but his mother is First Mate Hawthorn."

Maya tried to keep her voice neutral. "Oh?" Finneas hadn't told her about the relationship between Braird and the first mate.

Braird spoke in the same blunt way Hawthorn did. "My mother doesn't like you much."

"Braird!" Proko and Takis said together.

Maya felt her cheeks flush. "I guess that's settled, then," came her cool reply.

"No," came Braird's equally cool answer. "I don't always agree with my mother. Time will tell if she's right."

"How big of you," Maya said.

Braird's fierce eyes didn't blink. Sitting very straight, Maya didn't back down, and she stared directly at him. Maya thought, *I've faced far worse than you.*

59

Braird's thoughts replied, *Have you? You're one cocky little human.*

Proko and Takis made distressed chittering sounds, and Larz laughed nervously. Feeling a soft touch on her arm, Maya saw Alie was back, and the grenog handed her a cup.

"Don't mind him," Alie said in a low voice. "He's hard but fair."

Somehow, this made Maya even angrier. Who was Braird to judge her? Especially when she had come so far and had done so much to help Norlander.

Alie's gentle voice interrupted Maya's thoughts. "But we don't know anything at all about you."

Maya turned on Alie. "The captain thinks I'm fine! Why shouldn't the rest of you?"

The slender grenog shrank away from Maya, who immediately regretted taking her anger out on Alie.

"Sorry!" Maya said.

Alie whispered, "That's all right."

Clearing his throat, Larz spoke sternly, "Enough now. It's true. We don't know little..." there was a pause, "Maya, but she's right. The captain has taken her in, and if he thinks she's fine, then we should, too."

Everyone nodded except for Braird, and Larz nudged him. "Right?"

"Maybe," Braird replied, finally looking away from Maya.

Maya got the sense that for now, at least, this was the only concession she would get from him. Closing her thoughts from everyone, Maya wondered how in the world she would ever be able to work with Braird. They had gotten off to a bad start, and it was all because of Braird's mother, who had taken a dislike to Maya because she reminded the first mate of the captain's daughter. Clearly, Hawthorn thought Clarin was a fool for allowing herself to be enchanted by Rhye. Again, Maya felt herself getting angry. It wasn't Clarin's fault that Rhye had cast a spell on her. Maya felt that both Hawthorn and Braird were too critical, too harsh, and it made their judgments unfair.

Absorbed with her thoughts, it took Maya a while to realize everyone was staring at her, and they were regarding her with respect. Even Braird, although he was trying hard not to show it.

Larz said, "It's not every human who can hide their thoughts from us. Maya, there's more to you than meets the eye."

Maya realized the same was true for Larz, who was not exactly the big goofy elf he appeared to be.

Maya grinned. "Could be."

Larz grinned back. "Tell us your story. But first, Proko and Takis, put one of your bubbles over us. That way we won't bother the captain."

In fascination, Maya watched as the two castors stood and made weaving motions with their furry hands, much the way Hanss had done with his protection spells. A shimmering translucent bubble surrounded them all, and when it was done, Maya couldn't hear any of the sounds from the ship and the sea. But she could breathe easily. Somehow, the bubble provided all the oxygen they needed.

"Wow," Maya said. "That is some bubble."

Whiskers twitching, Proko and Takis smiled proudly at Maya.

Alie said, "When they have to repair the ship underwater, that's what they use. They can reach through the bubble to work and no water comes in."

Proko settled down beside Maya. "We can't hold our breath underwater as long as you can, Alie."

Alie said, "And the bubble keeps you dry, letting you stay down as long as you need to. Even I can't hold my breath underwater forever."

"Yes, yes," Larz agreed, his face already flushed slightly from drinking. Braird, on the other hand, looked as self-possessed as ever. Larz's large voice filled the bubble. "Now little Maya, tell us your story."

Maya looked upwards at the sky through the bubble. She supposed "little Maya" was better than "little human," but not by much. However, Larz radiated such good will that Maya wasn't irritated when he repeatedly called her "little."

"We'll work on him," Proko whispered. "He's not as foolish as he looks."

"I know," Maya whispered back.

"Anytime you're ready," Braird called.

Ignoring him, Maya took a long drink of what Alie had poured in her cup. It was light and fresh, and Maya felt its warmth spread through her body, relaxing her.

Putting the cup down, Maya thought, *I'd better not drink too much of this. At least not until I'm done with my story.*

Maya told them nearly everything. The only part Maya left out was the deal she had made with Captain Blythewood. Maya figured the captain should be the one to tell Braird that she would be helping him find *The Cuttlefish*. She didn't want to ruin the evening by having a big fight with Braird, which Maya sensed would happen if she proposed it right now. Thanks to his mother, Braird was too suspicious of Maya to go along with anything she suggested.

When Maya was finished, there was a long silence, the way there had been with the captain and Finneas a few hours earlier. Drinks were untouched, and everyone's expressions were serious, even Braird's.

But Maya was not surprised when Braird asked, "Why should we believe any of this? Hard to imagine that someone as small and as weak as you could do all these things."

Maya was about to respond, but Alie came to her defense. "Maya's telling the truth, Braird. I can tell. You know I can. And when it comes to seeing, it doesn't matter how big or how strong you are."

Braird looked from Alie to Maya. With her chin up, Maya sat straight, and while Alie trembled a little, she didn't back down, either.

"All right," Braird said at last, and everyone sighed, clearly relieved Braird wasn't going to make an issue about Maya's honesty. Maya understood that while Braird and his mother were invaluable crew members, their prickly natures and exacting standards made them hard to be around.

Alie whispered, "But when they finally trust you, they're on your side. No matter what."

"Right," Maya whispered back, wondering if Braird and his mother would ever be on her side.

Not hearing the conversation, Larz leaned forward and smiled. "I will never call you little Maya again. You might be short, but there's nothing small about you. You have enough courage for ten people."

Maya blushed. "Thank you, Larz." She shrugged. "Sometimes, I was scared. Especially when I was in the Office with Bigly. And at first when Cali scooped us up."

"Of course you were." Larz picked up his cup and took a drink.

"Only a fool wouldn't be afraid," Braird added. "And I hope you're not a fool."

"I try my best not to be a fool," Maya retorted.

"Be quiet, Braird," Proko said. "This human from the other side is risking her life to help bring Pawel Greenwood back to remove Tamick Ashglade from the ruling council. You should be thankful, not critical. What happens in Norlander affects many places, even as far away as the Blessed Mountains. You of all creatures should know this."

Braird glared at Proko and would have stormed away if the bubble hadn't been there, keeping everyone in place.

"Water creature," Braird said, his voice scornful.

"Air head," Proko and Takis shot back together.

Braird stood, and Maya saw feathers rise from his arms and shoulders.

"Enough! Braird, sit down," Larz said. Maya felt his voice as a firm nudge, bringing her and the others to attention.

"Do I have a choice?" Braird asked. "I'm trapped in this damned bubble."

Alie replied, "I'm sure either Proko or Takis would let you leave if you really wanted to." She turned to the castors. "Wouldn't you?"

Proko said, "Braird, we would never keep you here against your will. You should know this by now."

Braird's shoulders twitched, but his feathers disappeared back into his arms and shoulders.

"Come on, buddy," Larz urged. "Sit down. Let's show Maya our stories."

Braird didn't say anything, but he sat down.

With his hands, Larz wove a story, which sprang into focus the way a movie or a television show would. Images of a frozen land appeared with a town filled with stone and wood homes with sweeping domed roofs. Large elves moved lightly through the snow, and they always seemed to be laughing, even when they were chased by huge white furry animals that looked like a cross between a leopard and a lion. Without killing or hurting the creatures, the elves worked together and used magic to keep them at bay. The creatures had their own magic, but Maya got the feeling that when the strong elves were in a group, they were not in any danger. Bringing his hands together

63

and then pulling them apart, Larz homed in on a scene where a much younger image of himself was being chased by one of the animals, whose mouth was wide open, revealing sharp teeth. Nobody was around to help. Larz was alone.

Maya and Alie gasped.

"Run!" Takis and Proko urged.

Braird laughed, and it lightened his fierce face. "If the leupart had caught Larz, then he wouldn't be here showing us the story."

Grinning, Larz didn't reply, focusing instead on the scene between his hands. Maya and the others watched as young Larz looked over his shoulder at the advancing leupart. Then, in an astonishing burst of speed, the elf ran until the creature was left far behind. Cheated out of a meal, the leupart's roar of disappointment burst from the confines of Larz's hand and bounced around the bubble until it gradually dissipated.

Everyone clapped—even Braird—and Takis said, "We've never seen that one before, Larz."

"Oh, I've got plenty of tales you've never seen," Larz replied. "I don't want to show everything at once. Who knows how long we'll be out here searching for the captain's daughter?"

"Did you think about blasting the leupart with magic?" Braird asked.

"Yup," Larz answered. "But first I wanted to try to get away without killing or hurting her. And I did."

Alie's soft voice chimed in. "You must have been pretty tired after using all that magic to escape."

"I was," Larz said. "I had to rest for a couple of days. I couldn't even go to school. My mother and father weren't too happy with me." Shrugging, Larz laughed as he remembered. "They got over it."

"Did you learn your lesson?" This question came from Maya, and it just popped out, surprising her as much as it surprised everyone in the bubble.

Larz frowned. "My lesson?"

Braird astounded Maya by siding with her. "Not to go out on the tundra by yourself, you idiot. You might be big, but there are things out there that are bigger, and they have their own magic. Some of them would be happy to eat you. Like the leupart."

"Yeah," Larz said, staring at a point somewhere out of the bubble. "Never did that again." Blinking, he looked around the circle. "An elf at school dared me to go out by myself."

"And you fell for it?" Proko asked.

"I did." Larz looked sheepish. "Never could resist a dare." He shook his head. "Never mind about that. Proko and Takis, show Maya something from your lives."

Sitting side by side, the two castors turned to face each other, putting their furry hands up. Their four palms nearly touched, and Proko's and Takis's synchronized motions became a kind of entrancing dance. No one could look away.

The castors took everyone deep into a forest, by a lake too large to see one end from the other. Maya got the feeling this was not Darkwood Forest, where the ogres were confined and where Novok had pulled her into the ravine. There was a feeling of peace and security rather than the radiating tension that came from the ogres' fierce hatred of being imprisoned. On one side of the lake, the castors had their village, homes built from logs and branches. The village, encircled and connected by ramps, was in the water rather than on the banks. All around, castors young and old splashed in the water, not minding if their clothes got wet. Some of the very young castors didn't even bother with clothes as they leaped and swam.

Maya murmured, "What a beautiful place."

"Someday, after we've sailed Elferterre's seas, we'll go back," Proko said, and Takis chittered in agreement. "But not before we've had a few adventures of our own. Right, Takis?"

"Right," Takis answered.

Then Takis and Proko showed another village, far across the lake, this one built high into large sloping banks, and Maya saw grenogs going in and out of round doors with decks that had long stairs leading to the water.

Maya turned to Alie. "Is that your village?"

"It is," Alie told her.

Proko said, "Alie doesn't have the same kind of magic we do, and we wanted to show you where she came from."

"Thank you," Alie replied. "That's very good of you."

Maya asked, "Did you three know each other before you came to work on *The Resolute*?"

"No," Takis answered. "Grenogs and castors don't mix much. But maybe we can work on this when we go home. We get along fine, even though we look different."

She might have said more, but Larz nudged Braird. "Show Maya where you're from."

Braird extended his arms, and again Maya got the impression of feathers and a faint unfurling of wings coming from his shoulders. But the feathers went away as Braird showed his story.

Braird's image took everyone high into the mountains, where various homes were tucked into caverns big and small. The corbeaus, sometimes in elf form and sometimes in bird form, lived in the largest caverns, which all had ramps that looked like runways. In the smaller holes were winged creatures that were a cross between a rabbit and a dog but with feathers rather than fur. As Maya watched the corbeaus soar and dip, she got the impression they were somehow guarding the smaller creatures, who clambered without concern on the sides of the mountains and nibbled on the various plants and flowers that somehow managed to thrive there.

The scene changed to show a very young Braird, who was being taught to fly by an older corbeau who could only be his father. In fascination, Maya watched as the two easily transformed from elf to bird with glossy indigo feathers. While Braird flew hesitantly up and down, never going too far from the ramp by his home, an elf came to stand by the older corbeau who was coaching Braird.

Maya blinked. The elf was Hawthorn, and her face didn't have the long scar. She was even smiling as she watched Braird. There was no hint of the hardness or bitterness Maya had felt when she first met Hawthorn. Maya thought, *Something bad happened between then and now.*

But Braird was too busy with his story to notice Maya's thoughts. In the image, as Braird practiced flying, he flew farther and farther away from his ramp and his home. His father accompanied him, and together they soared in a circle around the peaks of the mountains.

"Wow," Maya said as the image faded.

"Can't compete with the Blessed Mountains," Larz replied, but there was no envy or resentment in his voice. "One of the most beautiful places in Elferterre."

For the first time, Braird's sharp expression softened, and while he didn't say anything, he actually looked pleased.

Larz clapped his hands. "All right. Time for some music. Alie, do your thing. You might not be able to show stories the way we can, but when it comes to music, you can't be beat."

Bobbing, the grenog stood.

Maya wondered what kind of music the nervous grenog could make, but as soon as Alie began to sing, her tentativeness dropped away to be replaced by a confidence and verve that Maya, even with her ability to see to the heart of things, hadn't known was there. Alie's voice was full and strong, with an astounding range of notes and melodies.

"How does she do it?" Maya asked in wonder.

"Grenogs have several vocal chords," Proko answered. "Amazing, isn't it?"

"It sure is," Maya said as Alie began to sing a lively song, all the while providing an accompanying melody.

Maya wasn't much of a dancer, but the music urged Maya to her feet. The notes and the songs surrounded her in a swirl, and she forgot about everything else except for dancing and taking a drink when she was thirsty. The more Maya drank, the more she felt like dancing until she was giddy and out of breath. Larz, Proko, and Takis whirled merrily, but to Maya's surprise, Braird's dancing was the most beautiful, a series of intricate spins and steps. As Alie sang one song after another, Braird danced closer and closer to Maya until they were nearly touching. She put her hand on his chest, feeling his warmth and the beating of his heart. This made her feel even giddier, and Maya left her hand on his chest for a long time as they danced together. And even though Braird had not transformed into a bird, Maya felt as though she were enveloped by his wings.

8: STORM ON THE RESOLUTE

The next morning, Maya felt worse than she ever had in her life, even when she'd had a bad case of the flu. Her head throbbed, and sitting up made everything spin around so alarmingly that Maya collapsed back onto the bed. Even worse, her stomach churned in a sickening way, and moaning, Maya wrapped her arms around her stomach.

With a flushing face, Maya remembered how the night before, Braird had guided her down the stairs that led to the lower deck. He had held her gently but firmly to stop her from careening from side to side and falling. The crew had all decided it would be better for Maya, in the state she was in, to stay with Alie rather than stumble back to her own room in the captain's quarters.

"Can't hold your drink, can you?" Braird had asked as he helped tuck her into Alie's bed. But his tone was not sharp.

"Hush, Braird," Alie said. "Maya's not from here. She doesn't know how strong our drinks are."

"No, I suppose not," Braird conceded, briefly putting his hand on Maya's cheek.

With the music gone, Maya felt cross and queasy. She wanted to slap Braird's hand away, but all she could manage was a half-hearted retort. "Leave me alone."

But instead of coming back with a snappy response, Braird laughed. "That's exactly what I'm going to do. Alie, have fun with her tomorrow morning."

"I'll give Maya a tonic tonight, and it will help her feel better in the morning," Alie said.

Closing her eyes, Maya clamped her mouth shut. There was no way she was going to drink anything else.

Braird laughed again. "Good luck with that. My prediction? She'll be puking her guts out tomorrow."

"Oh, Braird," Alie said with a sigh. "Why can't you be nice?"

Maya thought, *Yeah, Braird, why can't you be nice?*

Braird's thoughts replied, *I am being nice. I could have let you fall down the stairs.*

"Larz wouldn't have let me fall. So there!" was Maya's last triumphant retort out loud before she fell into a dreamless sleep.

But in the cold hard light of morning, as Maya lay in bed, clutching her stomach, she knew Braird was right. She was going to be sick. Looking desperately around, Maya saw a small bathroom across the room. Despite being dizzy, she leaped out of bed and somehow managed not to trip over Alie, who was wrapped in a blanket and curled up on some cushions on the floor. Maya made it to the bathroom just in time and stayed there for a long while.

When Maya, pale and on shaky legs, finally came out, Alie was waiting for her with a glass of something in such a bright shade of green that Maya's stomach twisted as she looked at it.

"Drink," Alie commanded as sternly as her gentle nature allowed.

"I can't," Maya whispered, licking dry lips. "I'll be sick again."

"No you won't," Alie said, putting the cup to Maya's lips. "Drink!"

Groaning a little, Maya opened her mouth and let Alie trickle in some of the liquid. To Maya's surprise, the drink didn't taste as bad as it looked. It was fresh and smooth, and Maya drank it all. Almost immediately, her stomach settled down, but Maya was exhausted, and she didn't think she'd be able to make it up the stairs by herself, much less face the captain and Finneas.

"Sleep it off," Alie said. "I'll come back and check on you after breakfast."

Maya didn't argue as she crept back into bed. "Sorry, Alie!"

"Oh, this happens to all of us at first. Hope it won't happen to you again too many times," Alie replied.

"It won't. I never, ever want to feel this way again."

Not saying anything, Alie patted Maya's shoulder and left.

Before Maya fell asleep, she remembered how Will, Jay, and Lexie had drunk too much at The Trotting Horse. At the time, Maya had had little pity for her friends the day after, but now that Maya understood how bad it could feel to drink too much, she was more sympathetic.

Maya slept for most of the morning. She woke up briefly when she felt something move on her pillow. Opening her eyes, Maya saw it was Aiken, Orlaith, and Eloise, who were watching over her.

Maya smiled wanly at them.

Eloise said, "Last night, I was going to warn you not to have too much to drink if the younger crew came out on the upper deck."

"Probably wouldn't have done any good," Orlaith replied.

"Probably not," Eloise agreed. "That's why I didn't bother to say anything."

Sighing but comforted by the relics, Maya went back to sleep. She was aware when Alie came in periodically to check on her, but she only woke slightly before falling asleep again. Then someone else came in, someone whose personality had more of a pull, and Maya opened her eyes to see Symi, the cook, sitting on a chair by the bed. Symi was tall, dark, and slender like Pawel and the elves at The Other Green Door, but there was something about the cook that reminded Maya of her mémère, even though her grandmother was short and plump. Symi had the same aura of concern, sympathy, and warmth as Mémère did, and Maya had the feeling Symi did not judge people harshly for the mistakes they made. Around Symi's neck was a necklace, a sliver of a moon that changed color as Maya stared at it, going from silver to white to blue.

"Hello," Maya said shyly as Aiken, Orlaith, and Eloise calmly regarded the cook.

"Hello." Symi smiled. Her warmth radiated out, enveloping them all, and Maya relaxed. "Lunch is winding down, and I thought I'd come in and check on you. Feeling better?"

"Yes, I am." Maya sat up. "Alie gave me something green to drink this morning, and it really helped a lot."

"Our Alie can do a lot of things," Symi said. "I don't know what I'd do without her."

"Too bad she's so timid," Maya said.

"I'm working on that," Symi replied. "But I've still got a long way to go."

Maya nodded. "It's not easy to change, is it?"

"No, it's not. Somehow, I wonder if we ever do. I'm thinking that as we age, we just become more of who we really are." The smile went away to be replaced by a little frown, but soon the smile came back. "I've brought you a cup of tea. Thought it might help settle your stomach even more. Would you like it?"

"Yes, please."

Symi passed a white mug to Maya, who took a sip and was astonished to find it was chamomile tea.

The cook laughed. "I can see by your expression that you're surprised. But it seemed to me that a human girl who traveled the sea in a web boat deserved a special cup of tea."

Maya said, "Thank you."

Symi stood. "My pleasure. And, Maya, please feel free to come down and talk to me whenever you need to. The captain told us you'll be working with Braird." Symi hesitated. "Braird is good, but he isn't always nice." She shrugged. "Anyway, if you need a sympathetic ear, you know where to find me. In the kitchen."

"Thanks," Maya said, grateful for Symi's warm offer.

After finishing the tea, Maya thought the time had come to go to the deck house to take a shower. Feeling better but bedraggled, she hoped she wouldn't meet anyone, and slipping the relics into her pockets, Maya crept up the stairs. Down below, she could hear a happy chatter as the crew finished their lunch, and some of the smells—warm, spicy, buttery—drifted up. By now, Maya was hungry, and after her shower, Maya decided to return to the kitchen to see if there were any leftovers. And perhaps talk to Symi, if she wasn't busy.

Maya almost got her wish about not meeting anyone. The upper deck was nearly empty. Most everyone was still in the dining room on the lower deck, having their lunch. Everyone except for Braird, who looked furious as he paced from side to side.

Immediately, Maya sensed Braird was angry with her. Maya wished she could slip around him, undetected, but he was between her and the deck house, and there was no way to avoid him. Maya lifted her chin, readying herself for the fight she knew was coming.

She didn't have long to wait. Spotting her from across the deck, Braird strode toward Maya, and she was amazed at how fast he could move. As Braird rushed over, Maya got the impression of a bird of prey. But Maya was neither a mouse nor a rabbit, and standing as tall as she could, she glared defiantly at him.

"What's the matter with you?" Maya asked, deciding to get in the first strike.

Braird loomed over her, and there was the impression of feathers. "You're a sneaky little human, that's what. Last night, You knew about the plan to fly with me to find Clarin, didn't you? But you never said a word. You danced like you didn't have a care in the world."

Maya didn't back down. "So what if I did? What difference does it make?"

Braird drew himself up to his full considerable height. "It means I can't trust you to be honest. You might not actually lie, but you don't tell the whole truth."

Maya flinched a little, knowing Braird wasn't wrong. Ever since the Book of Everything had come into her life, Maya had been keeping secrets from the people who mattered the most to her. Maya told herself it was for their own good, but was it really? Or was she simply being devious?

Looking up at Braird, Maya was about to concede that he had a point, but his expression, judgmental and harsh, made her angry.

She shook her finger at him. "You think you know it all, don't you? Because you're half elf, half bird? Far superior to a little human."

"I'm a corbeau," Braird retorted. "Get it right."

"Whatever!" Maya caught a glimpse of his pride, of how thin skinned he was, and she knew where to strike. "But you don't know much, and that's a fact. In your universe and mine, things are moving in a bad direction, and all you can do is worry about your little reactions to things. I've got news for you, Braird. It's not always about you. This time it's about the captain and his daughter. I can help. I can see in a different way than you can. Have you found Clarin yet? No, you haven't. You should be grateful this little human is here to help. Stop moping and grow up. Don't be such a stupid baby."

Braird's head snapped back, and Maya knew that once again, in her anger, she had said too much.

"Braird..." Maya began, but he was gone. Half-way across the deck was the largest bird she had ever seen, and his indigo feathers gleamed in the sunlight. The bird gave her one piercing look before taking flight, leaving the deck in a silent but furious flap and taking to the sky. Maya watched as Braird soared higher and higher until she could hardly see him anymore.

The relics had crawled out of her pockets and were perched on her arm.

Eloise's voice was reproachful. "Maya."

"He's really mad," Orlaith said.

Aiken whistled in admiration. "That boy sure can fly." Then he turned to Maya. "Went a bit too far, didn't you?"

"Yeah," Maya replied, her shoulders drooping. "But he's one of the most irritating boys I know." However, this was no excuse, and Maya realized it. Her eyes stung with tears, and by the time she reached the deck house, she was crying.

"My, oh my!" Finneas said as she entered. "What now? Did you have a dustup with Braird?" Maya nodded brusquely, angry with herself for crying yet again in front of Finneas. "I saw him pacing the deck when I returned from lunch. Go take a shower. I'll have a nice cup of tea ready for you when you're done."

After Maya's shower, as they settled in the sitting area, Finneas said, "I'm not surprised. The captain made his announcement over lunch, and while Braird didn't say much, I could tell he was upset. He left as soon as it was polite to do so, and that's when you came upon him. Too bad you had to meet him just then."

Maya sighed. "Bad timing."

The relics were on the coffee table.

Orlaith blinked. "And rude words."

"Yes, rude words," Maya admitted. "Now that I can really see, I know just what to say that will be the most cutting."

"I know," Finneas replied. "I can see a little, too. Not as much as you can, but enough for me to have to bite my tongue from time to time."

"Do you have a hard time doing it?" Maya asked.

"A little. But my nature isn't as fiery as yours is. I think it's easier for me. I just wait until my anger subsides a little. Then I know whether to say something. Or not."

Maya ran her fingers through her wet curls. "I wish I was more like you and didn't lose my temper so easily."

Finneas regarded her. "Do you? And if you were more like me, would you have come to Elferterre? Would you have gone across two universes?"

"You're here on the ocean with the captain," Maya pointed out. "Far from the lake in the woods where you were born."

"True," Finneas replied. "But on this ship I am protected by the elves and their magic. And there you were, on that little boat out to sea."

"I had the relics," Maya said, smiling at the three on the table.

"Yes, you had the relics," Finneas agreed.

"But you're the one who came up with the idea of Orlaith building a boat," Aiken said.

"And you're the one who talked to Cali and found out we were in no danger," Eloise added. "After that, you were actually enjoying the adventure, weren't you?"

"Maybe," Maya conceded.

"And you're the one who went over the cliff with the ogre so that her friends could escape with the lock and key," Finneas said. "Do you think a girl without a fiery nature could have done all those things?"

"I don't know. But there's more than one way to be brave, isn't there?"

Finneas answered, "There is. All I'm saying is that without the qualities you have, you might not have gotten this far."

"Finneas is right," Eloise said. "Nevertheless, you shouldn't use your ability to see to hurt others' feelings."

Orlaith tapped the table with her two front legs. "Don't mistake being blunt for being frank."

Maya smiled ruefully. "I know, I know." But then her stomach rumbled, reminding Maya how hungry she was. "Do you suppose there are any leftovers from lunch?"

Finneas set his empty cup on the table. "I bet there are. Symi usually makes a lot. She doesn't want anyone to go hungry."

Maya said, "Just like my grandmother."

Finneas laughed. "From universe to universe, some things don't change. Go down and see what Symi has left."

As Finneas had predicted, there were plenty of leftovers: a smashed chickpea salad, more of the dark bread, raw vegetables with a creamy dip, and crunchy cookies for dessert. Leaving the relics behind in the deck house, Maya ate at a small red enamel table in the corner of the kitchen rather than in the dining room by herself.

On the counter, there was a huge mound of vegetables for Symi and Alie to chop, and there was just enough room for them to stand side by side and work without bumping elbows.

"Did you see Braird on deck?" Symi asked, chopping with a speed and precision that dazzled Maya.

"Yeah," Maya said between bites of the tasty chickpea salad.

"How did it go? He left pretty fast after the captain said you'd be working together."

"Not good," Maya answered. "We had a fight. And then he turned into a bird and flew away."

Alie shook her head, and Symi told Maya, "You know, maybe it would be better for Braird to search the sea on his own. The boy's a loner, just like his mother."

"Maybe." Maya scooped up some dip with a long thin green vegetable. "But I really think I could help. We see in different ways. We could make a good team if we didn't fight so much."

Symi turned back to her chopping. "Braird's not really a team player. No doubt his pride is wounded by being aided by a small human."

"Yeah, it is," Maya replied, sorry that she had spoken in anger.

"Braird can be a good friend when he trusts you," Alie said, glancing quickly from her chopping to Symi and then back again.

Symi didn't stop chopping. "Yes, but getting him to trust you can take a long time. And things can be pretty unpleasant until he does."

Maya had finished eating and sat quietly while Symi and Alie made their way through the vegetables. No doubt Symi was right. After the fight on the deck, Maya decided that it probably would be better for Braird to search on his own. She and Braird wouldn't make much of a team if he didn't trust her. After working with Will, Jay, and Lexie, Maya knew firsthand how important trust was, how it could mean the difference between a successful mission and one that ended in disaster. Even then, things didn't always turn out the way they should. And without trust? Maya shuddered as she thought about it.

Maya stood. "I'm going to talk to Braird before I go to the captain. Because Braird was right. I should have mentioned something last night when we were on the upper deck. But I was having a good time. I didn't want to spoil things by making Braird mad."

"Which he would have been," Symi replied. "And that would have ended the fun."

"Probably, but still."

Symi said, "You must do what you think is right. But tread carefully. Corbeaus are touchy by nature, and you're already on his bad side."

Alie looked as though she wanted to say something, but she didn't.

As Maya headed up the stairs to the deck, she thought about what Symi had said. Maya agreed with the cook: Braird was one of the prickliest guys she had ever met, and it was unlikely he would bend enough to work with her. Nevertheless, Maya had said things she shouldn't have, and it was up to her to apologize.

Braird had come back from his flight and was by the prow of the ship. Proko and Takis were with him, and before Maya got halfway to the prow, Braird spotted her and scowled fiercely.

Oh, great, Maya thought, even though his expression didn't surprise her. Braird had left in a rage, and not enough time had passed for him to calm down.

"What do you want?" Braird asked as soon as Maya was close enough.

"Can we talk?" Maya stopped a little ways from him and the castors.

"Do I have a choice?" Braird asked. "Can anyone stop you from talking?"

Maya frowned. "If you want me to go away, I will."

Proko put her hand on Braird's arm. "Let's hear what Maya has to say."

Shaking his head, Braird swung around and gazed moodily out to sea.

"Give Maya a chance," came Chantay's melodious voice. "For a small human, she has a lot of pluck."

"She sure does." Braird laughed shortly, but Maya could tell he was not amused.

Remembering Finneas's advice, Maya waited a few beats before responding. "Okay, if you don't want to talk to me, I get it. I said some mean things, and I'm sorry. I'll go to the captain and explain."

Braird whipped back around to stare at her. "Explain what?"

"That we can't work together after all. We get on each other's nerves too much. You know we do."

"You're going to tell that to the captain?" Braird asked in astonishment.

Maya shrugged. "Sure, why not?"

Takis said, "Maya, the captain gave an order. He's the commander of the ship. You can't just tell him you're going to back down. Especially when it's about something as important as finding his daughter. Do you understand?"

Chastened, Maya did understand. She had overstepped her bounds by impulsively making a suggestion that involved Braird, someone she hadn't even met. She had never stopped to consider how Braird might feel. "Braird, I'm sorry. I truly am. I just wanted to help the captain. He loves his daughter so much that he would never desert her. Never, ever in a million years." Maya's eyes filled with tears, and she angrily rubbed them. She would not cry again, especially in front of Braird.

Stumbling, Maya turned to leave, but was stopped by Braird's command: "Wait!"

Turning, she faced Braird. "What?"

"You really want to help the captain, don't you?" Braird asked.

"Of course I do!" Maya retorted. "Did you think I offered to help because I wanted to fly on the back of a large bird?" Then, despite herself, she grinned a little. "Even though it does sound like fun to go up high over the sea."

Proko and Takis laughed, and Chantay chimed in, "See what I mean, Braird?"

There might have been a softening of Braird's expression, but there was no hint of a smile. "Did you ever think about how slippery my feathers would be?"

"No," Maya admitted. "I didn't."

Braird flexed his arms and there was a fluff of blue. "And how if you fell, something in the sea might eat you? There's a lot out there, waiting. You're lucky Cali found your little boat before something else did."

"I didn't think of that either," Maya said. She understood now that Braird's concern was not only for his pride but also for her safety. However, his pride was like a glittering light that shined with such force it obscured his other virtues.

Braird shook his head. "You just act first and think later, don't you?"

"Pretty much," Maya replied.

Proko said, "Well, lucky you have us here to help you because we're going to build you a small saddle with a safety strap to help with the slippery feathers."

"They should work, Braird, don't you think?" Takis asked. "We're castors, and we're pretty good at making things."

"Maybe," Braird replied, and there was a glimmer of a smile as he considered Maya.

9: VIOLA'S DECISION

Viola stood in front of the impassive Toad Queen and the Old Oak. The Forest of Arden was so still that it seemed as though the forest was holding its breath as it waited for her answer. Viola wanted to say no. To Viola, having her eyes peeled sounded like nasty business and just thinking about it made her toes curl in her shoes. Plus, she had seen what it had done to Maya, who seemed more like an adult than a teenage girl. Viola understood that being able to see deeply was a burden that had aged Maya in an astonishingly short amount of time. As the president's daughter, Viola felt as though she had enough burdens to carry her through her teenage years. She didn't need the added weight of really being able to see to the heart of things. And then what would she do? Advise her father on the sly after catching glimpses of what leaders and their aides hid deep inside? No, Viola didn't want to be in that position. She wanted to be a teenager, not a mini-spy who tricked unsuspecting adults.

The Toad Queen didn't hurry Viola. Instead, she sat patiently beneath the Old Oak, who thrummed softly, even sympathetically. In the moonlit clearing, the smaller toads were still, leaning toward Viola, and they were as patient as the Toad Queen.

Viola was about to say no, she would not have her eyes peeled. But then a flash came to her of a white castle with towers and turrets. This could only be the Great Library. Inside was a man, dark and beautiful but with a coiled intensity.

Cinnial, Viola thought.

"Yes," the Toad Queen answered, and there was the slightest tremor in her voice. "He has just taken the Great Library and killed Sydda."

"How do you know this?" Viola asked in a shocked whisper. She had never thought this would happen. Somehow, she thought that Maya and everyone working to help the Great Library would prevail.

"The universe chirrs with the news. Everything has changed."

As Viola thought about this and all the various implications, another image came to her. At the Great Library, Cinnial's armored troops faced a large group that had surrounded the castle. Without a doubt, Viola knew this group had come to liberate the Great Library. Nobody in the group had any weapons, but it was clear to Viola that they had a power, formidable in its own right, even though Viola wasn't exactly sure what that power was. To Viola's surprise, Mémère was there, and beside her were teenagers Viola had never seen. One was a beautiful blonde girl and the other a boy with dark hair and eyes.

"I should be at the Great Library, too," Viola murmured as the image faded.

"Should you?" the Toad Queen asked. Above her, the Old Oak creaked.

Viola sighed. "Yes."

Not blinking, the Toad Queen stared at Viola. "But do you need to have your eyes peeled to be there?"

"Maybe not," Viola answered, ready to grasp at the way out the Toad Queen was offering. After all, in Viola's flash, Mémère was at the Great Library, and Viola thought it highly unlikely that she would be coming to the Toad Queen to have her eyes peeled. But then the Old Oak creaked again, and the Toad Queen looked up into the massive branches. The creaking stopped, and the Toad Queen turned back to Viola.

However, Viola had heard the Old Oak's message. The tree was urging Viola to have her eyes peeled, and she understood why. Cinnial was such a formidable adversary that the opposition needed each member to be as strong as possible. Even though she was strong in other ways, seeing was not Mémère's power. But seeing was Viola's power, and by refusing to have her eyes peeled, that power would be diminished. Viola sensed this missed opportunity would ripple forward in unexpected ways, holding her back when she should be surging forward. Even at twelve, Viola understood this would make a big difference in the outcome of many things, perhaps even be a matter of life and death for her as well as for others whom she cared about.

Viola squared her shoulders. "Yes, I'll have my eyes peeled."

"Are you certain?" the Toad Queen asked. "It will change your life, and you will never be the same again."

Viola's palms were wet, and she wiped them on her dress. "Yes, I'm certain."

"I will ask you one more time. Think carefully, Viola. I sense you are unsure. Will you have your eyes peeled?"

Viola looked up into the Old Oak's dark branches, but the tree remained silent. "Yes, I'll have my eyes peeled."

"Very well, come closer. Back at the lodge, the stewards Sophie and Elwyn know you are making this decision. The Book of Everything is helping them keep track of things. They will help you."

"Okay. Will it hurt?"

"It will hurt a lot."

"Do it, then," Viola said, her voice fierce. "Do it now. Get it over with."

"I will in a moment. But before I peel your eyes, I have a gift for you from the Old Oak." Holding out her left arm, the Toad Queen opened her hand to reveal three golden acorns.

Viola's eyes were wide. "Just like the ones the Old Oak gave to Maya."

For the first time, there was a glimmer of humor in the Toad Queen's voice. "It seems the Old Oak has taken a shine to both of you girls from Earth." Then her voice became grave. "These are not given lightly, but the situation is very serious. The Old Oak thinks you need all the help you can get. And I concur."

Viola looked up into the dark branches. "Thank you," she whispered, and the branches creaked in response.

After putting the acorns in the pocket of her dress, Viola stepped forward. "Do it," she repeated.

The Toad Queen's right arm shot forward, and the last thing Viola saw was a gleaming claw. Then there was blood and pain so intense that she passed out. Viola would have fallen, but the small toads were ready, and their voices leaped from their throats, surrounding Viola in a cocoon of sound, stopping her from hitting the ground, propelling her through the woods, bringing her to the lodge, where Sophie and Elwyn waited.

Viola came to a little and heard Elwyn say, "Oh my, oh my, oh my!"

Sophie said, "Not a pretty sight, that's for sure." This was followed by a sigh. "Poor girl."

Then Viola lost consciousness again. When she woke up, she was in bed. The pain was gone, but everything was dark. In a panic, Viola sat up, but a hand patted her shoulder.

"You're all right," Sophie said. "Your eyes are bandaged. I'll take them off soon."

Viola choked a little. "I thought I had gone blind."

"No, you are not blind. When I remove the bandages, you will see all too well."

There was an edge to Sophie's voice, and Viola asked, "Have you had your eyes peeled?"

"I have. Many years ago, but when it was done, I was much older than you are. With Feste gone so much, it seemed that it would be a great help if someone else here could really see. Not much gets through the trees in the Forest of Arden, but there is always a chance that someone will slip through and betray us."

"Did someone slip through?"

Sophie didn't answer right away. "Yes," she finally said. "But the person was so close that even I didn't see it."

"Sir John," Viola whispered.

"Sir John," Sophie repeated. "A lesson, Viola. Even those of us who have had our eyes peeled can't see everything. Sometimes, our feelings get in the way. It did with Feste, and it did with me. We both loved Sir John. We didn't think he'd steal a Book of Everything and then attack the garrison in Greendale."

"So terrible," Viola said, her voice catching. "And my father helped him."

"I expect they both thought they were doing the right thing. Even though they weren't."

"How do we know when we're doing the right thing?" Viola asked.

Sophie hesitated. "Sometimes there's a bad feeling, deep inside, telling us when we shouldn't do something. When we ignore that feeling, the results are usually not good."

"Do you think my father and Sir John had a bad feeling before stealing Earth's Book of Everything?"

"I don't know," Sophie answered. "When emotions are high, you can be sure you're making the right choice when really you aren't. That's why it's best, if you can, to make decisions when you've had time to think about things."

"But we don't always have time to think about things first, do we?" Viola asked, remembering how quickly she had whisked Earth's Book of Everything and the duke's children, Sebastian and Rosalind, away from Chet. But Viola had no doubt this had been a good decision.

"No, life doesn't always give us the chance to sit and reflect. Sometimes we have to act fast and let the chips fall where they may. Now let's take a look at your eyes and see how they are doing."

Sophie unwrapped the bandages, and Viola blinked in the bright light of a small bedroom that was not the one she had been sleeping in next to Rosalind and Sebastian's room. Everything looked crisp, standing out in sharp detail. It was as though there had been a slight fog over everything before she'd had her eyes peeled, and now it was lifted. The clarity of her vision took her by surprise, and Viola shook her head as she regarded Sophie.

"Everything seems different, doesn't it?" Sophie asked.

"It sure does," Viola answered in amazement, and as she regarded Sophie, various images of the woman's life came to Viola: Sophie, as a young girl, running with friends in broad green fields; Sophie, as an older girl, helping her mother around the house; and Sophie, as a young woman, being rejected by a man she loved.

"That's enough," Sophie said. "Don't pry."

Viola pulled back. "Sorry!"

Sophie patted Viola's shoulder again. "Seeing like this takes some getting used to. But pretty soon you'll learn to look only when you should."

"Maya must have had to learn," Viola said.

"She did."

"My seeing is not as good as hers is."

Sophie stood. "Maybe not, but it's good enough. Better than mine. Are you hungry? I'll go get a tray from the kitchen if you are."

Viola's stomach rumbled. "Yes, please."

As Sophie turned to leave, there was a soft knock on the door.

"Viola?" Rosalind's crisp voice called. "Are you all right? Can we come in?"

"Please?" Sebastian added in his best pleading voice. "We really want to see you."

Viola looked up at Sophie, who nodded. "Come in," Viola said.

The door opened with a snap, and the children bounded into the room.

"Viola," Sebastian said, his eyes wide, "you've been in bed for two nights and a day. And they put you in a room away from us so that it would be quiet for you."

"Meg told us you went to the Toad Queen to have your eyes peeled. Is that true?" Rosalind asked.

"It's true," Viola answered.

As the children gazed at Viola's eyes, Sebastian wrinkled his nose. "Your eyes are red."

"Sebastian," Rosalind chided, "of course Viola's eyes are red. She just had her eyes peeled. Meg told us Viola's eyes would be red. Remember?"

"Speaking of Meg," Sophie said. "Where is she?"

"They gave me the slip." Meg, their new young nanny at the lodge, was standing in the doorway. Her arms were crossed, and she wasn't smiling.

"Now that wasn't a good thing to do, was it?" Sophie's expression was stern, but Viola could tell she was trying not to smile.

Rosalind looked anxiously from Sophie to Meg. "Sorry."

With grubby hands, Sebastian pulled at Viola's arm. "We knew it was the only way we'd get to see you."

"We missed having you in the next room, and everyone kept saying no when we asked if we could visit you," Rosalind said. "And finally they told us not to ask anymore."

Viola studied the children. From them she got feelings of loneliness and confusion. They missed their mother and father, and they missed their busy life in Caxton, where everyone knew and catered to them because they were the duke's children. In the span of a night, all that had changed. First their mother had been murdered and then their father. While the children didn't know this, they did know that they had been bundled away from Caxton and taken on a long journey to a place they had never been, to a lodge and a tiny village in a deep forest. Even though Viola hadn't known the children long, she was their only tie with Caxton.

Viola glanced at Sophie, who understood and nodded slightly.

Viola patted the bed. "Do you want to come up here with me?"

"Yes!" Sebastian scrambled joyfully onto the bed, and Rosalind quickly followed him. Soon, there was a child tucked on either side of Viola, who put her arms around them.

Meg sniffed. "Well, that certainly rewards naughty behavior." But as she stared at the children nestled beside Viola, her expression softened.

"They've been through a lot," Sophie said.

"I know." Meg's lips quirked into a reluctant grin. "And I suppose we have to make allowances." Then she shook her finger at the children. "For now."

"Sorry, Meg," the two children said together, giving her contrite looks.

"Apology accepted," Meg replied.

Sophie put her hand on the door. "I'm going to go downstairs to make a tray for Viola. Meg, will you come down with me and then bring it to her?"

"Will do," Meg answered cheerfully, and Viola could see that she was no longer grumpy with the children. *Good*, Viola thought. *She doesn't stay mad long.*

"Okay, then." Sophie paused. "That will give Viola and Rosalind and Sebastian a chance to talk."

"Yes," Meg replied, looking thoughtfully at Viola and the children. Then they left.

A chance to talk. Viola knew exactly what Sophie meant. It was time to tell the children that they would be staying at the lodge until things were safe in Caxton, whenever that might be. Perhaps even tell them that their parents were dead, but Viola wasn't sure about that. It all depended on how the conversation went. Finally, Viola needed to tell the children that she would be leaving soon, in a day or two, when her eyes had fully healed. Even though she had not consulted the Book of Everything yet, Viola knew it was time to return to her father, Mémère, Diana, and Simon. And to Chet, who was surely plotting his escape.

"What do you want to talk to us about?" Rosalind asked. "We're good most of the time. We hardly ever run away from our nanny."

Viola stroked the little girl's smooth hair. "Yes, you are."

"We just wanted to see you," Sebastian said.

Viola ruffled his curly hair. "I know."

Rosalind sat up straight. "It's about Mama and Papa, isn't it?"

Another one who could see. Viola suspected now that she'd had her eyes peeled, she would notice that many other people could see in varying degrees. It would jump out at her, the way it had with Maya when they had first met. Immediately, Maya had known that Viola could see, even though Viola hadn't known it herself. Well, a part of her had known, but she hadn't been able to understand why she always sensed things that other people didn't seem to notice.

"It is." Viola decided that the children, young though they were, needed to hear the truth. She didn't want to leave them with the memory of being lied to about their parents.

Rosalind's small face was sober. "Are Mama and Papa dead?"

"Yes, they are," Viola answered, her voice soft and gentle. She turned to Sebastian. "Do you know what dead means?"

The little boy nodded. "Like when Manda kills a chicken? When she snaps its neck, it closes its eyes. Then it goes all limp. It doesn't move or run around or cluck anymore."

"Or lay eggs," Rosalind added.

"Manda?" Viola asked.

"One of Cook Molly's helpers," Rosalind answered.

"Yes, something like that," Viola said, thinking she had never seen anyone kill a chicken and was glad she hadn't. Viola realized that in many ways, despite having traveled to lots of different places, her life had been much more sheltered than Rosalind's and Sebastian's. But not anymore.

Sebastian's eyes were big. "Did someone snap Mama's and Papa's necks?"

"No," Viola answered slowly. In graphic detail, the Book of Everything had told her exactly what had happened, but Viola didn't want to get too explicit.

"But Mama and Papa were killed, weren't they?" Rosalind asked. "Did someone stab them?"

Viola's voice was sad. "Yes, someone stabbed them."

Rosalind frowned fiercely. "Who did this?"

"A very bad man," Viola replied, thinking of Chet.

Staring into the distance, Rosalind was still. "The man in the tower. He's after us, isn't he?"

"He is." Viola drew the children close. "But he can't get you in the Forest of Arden. That's why I brought you here. The forest has magic trees, and they'll protect you. So will Sophie and Elwyn and Meg and everyone else who lives in the village."

"And you, too?" Sebastian asked. Both children stared hopefully at Viola.

Viola shook her head. "I have to go soon. I can't stay here. Meg will look after you."

"I like Meg," Sebastian said. "She gives us sweets and lets us play with Luna, who runs and barks whenever we throw the ball."

Rosalind's eyes were shiny, and tears trickled down her cheeks. "I like Meg, too. But I don't want you to leave."

Seeing his sister cry, Sebastian began to cry as well. He slipped his little hand into Viola's larger one. "I don't want you to leave either. Stay here with us."

Blinking rapidly, Viola squeezed Sebastian's hand. "I wish I could stay."

Rosalind rubbed her eyes. "I miss Mama and Papa."

"Me, too," Sebastian gulped.

Feeling their misery, Viola cried along with them. At the lodge, Rosalind and Sebastian would be well cared for, loved even, but it wouldn't be the same as having their mother and father to guide and nurture them.

Finally, they all stopped crying. There were clean cloths on the stand by the bed, and they wiped their faces and blew their noses.

"Please stay here with us," Rosalind whispered.

"I can't. I wish I could, but I have to go back to my own family." Viola wistfully thought about the lodge, where everything seemed calm and free, protected and ordered. She could go where she wanted and talk to anyone she pleased. Fanning out from the lodge, the small village, aptly called Forest Village, provided necessities for those who lived in the forest. Aside from taking care of Rosalind and Sebastian, Viola wasn't sure what she would do if she stayed in Forest Village, but she suspected it would have something to do with the lodge. Like her mother, Viola was organized, and she knew she could be a big help to Sophie and Elwyn.

"Couldn't you stay just a little longer?" Sebastian asked. "Please?"

Viola was tempted. Perhaps she could stay a little longer, maybe a week or so. Viola thought of how danger and Chaos waited for her outside the Forest of Arden. *But they're not going anywhere,* Viola thought. *Maybe I don't have to go back just yet.*

"Ask the Book that brought us here," Rosalind suggested.

"Good idea," Viola said, thinking that the Book would be able to guide her and perhaps give her more time to stay in the forest she had come to love.

But later that day, after Meg had hustled away the children so that Viola could rest, she picked up the Book of Everything, which Sophie had placed on the chair by her bed. As soon as Viola finished asking if she could stay in the forest a little longer, the Book said, "No, it is time for you to go back."

For the first time, Viola heard the clear voice of the Book and didn't have to read its response. Viola supposed it was because she'd had her eyes peeled.

"I'm sorry," the Book added. "I know you would like to have more time with the children. But your father, Mémère, and Simon need help dealing with Chet. We should go to the hunting lodge where Rhys, Molly, Jem, and Sir John are staying in Oakton Forest. I will bring Rhys and Sir John to the clearing to take care of Chet. If I don't, it's likely that Chet will escape."

"And kill my father, Mémère, Simon, and Diana?" Viola asked in a whisper.

"Yes, in all probability someone will die. Perhaps even more than one person," the Book answered. "Then Chet would make his way back to Humphrey and let him know about all that's happened, that I brought your father to Caxton, that you escaped with the children to the lodge. Humphrey would send everyone he's got to the Forest of Arden. Years ago, he had planned to burn down the forest but left before he had the chance. Now Humphrey would have a second chance."

Viola trembled, thinking of the forest on fire. Then: "What will Sir John and Rhys do with Chet?"

The Book was blunt. "I expect they will kill him rather than take him prisoner."

"Kill him," Viola whispered.

"Chet will never change, and he is very dangerous. But to kill in cold blood goes against every principle we Books have." Here the Book actually sighed. "With Chet, we have a real problem. We Books thought he'd be out of the way in Caxton. We didn't foresee the chain of events set in motion by Nemesis. And if Chet escaped once, he will escape again."

The Book and Viola were silent as they thought about this, and the Book asked, "The Toad Queen told you the Great Library has fallen, and Cinnial killed Sydda?"

Viola shook her head. "I can hardly believe it."

The Book's voice was sad. "It is the truth. A terrible day for the Great Library, for us Books, for the universe." The Book hesitated. "And there is something else you should know."

"What?"

"With Cinnial at the Great Library and the Great Library's Book in hiding, we Books are no longer connected to the center, where all information flows. As a result, Chaos has become very strong. I can no longer see the various possibilities the way I once did. The timeline is in flux, as Chaos knocks it off course again and again. For now, Time still has the upper hand, but for how long, we Books do not know."

"Terrible," Viola whispered.

"Terrible," the Book repeated. "This means I can't guide you the way I have usually guided my human companions. I will help as best I can, but you will have to rely more on your own intuition. And, your intelligence and common sense, gifts you received from both your mother and father."

"I hope I do a better job than my father did," Viola muttered.

"Viola, you have had a different life than your father did."

"I know." Viola thought of how her father had grown up poor, deserted by a father who hardly took an interest in his family after he left.

"It makes a difference," the Book insisted. "You are more secure than he ever was."

"I guess," Viola said, still upset by what her father had done.

The Book's voice was stern. "You will have to do what you can. You had your eyes peeled, and we are depending on you."

Viola sat up straight. "All right, all right." She thought of Maya, who never hesitated to rush toward danger. "I'll do my best."

"I know," the Book replied in a softer tone. "We will go to the lodge outside of Oakton tomorrow?"

"Yes," Viola answered. "But first I have to talk to my father."

"Are you sure?" the Book asked. "It seems to me that Chet should be the first priority."

Viola didn't hesitate. "I'm sure." She had to see her father and find out from him what had happened long ago when he had been here with Maya. With all the chaos swirling around Chet, Cinnial, and the Great Library, Viola had the feeling it would be better to speak to her father sooner rather than later. Viola thought, *Who knows when I'll get another chance?*

Aloud, Viola said, "I really, really need to talk to him. Please, Book, take me there first when we leave tomorrow."

The Book sighed. "All right, then. First to the clearing where Chet is being held and then to the lodge in Oakton Forest. How this will end, I cannot see."

"Yeah," Viola said with a slight shudder. It seemed to her that she was on the edge of something big, getting ready to jump. Just like Maya always did.

10: FROM ONE FOREST TO ANOTHER

Viola's last day at the lodge was bittersweet. After sleeping much of the morning, Viola felt as though she was pretty much back to normal—whatever that was now that she'd had her eyes peeled—and in the afternoon she roamed the forest with Meg, Rosalind, and Sebastian. The vast trees spread out as far as Viola could see, tall columns that ended in green canopies against the deep blue sky.

Hearing the deep roar of something in the distance, Viola asked, "Aren't you afraid of the animals here?"

"Nay," Meg replied. "The trees protect us. They keep the wild creatures away."

The trees protect us, Viola thought, putting her hand on the rough trunk of a young oak, which thrummed in response, a comforting sound that made Viola even more sorry to leave the Forest of Arden.

When he was done with his work in the stables, Robbie—Meg's brother—joined them, and with other children and teenagers from the village, they all splashed and paddled in a stream not far from the lodge. Unlike the stream by the Old Oak, this one did not glitter with magic, and there were no sprites zipping in and out of the sparkling water.

Stripped to their underwear, girls and boys swam together without any self-consciousness, and Viola realized this was much different from back in the day on Earth, when girls wore clothes that covered them from their necks to their ankles and never would have dreamed of swimming with boys. But this was not Earth. This was Ilyria, and many things were different here.

Freer, Viola thought. *And more fun.*

As if in response, Robbie splashed Viola, and she splashed him back. His hair, so blond it was almost white, was slicked to his head, and he grinned at her. Viola grinned, too.

After swimming, the kids went to a grassy area by the edge of the gardens in back of the lodge, where they sat in the warm sun. Before long, they were dry, and they put on their clothes. Robbie and Meg made a fire in a rock fire pit while other children searched the woods for long sticks that had fallen from the trees. Annie and Gwen Littleton, the two sisters who helped Sophie in the lodge, brought out trays of sausages and bread. Emilie, the cook's assistant, came with a tray of cookies. Sophie and Elwyn also joined them. So did Max, the cook, who carried big pitchers of cider.

Soon there were sausages on sticks sizzling over the fire, and even the youngest children, watched carefully by the older teens and adults, were allowed to roast their own sausages. Rosalind and Sebastian frowned with concentration as their sausages browned. Sebastian yipped with pleasure when his was done, and Meg produced a slice of soft bread for him to wrap around it.

Rosalind gave Sebastian a reproving look, but Meg said, "Little miss, let your brother have his fun. We're in the Forest of Arden. Things are not as strict here as they were in Caxton, the big city."

Looking chastened, Rosalind said, "Yes, Meg."

Sophie, who was nearby, patted Rosalind's shoulder. "Not easy being the eldest, I know."

"Were you the eldest?" Rosalind asked.

"I was," Sophie answered. "And it was my job to keep everyone in line."

"Sebastian doesn't always remember his manners," Rosalind said.

"He's just a little boy," Sophie replied. "And Meg is right. We're more relaxed here than you were in Caxton."

Rosalind frowned. "But Sebastian is the duke now. He needs to learn how to behave."

Sophie glanced at Viola, who nodded sadly, confirming that she had indeed told the children about the murder of their parents.

91

Sophie turned back to Rosalind. "Aye, but didn't your father play with you sometimes?"

Rosalind smiled as she remembered. "Yes, and Mama, too."

Sophie said, "Good leaders know when to have fun, when to relax, and when to remember their manners. Sebastian will learn."

Viola watched Rosalind as she considered this. Viola understood Rosalind would always be the serious one and Sebastian would be more fun loving, but she saw that each would grow into thoughtful adults with a passion for justice and a keen respect for facts.

"They'll be all right," Viola said, her voice soft.

"That they will," Sophie replied just as softly. "As long as Chaos doesn't continue to have the upper hand."

Viola rubbed her face. "That's why I had my eyes peeled. To help Time."

"Aye," came Sophie's response. "There's a lot that will be asked of you. I wish we could help, but unfortunately we can't."

Viola said, "You have to stay here in the Forest of Arden with Rosalind and Sebastian. That's your job. Leaving the forest is my job."

"And even though we can't help you, there are others who will. You won't be alone."

Good, Viola thought because as she watched how easy the children and adults were with each other, she felt extremely alone.

As the afternoon shadows lengthened, adults from the village joined them. There were music and dancing and more food. Viola remembered the bonfire in Caxton, which had started out as a celebration of summer and had ended in tragedy and exile. So much had happened in such a short time, and Viola shivered as she thought about it. Sitting to one side, Viola watched the dancing, and it wasn't long before Robbie, sweaty and flushed, dropped beside her.

"Don't want to dance?" he asked, and Viola shook her head. "How do you feel after having your eyes peeled? Are you tired?"

"Not really," Viola answered, resting her head against her knees. "I just don't feel like dancing." There was a slight pause. "Everything looks so sharp. And I catch all sorts of images from people."

"From me, too?"

Viola studied Robbie. She could see that he wanted to have his own cottage, his own family, and live out his days in the Forest of Arden. At the same time, Robbie yearned to leave the forest, to see what was out there beyond the trees. Viola understood how the desire to stay and the wish to leave were in constant opposition with each other, but so far, Robbie had stayed.

"Yes, from you, too," Viola told him.

"You'll be going soon." Robbie gave her a wistful look as though he sensed which impressions she had caught from him.

"Tomorrow."

"Will you ever come back, do you think?"

"I don't know," Viola answered. "I can't see everything."

Robbie ran his hand over the grass. "No, I don't suppose you can."

"I probably won't come back, Robbie. My father is the leader of the country I live in, and I have a busy life back home. My parents expect me to do what other kids do in my time—go to school and have a career."

Robbie stared at the fire. "Not settle in the Forest of Arden."

Viola shook her head. "Definitely not settle in the Forest of Arden."

Robbie's expression was serious. "But your heart's home is here. I can tell."

Viola sighed. "You're right. But I have to go. The Great Library needs me."

As soon as Viola had finished speaking, she felt as though she was surrounded by a strange shimmer. Then a vision came to her, of Maya going over a cliff with what looked like an ogre. Crying out, Viola put her hand over her mouth, and the shimmer disappeared with a snap.

"What's wrong?" Robbie asked. "What just happened? You looked all wavy there for a minute."

"I don't know," Viola answered in a halting voice. "But I had a vision of Maya going over the cliff with some kind of creature. An ogre, maybe. And this will change everything."

Robbie put his arm around her. "Let me come with you," he whispered. "I can't see the way you do. But I can help. I know I can. I've been wanting to leave the forest for some time. Not forever. Just for a little while. To see what's out there."

93

"No, Robbie. You should stay here. It's dangerous outside the forest."

"And what about you?" Robbie frowned. "A young lass. Isn't it dangerous for you?"

"Well, yes, but..." Viola couldn't think of any good reason why she should face the dangers and Robbie shouldn't. "What about your chores here?"

"Someone else can muck out those stables and take care of the horses. And I have other brothers who help my father in the forest. Please, let me come with you. Let me help in whatever way I can."

As Viola regarded Robbie, she had the feeling that he would be a help, even though she didn't know exactly how. "All right," Viola said reluctantly, not wanting to get him involved. With a shudder, she thought about Chet and how he would not hesitate to kill her and Robbie if given the chance. After all, Chet would have had no qualms about killing Rosalind and Sebastian, two innocent children. Then there was Cinnial, who with Chaos, was a driving force to be confronted. Cinnial had brutally murdered his own teacher, Sydda. Like Chet, he would not hesitate to kill them. "But you might not come back," Viola added in a low voice.

Robbie didn't back down. "Aye, but the same is true for you. Viola, this is our forest and our land. And you, a stranger, a young lass, are going out there to do what you can to help us. It seems only fitting that someone from the forest should go with you."

"But what will your parents say?"

Robbie's mouth was a firm line. "I'm sixteen. I'm old enough to make my own decisions."

As it turned out, Robbie's parents agreed with him as did Sophie and Elwyn and all the other adults and teens in the forest. So much so that others clamored to come, too, but here Viola remained firm. She felt it was more than enough to be responsible for Robbie.

"No," Viola said in a tone that she had heard her father use many times, sometimes with her. It was a tone that suggested there would be no more arguments, and the group that had gathered around Viola and Robbie regarded her with respect. Viola continued, "I need to be able to move fast, if I have to. One person is enough to keep track of. The Books can only travel with two at a time. I was able to take both Rosalind and Sebastian because they are small. The rest of you need to stay here and do what you can to protect the children and the Forest of Arden."

Although there were a few halfhearted arguments, no one objected too much—what Viola said made sense to everyone—and in the end it was agreed that Robbie should be the one to go with Viola.

After everyone had returned to their cottages or the lodge for the night, Robbie grinned at Viola. "Okay, then."

Viola grinned back. "Okay, then." She had not seen Robbie in any of her flashes and had not thought about asking him to come with her, but somehow it seemed like the right thing to do. Viola got the sense that he would be a good friend, brave and loyal, some- one who knew about the Books of Everything, the Toad Queen, and the Great Library. *He's up to speed*, Viola thought, borrowing an expression that her mother often used. And even more import- ant, she would not be alone.

Robbie nodded. "Tomorrow at dawn?"

"Yes," Viola answered. "Tomorrow at dawn."

All the farewells had been said around the fire. Viola had cried as she said goodbye to Rosalind, Sebastian, Meg, Sophie, and Elwyn. Would she ever see any of them again? Viola's intuition was silent on this point, and she realized that too much was in flux for a clear answer.

The next morning, before the sun had even risen, Viola dressed quietly and slipped outside the lodge, waiting by the big front door for Robbie to join her. She had a backpack with a change of clothes, a cloak, some food, and a water skin. The Book of Everything was in the pocket of her dress.

Settling on the lodge's massive granite steps, Viola watched the dark sky fade into morning. The cries of night creatures went away to be replaced by the songs of birds as they woke up and greeted the day. Viola let the sounds, smells, and sights fill her senses until she was hardly aware of herself anymore. Instead, Viola felt as though she was a part of the village and the forest and all that was in it.

Viola was so absorbed with everything around her that she jumped when Robbie put a hand on her arm. He had come around from the side, from the stables, where he had gone to say goodbye to the horses.

"Sorry," Robbie said. "I didn't mean to scare you."

"No worries," Viola told him. "I was just taking everything in. To remember."

Robbie's bright face was serious. "Aye, it's special here, isn't it?"

"Yes," Viola answered. "I've traveled all around my planet, but I've never been anywhere like the Forest of Arden. I wonder if Earth has a forest like this. And if other planets do."

Robbie looked around. "I expect that where there's a tree with golden acorns, there's a forest like this."

"I think you must be right." Viola stood. "Well, it's time for us to get going. You'll probably feel sick when you travel with the Book. I did. The first time, I threw up in Sir John's cottage. But after a while, you get used to it."

Robbie grimaced. "Thank you for the warning."

"Are you ready?" Viola asked, reaching for the Book.

"Ready," Robbie answered.

When they traveled with the Book, Robbie didn't throw up, but he clutched his stomach and fell to his knees. After tucking the Book back into her pocket, Viola put her hand on Robbie's shoulder as he took deep breaths and waited for his stomach to settle down. Simon, who had been dozing nearby as he kept guard over Chet, scrambled to his feet.

As Simon reached for his knife, Viola called, "Simon, it's me. Viola. And this is Robbie from the Forest of Arden."

Simon's hand stopped on the hilt of his knife, and he gazed from Robbie to Viola. "Viola!"

Chet, who was tied to a nearby tree, was awake, and as he stared coldly at her, Viola wondered if he ever slept. "She returns," Chet said, his lips curling as though he had a bad taste in his mouth. "And she can see more than she used to."

Before Viola could reply, she heard her father call, "Viola?"

"I'm back, Dad," Viola answered. She saw him not far from the fire pit. Wrapped in a blanket, he sat up quickly. Mémère and Diana were beside him, and Mémère sat up quickly, too. Diana lifted her head, but Viola could tell that she was too weak to do anything more.

Viola glanced from Simon to Robbie, who were warily regarding each other.

Viola said, "I need to talk to my dad and Mémère. And see how Diana is doing."

Chet snorted. "Should have killed her when I had the chance."

Viola whirled around to face him. "Then why didn't you?" she asked, her voice fierce.

Chet answered, "I was hoping to get some information from Diana."

"She wouldn't tell you anything," Viola replied. "No matter what you did to her."

Chet shrugged. "Maybe. Maybe not. But it was worth a try. And now look at her. She's probably going to die anyway."

Viola knew Chet was right, but she didn't say anything else to him. Instead, she turned to Simon and Robbie. "Guard him carefully."

Simon frowned. "Of course I will. Who do you think's been keeping watch over him while you were gone?" Then he considered her. "You've changed."

"Idiot," Chet muttered. "Viola had her eyes peeled."

As Viola considered Chet, she realized that he could see, too. Viola thought, *Boy, does that ever make sense.*

But Chet wasn't paying attention to Viola. His attention was still on Simon. "Better guard what you think, boy, because she can see deep now."

Simon winced, and even though Viola hadn't looked deep inside him, she knew what Sophie had said about Simon was true: He had betrayed Greendale. Viola felt sad, let down, and her expression mirrored her feelings.

Simon leaned forward. "Viola..."

Viola shook her head. "Not now. I need to talk to my father." She glanced at Chet, who was smirking. "Robbie, help Simon. Chet's a rotter."

Robbie glanced sternly at Chet. "Aye, one look is all it takes to know that. Go talk to your father. Simon and I will take care of Chet."

Her father and Mémère were slowly making their way toward Viola. Her father had a stick, which he used for support, and Mémère kept an anxious eye on him as he walked carefully across the clearing.

Despite her disappointment with her father over the part he had played in stealing Earth's Book of Everything, Viola felt a swell of love for him. She ran to her father, giving him a fierce hug. Drew winced but hugged her back just as fiercely.

97

"Tiens," Mémère said, sniffing a little. "Rosalind and Sebastian are safe and sound?"

Viola let go of her father. "They are. Rosalind and Sebastian have a new nanny and are settling into life in the lodge in the Forest of Arden." Viola's expression was wistful as she remembered swimming in the stream and sitting by the fire and watching everyone dance.

Drew said, "I know how you feel. It's a beautiful place."

Glancing at her father, Viola thought about what he had done. "Dad, I need to talk to you. Alone. Sorry, Mémère."

Mémère's expression was serious. "That's all right."

"Can we go just a little bit away from the clearing?" Viola asked.

Drew looked at Chet, tied to the tree, and at Simon and Robbie who were guarding him. "I don't see why not." His somber expression indicated that he had guessed what Viola wanted to talk to him about. He sighed. "Come on."

Leaving the clearing, Viola and her father walked until they were out of earshot. Gingerly, Drew sat down by a massive pine tree, and Viola settled next to him.

"Dad, how are you feeling?" Viola asked anxiously. Although her father was able to walk, his face was pale, and it was clear that he was in pain.

Her father tried to smile. "Oh, not too bad. Better than Diana."

Feeling the Book of Everything in her pocket, Viola kicked at the dirt. "The Book told me she was all right."

Drew shrugged. "She was at first. But then one of her wounds became infected. And then she came down with a fever. And now she's not all right."

"The Book never said Diana was getting worse."

Again, her father shrugged. "Sometimes the Book is like that. It might not lie, but it doesn't always tell the whole truth."

"Yeah." Viola looked at her father. "Dad, there's something you should know."

He put his hand on her shoulder. "What?"

"I've had my eyes peeled."

Except for a slight tightening of his hand, her father was still. "I was wondering if you would."

"I didn't want to. I didn't want to see more than I could before I had my eyes peeled."

"Then why did you?" Drew asked in such a gentle voice that it made Viola want to cry, and she blinked fiercely to keep back the tears.

Viola said, "Because it seemed like the right thing to do. The Toad Queen told me the Great Library has fallen. Sydda is dead, and Cinnial is now in charge."

Her father winced. "Terrible, terrible news. I had hoped it wouldn't come to this."

"Me, too. I always thought that Maya would win in the end. She's so..." Viola paused, searching for the right word.

"Determined?" her father suggested.

"Yeah, determined. Maya just keeps going, no matter what."

Drew smiled a little. "That she does. Maya's quite the girl."

As Viola studied her father, a flash came to her. Her father and Maya were on a stone wall surrounding a small city. He was a teenager, not much older than Maya, and they were holding hands. With a start, Viola realized there had been more than friendship between the two of them. Her father and Maya leaned toward each other, and with a snap, Viola cut off the vision. She had seen enough.

Thrown off-guard, Viola didn't ask her father about stealing Earth's Book of Everything. Instead, she blurted out, "Did you and Maya?" Stopping, Viola flushed, embarrassed that she had asked what had happened between Maya and her father when they were together as teenagers. She averted her gaze, not wanting to look too closely at her father.

Drew studied her, and glancing back at him, Viola could tell he was trying to decide what he should say. "Maya and I had an extraordinary adventure. I saw things I had never even imagined, and it set me on the path I took when I returned to Earth. Here in Caxton, Maya and I became...close."

Viola thought, *How close?* But she couldn't bring herself to ask the question.

Noting her expression, her father shook his head. "Not much actually happened. It was the beginning of something. We made a good team. Our personalities meshed. She is fiery and impulsive. I am cooler and more deliberate."

"Kind of like you and Mom?"

"Yes, I suppose so," Drew answered slowly. "I never really thought about it that way."

"Do you love Mom?" Viola asked in a small voice.

"Of course I do," her father answered without hesitation. "By the time I met your mother, a lot of years had passed since I had traveled with Maya. I didn't forget Maya. How could I? But the Book of Everything had brought us together from different times for a specific purpose, and there was no future for us as a couple. I knew that as soon as I got back to Earth, to Waterville, Maine. At first, I thought about Maya a lot, and I waited for her to come back. But she didn't, and as time went by, I realized she never would. I met other girls. Most important, I met your mother. And that was that."

Viola listened attentively. "Really?" Her parents had never talked about how they met, and Viola hadn't given it much thought. To her, they were her parents. They were together, a tight pair, and that was all that mattered.

Her father smiled. "Really. I was smitten the first time I saw your mother. She, on the other hand, was not that impressed with me." He winked at Viola. "But I grew on her." Then her father became serious. "We come from very different families. Hers have money. And as you know, my family was poor." He shook his head. "To tell the truth, at first your mother's parents weren't impressed with me either."

Shocked, Viola regarded her father. "Gigi and Pup-pup didn't like you?" Viola had never felt any tension between her grandparents and her father. Instead, Viola got the sense that Gigi and Pup-pup had a tremendous respect for him. "Why?"

Drew's tone was rueful. "Because I grew up so poor, there was a lot I didn't know, right down to what I should be eating. Spam and Wonder Bread sure didn't cut it for your grandparents." His voice became low and intense. "My mother did the best she could. She had nothing, but she worked hard, and there was always food in the house. The rent was paid on time. And she didn't drink too much." His lips quirked into a grin. "All right. Maybe a little more than she should have. Your mémère liked to have a good time. But it wasn't excessive, especially compared with the way some of the other parents in my neighborhood drank."

Viola thought about the grandmother she had never known, who had died before she was born. Viola had seen pictures of her mémère and had always been drawn to the snappy spark in her face and her dark, dark eyes. "I wish I had known her."

Drew put his hand on Viola's head. "She would have loved you as much as she loved me." He was silent for a moment. "But the life we live now is so outside her experience that I'm not sure how she would have handled it. She would have been very uncomfortable."

"Unlike Gigi and Pup-pup," Viola said, thinking about how confident they were at any gathering or party her parents had.

"Right." He stared off into the distance. "They're the ones who suggested I change my name."

Viola stared at her father. This was another story she had never heard, and she had the uncomfortable feeling that although she had always been able to grasp things that were hidden, her family's life was even more complicated than she had realized it was.

"Your name?" Viola asked.

"My name. Gigi and Pup-pup thought that Andy sounded too casual for a politician, not serious enough." Her father shrugged. "But somehow Andrew just didn't seem quite right to me. A little too formal. So we hit upon Drew."

Sensing how hard it had been for her father to give up the name he'd had for so many years, Viola said, "Oh, Dad."

Her father drew her close, and his voice was gentle. "It's all right, Viola. It took a lot of years for me to feel comfortable with my new name, but now I really do feel like Drew Murphy."

For a while neither of them spoke. Then her father shifted. "Was there something else you wanted to discuss?" he asked, sounding like the law professor he had once been.

Sitting up, Viola hesitated. Although it wasn't even midmorning, she was tired, weary from all she had learned from her father. Yet Viola had to ask her father about why he had stolen Earth's Book of Everything. She couldn't just let this hang between them, an unspoken issue that Viola knew would eventually become a barrier in their relationship as father and daughter.

However, Drew preempted her question. "You want to know why I stole Earth's Book of Everything from Maya." Viola nodded miserably. "There hasn't been a day that's gone by when I haven't regretted it. Maya forgave me, and I tried to make up for what I did. To this day, I'm still trying. But anyway..."

"There it is," Viola said quietly.

"There it is."

"Why did you do it?"

Drew frowned. "I'm not really sure. I think it had something to do with the way I identified with Sir John, how mad I was that people like Feste disregarded him and left him out of the loop. I know what that's like. When I was young, it happened to me all the time because I didn't come from the right neighborhood or wear the right clothes." Drew shook his head. "Anyway, it's not an excuse. It's an explanation. My buttons were pushed, and I did the wrong thing."

Viola felt her father's disappointment with himself. It came to her in a wave, and although her own disappointment with him didn't go away—she sensed it never really would—Viola felt sympathy for the poor boy her father had once been. Reaching over, Viola took one of her father's hands and squeezed it. Drew returned the squeeze, and together they sat in silence.

11: NEEDLE DROP FROM NEW YORK

When Viola and Drew returned to the clearing, Mémère had started a small fire and was heating water in a pot resting on three flat rocks placed over the fire. Immediately, Viola got different impressions from Mémère—her zeal for cooking and for taking care of people, her unwavering love for Maya, and her affection for her makeshift family—Simon, Diana, Viola's father, Viola.

For the first time, Viola realized that in addition to being able to see to the heart of things, she and Maya had a lot in common. They both had Franco-American grandmothers, mémères from Waterville, Maine. Although neither Viola nor Maya had grown up in a Franco-American community, Viola understood how the culture was always there, humming in the background, passed down in various ways from grandparents to parents to children. Viola thought about her father's easy laugh and the delight he took in simple pleasures, even though he was president of the United States. Her father worked hard—*Nobody works harder*, Viola thought loyally—but he always found time to have fun, to read or play games with her, no matter how tired or frazzled he felt at the end of a long day. Glancing at her father, Viola knew that despite his crushing responsibilities, she and her mother were the center for him, and that devotion to family was also part of being Franco-American. The same was true for Mémère and Maya, and Viola remembered how without hesitation, Mémère had allowed Maya to take her across the universe.

Several small stumps for sitting had been arranged by the fire. In a daze from all that she had seen, Viola sat down on one of them. Mémère glanced sympathetically but shrewdly at Viola. "You look tired. And different."

Viola decided to be straightforward with Mémère, who, after all, had seen things most grandmothers from Earth could never even imagine. "I've had my eyes peeled by the Toad Queen. Maya has, too. Did she tell you about that?"

"Yes," Mémère replied. "A giant toad scraped Maya's eyes, and now her sixth sense is stronger than ever."

Viola sighed. "That's right."

"Did it hurt?" Mémère asked in a low voice.

Viola nodded. "A lot."

Mémère put her hand on Viola's shoulder. "I'm so sorry..." Her voice caught, and she cleared her throat. "I'm sorry that you and Maya had to go through something like that. You'll never be the same kids again, will you?"

Viola stared at the sky, a soft blue as the sun rose. She turned to Mémère. "No, but we did what we had to."

Drew had come over to the fire. As he and Mémère sat down on the two remaining stumps, Viola knew the time had come to tell them what she had seen in her flashes about the Great Library and about Maya and the ogre.

Even though her father couldn't see the way she did, he was able to sense her moods. "What is it? What's wrong?"

Viola said, "Some big things have happened." Turning toward Simon, Robbie, and Chet, Viola called, "Simon, come here. That way you can listen, too, and I only have to say everything once. Robbie, you already know the things I'm going to tell them."

Leaving Robbie to guard Chet, Simon came over but before he sat down, Drew glanced at Chet, who, with his eyes closed, seemed to be resting. However, there was an alertness to the tracker that indicated he was listening to all that was being said.

Drew frowned. "Viola, before you tell us what's happened, let's move farther away, to the edge of the clearing by the pond, where we can see Chet, but he won't be able to hear us."

Mémère stood up. "Good idea. The last thing we need is that stinker overhearing what Viola has to say."

Viola thought about how Sir John and Rhys were soon going to come for Chet, but she didn't argue, figuring that no matter what, the less Chet heard, the better it would be.

Glancing at Mémère, Simon picked up one of the stumps. Noting how drawn and tired her father looked, Viola picked up a stump, too. They all moved to the edge of the pond, to a spot where they could still see Robbie and Chet and the unmoving figure of Diana, who lay not far from the fire. But they were clearly out of earshot, even for someone as vigilant as Chet.

Simon set the stump down for Mémère. "Oh, thank you," she said gratefully. "This stump gives me a boost. I can't get up from the ground the way I used to." She laughed. "And let me tell you, getting off that hard ground once in the morning is enough."

Setting her stump down, Viola said, "Here, Dad. I know it's not that easy for you, either."

"I can still get off the ground," Drew protested, leaning wearily against his walking stick.

"Sit," Viola said, her voice stern.

Shaking his head, Drew sat down. "Okay, Viola. Thank you."

Mémère patted his arm. "We're the elders here. Let's take whatever advantages we can."

Grinning ruefully, Drew nodded. Then he looked at Chet. "It should be safe to talk now."

Viola told them what she had seen in the flash where Mémère was part of a large group surrounding the Great Library, to take it back from Cinnial, who had killed Sydda.

"Me at the Great Library?" Mémère asked in surprise.

"Yes," Viola replied.

Drew frowned. "What about me?"

Viola shook her head. "I didn't see either you or Simon. Or me and Robbie. So I don't know about us."

"Well, I wouldn't be there by myself," Mémère said.

"No, I guess you wouldn't," Viola replied. "So that must mean we're there somewhere. For some reason, I just didn't see us. My focus was on you. And two teenagers I've never seen before."

"What about Maya?" Mémère asked, and Viola bit her bottom lip. "Something's wrong, isn't it?

"Yes," Viola answered. "I had another flash where I saw Maya going over a cliff with what looked like an ogre." The night before, at the lodge in the Forest of Arden, the Book of Everything had told Viola where this vision had come from, and she explained, "Maya went to another dimension called Elferterre, where Magic rules. Usually, our dimension and Elferterre are pretty separate from each other. Time and Magic like to keep it that way. The Books of Everything aren't connected with what's going on in Elferterre, and Magic is a minor force in our dimension. But because of Cinnial and how strong Chaos is getting, Magic and Time have relaxed the rules and are kind of working together. That's how come I got a flash from Elferterre and saw Maya going over the cliff."

There was silence. Closing her eyes, Mémère balled one of her hands into a fist and pressed it against her mouth. Drew looked off into the distance, and Simon stared at the pond.

A voice to the side said, "If anyone can survive going over a cliff with an ogre, it's Maya."

"Yeah," another voice added. "She's tougher than anyone I know."

Two teenagers, a boy and a girl, came into the clearing and walked to where Viola, her father, Mémère, and Simon were sitting. Everyone jumped. Drew grabbed his walking stick, Simon reached for his knife, and Mémère glowered at the boy and girl.

Viola, on the other hand, was not afraid of the teenagers. "It's all right. I saw them in my flash of the Great Library. They were with you, Mémère, and they're here to help. I know they are."

The girl, even lovelier in person than she had been in Viola's vision, said, "You must be Viola." She stood straight, and her voice was confident as she appraised Viola. "You're a cute little thing."

The boy, who had black hair and a puckish expression, turned to Viola's father. "And you must be President Murphy."

The girl glanced at the tree, where Chet was tied. Her lips curled. "And there's the infamous man who doesn't smile. Maya sure had him pegged right. Even from here I can catch his bad vibes."

Alert now, Chet stared intently at the boy and the girl as he tried to figure out who they were. Although he couldn't hear what was being said, Chet could tell the girl was talking about him. Viola caught a flicker of apprehension, and she understood that Chet was used to being unnoticed, working mostly in the shadows. Being recognized by an unknown teenager, clearly not from Caxton, was not to his liking.

Drew held up his hand. "All right. Slow down. Who are you two? And why are you here?" He spoke with such cool authority that both the girl and the boy nodded with respect.

"May we join you?" the boy asked. "I'm Jay, and this is Lexie."

He was holding a small black Book, which he tucked in the pocket of his jeans. Lexie had a red Book, which she put into the pocket of her jeans.

"Yes," Viola said. "Sit down and join us. Are those Books of Everything?"

"Apprentice Books," Lexie answered, settling on the ground beside Viola. "That's how we got here. Alani and Alexander, two librarians in exile from the Great Library, let us borrow them. They live in Brooklyn now, and we're from New York, too."

Patting his pocket, Jay sat down beside Mémère. "It was a hell of a trip. We had to stay in the forest for a little while to let our stomachs settle down."

"Someone might have thrown up as soon as we got here," Lexie replied.

"And someone was not far behind," Jay retorted, and Lexie stuck out her tongue at him.

Viola's father studied their clothes. "You're from our time?"

"Ten years in the past," Jay answered. "But everything is so mixed up I'm not really sure where we're from now."

Eyes glittering, Mémère leaned forward. "Tell me what happened to Maya. I'm her grandmother."

Jay looked around the clearing. "We know who all of you are. The Apprentice Books told us."

"Robbie might as well join us," Lexie said. "That creep Chet is tied to a tree. He's not going anywhere."

"Aye," Simon agreed. "I tied those knots nice and tight."

Standing, Lexie motioned to Robbie, who was also staring intently at her and Jay. Robbie pointed to himself, and Lexie nodded. Still, Robbie hesitated.

"Do you think it's okay, Dad?" Viola asked.

Drew looked from Simon to Chet. "I do. Simon's clever at things like tying knots. If he thinks Chet is secure, then Chet's secure."

Simon blushed proudly but didn't say anything.

Viola stood and motioned to Robbie.

After giving Chet a look that implied he would still be keeping track of him, Robbie left and joined the group by the edge of the pond.

"Good, good. Go," Chet muttered but nobody heard him.

As soon as Robbie, Viola, and Lexie settled on the grass beside Simon and Jay, Mémère said, "Tell me about Maya." She was trembling. "What happened to her?"

"It's a long story," Lexie said, biting her lip, and Viola sensed that the blonde girl felt guilty about something. But Lexie blocked her thoughts from Viola's speculative gaze, and no images came to her.

Glancing sympathetically at Lexie, Jay continued, "Lexie and I and another boy named Will met Maya at the Little Bard Theater in Brooklyn."

"Where Maya's father used to work in the summer, putting on teen productions of Shakespeare's plays?" Mémère asked in surprise.

"The one and the same," Jay replied. "It was his first year there."

Mémère scowled. "It's where Giles met that red head."

Lexie's voice was thoughtful. "Inga Peterson. But I don't think there was anything between them that first year."

"How old was Maya?" Drew asked, and Viola could tell he thought it was best to change the subject away from "that red head."

Jay smiled. "Sixteen. And full of jazz. I liked Maya the minute I saw her."

Lexie snorted. "I didn't. Sorry," she added, noting all the frowns coming her way. "She took Will away from me."

"Lexie," Jay said, "you know that's not strictly true. Will was never really with you. Your relationship was always going to be short term even without Maya."

Lexie replied, "I know. But still. Will and I were going out, and when Maya came on the scene, that was that. He didn't have eyes for anyone else." The blonde girl shook her head in disbelief.

"And probably never will," Jay said. "I think Maya's the one for Will even though he's only seventeen."

Lexie sighed. "Yeah." Then she grinned at the frowning faces. "But don't worry. Maya grew on me. The same way she does with everyone."

Drew summed up the situation. "You two and a boy named Will met Maya as teenagers at a place called the Little Bard Theater in New York City. Where Maya's father was working. Did he recognize her?"

Jay grinned. "Not really, although he could sense there was something about her that seemed familiar. Man, right away, the sparks flew between Maya and her father."

Here Mémère laughed. "Oh, yes. Those two could butt heads. My Lily always had to calm them down."

Jay said, "Actually, at the Little Bard Theater, Maya backed down on her own. I think she knew she'd get kicked out if she didn't."

"That would have ruined her mission," Lexie put in. "And when it comes to the mission, Maya is relentless."

Drew said, "Lexie and Jay, tell the story as straightforwardly as you can. We all want to know how and why Maya went over the cliff with an ogre. And what the mission is."

With some starts and stops, Jay and Lexie told the story of their adventures in Elferterre and how it had ended. Viola got the sense that Lexie had left something out about when she had been captured by the ogres, but both Jay and Lexie firmly kept this memory away from Viola, and she knew it would be rude to push back against them.

When Lexie and Jay were done, everyone was quiet for a while. Simon pulled at the grass as Mémère sniffed and stared off into the distance.

Drew asked, "Will's quite sure that Maya survived the fall with the ogre?"

"Oh, yeah," Lexie answered. "And when Will's sure, he's sure. Nothing can make him change his mind."

Jay looked sympathetically at Mémère, who was wiping tears from her cheeks. Gently, he said to her, "Will called to Maya across two universes, and she heard him. He helped bring her back. Without Will's help, Maya's spirit might not have returned to her body. If anyone knows, it's Will."

Mémère said, "But they're just teenagers. Maudit, he's seventeen and she's fifteen. Well, sixteen, I guess, by now. How can they have such a bond?"

"I don't know," Jay replied. "But they do."

Drew asked, "And Thirret, from The Other Green Door, is going with Will to Elferterre to find Maya?"

"That's right," Jay answered.

Elferterre, Viola thought, catching her breath. *A dimension where Magic rules.* How she longed to go there.

Drew considered Jay and Lexie. "You're taking over Maya's mission, and you have the lock to trap Cinnial?" They both nodded. "Then why did you come here? Why didn't you just go to the Great Library?"

Jay looked away, but Lexie stared directly at Drew. "We're just the sidekicks." Lexie grimaced, clearly not relishing that role. "We came for Viola. To help trap Cinnial."

"Me?" Viola squeaked as her father shook his head. "But I've just had my eyes peeled."

Jay said, "The Books told us that while you're not as good as Maya, you're pretty damn good. You're better than Lexie and me. You can see more, and your intuition is a better guide."

"But in Caxton, I saw Julian at the midsummer festival. He might recognize me."

Jay replied, "The Books also told us that it's not likely that Julian will remember you from Caxton, but to be sure you can cut and dye your hair before you go to the Great Library."

"The way Maya did when she came to my party," Drew murmured to himself. "I nearly didn't recognize her."

As Viola put a hand to her smooth dark hair, she stared in astonishment at Jay and Lexie and realized they were right. That's why, in her flash, she hadn't been outside the Great Library with the others. Instead, she was inside, trying to trap Cinnial. Not a comforting thought but true nonetheless. And she guessed Robbie was with her, which was why he wasn't outside with the others. And maybe her father, too. As for Simon, Viola suspected his role was here, in Caxton, tangled up with Chet and Rhys and Sir John. Viola had an uneasy feeling about this, but she knew there wasn't much she could do about it. Soon, she would be leaving Caxton to go to the Great Library.

Jay was watching her closely. "But first we have to go somewhere else."

Startled, Viola asked, "Where?"

"To a planet called Aarde to find someone to help you. We'll be going to Camber, the capital city of the island nation of Daywen," he answered. "It's where some of the exiled librarians from the Great Library are staying. The Books said that in Camber there are some kids whose ability to see is really strong. Like yours. There is somebody there who can peel eyes, the way Myranda and the Toad Queen can. So these kids have had their eyes peeled. With some extra help, you should be able to trap Cinnial. And, of course, we'll help, too, in any way we can."

Drew frowned. "No. The only place Viola is going is home. She's twelve years old. Even with help, Viola is too young to face Cinnial at the Great Library." He said this so firmly that at first no one dared to contradict him, not even Lexie.

Finally Viola, her voice soft but urgent, spoke, "Dad, why do you think I got my eyes peeled? So I could just hang back and let others do things?"

Drew said, "It's one thing to help. It's quite another to go up directly against Cinnial and try to trap him. Cinnial killed Sydda. He's taken over the Great Library. He's much too dangerous for someone your age to go up against."

But Viola didn't back down. "That's what Maya was planning on doing, and she's not that much older than me. Because we're kids, Cinnial won't suspect us."

"And with Cinnial in charge, how exactly are you supposed to sneak into the Great Library and trap him?" her father asked. He turned to Jay and Lexie. "All the teenage apprentices evacuated with the others, didn't they?"

"They did," Jay admitted.

Drew continued, "And I bet all of Cinnial's crew are adults. Don't you think Cinnial would notice if teenagers started roaming the halls?"

Jay said, "Sir, you're right, but we have a solution. When Maya went to the Great Library, she met a guy named Kip, who lives with his boyfriend Isik in Watertown, the city across from the library. Kip said he'd be there to help whenever she needed it. The exiled librarians have found out that Kip has just been hired to take care of the atrium inside and the gardens outside the Great Library. That's where Viola and whoever she chooses will come in. They can be part of his crew to help him pick potatoes, which are ready to be harvested. The schools in Watertown have something called potato recess. It lasts for two weeks, and no one will think it's weird if kids are at the Great Library helping to pick potatoes."

111

Drew continued to frown, but he didn't say anything.

Viola said, "I have to go. Can't you see that?"

Her father sighed. "In a way, I do." Then in a low voice, he asked, "But what in the world would your mother say if she knew about this?"

Viola smiled a little. "You know what she'd say. She'd have a fit. Have you told Mom about any of this, how Maya came to you when you were seventeen and took you to Caxton? Does she know we're both here now?"

Her father shook his head. "No, I never told her, and she doesn't know we're here."

Viola took a deep breath. "Maybe it's better that way. Then she won't worry." She might have added, "Either we come back or we don't." But she didn't. Viola understood her father was all too aware of this.

"That's no way to treat your mother," Mémère said. "You shouldn't keep something big like this from her."

"Did Maya tell her mother what she was doing?" Viola asked. "How she went across the universe to the Great Library?"

"No," Mémère admitted in a small voice.

"That's what I thought." Viola regarded her father, and two pairs of deep blue eyes stared fixedly at each other. "Dad, I'm going to Aarde and then the Great Library. I'm sorry you don't like it, but that's what I have to do. And I bet you'll be there, too. We'll be together."

"I'll be there as well," Jay put in.

"And so will I," Lexie added.

"Me, too," Mémère said.

Robbie grinned. "Where Viola goes, I go."

Simon remained silent, and Viola's suspicions were confirmed. "You're not coming, are you?"

"Nay," Simon answered. "My place is here. It always has been. I'll stay and look after the horses."

"Right," Viola said, her voice brisk. "As soon as we're done talking, I'm going to the lodge in Oakton Forest, and the Book will come back with Rhys and Sir John, who are staying there." Nobody said anything. They all knew why the Book was coming back with Rhys and Sir John. Viola glanced at Chet, who was standing still and straight. Too still and too straight, Viola would realize later, as though he was coiled for action.

But distracted by Jay and Lexie, and the plans they were making, Viola turned to Simon. Everyone else was looking at him, too. Viola asked, "Afterwards, will you join Rhys and Sir John at the lodge?"

"Aye," Simon answered. "And I'll help them take Caxton back from Humphrey." He sighed and looked at Drew, who nodded. "Again."

As Viola thought about Humphrey, Rosalind, Sebastian, and the Forest of Arden, she felt the Book sag in the pocket of her dress. It seemed as though it was becoming heavier and heavier and might even rip through. She saw Jay and Lexie look down at their pockets and realized the same thing must be happening to them.

Reaching into their pockets at more or less the same time, Viola, Jay, and Lexie pulled out their Books and opened them.

"It's Chet!" they cried in unison. "He's escaped."

Viola, Jay, and Lexie were the only ones who could hear the Books, and with a start, they jumped up to find that Chet was indeed gone. The others looked, too, and saw that the tracker was no longer tied to the tree.

Simon and Robbie raced to the tree and found the cut rope that had once bound Chet.

"One moment he was there," Viola murmured. "And then he was gone."

"I should have stayed with him," Robbie said when they came back with the rope.

Mémère scowled. "We all should have kept a closer eye on that stinker."

"I checked the knots before I joined you," Robbie added, "and Simon was right. They were nice and tight."

His face red with anger and embarrassment, Simon stared at the rope, which he twisted in his hands. "The knots were tight, but someone cut him loose."

"You should have had me out," Earth's Book of Everything told Viola. "You shouldn't have kept me in your pocket."

"Right!" Alani's Book agreed.

"We could have warned you as it was happening," Alexander's Book said.

Lexie's face flushed. "Why didn't you tell us ahead of time that this would happen? You told us to be careful, and we were careful.

Chet was tied to the tree. President Murphy said the knots were secure because Simon had tied them. And they were secure. Chet got away because someone cut the rope."

There was a sheepish silence, and finally Earth's Book replied, "We didn't tell you because we didn't know until Chet was actually being cut free. Unfortunately, we can't see things the way we once did."

"Who helped him?" Lexie asked.

"We don't know that either," Alexander's Book answered. "One moment, Chet was being cut free by someone we couldn't see, and the next minute they were both hidden from us."

Earth's Book said, "Earlier, just after Viola and I arrived here at the clearing, I felt something. Someone with one of Cinnial's Books has come to Caxton, and no doubt that person freed Chet. But I was in Viola's pocket, and I couldn't warn her."

Alexander's Book sighed. "Bad."

"Very bad," Alani's Book agreed.

Viola told those who couldn't hear the Books what they had said.

Drew asked, "Should we go after Chet?"

"No," Earth's Book answered. "Who knows where he is? He might not even be on this planet. And, of course, there's no point in going to get Rhys and Sir John now that Chet is gone."

After Viola related the answer, she glanced at Diana, who was huddled and still.

"What about Diana?" Viola asked, considering her for the first time. "What are we going to do with her?"

"She'll be coming with us to Aarde," Lexie answered. "They'll be able to take care of her there."

Viola frowned. "But how? We don't have enough Books for everyone to travel."

Jay grinned. "What has it got in its pocketses?"

Lexie rolled her eyes. "You've just been waiting for the opportunity to ask that, haven't you?"

"All my life," came Jay's prompt reply.

With a start, Viola slid her hand into her dress's pocket and felt three acorns. "That's why the Old Oak gave them to me, wasn't it?"

"The Old Oak had a feeling you would need the acorns," Earth's Book agreed.

As everyone nodded, Earth's Book said, "So now it's time to go to Camber, where Viola can choose whom she wants to take to the Great Library."

Viola blinked at the Book. "I'm going to choose?"

"Of course you are," Alani's Book replied. "You need to pick someone who will work well with you."

Work well with me, Viola thought, a little bemused. *But how will I know?*

Earth's Book, as if sensing her concern, said, "Don't worry. You'll know."

12: OF TIME AND MAGIC

And Viola did know. As soon as she saw Wren's round brown face and dark eyes, the choice was clear. Wren was the one. Although Wren waited patiently, the way the other two did, Viola sensed what the girl really wanted was to move around and examine everything around her. Clearly, Wren had never been in this back room in Camber's city library, and when she thought Viola wasn't looking, Wren glanced longingly at the books arranged in the bookcases, at a big globe on a nearby table, at the framed maps on the walls. It was this curiosity and the sparkling attention that went with it that drew Viola to Wren.

But wanting to be fair, Viola reconsidered the other two candidates—a girl and a boy, both about the same age as Jay and Lexie. The girl, Helgin, stood confidently, and at school on Earth, Viola had met her type many times. Helgin was someone who liked to tell people what to do, and because of the force of her personality, most everyone fell in line. If Viola was going to be honest, she had to admit it would be somewhat of a relief to follow a decisive girl like Helgin, whose gaze was sharp and penetrating. Because even though Viola had argued with her father about going to the Great Library, she realized he was right. She was only twelve years old and all too aware of her limitations in going up against someone as powerful as Cinnial.

Viola's impression of the boy, Isold, was that he was more like Maya, always ready for action, someone who never hesitated when it came to doing something bold or dangerous. After being with Maya, Viola had come to realize how useful this was, how hesitating could make a difference between living and dying, between failing and succeeding.

Viola turned back to Wren, who smiled shyly at her. *Yes*, Viola thought, *she's the one. We'll make a good team. And she'll get along with Robbie.* From being in the White House with her father, Viola understood the importance of having a good team, even if that team was small.

Nodding at Wren, Viola turned regretfully to Helgin and Isold. Knowing that no one liked being rejected, Viola really didn't want to say she had chosen Wren over them. As it turned out, Viola didn't need to say anything. Helgin and Isold could tell by Viola's expression that they had not been picked.

Helgin blinked in disbelief. "Really? Wren?"

Isold shook his head in disappointment.

As Wren stared down at her scuffed shoes, Viola knew exactly what Helgin meant. Wren's family was not as wealthy as Helgin's and Isold's families were. It was clear that Wren's clothes had been washed and worn many times, perhaps passed down from an older relative. On the other hand, Helgin's and Isold's clothes were crisp and new. Their expressions and the way they held themselves told Viola that Helgin and Isold were used to getting what they wanted. Here in Camber they were at the top of society. They knew it, and so did everyone else, including Wren.

Just like me in the United States, Viola thought. Although she had a confidence similar to Helgin's and Isold's, there was a difference. And that difference was Viola's father, whose family was a reminder that talent came to the rich and poor alike. But, as her father had told her many times, the rich could afford to nourish their talents while the poor had to scrabble for a living and often weren't able to take advantage of the talents they were born with.

"I got lucky," her father had often said. "My mother encouraged me to go to college even though nobody in our family had ever gone before. Most of my aunts and uncles hadn't even graduated from high school. They went to work in the mills as soon as they could."

Thinking of her father, Viola turned to Helgin and Isold. "I'm sorry. You'd both be good. It was hard choosing."

Helgin arched her eyebrows. "No, it wasn't. I could tell right off that you connected with Wren."

"Me, too," Isold said.

117

"You're right," Viola admitted, sorry she had told a lie to these two who could see right through what she said. "There's just something about Wren."

Helgin stared at Wren. "There always has been."

Looking up and grinning faintly, Wren shrugged.

Isold laughed. "Wren, we could see it the first day you started school at Chêne Grove Academy." Then Isold became serious, and he put his hand on Wren's shoulder. "Be careful, little bird. This mission's a dangerous one."

"I will," Wren replied, her voice clear, fresh, and confident. She smiled at Isold. "But I can take care of myself. You know that."

Isold's lips quirked into a grin. "I do know that."

Gathering herself together, Helgin nodded regally. "Nevertheless, Wren, do be careful."

Isold shook his head.

"What?" she asked.

"Oh, never mind," Isold replied, and although his lips twitched, he maintained a serious expression.

Helgin sniffed. "Let's go."

After Helgin and Isold left, Viola and Wren looked at each other. First they grinned, and then they began to laugh.

Wren wiped her eyes. "Goodness, Helgin didn't like it that you chose me. Not one bit."

"No, she didn't," Viola agreed, also wiping her eyes. "She acts like royalty."

Wren glanced at Viola. "In a way, she is. Her family runs a lot of things in Camber. And she thinks she's better than me."

"No," Viola replied, her voice firm. "She's not better. Just different. And you know what? Helgin would stand out too much. We're supposed to be gathering information and then trapping Cinnial when he's off guard." Viola pushed away the uncomfortable feeling that like Chet, Cinnial was seldom caught off guard. She continued, "There's no way Helgin would stay in the background. She'd be noticed right away. And so would Isold."

"And maybe you, too," Wren said. "Not as much as they would. Mostly because you're not as tall as they are, and you're younger. But you walk the way they do."

Seeing two chairs by the big globe, Viola said, "Let's sit and talk. We might not get another chance to be alone before we go."

"Right," Wren said with a brisk nod, and they sat down on the big wooden chairs, which had padded cushions.

"Can you teach me how not to be noticed?" Viola asked.

With a slight frown, Wren regarded her. "I don't know. You're really confident."

Viola sighed. "Yeah. But I have to try. None of this will work if Cinnial figures out that we've come to trap him."

Wren's bright eyes became even brighter. "I'll do my best to teach you."

Viola smiled at her. "Yup, I know you'll be a big help. That's why I picked you."

Wren's expression became even more serious. "Exactly how old are you?"

"I'm twelve," Viola admitted reluctantly. "But I'll be thirteen in a couple of months. How old are you?"

"Fifteen."

The two girls were silent as they thought about their ages and how young they were.

To lighten the mood, Viola asked, "What's your favorite color?"

"Brown." Wren's expression became dreamy. "Lovely soothing brown, like in the autumn when the leaves fall and there's that nutty smell and the feeling that change is coming. Chilly weather. Fresher breezes from the ocean. What's your favorite color?"

"Blue," came Viola's quick answer. "True blue. Cool blue. Loyal blue."

"Like your eyes." There was wonder in Wren's voice. "Until Astrid, Elspeth, and the others from the Great Library came to stay here in Camber, I had never seen blue eyes before."

"Never?" Viola asked in surprise.

"No, we don't have blue eyes in our country, only shades of brown and black."

"Huh," Viola said.

"You don't know much about our country and this planet, do you?"

"No, I only heard about it a few hours ago," Viola answered. "The Book told me that the exiled librarians had made their headquarters here in Camber in the island nation of Daywen. And the planet was called Aarde. That's all."

"Do you know why the librarians came here?"

Shaking her head, Viola thought about the glimpses she had gotten of Camber, of the parks and the gardens and the streetcars and the lack of traffic. She had seen a few small electric cars, mostly driven by older people. Everyone else seemed to walk, bike, or take the street cars, which clanged merrily as they whizzed by.

Wren said in sorrow, "Hundreds of years ago, our planet Aarde was wrecked. There were floods and fires. Storms and diseases. Wars. Lots and lots of people died. In the end, hardly any were left. Only small pockets here and there." Clearly, Wren was reciting what she had learned in school, but her emotion was genuine, and Viola listened attentively.

"Who wrecked your planet?" Viola asked.

"I think you know," Wren whispered.

Viola sighed. "People wrecked the planet, didn't they? By burning fuel that caused climate change."

"You guessed that pretty fast."

Viola thought of the discussions her mother and father had had. "It's happening on Earth, where I come from. We just haven't destroyed the planet. At least not yet." She gazed out one of the windows at a small green park with trees and flowers. "But it's beautiful here. It doesn't look ruined at all."

"My country is far out in the ocean, away from everything else," Wren said. "Somehow, with the wind and the currents, even with climate change, the storms weren't as bad here, and we still had plenty of rain. But not too much. We just got lucky that we're so isolated. Not many died in Daywen because of the pandemics. And the wars never came here. The people on the mainlands were too busy fighting among themselves. They didn't care about our little island nation, way out in the ocean. They left us alone."

"I'm glad they left you alone," Viola replied. Getting different impressions from Wren, Viola understood that the planet Aarde, ruined except for a few lucky spots like Daywen, was the perfect place for the librarians fleeing from the Great Library. The planet was in such bad shape, especially compared with Bellefour, the Great Library's planet, that it was the last place Cinnial would expect Astrid and some of the exiled librarians to hide.

Viola asked, "Does Aarde have one of Cinnial's Books?"

Wren shook her head. "Not anymore. It burned in the chaos it helped create. And thank the blue waters, Aarde never got another one of his books. After all the destruction, Cinnial must have thought we weren't worth bothering with anymore."

"But you have a Book of Everything?"

"Yes," Wren replied. "It had come to Daywen long ago, and it helped us get through the chaos."

Viola hesitated before asking the next question. "Did your parents give you any trouble about maybe being chosen to come to the Great Library with me to trap Cinnial?"

"My parents are dead," Wren said, staring down at her hands. "They were killed in an accident at sea. They had taken the day off to go fishing. A storm came and capsized their boat, and they drowned."

Viola felt Wren's great sorrow. Leaning forward, she took one of Wren's hands and held it.

Wren sniffed sadly. "I wanted to go with my parents, but they wouldn't let me skip a day of school. I was so mad at them that I didn't even say goodbye when I left that morning. I just slammed the door as I went out."

"You couldn't have known what was going to happen," Viola said.

Wren looked up. "True, but I didn't have to leave in such a snit." Her voice was so soft that Viola could hardly hear her. "I could have said goodbye."

Viola knew there was nothing she could say to make Wren feel better, and the two sat in silence, hands clasped, until Wren's sadness passed. Finally, Wren nodded at Viola, and their hands unclasped.

"What happened to you after your parents died?" Viola asked.

"For a while I lived with my aunt." Wren shrugged. "But my aunt's always busy. She works a lot of hours at the spinning mill. And when she isn't working, she likes to go out. I was alone a lot. When I was accepted at Chêne Grove Academy, I became a boarder even though I lived close enough to be a day student. On holidays, I stay with friends. I hardly ever see my aunt anymore. But she's still my guardian, and she said yes right away when the headmistress, Ensante Madeleine, asked my aunt for permission for me to go to the Great Library if I was chosen."

"Wow." Viola thought about her father's response when Lexie and Jay had told everyone about their plans to take Viola to the Great Library.

"It's not as bad as it sounds." Wren scrunched up her face. "In Daywen, we hate Chaos. We've seen what it can do to a planet. We know we have to be on guard against it all the time. If someone can help, she helps, no matter how old she is. Well, maybe not four or five, but you know what I mean."

"I do." Viola reflected on how her father had finally given in. *But only because he thinks he's going to be there, too,* she thought.

"Have you had your eyes peeled?" Wren asked.

"About a week ago. Have you?"

"Yes, just before I came here. Also, you should know that my real name is Elowren. But I'd much rather be called Wren."

Viola smiled. "All right. Elowren is a pretty name, but somehow Wren is better for you."

Wren was about to reply, but a knock on the door interrupted them, and an old woman, tall and dark, came into the room. Her short hair was silver, and although she walked slowly, her back was straight. The woman's face was serene but stern, and Viola got the impression of power and confidence.

Immediately, Wren leaped from the wooden chair. "Ensante Madeleine!"

Following Wren's example, Viola also stood.

Ensante Madeleine said, "I can already see that you two will make a good team. Wren, because I am an old woman, I am going to take your chair. But do bring another one over so that we can talk for a while. Viola, please sit down."

Wren found another chair across the room, carried it over, and sat down.

Viola had briefly met Ensante Madeleine before being brought to the room where the students were waiting. Viola knew that the old woman's sharp eyes had seen a lot in that short time.

Sitting down, Viola asked, "Ensante Madeleine, did you think I'd pick Wren?"

The old woman hesitated. "In a way. And yet I knew that Isold and Helgin, so different from Wren, also had qualities that would appeal to you."

"Yes, they do," Viola said. "I wish I could have chosen all three."

"We thought of that," Ensante Madeleine admitted. "But Astrid can only spare five acorns to add to your two. She needs to have some in reserve, just in case. Our own Old Oak could spare some acorns, but it's best if you use ones that come directly from the Ancient Oak. Their magic is stronger, and they can more easily avoid Chaos."

Viola asked in surprise, "Seven acorns? One for each of us to go to Kip and Isik's home in Watertown?"

Ensante Madeleine stared evenly at Viola. "That's right."

"Won't the Books be taking some of us?"

The old woman leaned forward. "Cinnial might be distracted by all his duties at the Great Library, but he is no fool. Never think for one minute that he is." Ensante Madeleine stared sternly at Viola and Wren, and they both nodded solemnly. "If Earth's Book and the Apprentice Books followed the acorns' path and took some of you to Kip and Isik's home, Cinnial's Book would feel their energy immediately and warn Cinnial that the Books were nearby. Books are always on the lookout for other Books, no matter where they come from. Then Cinnial would be on high alert, and so would his staff."

"He mustn't know we've come," Wren murmured. "This will only work if we can take him by surprise."

"Yes," Ensante Madeleine said. "With Magic crackling all around them at the Great Library, Cinnial and his Books, who have been away for so long, are unlikely to notice the magic of the acorns. In this universe, traveling with acorns is not common, and Cinnial won't be looking for their magic. The Ancient One's acorns should be able to slide you into Kip's house without anyone noticing. Time will help, too."

Viola didn't say anything. She had used an acorn to travel from Caxton to Camber, and the way had been bumpy and rough. At times, Viola had felt as though the acorn might slip from her grasp, and she had clenched her hand into such a tight fist that the acorn had dug into her palm. Viola wondered what it would be like to travel with an acorn to the Great Library, to the center of the universe. *I'll soon find out*, Viola thought. *But I can make it. I know I can.* Then she thought about her father, who was still weak from being shot. And about Mémère, who seemed very old to Viola. How would she do?

"The Book never told me that the acorns would be taking all of us to Kip's home," Viola said in a low voice.

Ensante Madeleine's expression softened, and her warm hand covered Viola's smaller one. "I'm not surprised. You know how those Books are."

"I do. And this happens with your Book, too?" But Viola knew the answer even as she asked the question.

"All the time," Ensante Madeleine replied. "Its guidance is invaluable. Our nation would not be what it is without our Book.

However, I have discovered the Book only tells me what it thinks I should hear. And the Book from the Great Library, which Astrid brought, is even more adamant. In the past week or so, I've gone up against both of them several times, and together they never budge when they don't want to tell me something."

Dropping her great reserve for a few moments, the old woman made a face, and Viola nearly laughed. She could see that across from her, Wren was biting her lip.

Ensante Madeleine grinned a little. "After all these years, I should know better. But because I am a stubborn old woman, I keep trying. And every once in a while, when it was by itself, our Book would slip, and I'd get a nugget of information it didn't intend to give me." The grin went away. "Viola and Wren, you are both young, and the trip across the universe will be hard and dangerous. If you let go of the acorn..." Ensante Madeleine shook her head. "Well, don't let go." She paused. "And there is one more thing you should know."

Viola thought, *Oh, no.* Aloud she asked, "What is that?"

"The Books can't come with you when you go to the Isle of Samaras, where the Great Library is," Ensante Madeleine answered. "You'll have to leave the Books behind at Kip and Isik's house when you go to the island. You can confer with the Books when you come back at night."

Wren gasped, and Viola put a hand to her cheek. "Why?"

"Normally, as long as they aren't traveling, the Books of Everything can shield themselves from Cinnial's Books. But on the Isle of Samaras, they can't hide from Cinnial's Books. Because of the Ancient Oak and the acorns, the island is bound to Magic as well as to Time. Magic is strong on the island, and it keeps everything open. That's why at the Great Library everything works, and nothing can be hidden, despite what Cinnial might want. Cinnial's Book was in plain sight until he left. And the Book was in plain sight when Cinnial came back to murder Sydda."

"If everything is open, then how can Cinnial close the Great Library off from the Books of Everything?" Viola asked.

Ensante Madeleine answered, "Because the way to the Great Library is mostly outside the library, across the universe, where Time is strong, and Magic is weaker. Magic can't keep things open the way it can on the Isle of Samaras. Unfortunately, it's easier for Chaos to knock Time off course."

Wren frowned. "But why?"

Ensante Madeleine replied, "Think of Time and Magic as though they are siblings. Although Time is mysterious, it has a strong, steady flow that Chaos can chip away at. Magic is dazzling and flamboyant with a crazy energy that is akin to Chaos. Because of this, Magic is harder for Chaos to control." She tapped on the arm of her chair. "Know this. Cinnial is strong with Chaos, but in taking over the Great Library, he has his hands full coping with both Magic and Time, a new experience for him. In Mortmain, where Cinnial came from, Magic was weak. At the Great Library, Magic is waiting for you and your team. And Time will be there, too, with its own quiet strength. You won't be alone. Because Cinnial's not expecting to be trapped by teenagers, maybe, just maybe, you'll be able to catch him and his Book unawares."

Viola said, "Okay then, but I don't know what my father is going to say about this. He won't like it that we have to leave the Books behind when we go to the Great Library."

Ensante Madeleine replied, "Your father is a smart man. He realizes how much is at stake." Then the old woman frowned slightly, and Viola frowned back at her, sensing Ensante Madeleine was keeping something from her.

Later that day, when her father, flushed and feverish, collapsed after dinner and was rushed to the hospital where Diana was being treated, Viola knew why the old woman had frowned. Ensante Madeleine had seen that Drew's wound was becoming infected and thought it might get in the way of him going to the Great Library. Viola, intent on her mission, had missed how sick her father was.

The Camberside Hotel, where Viola, her father, and the others were staying, was not far from the hospital. The city was so small that nothing was very far from anything else. Still, to Viola, it seemed to take ages for the ambulance to reach the hospital. Sitting beside her father, Viola held his hand, and he was too weak and feverish to even talk to her. Eyes closed, Drew shivered until his teeth chattered.

Viola thought, *Oh, Dad.*

One of the paramedics, a middle-aged woman, said to Viola, "Don't worry. They'll be able to treat him at the hospital. He'll be fine."

The other paramedic, also a woman, agreed. "We've seen worse, and they've all recovered."

Viola didn't say anything, not knowing if they were right or wrong. Viola's fear for her father was strong enough to damp down her intuition, her sense of how things might turn out. She wished her mother, brisk and capable, were beside her to take charge, the way she always did on Earth. For the first time, Viola was sorry she was so far from home.

But at least we're someplace where Dad can be treated, Viola thought. *At least we're not in the middle of the forest in Caxton.*

And that was something.

13: DARK CLOUDS AT SEA

Even with the safety strap and the small saddle, Maya was more than a little nervous on Braird's back. Because Braird was right. His feathers were slippery, and if it hadn't been for the saddle, Maya wouldn't have made it around the deck much less over the sea. The strap around her waist gave Maya an extra feeling of safety. If she did somehow slip, at least she wouldn't fall into the water. Nevertheless, Maya had a tight grip on the edge of the saddle and on the feathers on Braird's back.

"You're pinching me," Braird said as they flew around the upper deck on a test run. "Hold onto the saddle instead."

"Sorry!" Maya moved her hands away from his feathers and more onto the saddle. When Braird dipped to one side, Maya squeaked a little, but she didn't fall off.

Braird turned to look at her. "I think the strap and saddle are holding. Do you want to go a little ways over the sea?"

Maya took a deep breath. "All right."

Everyone was watching on the deck, even Symi and Alie, who had taken a short break from cooking. Standing with his arms folded across his chest, the captain smiled as Braird and Maya came to a stop in front of him.

"Sir," Braird said, "with your permission, we're going to try going a little ways out to sea."

"Maya, are you ready?" the captain asked.

"I am," Maya answered. "Thanks to Proko and Takis. I don't think I would be able to stay on without the strap and saddle."

Zeynip, the bosun, nodded proudly at Proko and Takis, who chittered softly.

Smiling, Maya looked down at the blue feathers gleaming in the sunlight. *So pretty*, Maya thought.

The feathers might have puffed slightly. *What? A compliment?* Braird's thoughts asked.

Don't intrude, Maya's thoughts replied. *But, yeah. That was a compliment.*

First Mate Hawthorn asked, "Are you two done?"

The feathers quickly smoothed back down. "We're ready," came Braird's quick response.

The captain nodded. "Permission granted, then."

"Stay steady, you two," Larz said, watching anxiously. He had double-checked the straps after helping Maya get settled.

Alie's soft voice followed. "Come back safely."

"Bon voyage!" Finneas sang out.

Symi didn't say anything.

With a mighty rush and a flap of his powerful wings, Braird flew from the deck, up into the sky, over the vast sea.

Braird's thoughts asked, *Are you all right? And is it okay to talk like this when we fly? I think we'll be able to hear each other better.*

The whistling wind blew Maya's curls around. *Yes. And thanks for asking.*

I'm not going to go too high. When I look for The Cuttlefish, I fly high enough to avoid anything that might want to eat me yet low enough to see any signs of the submarine.

Like what kind of signs?

From the magic that powers the submarine. No matter how deep The Cuttlefish goes, the magic comes up in little waves. But I haven't spotted anything like that yet. And I've been looking for about a month.

Maya was silent for a moment, thinking about how hard it would be to track a submarine in the vast sea. Then Maya remembered the line she had followed when she had escaped from Bigly and the Office, back in time to her younger self on Earth. Maya wondered if Magic would leave a similar line that could be traced under water, too deep for Braird to see but strong enough for Maya to sense and follow.

Braird asked, *Where would you start? From Isleros, where The Cuttlefish left? The captain has maps. Maybe one of them would help you connect. I've tried, but that's not how I see things. Even the magic engineers haven't had any luck, and their magic is pretty strong. It's like there's something hiding The Cuttlefish's trail.*

There probably is, Maya replied. *But maybe Time can help me in a way that it can't help you and the magic engineers.*

Let's go back and try, Braird said.

Not yet. Let's fly a little farther. Now that Maya trusted the saddle and the safety strap to keep her safe, she was enjoying the flight. With deep blue above and below her, Maya loved the feeling of soaring through the air, similar to the way she had felt when Kai's potion had turned her into a dragonfly.

Braird asked, *Really?*

It's wonderful to go through the air, Maya said. *And see everything from above. You're lucky you can fly.*

Maya could tell Braird was pleased, but his response was matter-of-fact. *I never thought of it that way. Where I grew up, most everyone can fly. Except my mother and a few other elves who live with us to help protect the onneas.*

Onneas?

Do you remember those creatures I showed you in my vision-story?

I do, Maya answered, thinking of the little winged animals who lived in small burrows and were feeding on grass and flowers that grew on the side of one of the Blessed Mountains.

The onneas are a protected species. Everything about them is lucky, from their feathers right down to their toes. The Blessed Mountains are the prime source of magic in this part of Elferterre, and the onneas help regulate the flow. They eat and take in some of the magic, and in return they reinforce the magic.

Who would have thought those cute little animals could be so powerful, Maya mused.

Looks can be deceptive, Braird responded sharply.

But Maya didn't take offense. Instead, she thought of the two trolls, Jeam and Captain Creb, who had helped her on Tufrak when she had run away from Bigly and the Office. The trolls' homely looks had belied their kind, generous natures.

I know, she said. *I've learned that in my travels across the two universes.*

129

You've come a long way, haven't you?

Yeah, Maya answered.

Braird's voice was gentler than usual as he asked, *Do you ever get tired?*

Sometimes, Maya admitted. *But I have to keep going. I can't stop.*

Kind of like the captain.

Kind of. And after I'm done here, I need to go back to my own universe to see what's happening with Cinnial and the Great Library. And help if I can.

Let's go back to the ship, Braird said. *So that you can take a look at a map.*

Okay, Maya replied, and Braird turned around. The ship was no longer in sight. There was just the wide expanse of the dark sea.

Maya asked, *How do you find your way back?*

I follow my beak. Once I've been somewhere, even on a boat, I can always find my way back. But the problem is, I've never been on The Cuttlefish.

Maybe a map will help, and between the two of us, we can find that submarine.

Maybe, Braird replied.

But the map didn't help. The captain tried not to hover as Maya inspected *The Resolute*'s trail, which started in Port Isleros and led to the ship's current position. Standing nearby, First Mate Hawthorn watched closely. The map was on a huge screen in the wheelhouse, and Maya got absolutely nothing from it about where *The Cuttlefish* might be. No flash, no images of either Clarin or Rhye. They were blocked by a great yawning silence that Maya didn't know how to bridge, and there was something about it that didn't feel right.

Disappointed, Maya shook her head.

Equally disappointed, the captain sighed.

"I'll keep trying," Maya assured him.

"I know you will," the captain answered.

First Mate Hawthorn didn't say anything. There might even have been an expression of sympathy before she quickly turned away. Braird didn't say anything, either. Looking sharp and moody, he left the wheelhouse with his mother, who put a hand on his shoulder. As they left, the captain silently studied the map.

Maya felt as though she had let them all down, and despondent, she went down to the kitchen to talk to Symi and Alie. Dinner was ready, and the grenog and the elf actually had time to sit down with her at the red enamel table in the kitchen. A third red chair was at the table as though it were waiting for her, and the kitchen, with its cozy size and delectable smells, was fast becoming one of Maya's favorite places on the ship.

Symi and Alie were drinking tea and eating cookies. As soon as Maya came into the kitchen, Alie produced a steaming mug of tea—not chamomile—and a small plate for Maya for cookies, nutty and buttery with jam in the middle.

"No luck?" Symi asked sympathetically.

Maya sat down heavily. "None. Usually I get some kind of flash that helps me, but aside from when I first met the captain and got a sense of his daughter, there's nothing."

"The sea is vast," Alie said, her eyes big.

Maya took a cookie. "So is my universe. But I found my mother and my younger self all the way across from another planet."

"You had Time to help, didn't you?" Symi asked.

"Yeah. But Magic has helped me before. Something's blocking me. I know it."

Symi took a sip of tea. "Could be. But keep in mind that it's different here, Maya. You can't expect to do things the way you did when you were in your universe, when Time was on your side."

Maya realized Symi was right. In Earth's universe, in the battle against Chaos and with the fall of the Great Library, it was only natural that Time would help her in any way possible. On Elferterre, with Magic in charge, Maya had no idea what the natural order was.

Maya said, "Maybe Magic doesn't want me to find Clarin. But why?"

Symi shrugged. "Who knows? Magic moves in mysterious ways. Even at my age, I'm surprised by its workings." Symi frowned as she remembered, but her thoughts were blocked from Maya, who pulled quickly away, knowing she was intruding.

Maya's words came out in a rush. "Sorry! I'm still new at this."

Symi just smiled. Maya got the sense that the elf was not at all concerned, that it would take someone more powerful than Maya to intrude on Symi's thoughts.

Alie said, "Maybe you haven't found the right way to connect with the submarine."

131

"But what could that way be?" Maya asked.

"That is the big question." Symi patted Maya's shoulder, exactly the way Mémère would have.

The next day, the weather was clear and still. Maya and Braird were ready to search for the submarine. Again, the crew and the captain were on the deck to see them off.

Despite the previous day's failure, the captain's expression was bright with anticipation. "Magic be with you."

Finneas's hands were clasped. "Find our dear Clarin."

Eloise, Aiken, and Orlaith were perched on a section of the ship's rail near Maya and Braird.

"Are you sure you don't want us to come with you?" Eloise asked. "You're going out farther today."

Maya shook her head. "No need. The weather couldn't be any calmer. Braird is a strong flier, and I have the saddle and harness. I'll be fine."

"Okay, then," Aiken said as Eloise and Orlaith nodded.

Proko and Takis double-checked the straps and the saddle. "Everything's good."

Larz clapped Braird on one of his strong wings. "Magic speed, buddy."

As Braird nodded curtly, Larz cupped his hands together for Maya's foot, and hoisted her onto the saddle. After helping her strap in, he patted Maya's leg. "Hope you find that submarine."

Maya took a deep breath. "Me, too."

Even Hawthorn came over and murmured, "Good luck."

"Thanks, Mom," Braird murmured back.

Despite their reserved natures, Maya could feel the strong affection between Braird and his mother.

Braird turned to Maya. "Ready?"

"Ready!" With great resolve, Maya stared out to sea. As she concentrated, it seemed as though she pierced through something, and Maya got a faint impression of Clarin. Would today be the day that Time, or even Magic, helped her? Feeling hopeful, Maya leaned forward in anticipation. "Let's go!"

Braird took to the air, and as they left the ship, Maya heard Alie ask Symi, "Do you think Maya found the way? She looks as though she might have."

"I don't have a clue," Symi replied. "But Maya is one determined human."

Yes, I am, Maya thought.

The voices faded as Braird and Maya flew over the sea, and they left *The Resolute* far behind. Maya focused fiercely on the image of Clarin, which flared brightly. Maya's senses shot at a breakneck speed over the ocean, and she saw a faint line belonging to *The Cuttlefish*. The line headed back toward Port Isleros but then swerved around and went much farther north. But *The Resolute* was sailing southwest, away from Clarin and Rhye, away from *The Cuttlefish*.

"I saw the line!" Maya cried aloud as her senses returned to her. "*The Resolute* is going in the wrong direction. Clarin and Rhye are heading north, not south."

"To throw us off," Braird muttered, also aloud. "We didn't expect them to double back. We thought they'd head south toward the open sea and try to get as far away as they could from Port Isleros."

Then the image of Clarin and the line blinked out. It was as though something strong had pushed back against her, blocking her from Magic's line.

Maya exclaimed, "Oh, no!"

"What?"

"I lost the line. It just disappeared."

"But we know where they are. We can go back to the ship and tell the captain."

"Yeah," Maya agreed. However, a bad feeling came to her. Maya wanted to ignore it, but she couldn't. Maya had had the feeling before, when she had looked at the map in the wheelhouse. "We can do that. But will it do any good?"

"What do you mean?" Braird asked, tilting to turn around.

Maya had a tight grip on the saddle. "Will *The Cuttlefish* immediately change course and throw us off again? Do you think it's an accident that *The Cuttlefish* is always one step ahead? The sea is big, I know, but the captain has his maps and his magic engineers. He has you and Cali. But the captain gets nothing, absolutely nothing. A big fat zero."

"Someone aboard the ship is skunking us," Braird said. "But who could it be? Everyone is chosen so carefully. Chantay has to give final permission for anyone to board her ship. And let me tell you, she can see pretty deep."

"I don't know who it could be," Maya answered in sorrow. In her short time aboard *The Resolute*, she had come to know the crew, and while there were some Maya liked better than others—Alie and Symi were two of her favorites—she respected them all, even Braird and his mother. And after working so closely with Braird for the past two days, Maya realized that she was beginning to feel something more than respect for the corbeau, but she didn't want to think too much about that right now. Later, when things had settled down, Maya would try to sort out her emotions.

As they flew back toward the ship, which was just coming into sight, a small dot on the horizon, the wind began to pick up. Dark clouds swirled overhead, covering the blue sky. Below them, the water was choppy, and just beneath the surface, a creature was following them. Maya could see its spiny back break the surface and then go back under. Even from above, Maya could sense the creature's hungry intensity.

"A cerpetin," Braird said. "It's been following us for a while. Fortunately, it can't strike too far above the water, but it is one fast swimmer."

Catching a glimpse of a long sinuous body, Maya shivered and squeezed the edge of the small saddle.

As the wind pushed against them, Braird didn't falter, but Maya knew how tiring it must be for him to fly into the wind with someone on his back, even if that someone was a little human, as Larz would put it. Leaning forward, she shifted her weight away from Braird's back toward his neck.

"Better," Braird said. "You're small, but..."

"I know," Maya replied, anxiously watching the clouds as they dropped lower and lower until Maya could barely see beyond Braird's beak. The wind became stronger. Swearing, Braird flew, but it hardly felt as though they were moving, and it seemed to Maya that no matter how hard Braird's wings flapped, they were staying in one place.

The wind blew harder still, buffeting them, and Braird tipped from side to side. Maya felt herself slip at a crazy tilt, and when she looked down, Maya saw the safety strap had broken away from the small saddle. Before she could even cry out, down Maya tumbled, through the clouds, away from Braird and toward the dark sea, where the cerpetin, with its sharp teeth, was waiting for her as it tracked her fall.

Readying herself, Maya took a deep breath. *All right, then.* Maya balled her hands into fists. She would not go down without a fight, no matter how futile it was.

However, before Maya hit the water, she felt something rake against her back, sharp enough to split her skin and make her bleed. Crying out, she saw two large hopeful eyes beneath the water, marking her progress. However, instead of plunging to her death, Maya was yanked away from the waiting cerpetin. Braird's talons gripped the strap that was still cinched around her waist, and the searing pain had come as his talons had grazed her back. The wind wasn't blowing as hard, and up, up she went, carried by Braird and the strong, steady beating of his wings.

Below Maya came a roar as the head of the green crested cerpetin lunged at her. But too late. Braird had pulled her out of range. The cerpetin, overconfident that a meal was coming its way, had waited instead of striking and had lost its chance for a meal.

Maya could hear singing, beautiful but commanding. It was Chantay, and her song was dispelling the dark clouds and the wind. The sky was blue once again, and *The Resolute* raced toward Maya and Braird. Although it seemed like hours, it was only minutes until Braird and Maya both collapsed on the deck, and the crew clustered around them.

There were so many hands trying to help and voices calling out that everything seemed like a blur to Maya. But Braird's voice came through. "Maya, are you all right? I hurt you, didn't I?"

Braird was no longer a bird, and they were lying side by side as the crew milled around them. Even though Maya's back was soaked with blood and burned with pain, she turned toward Braird, grasping his arm. "It doesn't matter. You saved my life."

Sighing with relief, he grabbed her hand and squeezed it.

Then the captain took charge. "Bring Maya and Braird to the sick bay."

Down they were whisked to the small sick bay on the lower deck, where Maya's wounds were treated by Hannie. The chief magic engineer could heal as well as sort out magic. Murmuring, Hannie rubbed a salve on Maya's back. It smelled similar to the one from Tagen's cottage, which Lexie had applied to the deep wound in Maya's arm made by the imp's knife. Wincing as the salve went into her broken skin, Maya remembered how Tagen's salve

135

had stung, too. But whatever was in that ointment had worked fast. Maya's arm was nearly healed even though she had only been stabbed a few days ago.

Seeing the faint outline of a wound on Maya's arm, Hannie asked, "What happened here?"

"Stabbed by an imp," Maya answered.

"You certainly lead an exciting life, don't you?"

Maya sighed. "I sure do."

After bandaging Maya's back, Hannie gave her a pill and a cup of water. "Here, take this and sleep a little. I know the captain is anxious for a report, but it can wait."

Maya shook her head. "No, it can't wait. Send him down here. I'll take the pill afterward."

Hannie looked from Maya to Braird, who nodded in agreement. "Maya's right. Send him down."

"Okay, then," Hannie said, tucking a blanket around Maya, who except for the bandages, was bare from the waist up. "But first I'm going to examine Braird for sprains or breaks."

"As soon as you're done, go get the captain," Maya said. "It's really important that we talk to him."

Hannie's broad lips quirked into a grin. "Aye-aye. Maya's a bossy one, isn't she?" the elf asked as she checked Braird to see if he was seriously hurt.

Braird winced. "Oh, yes. Don't let her size fool you."

Hannie laughed. "That I will not do. After all, it's not every human who thinks it's a swell idea to ride on the back of a corbeau. And it's not every corbeau who would allow it." She squeezed Braird's arm, and he winced again. "You're all right. Nothing's broken."

"Good to hear." Then Braird grimaced. "But everything hurts."

"Of course it does," Hannie replied. "It was quite enough work to carry Maya on the saddle. But to carry her with your talons back to the ship? It's a wonder you made it."

"I had to," Braird said. "Or else the cerpetin would have gotten Maya."

"I know. Good thing you have some elf magic in you from your mother's side. Otherwise, you never could have carried Maya that far." Hannie gave a cup and a pill to Braird. "Take this after you've spoken with the captain. I want you two to get some rest. I'll be back down to check on you."

Hannie left, and Maya turned to Braird. "Thank you."

Braird shrugged. "Couldn't let you get eaten."

Maya would have reached for his hand to squeeze, but the beds were too far away. "Still."

"Wouldn't you have done the same?"

"Yes, I would have. I took a knife for Will, and I would take one for you, too."

"Well, there." Braird smiled at Maya, who was taken aback by his warmth. And affection.

"Well, there," she repeated in a low voice as the captain came into the room.

The captain pulled over a chair and sat between Maya and Braird. "Tell me everything that happened."

And they did.

When Maya and Braird were done, the captain didn't say anything. He simply sat and stared at them, and Maya got the impression that the captain, usually so decisive, didn't know what to do.

14: LET YOUR CONSCIENCE BE YOUR GUIDE

Maya slept into the middle of the night, and when she woke up, her back was stiff, but most of the pain was gone. Braird was asleep in the other bed, and Maya could hear his breathing, deep and slow. By the glow of a nightlight, Maya saw clean clothes on a nearby chair, and quietly slipping out of bed, she got dressed. Orlaith, Aiken, and Eloise had joined Maya in the sick bay. They waited silently on a side table by the bed, and Maya put the relics on her shoulders, where they could all cling with ease.

As Maya got dressed, Braird did not wake up. Slowly and on tiptoes, Maya left the sickbay. She went down the hall past the bedrooms, past the dining room, past the kitchen, past the lounge, and then to the stairs to the upper deck. By the glow of the mast lights, Maya saw that she was the only one on deck. Everyone else was sleeping.

There was a slight breeze, and Maya could hear the sea slap gently against the hull of the ship, which did not move at all. Maya went to the prow and leaned over.

Chantay's luminous face looked up at Maya. "That was quite an expedition for you and Braird, wasn't it?"

"Sure was," Maya answered. "Almost didn't make it. Again."

"A trend with you?"

"It's starting to look that way."

Chantay frowned. "I hurried the ship toward you and Braird as fast as I could, but there was a limit to how fast I could go for the safety of the crew."

"Of course," Maya said.

"Lucky for you that Braird is a mix of corbeau and elf. Otherwise, I don't think he would have found the strength to carry you in his talons all the way back to the ship."

Maya shivered. "That's what Hannie said."

Eloise's paw patted Maya's shoulder. "It just goes to show how a mix is good. You get the best of both."

"Yeah." Maya remembered how her parents had said the same thing about humans on Earth. But then her thoughts turned back to what had happened to her at sea. "Chantay?"

"Yes, Maya?"

"Something's not right on *The Resolute*. There's a traitor on board."

"I know. I've had that feeling for a while, but I can't see my way to the center of things the way I usually can."

"Same," Maya replied.

"And I can't either," Eloise added, her voice mournful.

"Whoever it is, the magic is strong," Aiken said, and Orlaith tapped her legs in agreement, tickling Maya.

Chantay rubbed her face. "Not only is it galling that the miscreant slipped by me, but it's also dangerous. The crew is in jeopardy. Look what happened to you and Braird today. That strap breaking was no accident. It was planned. And those storm clouds. They were being called. I could feel it. But I can't tell who's responsible."

Chantay, Maya, and the relics brooded together in silence. Nearby, a large creature leaped, making a big splash, and Maya saw the outline of a huge wedge-shaped head as it lifted out of the water for another leap.

"Keep your distance," Chantay commanded, and with the slap of its tail, the creature swam away.

"Do you think whoever is doing all this would hurt the ship?" Maya asked.

"Probably not. If the ship goes down, it would be bad for whoever is behind all this. But it's clear that if you and Braird go out again, you'll be in danger. Next time, you might not make it back."

"Yeah," Maya said. "For a moment, I saw where *The Cuttlefish* was. I saw the line going northeast from Port Isleros, not southwest.

But it blinked out. Right after that, the storm clouds came. Then the strap let go. Tonight, after Hannie examined us, I told the captain what I saw. Will we be heading northeast?"

"I don't know," Chantay answered. "For now, we're staying where we are until the captain determines what he should do. He's still undecided, which is very unlike him."

To the right of them there was another loud splash, and an enormous head came out of the water, but this time Chantay did not tell the creature to go away. "Cali," the figurehead murmured. "So glad you're here. There's been trouble. Big trouble."

Cali spoke as softly as his great size allowed. "I know. I heard the news about Braird and the little human from a school of rorquals." The sea beast rumbled in anger. "There's a traitor on board *The Resolute*. But the traitor made a mistake and used too much magic. A storm was called. Before that, the traitor could stay hidden. Now, the traitor's presence is known."

Maya thought sadly, *But who could it be?*

Chantay asked, "Cali? Could you find *The Cuttlefish*? Maya was able to break through the traitor's magic and catch a glimpse of *The Cuttlefish*'s trail."

"Maybe, if the little human can show me the way."

"Maya?" Chantay whispered.

Nodding, Maya sent her thoughts to Cali, showing him the line that went northeast to *The Cuttlefish*'s location the day before.

"Now, go," Chantay urged. "You know more or less where they were. *The Cuttlefish* has probably changed course, but you can swim very fast. You might be able to catch them."

"On my way," Cali said. And he was gone.

"Will the traitor know that Cali is tracking *The Cuttlefish*?" Maya asked.

"Not if Chance is on our side," Chantay answered. "This exchange was quick. Cali was here for a moment and then was gone again. It's late at night. Whoever is doing this has to sleep. Nobody, no matter how powerful, can see everything all the time. We'll just have to hope."

"Hope what?" a voice asked. Braird came over to the prow. Long and lean, he stood close to Maya and gazed down at Chantay. Maya did not move away, and she briefly told Braird about Cali and his plan to catch *The Cuttlefish*.

When Maya was finished, Chantay said, "Braird, do not discuss this with anyone else, not even your mother. I don't expect she's the traitor, but we don't know who we can trust."

Frowning, Braird tapped the rail of the ship. "I guess that means you think you can trust me."

Maya smiled. "Yes, Braird, we trust you. You could have let me fall into the water. Everybody would have thought it was an accident. Nobody would have thought it was on purpose. Instead you saved me, even though it wasn't easy."

"You might not always be pleasant," Chantay said. "But you are always good."

Braird snorted. "Thanks!"

Glancing sideways at him, Maya thought about how different Braird was from Will, who at seventeen was polished, sophisticated even. While Will did lose his temper sometimes, he had a cool control that Braird, a hot head, lacked. Maya realized that Braird, with his quick temper, was more like her. Maya thought, *But I'm nicer than he is, and he's a lot touchier than I am.*

Maya had kept these reflections from Braird, but he could tell she was thinking about him.

He scowled. "Is there something you want to say to me?"

All three relics tapped Maya on the shoulder, urging her to choose her words carefully. "No, I don't."

"You're not always nice all the time, either," Braird said.

Maya was not surprised that the corbeau, sharp and observant, had been able to guess her train of thought. "I know. I'm like my father. Sometimes we both say things that we shouldn't."

Eloise came to Maya's defense. "But you know how to apologize and how to forgive."

To Maya's surprise, Braird didn't argue. Instead, "I have a hard time forgiving. Like my mother. My father, on the other hand, didn't have a hard time at all."

Because she was so different from her mother, Maya understood what it was like for Braird to be so different from his father. She put her hand on Braird's arm. "My mother barely ever loses her temper. She just kind of sails through life, looking at colors and shapes. She doesn't really notice people. And she doesn't talk much at all. Unlike my father, who talks all the time."

"Like you?" Braird asked.

"Like me," Maya agreed. "When my father left us, the house was so quiet. No more discussions and arguments. No more laughing at funny shows. I could hardly stand it."

"Why did your father leave?" Braird asked.

Maya's eyes stung with tears. "He fell in love with someone else. Then he moved far away. My father's not loyal, the way the captain is."

"That's hard."

Maya blinked back the tears. "Yeah." She glanced at Braird. "Where's your father, Braird?" Quickly, he looked away from her, and Maya was sorry that she had asked. "You don't have to tell me if you don't want to."

Braird shrugged. "It's all right. Everyone on the ship knows about it. In fact, I think all of Norlander knows about it. Maybe even other countries."

Maya's eyes were wide. "What happened?"

As Braird shifted from leg to leg, Maya got a flash of how sore they were from carrying her.

"Let's sit down," she said. "I'm still a little tired from yesterday. I'd rather not stand."

Braird didn't argue. "All right. Chantay, you don't mind?"

"Not at all. Alas, I know the story very well. Sit down and rest your legs. Besides, I'll still be able to hear you. And if I have anything to add, you'll be able to hear me."

Turning around, Maya and Braird sat down and leaned against the side of the ship.

"I can't show you in a vision-story." Braird shook his head. "Even though it happened a few years ago, I still can't stand to watch."

"That's all right," Maya replied.

On Maya's shoulders, the relics shifted sympathetically. "Words will do," Eloise said.

"They certainly will," Aiken added. "Lots of times, words are better than images. They go deeper."

As was her way, Orlaith tapped in agreement, and Maya thought that the spider would be a good companion for her mother. Neither of them was much for conversation

"All right." Braird's voice was low. "I already told you about the onneas, about how they live in the Blessed Mountains."

"Yeah," Maya replied. "And you said they were lucky, from their feathers to their toes. You also told me that they helped with the magic in the Blessed Mountains."

Braird nodded. "The onneas are a protected species. Most everyone in Elferterre respects that, but there are always some who would love to get hold of an onnea to get its luck. And every once in a while someone tries to steal one of the onneas. Or an egg."

"I can picture it," Maya said. "The same thing would happen on Earth."

Braird shrugged. "It's the same across universes, isn't it?"

"It is. Unfortunately," Maya answered. "And I can see why the onneas are protected. They sound very special."

"They are. Along with helping with the magic, the onneas have another important job. They help tend the chênes."

"Chênes?" Maya asked.

"Big trees, with golden nuts we call galans, which are filled with magic. The chênes grow at the base of the Blessed Mountains, and the onneas keep the area around the trees clear. The chênes do better that way."

Taking a deep breath, Maya stared at Braird. "I know you don't want to show me what happened to your father, but could you show me what a chêne and a galan look like?"

"Sure." Murmuring, Braird put up his hands and held them a short distance apart. In between, a tree dotted with golden nuts snapped into focus, and Maya put her hand over her mouth as her suspicions were confirmed. The chêne was an oak tree. The galans were golden acorns, exactly like the ones the Old Oak had given Maya when the Toad Queen had peeled her eyes; it was a golden acorn that had taken her to the Great Library. Even more important, Maya realized that the Ancient One, which Cinnial had burnt, had been a chêne, suffused with magic, which was why all the townspeople across from the Great Library had been affected when they had inadvertently taken in its magic spread by the ashes.

As Braird glanced at Maya's astonished face, the image of tree and golden nuts flickered out. "What's the matter?"

"Those trees..." Maya said.

"What about them?"

"We have them in my universe."

"I know," Braird replied. "Did you think a regular galan just took you to the Great Library?"

"No," Maya answered. "I didn't think it was a regular galan. Or acorns, as we call them. But I didn't think it came from a tree from Elferterre."

"Technically, the Toad Queen's tree didn't come from Elferterre," Braird said. "It came from a galan from a tree at the Great Library."

Maya's voice was soft. "The Ancient One. How did the first golden acorn, the galan, get to the Great Library?"

"An elf brought it, of course."

"Of course." Maya thought about the tight connection between Earth's universe and Elferterre's. "Was the galan stolen?"

Braird frowned. "Sort of. An elf named Samlaren Samaras took a galan without anybody noticing. Apparently, he was so gentle and humble that no one guessed he would do such a thing, and nobody paid much attention to him. He was able to slip a galan in his pocket. Samlaren probably had some kind of relic to hide his intentions. At least that's what my mother thinks. Anyway, Samlaren planted the galan on the planet Bellefour, which is at the center of your universe."

Maya asked, "That's how the Great Library started, isn't it? With the help of Samlaren and the galan, which would become the Ancient One?"

"Yes," Braird replied. "Someday, maybe my mother will tell you about it. She knows more than I do."

"Okay." Dazed, Maya shook her head as she thought about how both Time and Magic were strong at the Great Library. "But we were talking about your father, weren't we?"

Braird rubbed his face. "Yes, my father. He died trying to protect an onnea's nest. A trio of powerful elves came to steal an egg. They were working for Donod Ashglade, another elf, equally powerful, who lives on Earth."

Maya asked, "Is Donod related to Tamick Ashglade?"

"His cousin," Braird answered. "Those Ashglades are a bad bunch. No wonder the captain wants to get his daughter away from Rhye."

Maya said, "Everything is so tangled between Earth and Elferterre."

"It sure is. Anyway, my father was on duty the night the egg was stolen. He and his team spotted the elves as they took the egg, and there was a fight. A big one. My father was killed and so were other corbeaus. My mother was hurt. That's how she got her scar."

Maya put her hand on Braird's arm. "I'm so sorry."

Braird looked away. "I miss him a lot. There's hardly a day that I don't think about him. He was something like your father. He liked to laugh and tell stories. And flying with him was the best thing. He was captain of the guard, and I was always so proud to be with him. My mother misses him, too, even though she doesn't talk about it. I can tell."

Maya thought about how Braird's mother had fallen in love with Captain Blythewood, but she didn't say anything. Instead, she asked, "Did the elves get away with the egg?"

Braird turned back to Maya, and his eyes glittered. "That's the worst part. After killing my father and so many other corbeaus and hurting my mother, the elves got away with the egg. As soon as I'm done helping the captain rescue his daughter, I'm going to go after those elves. I'm going to find them and make them pay."

From the prow, Chantay called, "Not a good idea, Braird."

Braird's jaw was tight. "I'm going to get them. And, Chantay, there's nothing you can say that will make me change my mind."

Maya knew Chantay was right but asked, "What are you going to do when you catch them?"

"I don't know," Braird admitted. "I haven't figured out that part yet. But I found out that the team leader's name is Lillian Pineglade, and when she's not trying to steal an onnea's egg, she spends most of her time on Earth, in Brooklyn. Have you ever heard of her?"

"No," Maya replied. "But I bet she works for APO, which is in Brooklyn, not far from The Other Green Door."

"Doesn't that Chet guy, the man who doesn't smile, work for APO?"

"Yeah." Maya shifted uneasily, wondering about Chet, who had been taken prisoner by Mémère and Simon. She hoped they were being careful. Maya thought about how Chet was dangerous, ruthless, and how he wouldn't hesitate to kill them if he broke loose. Shaking her head, Maya was sorry that she had brought Mémère to Caxton. It had been an impulsive decision, like so many decisions

Maya had made since getting involved with the Great Library. She had needed her grandmother's help and had hardly given any thought to how much danger there might be in whisking Mémère to another planet in a country with two feuding brothers—one of them a duke and the other one out for blood and revenge. Then there was Chet, a psychopath from Earth who, sooner or later, was bound to escape from his prison in the tower in Caxton. And then side with the brother who was out for blood and revenge. In retrospect, it all seemed inevitable, even though Maya knew this wasn't the case. Chance and Nemesis kept things in flux, and the Books had made the best decision they could based on the information they had.

Sighing, Maya thought about her grandmother, who without question, had let Maya take her to Caxton into the middle of what could only be called a dangerous mess.

"What's the matter?" Braird asked.

"I use people," Maya answered in a low voice. "Just like the Books of Everything."

"But it's for a good cause, isn't it?"

Maya stared soberly at Braird. "I don't know. Is it? Do I have the right to put people in danger?"

"Do you have a choice?" Braird asked.

Eloise answered for Maya. "There's always a choice."

"But not necessarily a good one," Chantay said.

For a while nobody said anything. Maya thought about how the battle between Time and Chaos affected the whole universe and maybe even beyond to Elferterre. On such a vast scale, individuals hardly mattered. Except for Maya, certain individuals did matter, including Mémère, Andy, Viola, Jeam, Captain Creb, Will, Lexie, Jay, and now Braird. Maya cared about them all as well as many others, and she didn't want bad things to happen to any of them. Maya had seen Duke Owen die, and it was something she would never forget. Yet on she pushed, getting various folks involved, putting them all in danger.

As Braird and Maya soberly regarded each other, she knew he wanted to kiss her. And despite feeling guilty because of Will, Maya wanted to kiss Braird, who smelled like clean feathers and the sea. Even though they fought about many things, Maya found Braird's intense nature exciting. But on Maya's shoulders sat the relics, and she could tell they didn't think she should kiss Braird. The relics were like three Jiminy Crickets from the old Disney movie *Pinocchio*, which Maya had watched with her father when she was young. Even now, Maya remembered Jiminy Cricket's refrain: "Always let your conscience be your guide."

Looking from the relics to Braird, Maya shrugged, and Braird glanced upward at the night sky. Then he shrugged, too. Taking her hand, Braird said, "We need to find out who the traitor on this ship is. Otherwise, the captain will never be able to rescue his daughter. When Clarin is back, I can go after those elves who killed my father, and you can go back to your own universe and help trap Cinnial."

"Yes," Maya replied. Despite the relics' disapproval, she leaned against Braird, feeling his warmth. Squeezing her hand, he leaned against her, and together they watched the night sky get lighter and lighter until dawn came and the stars went away and the sun rose over the shimmering sea.

15: IN THE DOLDRUMS

For three days, *The Resolute* stayed in one place, not even moving with the waves. Captain Blythewood didn't leave his quarters in the deckhouse, and First Mate Hawthorn ran the ship. Occasionally, Hawthorn would confer with the captain in his quarters, but whenever she came out, her mouth was set in a straight line of disapproval, and she was even more curt than usual.

Braird said, "My mother thinks we should bring Maya to Port Isleros so that she can return to her own dimension, and then after that we should head toward our job. We are weeks late as it is. Mother thinks Clarin can take care of herself, that the captain doesn't give her enough credit. But the captain won't budge. He wants to find his daughter."

It was late at night on the first becalmed day. Braird, Maya, Larz, Alie, Takis, and Proko were on the deck in a protective bubble, where they could speak freely without being heard. Braird and Maya sat side by side, their arms touching. The relics—Aiken, Orlaith, and Eloise—perched in vigilance on Maya's shoulders.

"The captain is devoted to his daughter," Maya murmured, and Braird squeezed her hand.

Taking a drink, Larz peered at Maya and Braird. "You two know something you're not sharing. I can feel it."

"So can I," Alie said, running her hand over her skirt.

Nodding their furry heads, Proko and Takis chittered together in agreement.

Maya and Braird looked at each other. Maya shook her head, and Braird shrugged. "Sorry. We can't tell you. Not yet."

Larz stared out into the dark night where under the still ship, the waves moved restlessly back and forth, back and forth. All around *The Resolute* there were various splashes, some large, some small, as creatures came to the surface and then dived back under water.

Maya listened for Cali, hoping to hear the sea beast's booming voice bring news of Clarin and her captor Rhye Ashglade. Although there were some big swooshes of water near *The Resolute*, none were big enough to be made by Cali's enormous bulk, and there was no great voice calling out to them.

In response to Maya's anxious thoughts, Chantay responded with her own chiming thoughts: *I am watching for him. I will let everyone know as soon as Cali arrives. Be patient.*

Sighing, Maya reflected on how patience wasn't one of her qualities. Always, her preference was to be moving rather than to be waiting, but with the captain and the ship in the doldrums, she didn't have much of a choice.

Proko's whiskers twitched, and the castor ran a hand over her sleek furry head. "You think we didn't know that something was wrong when the two of you went out to sea, looking for Clarin, and then nearly didn't come back?"

Takis leaned forward. "We're not stupid. And what a bloody state you two were in when you literally dropped on the deck."

Maya and Braird glanced at each other but didn't say anything.

Turning his attention away from the sea, Larz considered Maya and Braird. "You don't trust us."

Braird shook his head. "Sorry. Captain's orders."

Looking up from her skirt, Alie said in a soft but firm voice, "I'm going to say what nobody else wants to say. There's a traitor on board *The Resolute*. Maya's harness didn't break by itself. And that storm was called by somebody on this ship. Somebody who doesn't want the captain to find his daughter. And that somebody was willing to put Maya in danger to prevent her from locating Rhye Ashglade's submarine. That's why *The Resolute* isn't going anywhere. The captain doesn't know what to do."

There was a collective sigh of relief after Alie expressed what they had all been thinking but didn't dare talk about.

149

You might as well go ahead and discuss it now, Chantay's thoughts told Maya and Braird. *However, leave Cali's part out of it. Just in case.*

"But who could the traitor be?" Maya asked, relieved to be able to discuss this with the others. "Who wouldn't want the captain to be reunited with his daughter?"

Larz stared at Braird. "Your mother doesn't. Time and time again, she's made it clear that she thinks we shouldn't go after Clarin. Instead, she wants us to do what we were hired to do."

Blue feathers rose on Braird's arms and back. "My mother might not approve of the captain's decision to go after Clarin, but she's no traitor. You know that."

"Do I?" Larz asked coolly. "Your mother's in love with the captain. Any fool can see that. Maybe she doesn't want Clarin around, taking up all the captain's attention."

As Braird began to scramble angrily to his feet, blue feathers spilling across his chest, a bright light shined forth, sweeping over him. The beam came from Eloise, and the small wooden lioness radiated a steady, soothing glow. Gradually, Braird's feathers disappeared, and he reluctantly settled back down beside Maya, who took his hand and held it.

As her light dimmed, Eloise said, "Larz, do not let your hurt feelings make you lash out at your friend. You have no proof that First Mate Hawthorn is a traitor."

Larz flushed. "Sorry. I really am. Eloise is right. Braird, I lashed out at you because I was mad that you didn't trust me. There's no proof at all that your mother's a traitor."

Swallowing, Braird nodded but didn't say anything.

Alie's dark eyes were luminous. "Finneas has always said that First Mate Hawthorn is loyal to a fault."

Takis absently pulled at one of the straps of her overalls. "Still, somebody on board is doing this. The magic is not coming from afar. Don't you think?"

"Absolutely," Alie replied, and everyone else agreed.

"Well," Proko said practically, "we can strike Maya and Braird off the list of traitors. It's unlikely they would try to sabotage themselves in such a dangerous way."

Trembling as she remembered the snapping jaws of the sea serpent, Maya gazed at Braird. "If it wasn't for you, I would have been eaten."

Braird stared tenderly at Maya, and she knew that if the relics hadn't been perched on her shoulders, then Braird would have kissed her. Aiken's tiny nails dug into her, Orlaith tapped Maya with her slender legs, and Eloise's warm paws steadied Maya.

Larz grinned. "Maya, that's quite the little crew you have on your shoulders."

Maya sighed. "Yeah."

Larz said, "If we can discover who's skunking the captain, and we can find his daughter, then maybe we can all have a night on the town when we take you to Port Isleros." He winked at Maya. "With no little guardians to interfere."

"That would be great," Maya said as Aiken blew a puff of smoke at Larz, Eloise glowered, and Orlaith rapped her eight legs in disapproval, making Maya wince.

Braird looked upward and then back at the others seated around him. "Let's get back to the subject at hand."

As Maya considered the button-cute faces of Proko and Takis; blond Larz's rugged good looks; Alie's sweet froggy aspect; and dark brooding Braird, she knew with a deep certainty that nobody seated on the deck under the bubble was the traitor. Instead, it was one of the adults, and Maya made a mental note of each one: Zeynip, the bosun; Hannie, the chief magic engineer; Symi, the cook; or even Finneas, the captain's personal assistant. Also, even though it was unlikely, Braird's mother, First Mate Hawthorn, couldn't be ruled out.

Alie's face was scrunched into wrinkles. "It's one of the adults."

"I'm afraid you're right," Proko replied.

Takis said, "I hope it's not our Zeynip."

"Or Hannie," Larz added, subdued for once.

Alie picked at her skirt. "Or Symi."

Maya felt a pang as she thought about the cook, the elf who reminded her of Mémère. As Maya's intuition remained stubbornly silent, she thought, *Please don't let it be Symi.*

Braird looked away from everyone. "Or my mother. Much as I hate the idea, we have to include her, too."

Glancing up, Alie said, "And we can't forget Finneas."

Larz shook his head. "I think there's only one way forward."

"And what's that?" Braird asked.

"We each have to watch the adults we work with to see if we get any clues about who the traitor is."

151

"Yes," Maya said, "that's exactly what we should do." And everyone nodded in agreement.

"Even so," Proko said, "it might not be easy. Somehow, the traitor has something that hides him or her from the rest of us."

Maya stood. "Still, we have to try."

Alie jumped up gracefully. "And be on the lookout for anything that might be a relic but just looks like something normal. Like Finneas's waterlily tie tack."

As everyone else stood, Maya asked, "He always wears it, doesn't he?"

Alie nodded. "I've never seen him without it."

Takis said, "Zeynip has a bracelet made from varnished reeds. I thought her sweetheart gave it to her, but now I wonder."

"My mother has a leaf brooch," Braird added with reluctance.

Larz rubbed his face. "Hannie wears a silver ring with a leupart's head."

Maya said, "And then there's Symi's moon necklace." She thought of how the moon changed color, going from white to silver to blue. It was the most beautiful necklace Maya had ever seen.

Everybody had something, and as Maya headed to the deckhouse, she went over each of the adults and their potential relics, but nothing came to her. *Come on, come on*, Maya thought impatiently. Still, nothing came to her.

When Maya went into the deckhouse, she found the captain sitting in the living room. In his hand, he held a glass with a clear liquid, and Maya had a strong hunch it wasn't water. There was a fire in the fireplace, and he stared moodily into it. Maya hesitated. It was clear the captain wasn't waiting for her, and she wasn't sure if she should speak to him or not.

But the captain looked her way and even smiled a little. "Come sit down with me for a moment."

"All right." Walking over, Maya sat down in a chair next to the captain.

He swirled his drink. "I'm not going to offer you a drink. Officially, you're too young for anything this strong." His smile became broader. "Officially."

Maya blushed, remembering the night she had drunk too much. "I'm not thirsty," came her quick reply. "I'm fine."

"When I stepped out for a bit of air, I saw you talking with the younger crew. I was wondering if you had any..." The captain paused. "Insights?"

"We do," Maya answered but then added quickly when she saw the hopeful look on his face. "But we don't know who the traitor is. Yet."

"Ah," the captain said, clearly disappointed.

"We're working on it."

The captain regarded Maya affectionately. "You're a force of nature, just like my Clarin. Well, what conclusions have you come to?"

"We all have a feeling that the traitor is one of the adults who has a relic that's hiding everything from the rest of us," Maya said. Then she added, "We could be wrong, of course. It could be one of the younger crew."

"No, I don't think you're wrong. I, too, think the traitor is an adult with a relic. A younger person wouldn't be able to control such strong magic." The captain looked at the three relics still perched on Maya's shoulders. "As I'm sure you've figured out, relics have a will of their own, and the more powerful they are, the more they exert that will."

Maya muttered, "Don't I know it."

"Maya," Eloise said reprovingly.

"Ungrateful," Aiken added.

Orlaith merely sighed.

The captain laughed. "I guess you do know. Anyway, unless I'm very much mistaken, none of the younger crew has matured enough to handle a relic strong enough to trick my Chantay, whose powers of protection are very great indeed." The captain paused. "And the relic is far stronger than any magic I have."

Maya thought of the lovely figurehead that guarded *The Resolute*. "Captain, here's what we're going to do. Over the next couple of days, we're going to keep an eye on all the adults, even the ones who are at the bottom of our suspect list."

"And who might be at the bottom of your list?"

"First Mate Hawthorn and Finneas."

"I agree. However, we mustn't rule them out." The captain took a sip of his drink. "But how it would pain me to discover that either First Mate Hawthorn or Finneas are behind all this. In fact, the same is true no matter who it is. On this ship, we've become something like a family. Oh, I know. I'm in charge. I have the final word. But everyone on *The Resolute* has a job that's essential, even little Alie, who works hard to help feed us. Peeling and chopping all those vegetables is a daunting task, one that she does every single day. And she never, ever complains."

"She's so sweet," Maya said. "And even though Alie's shy, she always speaks up when she should."

"Despite their humble ways, grenogs are remarkable creatures." Nodding, Maya rubbed her eyes, weary with fatigue.

"You look tired."

"I am tired," Maya admitted.

"Go to bed. Tomorrow, you and the younger crew can keep an eye on the adults, and then you can report back to me." The captain shrugged. "And maybe, just maybe, Cali will bring us word about Clarin."

Maya stood. "I hope so. Goodnight, captain."

"Goodnight. And Maya? Thank you for all that you've done. I really appreciate it."

Maya smiled shyly. "You're welcome."

The next night, on the deck under the castors' bubble, there wasn't much to report. All of the adults, even the unflappable Finneas, were unnerved by the captain's withdrawal to his quarters and the becalming of *The Resolute*. When Symi dropped a whole bowl of cookie dough, smashing the crockery to bits, she sat down at the red enamel table and cried.

"And I've never seen Symi cry over anything," Alie said in a hushed voice. "Certainly not ruined cookie batter. Her moon pendant turned deep blue."

Larz made a face. "Hannie's no better. She can't stand keeping *The Resolute* still for so many days. She said it's not natural for any ship on the open sea to be stopped like this. In a harbor at port, yes. But not way out here. All day, Hannie paced the deck, and she snapped at me when I asked her even the smallest question. Finally, I stopped asking."

Proko and Takis chittered sympathetically, and Takis put a furry hand to her cheek. "Zeynip actually made a bubble that popped on deck. We were getting ready for an underwater ship inspection, and we hadn't even called the dinghy. Zeynip was so flustered that she postponed the inspection until next week. She said everything was fine last week, and it was probably all right this week, too."

None of the others said anything. They had all heard of the bubble's popping and how upset Zeynip had been.

"What about Finneas?" Alie asked after a while.

"Well," Maya answered, "I wouldn't say he's flustered like Symi and Hannie. And certainly not like Zeynip. But he's been very, very quiet. He hasn't been telling any of his little stories to cheer me up because things aren't going the way they should." Maya was silent as she realized how much she had come to depend on Finneas's gentle guidance. *Please don't let it be him*, she thought.

Larz glanced at Braird. "And First Mate Hawthorn?"

"If I didn't know my mother so well, I'd say it was business as usual running the ship. But even though my mother doesn't show it, she's tense underneath. Just like the rest of us."

Sheepishly, Larz shook his head. "But you know one of the things that bothers me the most? No board games after dinner." Larz's voice was wistful. "Every night when we're out at sea, we play them. It's a great way for everyone to come together and relax at the end of a long day. Now, nobody's in the mood."

"Board games?" Maya asked.

"Yes," Alie answered. "When you came, we took a little break, and now nobody wants to play anymore. Everyone is too tense."

Maya looked around the circle. "Sorry."

Alie said, "It's not your fault there's a traitor on board. And your coming here let us know there is one in our midst. In the end, this is a good thing. Otherwise, we would still be searching the sea for Clarin and going in the wrong direction." She glanced sideways at Larz. "But I miss playing board games, too."

"Same," Takis said, and Proko nodded in agreement.

Braird looked at Larz. "It was always fun to kick your butt."

Larz protested, "I kicked your butt plenty of times."

"Not as often as I kicked yours."

Alie whispered to Maya, "That's why we had to start playing cooperative games. Too much squabbling." Then she smiled. "And you know who was the best? Mild mannered Finneas." Her smile became broader until it seemed to cover most of her face.

"Alie, you're pretty good, too," Braird said in an offhanded voice.

Alie nodded humbly. "Why thank you, Braird. We grenogs have always had to be watchful and observant."

"Why?" Maya asked.

As Alie shivered, Proko explained, "A lot of creatures like to eat grenogs. Imps, especially. I've heard they think grenogs taste like chicken."

Maya stared in astonishment at Proko. "Really? That's just terrible."

Alie replied, "We always have to be on the jump. And on the lookout for danger."

Larz said, "That's why we elves are vegetarians. To eat another creature seems wrong."

"We castors have never even dreamed of eating meat," Proko said, her voice proud.

Maya looked around the circle. "Before I came here, I ate meat. But no more."

With nothing much else to report, the conference in the bubble broke up, and Maya returned to the deckhouse, where the captain was waiting for her. As with the previous night, the captain was alone.

"Finneas is in his quarters," the captain said as Maya looked around. "He went to bed early. He's exhausted." The captain sighed. "We all are. We have to find that traitor. Any luck?"

Maya grimaced. "No. All the adults are acting weird. We can't tell who might be guilty."

"Right," the captain said. "No surprise that everyone's upset."

"Yeah, I just hope we find out soon."

The next night, under the bubble, Alie said with dismay, "I think I know who it is."

Everyone leaned forward in expectation.

"Who?" Maya asked.

Alie shook her head. "I don't want to say just yet. I don't want to falsely accuse anyone. But, Maya, tomorrow at breakfast, make sure the captain comes down to join us. If I'm right, then we'll all know."

To Maya's surprise, Braird replied, "Alie, you don't have to carry this all by yourself. We're here."

Touched, Maya put her hand on Braird's arm, and Larz clapped him on the shoulder. "Couldn't have said it better myself."

Flushing, Braird looked down at his hands.

Alie's huge eyes were wet with tears. "Thank you so much, Braird. But it really is better this way. You can all carry on even if I'm in disgrace."

Then to everyone's surprise, Eloise said, "Let me come with you. I can help. And if you're wrong, there will be no repercussions for me, a relic who's not part of the crew."

Eloise, perched on Maya's shoulder, calmly stared down at the grenog.

"Maya?" Alie asked. "What do you think?"

Maya twisted around to look at Eloise, who nodded. "I think Eloise is right." She put her cupped hand beside Eloise, who slid into it, and then deposited the lioness on Alie's shoulder.

In awe, Alie stared at Eloise. "Thank you so much."

Eloise inclined her head. "My great pleasure. But don't thank me just yet. Wait until we've nabbed the traitor."

The next morning, the captain, breaking his solitude, was at the head table with First Mate Hawthorn, Zeynip, Hannie, and Finneas. The captain had told everyone he had an announcement to make after breakfast, and although the adults were able to maintain polite conversation, it was definitely subdued.

At the table nearby sat Maya, Braird, Larz, Proko, and Takis. They all picked at their food—even Larz who usually ate with gusto, tucking away twice as much food as everyone else did. Feeling Aiken and Orlaith on her shoulders, Maya pushed around the food in her bowl. She couldn't bring herself to take even one bite of the sweet and spicy grains that were sprinkled with roasted nuts and topped with some kind of cream. With a sigh, Maya set her spoon in her bowl.

Alie and Symi were still in the kitchen. Usually they ate first thing in the morning, before anyone came to the dining room. "We get up so early," Alie had told Maya, "that if we don't eat first, we feel kind of funny." Then, when everyone was done, Alie and Symi would bring out steaming mugs of tea and join the rest of the crew.

Maya thought, *Come out, Alie. Come out, Symi. Let's get this over with.*

Maya had no sooner thought this when she heard the clear ring of a chiming bell, and a bright light filled the kitchen. Then Symi cried, "Stay away!" And this was followed by a shriek of rage.

157

Maya took a deep breath. *Oh, no. It's her.*

The captain leaped to his feet, as did Hawthorn, Hannie, Larz, and Braird. But before any of them could head toward the kitchen, Symi marched stiffly into the dining room, and around the elf's neck was a garland made of dried blue flowers. Symi was surrounded by Eloise's light, so bright that Maya could barely stand looking at it. The light pushed Symi forward, and although the elf struggled, her magic was no match for Eloise's heartwood power. Right behind Symi came Alie, and in her hand dangled the moon pendant, almost black. Perched on Alie's shoulder, Eloise focused intently on Symi, and the light never wavered.

Maya thought, *There's the relic that gave Symi so much power.* Then, *Oh, Symi. Why did it have to be you?*

On alert, Aiken and Orlaith were ready should Eloise need help. But Eloise didn't need any help. The light forced Symi onto a chair and firmly held her in place.

Scowling, the captain moved toward Symi. "All this time, it was you."

Symi twisted and turned, trying not to say anything, but she couldn't stop the words. "Yes, it was me. All this time. I stopped you from finding Clarin. I let Rhye know where you were so he could evade you. I even fooled with the maps so you wouldn't see his true location."

Standing, Maya faced Symi. "You nearly killed me."

"You stupid little human," Symi said in a bitter voice as though she were the one who had been wronged. "I never wanted you to die. I just wanted to scare you. But you have too much persistence for your own good. And far more power than you deserve."

In astonishment, the captain stared from Symi to Alie. "What did you do to get her to talk like this?"

Finneas spoke, "It's the clochette garland around Symi's neck. Anyone who wears one must tell the truth." He turned to Alie. "Where did you get this? Clochettes are not easy to find."

"My granni," Alie answered. "She knows where a patch grows, and she made this for me before I left. Granni has a feeling about things and thought I might need it. Eloise's light held Symi in place while I took off the necklace and then put the garland around her neck. But the garland can only be used once, so I had to be really sure who the traitor was."

"How did you know it was Symi?" the captain asked Alie.

"Captain, you know that like my granni I can see things."

"I do," the captain said.

Alie stared at the glowing moon on the chain swinging from her hand. "There was something about that necklace. It seemed to change color depending on Symi's mood." Alie hesitated. "And from time to time a sort of hum came from it, one that I could barely hear. It tried to hide itself from me, but grenogs have sharp ears. For the past two days I have been listening especially hard." She shook her head. "And at last I knew it was the sound of a power that was shielding Symi, tricking everyone into believing she was just an innocent cook."

In a rage, Symi turned toward Alie. "And if you had been wrong, then that would have been it for you. No more working in the kitchen with me. You would have been dropped off at the next port. You're just a little grenog. Going up against an elf and wrongly accusing her, you would have been in complete disgrace. That would have been the end of your life at sea."

"I know," Alie whispered. "It was a risk. A big risk." Her eyes filled with tears. "I love working on *The Resolute*. And I loved working with you, Symi. You've taught me so much." Alie sniffed sadly. "Why did you do it?"

Symi's words rushed out in a rat-a-tat. "Because I'm Tamick Ashglade's cousin, and I was sent to protect Rhye, to stop the captain from finding him. We knew that if the captain managed to capture Rhye, it wouldn't be good for him." She turned her snarling face toward Hannie. "With your help, the captain would have placed some ugly spell on Rhye that would have affected him for years, even with the help of our best physicians."

Hannie shrugged. "I might have had a spell or two at the ready for when we found that little rat."

Symi struggled against Eloise's light but could not break free. "Rhye is not a rat," she said through gritted teeth. "He's a gifted scientist who will do much to further our knowledge of Elferterre's oceans."

The captain's voice was cold. "Gifted scientist or not, Rhye had no business kidnapping my daughter."

But before Symi could respond, there was a huge boom of a splash, and Chantay chimed in triumph, "Cali is back, and he has *The Cuttlefish* with Clarin and Rhye."

16: A BETTER STORY

For a moment, there was complete silence. With a cry, the captain raced from the dining room, taking the stairs two at a time as he bolted to the top deck, and almost everyone followed him.

But Maya and Alie stayed behind. Plucking Eloise from Alie's shoulder, Maya asked, "Can you hold Symi until we get back?"

"Yes," Eloise replied as Maya set her on a nearby table. "As long as you are back down here before noon. I don't think I can hold her any longer than that."

"I hope it doesn't take us that long to rescue Clarin," Maya said. "I hope Rhye isn't that powerful."

Alie's big eyes were wide. "I don't think Rhye can overcome both the captain and Hannie. He's just a young elf."

"Unlikely," Eloise agreed. "Now go."

Maya and Alie ran up the stairs. Everyone was on the starboard side of the ship. They watched as Cali's great bulk rose up, up, up from the ocean. His mouth was clamped firmly on the tail of a small submarine, which pulled urgently, trying to escape. But it was no use. Cali's strength was far greater than that of *The Cuttlefish*. Cali stopped when *The Cuttlefish* was mostly above the surface, but he didn't let go of the tail. The sea beast's thoughts roared, *Come out, Rhye Ashglade. There's no escaping now. I can hold you until the captain and Hannie neutralize your magic.*

For a while, there was no sound except for the slapping of the waves against *The Resolute* and *The Cuttlefish*. Not wanting to be caught in the battle between the ship and the submarine, every sea creature, large or small, had disappeared into the depths.

Finally, the hatch of *The Cuttlefish* opened, and out stepped a tall, trim elf with curly dark hair. Chin up, he stood straight. Behind came another elf, also tall. Her hair was the color of honey, and she seemed to glow, but underneath Maya caught a glimpse of a will that was even stronger than her own.

"Clarin!" the captain cried. "Oh, Clarin."

"Father," Clarin responded in a cool voice, folding her arms across her chest.

"Why couldn't you just leave us alone?" Rhye asked, putting his arm around Clarin's shoulders.

As Alie stirred uneasily beside her, Maya realized with a sickening feeling that all this time the captain and Finneas had been wrong: Rhye had not kidnapped Clarin. Instead, she had gone willingly with him. Even from the deck of *The Resolute*, Maya could tell how much they loved each other. There had been no spell involved. None at all. Because of their prejudice against the Ashglades, the captain and Finneas and everyone else, with the possible exception of Hawthorn, had come to the wrong conclusion. And Maya, hurt by the neglect of her own father, had been all too willing to side with the captain.

Slowly, the others on the deck of *The Resolute* came to the same realization.

Finneas clutched the rail of the ship. "Oh, my!"

Hannie turned uncertainly toward the captain. "Shall I bind them?"

"No," Chantay's clear voice rang out.

The captain stood very still. He took a ragged breath. "No."

"Father," Clarin called, "may we come aboard? We need to talk right now and end this foolishness."

Unable to speak any further, the captain swallowed, and Hawthorn said, "Let them come aboard, captain. Let them have their say."

Hannie looked at the captain. "Sir?"

"Yes," the captain whispered.

Hawthorn said to Cali, "Release *The Cuttlefish*."

As gently as a mother cat setting down her kitten, Cali released the submarine.

Hawthorn called, "Clarin and Rhye, prepare to come on board."

As Clarin and Rhye nodded in assent, Hannie turned to Larz. "Go ahead. Get the dinghy."

"Aye, Aye," came Larz's crisp response. Then he gave a piercing whistle. In the stern, a door popped open, and out flew the dinghy that Maya had never seen. With astonishment, she noted there was a small head on the bow. With its alert ears, folded down at the tips, and long nose, the small figurehead reminded Maya of a dog.

Larz said, "Passengers from the submarine coming aboard *The Resolute*."

With a responding yip, the dinghy raced to *The Cuttlefish* and hovered at just the right height to allow Clarin and Rhye to climb into the little boat with ease. After they were in and seated, up, up the dinghy floated, setting down gently on the deck not far from the captain.

Clarin and Rhye disembarked from the dinghy. With a slight inclination of her head, Clarin surveyed the crew. She frowned questioningly at Maya but didn't speak to her.

Instead, Clarin turned to the captain. "Father?"

The captain sighed, but his voice was gentle. "Let's go to my quarters."

Everyone watched as the captain, Clarin, and Rhye entered the deckhouse, and the door shut behind them with a firm snap.

Larz absently patted the dinghy, which chirped a little. "Well, that was a surprise."

Finneas shook his head. "How could we have been so wrong?"

Hawthorn replied, "Because Rhye is an Ashglade, you thought that he must be as rotten as his uncle."

"I did," Finneas answered, his voice sheepish.

"Same," Hannie admitted.

"Me, too," Zeynip added, and everyone else nodded.

Hawthorn said, "I have to admit that at first I did, too. However, none of us really considered Clarin, a spoiled pain-in-the butt who won't take no for an answer." She stared at Maya. "A lot like you."

Flushing, Maya looked away.

"Really," Finneas said in a gentle huff. "Hawthorn, you're not being fair to dear Clarin."

"Yes, I am. And you know it. The captain dotes on Clarin. She is the light of his life." Hawthorn's expression softened. "Understandable. The captain's wife died when she was so young.

Clarin is all the captain has left." Hawthorn glanced at Braird, who ducked his head in embarrassment.

Then Hawthorn surprised everyone by smiling, and Maya was amazed by how it transformed the first mate's stern face. "But did any of you ever stop and consider how unlikely it was that such a willful elf would ever let herself be enchanted by another elf?"

"If that elf was powerful enough, Clarin would have no choice," Finneas protested.

"True," Hawthorn replied. "But did you really think Rhye was powerful enough to enchant Clarin? I've met him a few times at various functions in Port Isleros. Rhye might be handsome, but that doesn't change the fact that he's a nerd at heart. All he wants to do is travel the seas and discover what's there."

Larz said, "First Mate Hawthorn has a point. Rhye is obsessed with his submarine and the sea. Those are the only things he really liked talking about when we all went out together. He doesn't care a fig about casting spells on anyone, elf or otherwise."

Hawthorn's eyes gleamed. "And what does Clarin like to do?"

"Draw and paint pictures of sea creatures," Maya answered, remembering the vibrant yet delicate pictures on the walls in her sleeping quarters that had once belonged to Clarin.

"Right," Hawthorn agreed. "And what does that make Clarin and Rhye?"

Finneas gulped. "A perfect pair."

"A perfect pair," Hawthorn repeated.

Maya sat down heavily by the dinghy and absently patted its head. "This is all my fault."

Here Hawthorn actually laughed. "Maya, you are one pain in the butt, just like Clarin. However, none of this is your fault. All this was set in motion long before you came on board *The Resolute*."

"But I was so wrong," Maya muttered.

"Imagine that," Hawthorn said in a gently mocking voice. "The little human was wrong. A new experience for you?"

Maya bit her lip. "I'm not wrong very often."

"Well, join the club," Hawthorn replied, looking out to sea at Cali, who was floating patiently by the submarine. "Even those of us who can see are sometimes wrong."

Zeynip tipped her furry head to one side. "Maya, you might have been wrong, but you helped bring things to a head."

"And that was a good thing," Hannie added. The large blonde elf leaned against the side of the ship. "Who knows how long we would have been going in the wrong direction, looking in vain for that dratted submarine? In the meantime, we would have been neglecting our jobs." She shook her head. "It might have even ruined our reputation, which until now has been impeccable."

Finneas said, "And Alie was a big help, too. Without her, it would have been much more difficult to discover who was sabotaging the captain's efforts."

Alie flushed as everyone stared in admiration at her. "I just did what needed to be done."

Hawthorn shook her head. "Still, it was a brave thing to do." She looked down the stairs. "Now we have to take care of Symi."

"The Elven Authority in Port Isleros must be called," Hannie said. "Symi will have to face charges for sabotaging the captain and for her assault on Braird and Maya."

Hawthorn looked at the stairway, and there was a grim expression on her face. Hannie put her hand on Hawthorn's arm. "No, Azal. Don't take matters into your own hands. Let the Elven Authority handle it."

Hawthorn's fists were clenched. "She went after my son."

Zeynip put her hand on Hawthorn's other arm. "Nevertheless..."

There was a long tense silence as everyone watched Hawthorn and wondered what she was going to do. She glanced back once at Braird, who nodded, and then turned back to Zeynip and Hannie.

"All right," Hawthorn said at last. "I'll call the authorities. Zeynip and Hannie, you'll go down and guard Symi?"

"That we will do," Hannie replied, and Zeynip chittered in agreement.

The three adults left the deck—Hawthorn went to the wheel house over the captain's quarters, and Hannie and Zeynip went to the dining room where Eloise was holding Symi.

Nobody said anything for a long time. Finneas, Maya, Braird, Larz, Alie, Proko, and Takis sat around the dinghy, and from time to time, Larz would pat its head.

Finally Maya asked, "Does the dinghy have a name?"

Larz laughed. "Of course."

Maya said, "Of course. This is Elferterre. Most everything has a name here."

"You got it," Larz replied.

"Well?" Maya asked.

"Well, what?"

Braird shook his head. "The dinghy's name is Ninon."

The little head swiveled to regard Braird, and Ninon actually barked.

Everyone laughed, and some of the tension went away, allowing them to talk more casually about all that had happened.

Finneas began the conversation. "What a morning."

Braird ran a hand through his hair, making it stand up in a crest. "What a week."

From there, in bits and pieces, with everyone adding something, they rehashed the events from the start, when Cali had first brought Maya to *The Resolute*. From time to time, Cali boomed a response, and Chantay chimed in.

When they were done, the door to the captain's deckhouse opened, and out walked the captain, Clarin, and Rhye. While the mood was subdued, the three looked to be at ease with each other, and Clarin held both her father's hand and Rhye's hand.

"Thank goodness," Finneas whispered in relief.

As the three walked to the dinghy, the group sitting by the small boat scrambled to their feet.

"At ease, at ease," the captain said gently. But nobody sat down.

Rhye gazed affectionately at his submarine. "Well, time to go back under and see what might be out there."

Clarin squeezed Rhye's hand. "We never know what we'll find." Then she said to her father, "Now that everything is sorted out, we'll be in touch. We'll let you know when we're near a port. If you're not too far, then we can meet up there."

"I would like that very much." The captain kissed the top of his daughter's head. "Go off and explore." Then he regarded Rhye sternly. "But take care."

"Oh, I will," Rhye said with a smile.

Looking from her father to Rhye, Clarin added in a firm voice, "We'll both take care."

Maya tried not to grin as she remembered Hawthorn's not exactly flattering description of Clarin.

With narrow eyes, Clarin regarded Maya. "For a little human, you certainly caused a big stir."

Maya did not look away. "Yeah, that seems to be how it goes with me."

Clarin stared at her for a few moments, but Maya didn't squirm. Clarin's lips quirked into a grin. "Keep on causing big stirs when you have to. Otherwise, nothing will change."

"I don't seem to have much choice in the matter."

"There is always a choice." Clarin's voice was soft as she looked at Rhye, who gazed lovingly back at her.

With a pang, Maya thought of Will, who seemed so far away. Would she see him again? And if she did, how old would he be? Would he be married, and would he have children? Maya's intuition was silent, and in confusion she glanced sideways at Braird, who stared steadily back at her.

Clarin's thoughts said gently, *Maya, you're even younger than I am. Whatever happens, you don't have to decide now.*

Nodding gratefully, Maya watched as Clarin and Rhye climbed into Ninon, and the little dinghy took them back to *The Cuttlefish*, which floated serenely next to Cali. With a wave, the two disappeared into the submarine, and Ninon returned to the upper deck. With his hands behind his back, the captain watched as *The Cuttlefish* submerged, leaving a slight shimmer of magic in its wake.

Hawthorn had returned from the wheelhouse and stood next to the captain. "I called the Elven Authorities. They're sending a team to pick up Symi."

The captain sighed. "Very good, Hawthorn."

Hawthorn hesitated and then put her hand on the captain's shoulder. "It's not easy when a child leaves."

The captain continued to look out to sea and did not pull away. "It's very hard."

In surprise, Maya thought, *Huh, maybe there is a chance for the captain and Hawthorn after all.*

Hawthorn turned from the captain to give Maya a warning look.

Maya smiled innocently, and Hawthorn shook her head in exasperation.

While everyone was still on the top deck, the Elven Authority arrived in an airship that could land on water. A small dinghy with the head of a standard poodle zipped out from one end of the ship and hovered by the airship's door, which slid open. Two women in bright blue uniforms settled into the dinghy, and soon they landed on *The Resolute*'s upper deck. Ninon barked a greeting, and the poodle woofed in response.

After asking the captain a few questions, the officers from the Elven Authority went to the lower deck and returned with Symi, who was silent and stared straight ahead. The garland was no longer around her neck, but there were a few blue petals on her shoulders. Behind them came Hannie and Zeynip.

Maya wondered, *Where did the garland go?*

Alie's thoughts answered, *They fall apart after their job is done.*

Maya murmured, "Its job sure is done."

"Yes, it is," Alie replied as Symi and the officers settled in the dinghy and returned to the airship. "What will happen to Symi?"

The captain answered, "Because Symi's an elf, she'll be tried quickly and no doubt will be found guilty."

Although the captain didn't mention it, Maya sensed that as a commanding officer and an elf, his testimony might carry enough weight on its own to convict Symi.

The captain said, "First Mate Hawthorn, let our clients know we will be delayed but that we will be on the job as soon as possible. Then set our course to Port Isleros."

"Aye aye, captain." First Mate Hawthorn left the upper deck to return to the wheelhouse.

Hannie said, "Captain, I'm a pretty good cook. I can help in the kitchen."

"I'm not too bad either," Zeynip added. "I can help, too."

Maya raised her hand. "So can I."

"Very good," the captain said. "And Alie, I have no doubt you'll be able to run the kitchen until we get to port."

Alie smiled proudly. "I'll do my best, captain."

"I'm absolutely sure of that," the captain said. "And, Alie? What you did today was not only brave, but it also set a lot of things to rights, and I will always be grateful to you. I won't forget what you did."

Alie wiped her eyes. "Oh, thank you, captain." Then she looked at the stairs going to the lower deck. "But if you'll excuse me, sir, I'd best go down to the kitchen, get the breakfast things cleaned up, and start thinking about lunch."

The captain nodded. "Carry on."

As Alie left, Hannie said, "I'll go with her and help get things sorted." Reaching into her pocket, Hannie pulled out Eloise, and set her on Maya's shoulder. "That is some relic you have."

Eloise nodded graciously. "Nice of you to say."

With a wave of the hand, Hannie followed Alie to the lower deck.

Zeynip said, "I'll go, too." And she was not far behind Hannie.

Larz looked down at Ninon, who with pleading eyes, gazed at the elf. "Captain, permission to take Maya for a little spin in Ninon. That is, if Braird will fly with us, and Cali will come along to protect us."

"Maya?" the captain asked.

Maya stared out at the bright blue sea, which seemed to be calling to her. "I'd love to!"

"Braird?"

Braird grinned. "Sounds good to me."

"Cali?"

"I'd be delighted," the sea beast rumbled.

"May we go, too?" Proko and Takis asked.

"As you like it," the captain answered.

Finneas said, "I'd best get things settled in the deckhouse."

Maya handed the relics to the grenog.

"Maya!" they all protested, and Finneas hesitated.

But Maya remained firm. "Sometimes I need to be on my own and just have fun."

Finneas held out his hand. "Maya is right. Come with me, and you can join her afterward."

Only grumbling slightly, the spider, the dragon, and the lioness settled in Finneas's hand to return with him to the deckhouse.

Ten minutes later, with Larz at the bow of the dinghy, and Maya, Takis, and Proko clinging to their seats, Ninon skimmed joyfully over the waves that were small and friendly and seemed to move them along with just enough bounce to be fun but not so much to be stomach churning. Above them flew a large blue bird who swooped and occasionally dipped low, brushing Maya with the feathers on the tips of his wings. Scanning the sea for danger, Cali swam beside them, most of his vast bulk below the surface.

But that day there was no danger—only water, sky, and sun and the delighted shrieks of Larz, Maya, Proko, and Takis as the wind blew past their faces.

17: IN THE HOSPITAL

Viola stayed with her father all night in the hospital. It was very much like the ones she had seen on Earth. As far as Viola could tell, Camber was a modern city with all the same comforts and services that any small city in the United States would have. There was, however, a big difference. Camber seemed calmer, more relaxed, than any of the places Viola had lived or visited. In the hotel and the hospital, nobody hurried, but everything that needed to be done was done. Earlier that day, as Viola had walked to and from the city library, she had admired the cleanliness of the streets. Despite the laid-back atmosphere, Viola felt a cheerful vitality, even in the hospital, where sick people were being cared for.

Not long after Viola and her father had arrived at the hospital and were settled in a room, the doctor, a young woman darker than Ensante Madeleine, examined Drew, groggy with the medication he had been given. In a calm voice she said to Viola, "Like Diana, the other sick traveler, he'll recover, but he'll be here for a while and will need plenty of rest when he gets out."

"For how long?" Viola asked.

The doctor shook her head. "I don't know. A week in the hospital and then a few more weeks for recovery. Maybe longer. It all depends on how fast he heals."

"Okay, then," Viola said, thinking that perhaps her father wouldn't be coming with her to the Great Library after all.

Not long after the doctor left, Mémère joined Viola. She carried two small packs with a change of clothes and other things they might need. Like Viola, Mémère was no longer wearing the long dress she had worn in Caxton. Instead, Mémère wore pants and a tunic, much as she would have on Earth, but on her feet were the pink sandals that had come across the universe with her.

"Mémère!" Viola called in a soft voice, feeling better as soon as Mémère walked into the room.

Mémère winked at Viola. "You didn't think I was going to let you stay here all by yourself, did you? Technically, we're not family. But after all we've gone through together, it seems as though we are. Anyway, nobody gave me a hard time when I said I'd be spending the night with you and your father."

There were two chairs by the bed, and Mémère sat down next to Viola. Mémère glanced at Drew, who still flushed, was sleeping. She shook her head. "Even though your father tried to hide it, he's been fighting this for a couple of days. I did my best to help him and keep the wound clean, but my little first aid kit didn't have much. The wound was deep, and it wasn't exactly clean out there in the woods." Mémère looked around the bright room. "I'm glad we came here, where he can be treated."

Viola's lips trembled, but she didn't cry. "Me, too." She was silent for a moment. "Mémère, I don't think Dad's going to come with us to the Great Library."

"Doesn't look like it."

"He's not going to want me to go without him," Viola said in a low voice.

"I don't blame him," Mémère replied. "When my daughter Lily was twelve, I wouldn't have wanted her to go anywhere near Cinnial, much less try to trap him." Mémère sighed. "But here we are. Maya's gone over a cliff with an ogre. A boy named Will thinks she survived, and he's going to find her. In a place called Elferterre, that's ruled by Magic."

"Elferterre," Viola murmured. "Mémère, wouldn't you like to go there?"

"I don't know," Mémère answered. "At times, I think I've already seen enough. More than I ever thought I'd see. I'm not sure this old body would survive going to a place that's ruled by Magic." She grinned at Viola, who grinned back. Then Mémère's expression became serious.

"But going to Caxton and then coming here has really shown me what happens when the bad guys win, and Chaos takes over."

Viola shivered. "And with Chaos in charge at the Great Library, things are going to get worse and worse everywhere."

"Oui." Mémère's voice was sad. "Chaos won't leave Earth alone, will it?"

"No."

"And everything I love is there. Well, almost everything. Not Maya. But if Will is right, she'll be back."

"She'll be back," Viola echoed, hoping this was true. As much as she wanted to, Viola couldn't see ahead, and she realized that even though she'd had her eyes peeled, a flash couldn't be forced. She had to wait for it to come when she least expected it.

A nurse in bright red scrubs came into the room. He told Viola and Mémère, "I'm going to give Drew a little more medication to help him sleep through the night."

Mémère nodded. "Good idea. Sleep is what he needs right now."

The nurse gave Mémère an appraising look. "Are you a nurse?"

"I am," came the prompt reply.

"I thought so." The nurse smiled. "Doesn't matter where you're from, does it?"

In return, Mémère smiled proudly. "No, it doesn't."

"Are you two staying all night?" the nurse asked.

"We are," Mémère answered.

The nurse pointed to a small closet on the wall by the bathroom door. "There are blankets and pillows in there. And how about if I bring you a snack?"

"A snack would be nice," Mémère replied. "After all, we have to keep our strength up."

The chairs Viola and Mémère sat in were small but comfortable recliners, and soon the two were tucked in with blankets and pillows. There was a table between them that held the promised snack—two mugs of something steaming hot and a plate of golden brown cookies.

Mémère sighed happily. "It's nice to know that all across the universe there are cookies."

"Right?" Viola also sighed happily as she bit into the seeded cookie, crisp and buttery.

171

The hot drinks were another matter, neither tea nor coffee. Or chocolate, which was what Viola had been hoping for.

Mémère took a considering drink. "Well, I've tasted worse. Probably made from some kind of grain they grow here."

Viola sipped hers, frowned a little, and then took another sip. "It's not too bad."

Mémère smiled affectionately at Viola. "That's a girl. When we travel like this, we're bound to come across different things, and we just have to go with it."

"Yeah." Viola thought of all the different things she had come across. While the drinks tasted a little odd, they were the least of it.

Night settled over the hospital. The lights dimmed in the halls, and the staff lowered their voices, making the place as quiet as possible. In the room, the overhead lights had been turned off, and for the nurses who came in periodically, there was one side light left on by the bed. Drew slept soundly, hardly moving.

Viola drew the soft blanket up to her chin. "Tell me what it was like growing up in Waterville. Did you know my mémère?"

"No." Mémère settled into the chair. "Unfortunately not. I'm a few years older than she was, and we lived at opposite ends of the neighborhood. Somehow, our paths never crossed. By the time she was in high school, I was married and wasn't living in Waterville anymore."

"Oh," Viola said, a little disappointed that the two mémères from Waterville, Maine, didn't know each other.

"What was it like to grow up in Waterville? Well, it was good, and it was bad." Viola frowned, and Mémère patted her shoulder. "First, the good. Family lived all around us, and no one was ever alone." Mémère laughed. "Now the bad. Family lived all around us, and no one was ever alone. Everyone knew everyone's business. There wasn't much privacy."

Viola thought about her life in the White House. "I know just what you mean."

"I'm sure you do. It's hard when you're a teenager and you want to go your own way and do your own thing. But when you do, there's ma tante, seeing you go somewhere you're not supposed to go, like to your friend's house when you should be babysitting your younger sisters who are perfectly able to take care of themselves. And does ma tante tell Maman? Mais, oui, she certainly does." Mémère laughed. "Oh, I got scolded for that one."

"Did you do it again?"

Mémère shook her head. "I did not. When Maman said I would be in big trouble if I ever did anything like that again, I believed her. So instead one day, when Maman went to play cards with her friends on Saturday afternoon, and Papa was working, I somehow came up with the idea of taking my sisters to the library. It was a rainy day, and everyone was bored. Before she left, Maman said it was all right, and my friend, Agnes, did the same thing with her sisters. What a troop we were. Eight of us with four big umbrellas. And how we all came to love that old brick library with so many books, more than we had ever seen in our lives, with books that we could take home and read. Although we were a little silly, we weren't rough with the books, and our hands were always clean. The librarians never minded seeing us come even though they had to shush us now and then. After that first Saturday, it became a tradition, and we each got our very own library card. Maman made book bags for all of us—even Agnes and her sisters—with a small zippered pocket for our cards. A lot of the other kids in our neighborhood thought we were weird because we liked to go to the library on Saturday afternoons, but we didn't care what anyone said. All we cared about were the books."

"My mémère took my father to the library, too. Dad said that my mémère loved to read."

Mémère smiled. "Your father didn't spring out of nowhere, did he?"

"No, he didn't," Viola answered slowly.

"That library gave us the world of books. We were poor kids from the South End, and there weren't any books in our house. Same for Agnes. To this day, Agnes and I are readers. Maybe we would have come to love books anyway. Who knows? But the library sure encouraged us."

"Did you have a favorite book?"

"Not one book but a series of books. Nancy Drew. Agnes and I adored her. Nancy had her own car. A blue roadster, or was it a convertible?"

"A convertible in the books I read," Viola said.

Mémère nodded. "Along with her car, Nancy had good looks, beautiful clothes, money, and freedom. Everything we didn't have. Agnes and I dreamed about being like Nancy Drew instead of

173

being stuck in the South End where our families didn't even own a car. No matter the weather, our fathers walked to work."

Viola caught Mémère's longing and wistfulness. Reaching over, Viola placed her hand on Mémère's arm. "I'm sorry, Mémère."

Mémère patted Viola's hand. "No, no. Don't feel sorry for me. I've had a good life. I married a smart, decent man who is devoted to me and Lily and Maya. I have a big house in the country and my own little red car that I can zip around in. And voyons, I'm having adventures that go far beyond what Nancy and Bess and George had."

Viola smiled. "That's for sure. I know I never imagined any of this."

"How could you? It's too much. Even with your sixth sense."

Viola's smile went away. "I'm scared. We won't be traveling to Kip and Isik's home with the Books of Everything."

"Why not?"

"The Books are worried that Cinnial will know something is up if they take us anywhere near the Great Library. His Book will feel their presence when they travel and let him know. So instead golden acorns, like the one I traveled with here, are going to take us there. Cinnial's Book isn't tied into Magic the way it is with the Books of Everything. Ensante Madeleine thinks that with all that's going on, the acorns will zip us in, and Cinnial's Book won't notice. But it's not easy traveling with an acorn. I found that out when I came to Camber."

Mémère was silent for a moment. "Will Earth's Book of Everything and the Apprentice Books be coming with us to Kip's?"

"Yes, once we're there, the Books can shield us and themselves from Cinnial. But there's something else. The Books can't come with us to the Isle of Samaras, where the Great Library is. Magic on the island is strong, and everything is open. Nothing can hide."

"It will be hard not to have the Books with you when you're at the Great Library," Mémère said, and for a while neither of them spoke as they tried to imagine the path ahead. Finally, Mémère asked, "Where are the Books now?"

"With the Great Library's Book at Camber Public Library. They wanted to spend the night together, even though they're connected. In that way, they're a little like us, aren't they Mémère? They like to be together."

"That they are." Mémère hesitated, and Viola could tell she was trying to decide what to say next. Finally: "I'm not going to mince words with you, Viola. Even though you're only twelve, you've seen and done things that most adults haven't done. So here it is—you have every reason to be scared. I'm not ashamed to admit that I'm scared, too. After we travel with the acorns, we'll be going up against the big bad guy of the universe, méchant Cinnial. Even with the lock, it will be no picnic taking him down. But, Viola, look how far we've all come. Maya in Elferterre getting the lock to trap Cinnial. Jay and Lexie bringing it to us. You taking Rosalind and Sebastian to the Forest of Arden and then having your eyes peeled." Mémère could have gone on longer listing all the impossible things they had accomplished, but she stopped, and the determined expression on Mémère's face reminded Viola of Maya.

"Mémère, we can't stop now, can we?"

"Non. After all that Maya went through to get that lock, it would be letting her down if we didn't carry on with the mission. And there's something else to keep in mind."

"What?"

"Chaos might be on Cinnial's side, but Time and Magic are on our side. And that's not nothing."

"That's what Ensante Madeleine said," Viola replied. "She said Magic would help us get across the universe and be waiting for us at the Great Library. And Time would help, too."

The more Viola thought about this, the more hopeful she felt. Closing her eyes, Viola breathed deeply, listening, sensing, reaching out, and it seemed to her that she got two responses—one deep, steady, and rhythmic and the other lighter but filled with energy and power. Time and Magic. Viola understood that Chaos's destructive power would be matched by Time's and Magic's creative forces, just as formidable in their own way.

Comforted, Viola fell asleep. When she woke up, Mémère's chair was empty, but her bag was on the floor, and Viola knew she couldn't be far away. Her father was awake, and although he was still drowsy from the medication, there was a familiar sharpness to him as he looked at her.

"Dad!" Viola slid from the chair, went to the bed, and kissed his cheek. "Dad," she said again.

Drew tried to smile. "Viola, I'm so sorry."

"Come on, Dad. Chet shot you. You're not Superman."

Drew shook his head. "No, I'm not. And if it hadn't been for Mémère, Chet would have killed us all."

Viola hadn't heard this story. "Really?"

This time Drew did smile. "When Chet wasn't looking, she clunked him over the head with a small log. Chet had dismissed Mémère. Because of her age, he thought he didn't have to worry about her at all."

Viola smiled, too. "But Chet didn't know Mémère, did he?"

"He did not. If he had, he would have known she was a force to be reckoned with."

"Just like Maya."

"Yes, just like Maya." Drew took Viola's hand. "I'm not going to be able to go with you to the Great Library."

"I know, Dad."

"I suppose it wouldn't do any good to ask you not to go either."

"No," Viola replied. "Last night, Mémère said we had come too far to stop now, that Maya had sacrificed too much getting the lock. We have to carry on with the mission."

Drew sighed. "She's right, of course."

"Mémère said something else, too. She said that Chaos might be strong, but so is Time and Magic, and they're on our side. And you know what? I felt them last night. They'll help us, Dad, as much as they can. In their own way, they're gathering forces to go against Cinnial. We won't be alone."

"And here I am. Stuck in the hospital."

Viola said, "I thought for sure we'd both be at the Great Library."

Drew squeezed her hand. "Well, no one's right all the time. Not even me."

"But you're the president of the United States," Viola teased. "How could you be wrong?"

"Neither you nor your mother ever let my head get too swelled, do you?"

An image of Cinnial came to Viola, and she got a sense of his arrogance, which would never allow him to admit he was wrong. "It wouldn't be good, Dad, if no one could tell you when you were wrong."

"Right." With a grimace, Drew shifted in bed. "That would make me a tyrant. Not good at all."

A tyrant, Viola thought, as she went into the bathroom to take a shower and change into the clean clothes Mémère had brought.

When she came out, a nurse—this time an older woman—was standing by the bed. "You don't look too bad this morning," she said to Drew. "How do you feel?"

"Better but not great."

"No surprise." The nurse turned to Viola. "I need to get your father ready for the day. You have friends waiting for you in the lounge down the hall. Your grandmother is there, too. How about if you go meet them and maybe grab a bite to eat in the food court downstairs?" She handed some tickets to Viola. "There should be enough meal vouchers for all of you."

Viola took the vouchers. "Thanks. I'll be back later, Dad." She didn't add that it would be to say goodbye. Her father already knew this.

Robbie, Jay, Lexie, and Mémère were waiting for Viola in the lounge, and they all stood up when she came in.

"How is President Murphy?" Jay asked. "Mémère said he looked pretty good this morning."

"Better but still weak," Viola answered.

"That's great," Jay said as Lexie and Robbie smiled.

"Diana's doing all right, too," Mémère added. "She's in a room next to President Murphy, and I checked on her this morning."

Relieved, Viola sighed. "Oh, good." Then she said, "The nurse gave us all meal vouchers for breakfast and told us to go get something to eat while she got Dad ready for the day. There's a food court downstairs."

The nurse had counted correctly. There were just enough vouchers for everyone, and Viola passed them out.

Lexie took a ticket, but she said, "We've already had breakfast at the hotel."

Jay gave her a look. "I could eat a little something."

Lexie looked upward. "Right."

Robbie shook his head. "Sure is different here than it is in the Forest of Arden. Pieces of paper so you can eat at something called a food court." He frowned. "A court for food? And outside, carts zip around on their own. Inside, lights come on out of nowhere."

Jay clapped his arm. "Buddy, just you wait. You ain't seen nothing yet."

177

Robbie said, "Aye, and I'm looking forward to it. I'm actually having a real adventure, and I'll have plenty of stories to tell when I get back to the forest."

"Enough for a lifetime," Jay agreed. His expression was serious and so was Lexie's.

With her father being so sick, Viola hadn't had much time to think about Robbie and how weird it must have been for him to come from the forest of Arden to a city like Camber that had electricity and cars.

Viola said, "Sorry, Robbie, that I haven't been able to explain things to you."

"Nay, don't apologize. Your place was with your father."

Lexie grinned. "Besides, Jay, Robbie, and I explored the city last night. Helgin, Isold, Wren and some other kids took us around. We filled Robbie in about technology. We also went dancing." Lexie gave Robbie an appraising look. "You're not too bad."

Robbie laughed. "Aye, you're pretty good, too, especially when you've had something to drink."

Lexie swatted Robbie's arm.

"Maybe it's just as well that Viola stayed with me," Mémère said, looking at Jay, Lexie, and Robbie. "She is only twelve."

Jay winked at Viola. "Maybe so. There's no drinking age here."

Mémère's voice was firm. "Much better to have Viola with me."

Over breakfast, Viola told everyone that her father wouldn't be coming with them to the Great Library. She also told them about how they would all have to travel across the universe with acorns and how the Books couldn't come with them to the Isle of Samaras, the Great Library's Island. There were nods and shrugs, but Jay, Lexie, and even Robbie took it in stride. Glad that they were coming with her, Viola smiled gratefully at them. After breakfast, while Jay, Lexie, and Robbie waited in the lounge, Mémère and Viola spoke with the doctor, who assured them Drew was making good progress, and it was safe to leave him. After that, they visited Diana, who was awake. She smiled at them when they came in, but her face was pale, and there was a peaked look to her that Viola had never seen.

Mémère squeezed her hand. "How are you doing?"

"I've been better," Diana replied in a low voice.

"Oui," Mémère said. "You're lucky you came here when you did."

"Almost didn't make it." Diana sighed. "And I'm the one who's supposed to be looking after President Murphy and the rest of you."

"That Chet's a tough cookie," Mémère replied. "And he had a gun."

Viola stared proudly at Mémère. "If Mémère hadn't hit Chet over the head with a log, probably none of you would be here."

Despite the pain she was in, Diana grinned. "Is that right? You took Chet down?"

Mémère shrugged. "Well, he wasn't paying any attention to me. An old lady. It was easy to hit him when he wasn't looking."

Diana shook her head. "No, you saw your chance, and you moved in. If you had hesitated or waited, the story might have a different ending." She stared at both of them. "Remember this when you two go to the Great Library." Diana shifted and winced. "And one more thing. In my years of work, I've learned that everyone—and I mean everyone—has a weak spot. Even Cinnial. Find it and exploit it. When you come back, I'll expect a full report."

Viola kissed Diana on the cheek. "All right."

"Thanks for the advice," Mémère said dryly.

Then they left, and walking down the hall to the lounge, Mémère asked, "CIA agent?"

"One of the best," Viola answered. "I'm not supposed to know this, but I do."

"Tough to keep things from you. Just like Maya. That kid always knew what was going on, even when we didn't want her to."

In the lounge, along with Jay, Lexie, and Robbie, was Wren.

"Wren!" Viola called, rushing over to the girl she hardly knew, and the two embraced warmly. Because Isold was right—there was something about Wren, a luminous quality that drew everyone in.

Wren asked, "Viola, are you ready to go?"

"As ready as I'll ever be," Viola replied. "But I need to say good-bye to my father first."

"Goodbyes are important," Wren said.

Lexie sat down. "We'll be here in the lounge. Fun to read some of the magazines that are amazingly not that different from what we have at home."

"How are you able to read them?" Mémère asked in wonder.

Lexie shrugged. "Don't know. But somehow I can."

Wren had the answer. "At school, Ensante Madeleine told us that when you travel with the Books, they connect you to the universe's common language, which allows you to understand and read any language."

Startled, Viola stared at Wren. "That's why my father can speak so many languages. I never knew why. I just thought he was good at it."

Wren laughed. "He is, but it's all because of Earth's Book of Everything. I bet he even knows more than he lets on."

"Right." Then Viola thought about traveling with the golden acorns and wondered how the magic might affect them. But she didn't say anything. They would deal with that later.

Viola and Mémère left the lounge to return to Drew's room. He was sleeping, but as soon as Viola touched his arm, Drew woke up, and it was clear he had been waiting for them.

Her voice gentle, Mémère said, "President Murphy, it's time for us to go."

"Please call me Drew. After all we've been through, you can call me by my first name."

"I don't know if I can. You'll always be President Murphy to me."

"Would you try?"

Mémère smiled. "I'll try." She paused. "Drew, I know how hard it must be for you to stay behind when we're all going to the Great Library, but I promise you that I will watch out for Viola. She's like a granddaughter to me, and I will guard her the way I would Maya."

Moved, Viola looked away, but before she did, she saw that her father's eyes were filled with tears.

He cleared his throat. "Thank you. I know I can trust you with Viola's life."

"I promise I'll watch out for her," Mémère repeated. Then squeezing Drew's arm, she left.

Glancing back at her father, Viola saw him rub his eyes. Leaning over, she kissed him on the cheek, and he put his hand on her head. "I'll be back, Dad."

"Go get Cinnial." Drew's voice was firm and strong. "And rescue the Great Library from Chaos."

Viola felt how much courage and effort it took for her father to let her go, to send her off to do something even an adult would have a hard time doing. And she admired him for it.

Viola stood straight. "We will, Dad—me, Wren, Robbie, Jay, Lexie, and Mémère."

As Viola left, a sense of purpose pushed down the last of her fear, and she joined the others in the lounge.

Wren looked at Viola. "Are you ready to have your hair cut and dyed?"

"I am," Viola answered.

Lexie asked, "What color?"

"Red," came the prompt reply.

Mémère said in approval, "That will be a change. Afterwards, we might not even recognize you."

And an hour or so later, with a pixie cut and deep red hair, Viola looked at herself in the mirror at the salon. Who was that girl staring back at her? "Perfect," Viola said, pushing down the uneasy feeling that her mother would not like this change at all. But first things first—trapping Cinnial at the Great Library. After that, back to Earth to face her mother. *If there is an afterward* came the unwanted thought, but Viola pushed that one down, too.

18: THE CONDUCTOR

Traveling to Kip's house with a golden acorn was just as bad as Viola had thought it would be. With Earth's Book of Everything, each journey had been instantaneous. One second Viola was in a certain place; the next she was somewhere else. Viola suspected this sudden lurch was what upset people's stomach until they had used the Books a time or two and were used to the motion.

With the acorn, it was more like racing on a bumpy back road through the universe with plenty of potholes and dips along the way. Clutching the acorn, Viola sometimes rocketed with her eyes closed and sometimes with them open. Streaking along beside her were Jay, Lexie, Robbie, Wren, and Mémère. Their bodies, faces, and backpacks were a blur, but Viola could tell them all apart, and she could even see the fear on Mémère's face.

Poor Mémère, Viola thought. *I wish I could be beside her. I wish I could hold her hand.* But traveling with the acorn took every bit of effort Viola had, and holding anybody's hand was out of the question. Remembering how Ensante Madeleine had admonished her not to drop the acorn, Viola hardly dared to imagine what might happen if she did let go of it.

Fortunately, Time was there along with Magic, enveloping the group, shielding and hiding them from Chaos. With a snap, the acorns deposited the travelers in Kip and Isik's house. They were sitting in a bright dining room overlooking the sea when the six travelers dropped into the connected living room. Kip sloshed his tea down the front of his shirt, and Isik's fork clattered onto his plate.

"Damn!" Jay yelled. "What a trip."

"Wasn't sure I'd make it," Robbie said. "Thought I might drop that acorn."

Smoothing her hair into place, Lexie nodded regally at the two men. "Hello, Kip. Hello, Isik."

"Who are you?" Kip managed to ask. "And how did you get here?"

Grinning disarmingly, Wren showed him the blackened acorn. "Astrid from the Great Library and my mentor Ensante Madeleine sent us here to help you defeat Cinnial. We're going to work with you in the gardens at the Great Library so that we can scope things out."

"Okay," Kip said slowly.

Wren's grin broadened into a smile. "The Books told us about you and Isik and showed us what you two looked like. So we know who you are. But you don't know us, do you?"

"No, but I can guess," Kip replied. "Are you friends of Maya?"

"We are," Viola answered. "And we've come to complete her mission." Steadying herself on the arm of the living room couch, she quickly introduced the travelers to Kip and Isik.

Kip frowned. "Where's Maya?"

Mémère swayed slightly. "It's a long story. May I sit down?"

Isik stood. "Yes, yes, of course. Sit down. Tea for everyone?"

"That would be nice." Mémère gratefully sat on the couch. "That was some journey. I thought traveling with a Book was rough. That's nothing compared with using an acorn."

Soon chairs were pulled from the dining room into the living room so that there were enough seats for everyone. While Isik made tea, Kip hurried to a small bakery down the street and bought a huge box of frosted spiced cookies, which were piled on a plate on the coffee table in front of the sofa and two comfortable chairs.

Robbie and Jay quickly helped themselves to cookies, and it wasn't long before the others did, too. When everyone had a mug of steaming tea, and Kip and Isik had settled onto dining room chairs, the travelers, starting with Jay and Lexie, told their stories.

Viola provided the order her father had once maintained. When Jay and Lexie got off track about their time in The Trotting

Horse and how they had sung for everyone, Viola gently guided them back. But she noticed that Isik was keenly interested in Jay and Lexie. When music again came into the story as Jay and Lexie told about distracting the imps with singing and playing while Maya and Will stole the lock and key, Isik looked even more interested in the two teenagers.

After Mémère related her part, explaining in a down-to-earth way how she had prevented Chet from killing all who were in the clearing in Oakton Forest, Kip and Isik respectfully inclined their heads in her direction.

Viola recounted her journey to the Toad Queen. She spoke about the decision to have her eyes peeled, how she didn't want to have it done, but in the end felt it was necessary.

"I just had a bad feeling about what would happen if I didn't have my eyes peeled," Viola said, and everyone nodded sympathetically, especially Isik. "And now I know why. I'm the one who has to trap Cinnial, and I wouldn't be able to do it if my eyes weren't peeled."

Next Robbie told why he was there, how he had to do his part in the fight against Chaos and Cinnial. "Because of our Old Oak, the Forest of Arden has a bit of Magic. Not as much as here, I guess, but enough to make the forest a really special place. It would break my heart to see it destroyed."

"Yeah," Kip said, and Isik reached for his hand, squeezing it.

Wren, the newest, was last. "I'll be working with Viola and Robbie. To help trap Cinnial. We'll make a good team." Then her bright face became serious. "On Aarde, my planet, we've seen what Chaos can do when it's in control. Chaos wrecked so many things, and it nearly wiped out all the people on Aarde. Chaos must be stopped." She stared levelly at Kip and Isik, and Viola got a sense of Wren's inner strength, as firm in its own luminous way as hers was.

"Absolutely," Isik replied, meeting Wren's stare.

From a zippered pocket in her trousers, Lexie removed the lock from its pouch and placed them both on the coffee table. Everyone was silent for a while as they stared at the lock on top of the pouch. At first glance, the lock, dull and tarnished, didn't look as though it would fasten a jewelry box much less trap Cinnial. But as they all studied the lock, there came a low, steady hum of intense power, and Viola knew that despite its humble appearance, the lock would capture Cinnial.

Lexie said, "Pawel told us that for the lock to work, Viola will have to get within six feet of Cinnial. There's no spell, exactly, but Viola will have to direct the lock's energy and tell it who she wants to trap."

There was more silence, and Viola uneasily wondered if she would be able to direct the lock's energy.

Mémère cleared her throat. "My Maya risked her life to get this lock, to make sure that it got to our universe. Will is sure Maya's alive, and I hope to God he's right. But now it's our duty to trap méchant Cinnial and take the Great Library back from Chaos."

"Magic will help you." Kip glanced from Viola to Jay to Lexie. Then finally to Isik, and it seemed to Viola that the two were communicating to each other with their thoughts.

"Okay, then," Isik replied, regarding Lexie and Jay.

"What do you have in mind for us?" Lexie asked.

Isik set his mug on the coffee table. "We've been getting ready, too. Did you know that one of the first things Cinnial did when he got here was to chop down our Ancient Oak and burn it?"

Robbie winced. "How could he do that?"

"Along with killing Sydda, Cinnial was willing to do a lot of things to take over the Great Library," Kip answered. "He thought the Ancient Oak, with its power and magic, would work against him."

"He was right, wasn't he?" Jay asked.

"That he was," Kip agreed. "No surprise that Cinnial decided it would be best to burn the Ancient One and get rid of it. Cinnial hoped it would diminish the magic on the island."

"Did it?" Viola asked fearfully.

"No." Kip laughed, and it had an otherworldly chime to it. "Magic runs all through that island. The Ancient One had a massive root system with fungi that moved to other trees and their roots, passing on the magic until the whole island was saturated with it. Cutting down one tree, no matter how old or powerful, would not diminish the magic. Cinnial should have known better, but he didn't. He doesn't think much about things that grow. He mainly thinks about himself and his resentments. Cinnial's so bitter that he often doesn't see what's in front of him."

Viola wondered, *is that his weakness*? Yes, but her intuition told her there was something else, too. Wren, understanding, glanced at Viola.

185

Isik grinned, and there was a strange glitter in his eyes that seemed almost golden to Viola. "And there was another problem that Cinnial didn't think about. When the tree burned, its ashes blew into Watertown. The ashes fell on our food and into our water. We even breathed some of it in. It changed us. Forever, I think. When Cinnial gives one of his smooth speeches, it doesn't move us. We can see right through him into his wizened heart."

"You can resist him," Viola said.

"We can do more than that," Isik replied. "I'm a music teacher in Watertown. In the classes I teach, I've discovered that with a lot of work, I can conduct music and direct voices in a way I never could before the ashes fell on our town."

Viola remembered the small toads by the Toad Queen and how their voices had carried her back to the lodge in the Forest of Arden.

"Conduct and direct how?" Mémère asked.

Isik said, "It's almost like the music is at my command, and the voices become a physical force that can leave the singers and move things."

Jay stared at Isik. "You're planning to use your voices to take back the Great Library, aren't you?"

"We are," Isik replied. "And our chance for success will be a whole lot better if Cinnial is trapped in that lock. I've formed a town choir with singers of all ages. Every afternoon, we get together in the school's performing arts center. We've been practicing for a while, and I'm getting better at directing the voices, at encouraging them to go farther and farther, to wrap themselves around objects and hold them tight."

"Lexie and I can help, can't we?" Jay asked.

"That's what I'm hoping," Isik said. "I could use assistants who understand both music and magic and really know how to sing."

"We distracted the imps," Lexie replied with a smile. "And they're tough. Really tough."

"Lexie, that was in Elferterre," Jay said. "We had Magic to help us."

"Magic will help you here, too," Isik told Jay.

Jay shrugged. "I hope so."

Viola spoke, "Kip is right. When I traveled with the acorn, I felt something." The others nodded. "Magic, I think. Just a little in us that might help us and make us better at the things we're good at."

Isik murmured, "Plus we just might be able to come up with something to boost the magic you got from the acorns." He stared at Kip, who at first looked puzzled and then understood.

"Oh, right!" Kip said aloud.

Mémère frowned. "What kind of boost?"

"Don't worry," Kip answered. "You won't have to swallow the ashes the way we did. A little charm that you wear on a chain should do the trick. Our friend, Dani, makes jewelry. When the ash fell, many of us gathered the ash that collected in our yards. At the time, we didn't understand why. It just seemed like something we should do."

"One last directive from the Ancient Oak," Isik said sadly.

"Right," Kip replied. "Later we figured that out and how the ash could be used to enhance magic. Dani will be able to work some oak ash she gathered into a charm. She was always a fantastic jewelry maker. And now she's beyond fantastic. I'm betting that the charms will give you a little glow like the one we all have here in Watertown. That way, you'll blend in and won't attract attention."

"Very good." Mémère's voice was brisk. "We've come this far. We'll do whatever we have to do even if it means swallowing ashes. But I have to admit I'm glad we don't have to. When this is over, I plan to return to Earth, and I don't want to have too much magic."

The others laughed a little and nodded.

Kip said, "I'm glad you're all here." Then he hesitated. "But there are a lot of you, and we don't have enough bedrooms for everyone. We only have one spare bedroom, and a little office that doesn't even have a couch."

"But we do have an attic," Isik added quickly. "It's small, but there should be room enough for five of you. And I think I can rustle up some camp cots from various friends. We'll say we have guests from out of town who are staying with us."

"We certainly are from out of town," Viola agreed. Then she took charge, the way she had seen her mother and father do so many times at the White House. "Mémère will have the spare bedroom. The rest of us can sleep in the attic. Me, Lexie, and Wren on one side and Jay and Robbie on the other. We can hang some kind of line with sheets or curtains to divide the space." She pointed at her backpack on the floor beside her. "We brought basic things like toothbrushes and hairbrushes and pajamas, so you won't have to worry about that."

Isik grinned. "That is a big relief."

Lexie stared at Viola. "You're one that likes to take charge, don't you?"

"I do," Viola admitted. "I see how things should be done, and mostly I'm right. But not always," she added quickly. "No one's right all the time."

Mémère smiled fondly at Viola. "Just like my Maya. Except I think you're a little more organized and a little less impulsive."

Lexie said, "I was thinking exactly the same thing."

"Well, it is the truth." Mémère gave Lexie a stern look. "But my Maya is one brave girl."

"She has the heart of a lion," Lexie replied quietly, and Mémère's expression softened.

Viola thought, *Thank goodness Lexie said that. The last thing we need is for Mémère to have bad feelings about Lexie.* But with that one sentence, Viola could tell that all was well between Lexie and Mémère.

That afternoon, trooping up to the third floor, the travelers cleaned and arranged the attic for sleeping. Mémère scrubbed, swept, and dusted along with the kids, working as hard as they did. Isik, true to his word, found five cots as well as bedding, and pillows. There were also curtains, rods, and brackets for a room divider.

"I'm good at scrounging. A great thing to be when you're a teacher," Isik said as he waved goodbye to a friend who had a van and was able to help transport the cots. The travelers and Kip were clustered on the sidewalk beside him. "I've helped my friends many times. Now, it's time for them to help me. And they did."

Neither Kip nor Isik liked clutter, which meant there wasn't much to move aside to make room for the cots. Before dinner time, the cots were set up and made—three on one side, two on the other, just as Viola had suggested.

Stretched across the room were the rods and curtains, dividing the attic into two rooms.

"That was a great idea," Mémère said. "A little privacy is a good thing." As she stood surveying the attic, Mémère's shoulders drooped, and Viola could tell how tired she was.

Viola patted Mémère's arm. "Go lie down, Mémère. We'll help Kip and Isik with dinner after we get our stuff settled up here. It won't take us long. We don't have that much."

Mémère hesitated. "Are you sure?"

Lexie replied, "There are five of us here to help with dinner. Go take a nap."

Jay grinned. "That's an order."

"All right, all right." Mémère kissed Viola's cheek, and nodding to the others, she left.

Viola looked around the attic. A window was open, and white curtains flapped as a fresh sea breeze blew in. By each cot there was just enough room for a small crate with a lamp. Isik had also found quilts for everyone to keep them warm on cool fall nights. Before leaving to rustle up the cots, he had asked everyone what their favorite colors were.

"No promises," he had said with a laugh. "I'll take whatever my friends can spare."

But somehow Isik had come through. Wren's quilt was brown, Viola's was blue, and Lexie's was purple. On the other side, Robbie had a green quilt, and Jay's was a bright mix of many colors.

Earth's Book of Everything and the Apprentice Books were on crates by Viola's, Jay's, and Lexie's cots. The Books had been consulted when the kids first arrived, but it had been a quick check-in as there was a lot of work to do getting the attic ready for sleeping.

Lexie considered the Books. "After dinner, we can have a longer talk. Let's go downstairs and see what we can do to help."

The kitchen was long with counters on both walls, and it was wide enough for everyone to have a place for chopping and dicing. By the time Mémère came downstairs, salad and vegetable soup were ready. Kip had gone to the bakery again but this time for loaves of bread and a cake to celebrate their arrival.

"Well, look at that," Mémère said, smiling at the set table. It had been extended with a smaller table, which had folding chairs around it.

Isik replied, "Lots of hands to help."

Plans were discussed over dinner. For Isik, Jay, and Lexie, their job was straightforward: Learn how to direct the choir's voices to immobilize Cinnial's forces.

For Viola, Wren, and Robbie, things were a little trickier.

Kip frowned. "Not only do you have to figure out how to get close to Cinnial, but we have to worry about his Book tipping him off about us. So far, so good. Otherwise, Julian never would have hired me."

189

Isik said, "I think Cinnial and his Book can't be bothered to worry about the gardeners. Cinnial has bigger things on his mind, like suppressing Time and Magic."

"What about Julian's Book?" Viola asked. "Can you tell if he carries it with him in one of his pockets?"

Kip shook his head. "I don't think Julian carries his Book with him. It doesn't seem to be in his pocket. I've never seen him refer to it when he comes out to the gardens to talk to us. And the few times I've been in his office, the Book has been on a shelf. Closed. And again, Julian never referred to it."

Isik pursed his lips. "Maybe, just maybe, Julian and his Book have had a falling out."

"Could be," Kip replied. "All I know is that I haven't been arrested, even though I've been scoping things out whenever I can."

"Good," Viola said. "Let's hope it stays that way, that we're too small to be noticed."

And around the two tables, everyone agreed.

After dinner, when everything had been picked up and the dishes washed, they all settled in the living room. On one wall was a bookcase crammed full of books. As she had done in Camber's Library when she was with Viola, Wren looked longingly at the books. Viola, too, was itching to take a look.

Kip said, "Rain is in the forecast for the next two days, which means we won't be going to the Great Library to harvest potatoes until the weather is good. This will give you some time to look over the books and maybe even read a little. Might come in handy with Julian, who is keen on books and even more keen on talking about them. If you get on Julian's good side, you might be allowed inside the Great Library."

"Where we can scope things out," Viola put in.

"Exactly," Kip said.

"I'm not much of a reader," Robbie admitted with a slight blush.

"That's all right," Wren replied, her voice gentle. "You'll be able to help in other ways. I can feel it."

"Me, too." Viola sensed that although Robbie's skills were different from hers and Wren's, his help would be invaluable. Robbie smiled gratefully at Viola and Wren.

Then Isik asked casually, "How about some music?"

"Sure," Jay and Lexie said together.

On one wall was a keyboard on a stand, and from a closet under the stairs, Isik took out a guitar.

Jay grinned. "Yes, please!"

After Isik handed Jay the guitar, he asked, "Anyone else?"

"I can play," Lexie said. "But not as well as Jay."

"Your voice is better than mine," Jay replied.

Lexie took the guitar Isik passed to her. "True."

Wren spoke up, "I can play and sing, too."

Another guitar came out for Wren.

"That's all I have for guitars," Isik said.

"No worries," Viola replied. "I don't play."

"Same here," Robbie added, and Mémère nodded her head in agreement.

"You can't just sit there," Isik muttered, and Viola understood it was the teacher in him that wanted everyone involved. Into the closet he went, and out came egg shakers, maracas, and wooden claves.

The egg shakers went to Mémère and the maracas to Viola.

Laughing, Robbie took the claves. "Aye, we're all set now, aren't we?"

"Not quite." Isik went back into the closet. He brought out three music stands and sheets of music, setting them up in front of Jay, Lexie, and Wren.

"Now we are." Isik turned the keyboard so that it was facing the room, and when he sat down, he could see everyone. "Ready?" Isik asked.

"Ready," they all replied.

What followed was an evening of swirling music, conducted by Isik, that surrounded everyone, keeping them in sync, urging them to play and sing. Lexie and Wren sang in counterpoint, and their voices were so clear and true that for a moment even Isik looked moved. But he quickly recovered, gesturing with his hand for Jay to sing, and soon Jay's baritone joined in. How did Jay, Lexie, and Wren follow the music and sing as though they had known those songs all their lives? Viola wasn't sure, but she suspected that music had its own common language, and somehow, thanks to Magic and to Isik's skill as a conductor, they were all tapping into it.

Almost without volition, Viola shook the maracas, keeping a perfect beat to every song. Mémère's cheeks were red, and her eyes

191

were bright as she kept time with the egg shakers. With the claves, Robbie looked as though he was having the time of his life.

With abandon, Kip played the tambourine, and leaping up, he skipped around the living and dining room, which seemed to shift and dip with the music. Viola couldn't remember when she had ever felt so joyous. Jumping up, she joined Kip, and it wasn't long before Mémère and Robbie were dancing around the room, too. With their guitars, Jay, Lexie, and Wren stayed in one place, but their bodies moved with the music.

Isik, ever keeping an eye on the manic energy and tempo of the music, began to play softer and softer, and everyone followed his lead. Mémère was the first to gratefully sit down, followed by Viola, then Robbie, and finally Kip. The music became gentle, and it ended with a suggestion rather than with any sense of finality, as though the song was far from over. Instead, it was everywhere, simply waiting to be called.

"Wow," Jay said. "We had some amazing experiences in Elferterre, but nothing like this."

"No kidding," Lexie agreed.

Kip smiled proudly. "You didn't have Isik. He's a natural conductor. The school is lucky to have him. The town is lucky to have him."

"Maybe the universe," Wren whispered.

Viola remembered the vision she'd had of the group surrounding the Great Library. She now realized that their weapons would be music and voices, directed by Isik. Without the ability to harness the music, Viola understood that retaking the Great Library, with its armed guards, would be impossible without a bloody battle, which the townspeople were nearly certain to lose. After all, how could everyday people go up against trained guards with lethal weapons?

But music, working with Magic, would be there to help them. Nevertheless, Viola knew that even with the power of music and Magic, it would not be an easy thing to go up against Cinnial and Chaos. However, in burning down the Ancient Oak, Cinnial had unknowingly unleashed a force in the citizens of Watertown that was out of his control. And although Viola had never met Cinnial, she knew with certainty that he craved control as much as he craved power. But if all went well, Cinnial would be trapped in the lock, where he wouldn't be able to control anything.

19: ROBBIE TAKES THE REINS

Two days later, when the weather had cleared, Kip, Viola, Wren, and Robbie stood on the edge of Samaras Bay. Ready for gardening, they were dressed in brown overalls. The morning air had a fall nip, and Viola was glad she was wearing a jacket and gloves. The three also wore wide brimmed hats, brown like their overalls and jackets. Viola reached under the hat to touch the short hair she still wasn't used to.

Kip studied them. "Those charms will help you blend in, just as Isik predicted. They give you the same glow as the rest of us have. Dani is some jewelry maker, that's for sure."

Viola, Wren, and Robbie put their hands to their chest, where the charms nestled under their jackets, overalls, and shirts. Even though the chains and charms contained ash from the Ancient Oak, they were translucent and nearly invisible when they were worn. From the charms came a slight warmth, and when Viola had put hers on the day before, there had been a slight crackle that energized her. As the day went by, the crackle had faded, but the snappy feeling remained, giving Viola the notion that she was more than capable of carrying out the mission to trap Cinnial. Beside her, Wren and Robbie grinned.

Kip shook a finger at them. "Don't be overconfident. Remember who you're up against."

"Yes, Kip," they said together.

With narrow eyes, Kip regarded them. "There will be a guard we have to pass when we go onto the island. Never used to be. People could come and go as they pleased. Right from the jump, I'll explain you're new workers. The guards are vigilant, and it's best to be upfront that you three are new. No doubt we'll be allowed to pass. However, after that there will be the captain of the guard, and we'll have to be very, very careful around him. Captain Braylon will want you to empty your pockets. He might even want you to take off your jackets. But it's unlikely that he'll see your charms. Only someone with an eye for magic would spot them, and the captain certainly doesn't have an eye for magic. None of Cinnial's guards do."

Wren glanced at Viola. "Don't stand too straight. And don't look the captain in the eyes."

"Yeah," Kip agreed, and Viola could tell he was nervous. Then straightening his shoulders, Kip shook his head. "I'll go get us a cart. I see the rest of the gardeners are here and are getting their carts."

As Kip walked to the place that rented, sold, and stored carts in a large shed nearby at the edge of the beach, Viola thought about what Wren had said. Would she be able to follow Wren's instructions and convince the captain that she was just an average kid who was going to help Kip in the gardens? Viola's parents had raised her to be confident, equal to any social situation that came her way. But the mission to trap Cinnial depended on not being noticed, on not attracting attention. Thinking of all that Maya had done, Viola's chin went up. She was determined to pull this off. After all, the universe depended on it.

Wren put her hand on Viola's arm. "You'll do fine. I know you will. Just remember what I told you."

"I will," Viola replied.

Wren turned away from Viola. "Look," she murmured, pointing across the bay to the glowing Great Library with its white towers and turrets. "It's even more beautiful than I imagined. Worth risking our lives for, don't you think?" Wren's dark eyes were shining, and Viola and Robbie gazed in wonder at the castle.

"Aye," Robbie said. "From the time I was little, I've heard stories about the Great Library, but there's nothing like seeing it, is there?"

"No, there isn't." Viola had seen pictures of the Great Library in Earth's Book of Everything, but Viola had been unprepared for how moved she would be when she actually saw the shimmering library, which truly did seem to be at the center of all things. *Wren is right*, Viola thought, blinking back tears. *It's definitely worth risking our lives for.*

As Viola stared at the Great Library, she felt as though she was being welcomed, but even across the bay, Viola felt a tension, and she knew it came from the conflict between Time and Magic and Chaos. She also knew that Time and Magic would keep Chaos occupied, off balance, so that three kids from another planet would remain unnoticed.

"Worth risking our lives for," Wren repeated, and Viola and Robbie nodded.

Driving a blue cart with four seats, Kip stopped beside Viola, Wren, and Robbie. On the back was a basket with a big cooler that held drinks and their lunch. Not far behind came three carts with other workers, and they waved to the kids, who waved back.

"Get in," said Kip.

A little dazed from the sight of the Great Library and the struggle between Time, Magic, and Chaos, Viola sat next to Kip. Robbie and Wren slid into the seats behind them.

"That Great Library's quite the sight, isn't it?" Kip asked as he drove across the causeway that connected Watertown to the Great Library. In a line, the other carts followed.

"It sure is," Viola replied, and in the back seats, Wren and Robbie agreed.

"I grew up with the Great Library just across the bay. I've gone there many times to get books," Kip said. "But every time I look at the library from Watertown, I get a little chill. I never imagined I'd be the Great Library's head gardener, but Julian chose me over the other applicants." Kip frowned. "I'm not sure why. I haven't been out of university for that many years. While I have worked in a few big gardens, I don't have the experience that some of the others had who applied. But I didn't dare look at Julian's thoughts to see why he picked me. First of all, it's rude. Second of all, with Julian, it could be dangerous."

"I had a feeling you and Isik could communicate with your thoughts," Viola said.

195

Kip grinned. "Another gift from the Ancient Oak." Then he stopped grinning. "While Julian's not as hard as Cinnial, he's sharp and loyal. Remember that." Kip turned his head to regard Viola, and he gave the two in back a quick look. "Always keep your guard up, even if he starts talking about books with you."

"We will," Viola replied. "The Great Library's beautiful, but even all the way across the sandbar, we could feel the fight between Chaos and Time and Magic."

"Yes." Kip's voice was sad. "The struggle hangs over everything. The Great Library used to be such a joyous place. There was always a hustle-bustle as people went from the mainland to study and to get books at the Great Library. But with Cinnial and his crew there, everything's changed. The Great Library's closed to the public. Cinnial spends his days trying to push down Time and Magic. So far he hasn't succeeded, but he's working on it. And most of the current staff came with him from Mortmain. They're all as loyal as Julian. And suspicious. So be careful, no matter who you're talking to."

Leaning forward, Wren patted Kip's shoulder. "Don't worry. We know why we're here. We'll be careful."

"I do worry about you," Kip admitted. "You're all so young. And, Viola, even if you manage to get into the Great Library, I don't know how you're ever going to get close enough to Cinnial to trap him. I've worked at the Great Library for over a month, and I've barely seen him. Plus he's well guarded."

"We don't know either," Wren said. "Our first step will be to scope things out, to meet Julian and see how that goes."

Kip replied, "That will be a good place to start. Because it seems to me that Julian, not Cinnial, is the one who's actually running things."

Robbie tightened the drawstring on his hat. "What does Julian look like?"

"You won't be able to miss Julian," Kip answered. "His hair's as white as yours, Robbie, except it's long, and he draws it back into a ponytail. He's tall and slender. He'll probably come over and talk to us about some book while we're having lunch." Frowning a little, Kip said, "Even though I've never looked at his thoughts, I get the feeling that what Julian really wants is to be a teacher, that he isn't happy being Cinnial's right-hand man."

"That might be Julian's weakness," Viola said, remembering what Diana had said about everyone having a weakness.

"But never forget, Julian is loyal to Cinnial," Kip repeated. "I've never felt such loyalty from anyone."

"We'll remember," Viola, Wren, and Robbie said together.

As they drove closer to the Great Library, more details came into focus. There was a small walled village facing Watertown, and the houses and walls were white, just like the Great Library.

"Pretty," Viola said.

"That's Samlaren Village," Kip replied, "for the Great Library's workers who want their own homes."

Samlaren Village was built at a slant, perched on a hill leading up to the Great Library, and a corkscrew road wound through the village up to the library.

Kip said, "When the librarians knew that Cinnial was coming to the Great Library, they cleared the village, sending all the workers away. They were afraid Cinnial would kill them when he took over. Which was very likely. So now everyone in the village comes from Mortmain—the baker, the head chef, staff with families who want their own homes."

"Flunkies," Wren said bluntly.

"Flunkies," Kip agreed.

"Why didn't he bring his own gardeners?" Robbie asked.

"Because there are no gardens near Mortmain." Kip shook his head. "Hard to believe, isn't it? But that's what Julian told me. All their food is shipped in from other places. And although Julian didn't say as much, I think he wanted somebody local who understood Magic, which supports everything on that island. He gets it even if Cinnial doesn't."

At the end of the causeway was a new and hastily constructed guard booth. An unsmiling woman in a gray uniform opened the window as Kip stopped by the booth.

She considered Kip and the carts behind him. "Good morning, Kip." Her voice was polite, but there was an undertone of suspicion in it.

"Good morning, Officer Carada," Kip said, keeping his tone polite and neutral. "These three here with me are new workers."

Officer Carada stared at Viola, Wren, and Robbie. "Why new workers?"

"As you probably know, Julian gave me leave to choose whoever I wanted. The potatoes are ready to be harvested, and I need extra hands."

"Right," the officer said crisply. "I'll let Captain Braylon know you're coming. Even though you have permission to bring whoever you want, the captain will want to see your new workers before you head to the fields."

"Of course."

Officer Carada waved him on. "Go ahead, then."

Kip drove past the guard booth, and the other carts followed him up the winding road to the Great Library. They went by small white cottages, and Viola saw men and women leaving them to head to work. Some of the younger ones walked up the big hill, and they stepped aside to let the gardeners' carts pass. Others had carts like the one Kip had gotten in Watertown, and there was a small procession of carts on the narrow road. As Kip drove by the various people, there were no smiles, but there were no frowns either. Viola glanced as casually as she could at the folks going to work—some fat, some thin, some tall, some short, some plain, some attractive— and it struck her how ordinary everyone looked. From a few of the cottages, men and women waved as their partners left to go to the Great Library. In many yards, there were sandboxes with trucks and shovels. In other yards, little swing sets.

From the cottages, Viola heard childish voices call, "Goodbye, Mommy."

Or, "Goodbye, Daddy."

Or sometimes both "Goodbye, Mommy and Daddy."

It gave Viola a funny feeling to think about how the people who lived in Samlaren Village looked pretty much the same as people did anywhere. They might be Cinnial's flunkies, but they had partners and children and mothers and fathers. They had people who loved them.

"Just like we do," Viola whispered to herself.

After a final push up the last steep part of the hill, they came to a grassy yard, and there was the Great Library, looking even more magnificent up close than it had from a distance. In astonishment, Viola, Wren, and Robbie gaped at the castle. As she stared, Viola got a mixture of impressions—the serenity and strength Time brought to the Great Library leavened with the snap of Magic.

And on the edge was Chaos, trying to break through but so far not succeeding. Finally, Viola got a strong sense that the Great Library was anticipating something.

"Us," Wren said in a soft voice.

"Aye," Robbie replied. "I can feel it even though I haven't had my eyes peeled."

Viola thought, *Yes, and it's waiting for Maya, too. But will she come?*

Captain Braylon was standing by the front of the Great Library, and he motioned for Kip and the other gardeners to stop and pull to one side to allow the other carts to pass. Dressed in a gray uniform, he regarded them all sternly, and although the slender captain was not tall, he had such an authority that Viola knew she would not want to cross him. Viola had seen his type many times in different countries, and she had the strong feeling that Captain Braylon wouldn't hesitate to use the gun he had in his holster if he thought anyone was threatening Cinnial's order.

Kip stopped the cart as did the other gardeners who were behind him.

There was no greeting. Instead, the captain said, "I want the new workers to get out of the cart."

Viola, Wren, and Robbie slid out of the cart as did Kip. Viola felt the captain scrutinize her first, then Robbie, and then Wren. Viola slouched a little, remembering what Wren had said about not looking too confident. Although Viola glanced at the captain a couple of times, she mostly kept her head down and did not look into his eyes. Her hand wanted to touch her charm, but Viola knew better than to do that. Even though the charm was nearly invisible, Viola did not want to call attention to it, and her hands stayed by her sides.

After what seemed like an age but was probably no more than a few minutes, Captain Braylon asked Kip, "A little young, aren't they? Why aren't they in school?"

"It's potato recess," Kip answered quickly. "In Watertown, schools close for a couple of weeks so that kids can help with the potato harvest in the big fields outside the city. I'm a little short handed so these kids agreed to come help me. And they'll work at a cheaper rate than the adults."

More silence. "Turn out your pockets," Captain Braylon said at last to Viola, Wren, and Robbie. "All of them."

199

The kids turned out the pockets of their jackets and overalls. In Viola's and Wren's there were small combs, some tissues, and packages of gummy candies. Robbie not only had gummy candies but two large chocolate bars that he had slipped into the long side pocket of his overalls. Isik had also given candy bars to Viola and Wren, but they had left theirs behind, deciding to save them for later.

"That's a lot of candy." The captain gave Robbie a look that Viola's own father had given her more than a few times, and Viola knew without a doubt that the captain had children.

"Aye, harvesting is hungry work," Robbie replied with the conviction of someone who had done his fair share of harvesting.

"I'm sure it is." The captain considered Robbie. "Your accent sounds different than Kip's. Where are you from?"

"The Outer Islands," Robbie responded without hesitation. "I'm staying with Kip and Isik while I go to school." Kip and Isik had prepared Viola, Wren, and Robbie for this question, and they all knew which parts of Bellefour they had come from before they had moved to Watertown. But the captain never addressed Viola and Wren directly, and with no need for their story, they remained silent.

"Right," the captain said as though he were familiar with the various accents folks had on Bellefour when, in fact, he had no clue what they sounded like. "Open your cooler."

Kip opened the cooler, and the captain poked around the sandwiches, fruit, cookies, and drinks.

The captain shut the lid. "Okay, then."

Kip said, "Okay, then. Are we cleared to go to work? Those potatoes won't pick themselves, and your cook will be happy to have fresh potatoes."

"I suppose she will." It was obvious the captain had never thought much about where his food had come from. "Yes, go on to the gardens." Then his expression softened ever so slightly. "And son? Better eat a candy bar before it gets too hot, and the sun melts it. The other one should go in the cooler."

"Yes, sir," Robbie replied with a grin. "I'll do that."

Kip, Viola, Wren, and Robbie got back into their cart, and with the other carts following, they drove around to the back of the Great Library, to the tool shed and the stable, to the edge of the big gardens that produced much of the food for the library and its village.

I'm glad we only brought candy and other little things, Viola thought. Kip and Isik had been right when they had told Viola, Wren, and Robbie not to bring anything important or suspicious like, say, a lock that could trap Cinnial. She was grateful her charm was safely hidden under layers of clothes and that the captain never thought about checking for a magic charm. *But why would he?,* Viola thought. *He comes from a place where there's not much magic.*

At home, Kip had said, "Once the captain's sure you're not a threat, he won't meet us every day. We'll just have to wait and see how long that takes. Then it will be safe to bring the lock."

Kip and the other gardeners parked in the shade under a line of evergreen trees by the shed and stable. As the captain had suggested, Robbie tucked one of his candy bars into the cooler. Not far away, a potato field stretched in a long, wide band to the edge of a small forest in the distance, and Viola wondered how long it would take to harvest a field that size with only ten workers.

To complicate the process, it turned out that horses were used to pull the potato digger. From the stable, one of the gardeners led two massive horses, one dark brown and the other a reddish brown. Another gardener brought out the digger from the shed. As the gardeners talked about the best way to manage the horses and hook them up to the digger, Viola and Wren stared at the huge creatures.

Kip grimaced. "Right? In Watertown, we have machines to do this. But Sydda liked horses, and he preferred to harvest potatoes the old-fashioned way. Unfortunately, none of us know how to work with horses. We're not even sure how to hook them up to the digger. Good thing those horses are easygoing."

Robbie regarded the horses, whose ears were back and tails were clamped down. "Aye, they're easygoing, but right now they're nervous. They can tell you don't know what you're doing."

Kip blinked in surprise at Robbie. "How do you know that?"

Robbie said, "I've been around horses all my life. I know when they're nervous. Back home, we use them in the fields and gardens. We even have a machine a lot like that." He hesitated. "I know I'm new, but would you like me to hook up the digger, ride behind the horses, and dig the potatoes?"

201

The other gardeners looked pleadingly at Kip, who laughed. "Yes, yes, Robbie, hook the horses up and dig those potatoes."

Robbie went over to the horses and put his hand on the neck of the dark brown horse. After murmuring something, he did the same with the reddish brown horse, who nuzzled his hair. Their ears flicked forward, and their tails went up, just a little.

Turning from the horses, Robbie asked, "Do they have names?"

"The reddish brown one is Pari," Kip said. "And the dark brown one is Faras."

Robbie turned back to the horses and put a hand on each of their necks. "There you go, Pari. There you go, Faras. I'm going to hook this digger up to you, and then we're going to dig some potatoes. I've done this before. You've nothing to worry about."

By the time Robbie was done talking, the horses' tails were no longer clamped down. Quickly and efficiently, he hooked Pari and Faras to the digger and then guided the horses to the edge of the field. Glancing over his shoulder, Robbie asked, "Are the rest of you ready?" He looked back into the fields. "I see the barrels are already out there."

While Robbie had been working with the horses, some of the other gardeners had brought out large baskets from the shed.

"We're ready," Kip said. "Go dig some potatoes."

"Okay, then." Robbie climbed onto the seat. "Walk on, Pari and Faras. Walk on."

Into the field Robbie, the horses, and the digger went. Viola and Wren watched in amazement as over and over Robbie leaped from the seat to the ground beside the horses to encourage them and then back to the seat again. In the digger's wake were potatoes, lots and lots of potatoes.

Grabbing a basket, Kip whistled. "That boy sure can handle horses."

"It's what he did back at his home," Viola said.

In admiration, Wren stared at Robbie and the horses. "He's a wonder."

"Thank goodness he's here," one of the other gardeners said.

"You got that right," Kip replied. "Okay folks, let's go pick some potatoes."

And into the field they all went.

20: INSIDE

That morning, Viola worked harder than she ever had in her life. By lunch time, her arms ached; her shoulders ached; her back ached.

"Pretty much everything hurts." Viola sat down next to Wren in the shade of the evergreen trees next to the shed and stables. From a spigot in the stables, they had washed their hands and faces and afterward had grabbed sandwiches from the cooler in the basket on the back of the cart.

"Me, too," Wren said. "I've never worked in the fields before."

Robbie, on the other hand, hardly looked tired at all. He plopped down between them. "Soft, that's what you are."

"Huh," Viola said, but she really couldn't argue with him. Like Wren, she had never worked in the fields. Viola was a diligent student at school, but except for gym classes and hikes with her parents, none of what she did involve physical labor.

Wren smiled at Robbie. "It's a wonder how you worked with those horses."

Robbie waved his hand. "I've been doing this since I was a small lad. In the forest, we don't get out much to buy supplies, and we grow almost everything we eat." He bit into a sandwich. After chewing and swallowing, Robbie asked, "This is good. Some kind of nut spread?"

"It is," Kip answered. "Isik made a big batch last night for everyone for their lunches. He's the cook in the family."

"But Mémère made the sandwiches for us," Viola said loyally. "So now Isik has some help."

Kip grinned. "That she did, and I heard plans about how there might be some homemade cookies when we come home. Among other things. With two to cook, there should be all sorts of goodies for us."

Viola looked at the fields spread out before them. "I'm glad Mémère decided to go with Isik, Lexie, and Jay to choir practice instead of coming here to pick potatoes with us like she wanted to at first. This is hard work even for someone my age."

Kip took a bite of sandwich. "Yup, farming and gardening require hard physical work."

"And besides, singing in the choir will give Mémère time to cook and bake, which she loves to do." Viola remembered Mémère cooking over a fire. "Even in the forest, Mémère fed us."

"Some people are like that," Kip said. "Thank goodness for those who cook."

"And for those who harvest our food," Wren added.

"And for those who harvest our food," Kip repeated.

"Robbie, did you eat your candy bar?" Viola asked.

"I did," Robbie answered. "I knew I would get hungry in the fields. But I'm glad Mémère packed two sandwiches for us all."

Viola was, too. Usually, one sandwich was more than enough for her. But under the trees she had gulped down both sandwiches as well as a piece of fruit that was a cross between a plum and peach, and three cookies from the bakery down the road from Kip and Isik's house.

Kip said, "Mémère made extra sandwiches, just in case, and there's one left. Go ahead and take it, Robbie. You've certainly earned it."

Robbie looked at Kip, Viola, and Wren. "You're sure?"

"I'm sure," Kip answered.

"Go for it," Viola replied.

"You know you want it," Wren said.

Robbie took the sandwich.

As Robbie ate, Viola lay back under the trees. "When do we have to go back out there?"

Robbie looked at Kip. "Not for a while. We need to let the horses rest a bit. They're big, but pulling that digger is hard work."

"Okay, Robbie," Kip said. "You let us know when you think they've had enough rest."

Robbie lay down. "Will do." He was between Viola and Wren, and after winking at them, he pulled his hat over his face. "It never hurts to rest while the horses are resting."

The cool morning had given way to a warm afternoon, and after being in the sunny field, the shade of the trees felt good. Beside Viola, Robbie snored softly. Curled on her side, Wren faced Robbie and slept quietly. On the other side of Viola, Kip rested, but she could tell he wasn't sleeping. Dozing, Viola dreamed about big horses and newly dug potatoes and the way the dirt smelled in the sun.

A hand on Viola's shoulder woke her, and she sat up with a start.

In a low voice, Kip said, "Julian's coming. Wake up Robbie and Wren."

By the time Julian had reached them, everyone, including the other gardeners, who had also been resting, were awake and alert. Viola pulled the brim of her hat down so that her face was in shadow. Even though her hair was cut short and dyed red, she didn't want to take any chances that Julian would recognize her.

"You'll be fine," Earth's Book of Everything had assured Viola that morning before she left to go to the Great Library. "You look very different, and Julian isn't expecting to see you here. Plus, the charm will help protect you. He'll just see a young girl in dirty overalls. Nothing more."

Viola thought, *I hope the Book of Everything is right*. If not, they'd be caught before they even started.

Tall, slender, and striking, Julian approached them, glancing at all the gardeners. But it was a quick look, more to acknowledge them than to discover if there were any spies in the midst. Viola glanced at Julian's pockets and was relieved to see that Kip had been right; Julian was not carrying his Book. Even though the Books could make themselves very small, there was always a telltale outline unless the pockets were loose and baggy. But Julian's pockets were not loose and baggy, and there was no telltale outline.

"Good afternoon, Kip," Julian said genially.

"Good afternoon, Julian," Kip replied in a friendly but reserved voice.

Julian gazed out at the fields. "Looks like things are going well."

"They are," Kip agreed. "There's quite a crop of potatoes this year."

Julian smiled. "Good, good. Our cook is anxious to have fresh potatoes."

Kip said, "I knew she would be. She'll have plenty of barrels tonight."

Thinking of the cooks in the White House, Viola thought, *Cooks are pretty much the same everywhere, even if they're from Mortmain.*

Julian sat down next to Kip, and Viola noticed how tired the blond man looked. There were circles under his eyes, and Julian's weary face suggested that he hadn't slept well for a while. But as Julian looked at the newly dug fields, his body relaxed and some of the fatigue went away.

Julian asked, "How did it go with the horses? I know you were worried about using them. But getting a tractor right now isn't..." Julian paused. "Practical. Cinnial has a lot on his mind. Maybe next year."

Kip answered, "We're doing just fine. Our new worker, Robbie, knows how to handle horses. With the horses and the digger, he dug those potatoes like a knife going through butter."

"Oh?" Julian asked.

Robbie said, "Aye, I'm from the Outer Islands, where there's a lot of farming done with horses."

Julian frowned. "And what are you doing here?"

"Boarding with Kip and Isik while I go to school." Robbie's answer was so smooth that Viola almost believed him. "There's no secondary school on the islands."

Julian's frown went away, and he considered Viola and Wren as Kip introduced them. Viola held her breath, trying to keep her mind neutral. She felt a slight spark from the charm, but rather than energizing her, it helped calm her down.

"And what about you two?" Julian asked Viola and Wren. "You're new here as well, aren't you?"

"We are," came Wren's prompt reply. "A couple of years ago our families moved to Watertown because of the schools, and we go to the same one as Robbie does. We're all on potato recess right now."

"I see," Julian said. "I've heard Watertown has topnotch schools." Pausing, he asked, "What are you reading in class?"

Again, Wren was ready with the answer. "We're studying the women writers of Bellefour of the past hundred years. Right now we're reading Linea Carvella, Bevelyn Tamarant, and Anyes Greenwood."

"Don't forget Bevelyn's sister Amerynth," Viola put in, grateful that they had studied the books in Kip and Isik's home and had even skimmed some of them. Isik, ever the teacher and as keen on reading as he was about music, had given them information about the various writers.

Wren wrinkled her nose. "Not a fan of Amerynth Tamarant. She's too preachy, and she just goes on and on."

Julian grinned. "I'm not a fan either, even though it's been a long time since I read Amerynth Tamarant." He was silent for a few moments. "Way back when I was a young apprentice at the Great Library, we spent a whole year studying the history and literature of Bellefour." Remembering, Julian shook his head. "What about the other writers?"

"I really like Linea Carvella," Wren said truthfully, having finished one of her books the night before. "Especially *Tales from the Edge.*"

Julian nodded. "It's a ripping good story, that's for sure. I remember that much about it. And what about you?" he asked Viola.

"I like Linea Carvella," Viola answered, thinking how odd it was that here they were on this warm fall day, discussing books while inside the Great Library, Cinnial was plotting against Time and Magic. "Who wouldn't? But I like Anyes Greenwood better."

"I can see why," Julian said. "Her writing is cleaner, more direct. She doesn't overwrite. We have a complete collection of all those writers at the Great Library."

"A complete collection of Linea Carvella's novels," Wren said in wonder.

"There's at least forty of them," Julian replied. "She was a prolific writer."

Staring at a point past Julian, Wren sighed. "It must be wonderful to have so many of her books. Our library has a lot, but it doesn't have all of them." She glanced wistfully at Julian and then quickly looked away.

Julian hesitated, then asked, "Would you like to come into the Great Library and see the collection?"

Wren took a deep breath. "I'd love to!"

"Me, too," Viola added.

Julian looked at Robbie. "How about you?"

Robbie blushed a little. "Nay, I'm not much of a reader. I'll stay with the horses."

Julian asked Kip, "Is it all right if I borrow these two for a while?"

"No problem," Kip said. "Anyway, the horses have to rest. Right, Robbie?"

"Right," Robbie answered promptly.

Kip gestured to Viola and Wren. "Besides, they're not used to working in the fields. It won't be a bad thing if they get a little more rest."

With a start, Viola realized Kip was sincere. And even though what Viola wanted most was a chance to see and scope out the inside of the Great Library, she was stung by what Kip had said. "We worked as hard as anyone."

Kip bit his lip and then replied, "That you did."

Even unflappable Wren protested, "We picked a lot of potatoes. We helped fill those barrels for the Great Library."

"I know, I know." Kip put a hand on each of their shoulders. "I'm not saying you didn't work hard. But a longer break will do you good. Go look at books, and when you're done, come back and help us pick those potatoes."

When Viola and Wren continued to look stubborn, Julian said, "Come on, you know you want to look at books. Kip has given you leave, and it would be foolish not to take him up on it. Nowadays, not many get to browse the library's collections." He stared at the Great Library, magnificent even from the back. His voice became soft. "I'm hoping that will change. In time."

Again, Viola made her mind as neutral as she could, and she knew that Wren was doing the same thing.

Viola gave Kip a sideways look that suggested she still wasn't pleased with him. Then her lips quirked into a grin. "All right."

Julian smiled. "There we go." He glanced at Kip, indicating that he understood very well how moody teenagers could be. Nodding a little, Kip glanced upward.

"Are you ready to see more books than you ever have in your life?" Julian asked.

"I sure am," Viola answered. She felt a flutter of excitement and was no longer hurt by what Kip had said.

"Me, too!" Wren said.

"Let's go, then," Julian replied, and the girls followed him to a back entrance into the Great Library.

In its own way, the inside of the Great Library was just as impressive as the outside. Because they had entered from the back there was no grand foyer to greet them, but it wasn't long before they came upon the huge glassed-in atrium in the center of the library.

Wren and Viola paused for a moment to stare through the glass. Viola could see an immense lush green space with ferns and moss and flowers that grew in shade. Even more amazing were the trees that were stories tall, and Viola could tell that one of the trees, the largest, was an oak that had come from an acorn from the Ancient One. She could feel magic radiating from the tree, a steady vital force.

Viola wondered, *Why does Cinnial leave that oak tree in the atrium?* Then the answer came in a rush: Cinnial didn't dare rip out the oak from the center of the Great Library. At least not while Time and Magic were in control. When Chaos was in control, and Magic wasn't as central to the Great Library, then Cinnial would have the tree removed. Until then, even though Cinnial had had no qualms about destroying the Ancient Oak outside in the forest, he didn't dare disturb the magic inside the Great Library.

"So lovely, green, and growing," Julian murmured as he, too, looked through the glass.

"Beautiful," Wren said.

"Very beautiful," Viola agreed.

But the staff and guards who went by didn't seem to share Julian's, Viola's, and Wren's delight with the atrium. Walking quickly, most of the staff and guards glanced nervously at it. One woman shook her head as though she couldn't believe something this green and vital was in the center of a library. Frowning, another woman stared straight ahead and refused to even glance at the atrium. And two guards actually sneered as they passed by the glowing green.

"They don't like it," Viola said in amazement.

Julian shook his head. "They come from a place where growing things is not encouraged." Then his expression brightened. "But, come! Let's go find Linea Carvella and all the others. They're mixed in with the history books. Sydda always felt that novels were a part of history, too, and that you could tell a lot about an era when you read writers from that time, regardless of whether they wrote fiction or nonfiction."

"Right," Viola said. She had never thought about history that way, but she understood Sydda's point of view and even agreed with it. Viola wished her father were here so that she could discuss it with him and hear his law-professor take on it, where he would lay out arguments both for and against Sydda's decision. But her father was not here. Instead, he was in a hospital in Camber, and Viola hoped he was doing as well as the doctor had predicted.

Viola and Wren had to hurry to keep up with Julian's long strides. They went through room after room of books, and each one seemed to have its own mood and personality. Some were bright, some were dark, some were in between. In many, long tables with chairs filled the center of the rooms. Others were more like lounges with sofas and comfortable chairs and side tables that looked as though they had seen more than their fair share of drinks. Some rooms even had fireplaces, and a few had nothing in the center, just a smattering of tables and chairs around the edges.

In all the rooms, different colored ladders went from the floor to the ceiling, and Viola was certain that many of them twitched when they went by. She thought, *How can ladders move on their own?* Then, *But this is the Great Library, where both Time and Magic rule together. Anything can happen here.*

As they went from room to room, Wren's gleeful expression indicated how thrilled she was to be in a place with so many books. Feeling exactly the same way, Viola grabbed Wren's hand and squeezed it. Turning, Julian noted their excitement, and some of his weariness lifted, just as it had when he was outside by the fields.

Stopping, Julian said, "I know. What a magnificent place."

Viola and Wren stopped, too, taking in the books, which seemed to wink at them from the shelves.

Wren sighed with pleasure. "Yes, it is."

Viola asked, "Is the Great Library bigger on the inside than it is on the outside? I mean, I know the library is big, but somehow the inside feels way bigger than it should."

"Yes," Julian answered. "The Great Library is larger on the inside than the outside. Something about being in the center of the universe, I think. But I'm not really sure. None of us really understands how it works. Even Sydda," Julian ended, his voice sad. "And he knew more about the Great Library than any of us did."

"Maybe Magic has something to do with it, too," Viola said cautiously, wanting to get Julian's take on Time and Magic. Viola was all too aware that their success in trapping Cinnial depended on Julian's unwitting help. Without Julian, there would be no access to the Great Library and no chance of trapping Cinnial.

Julian was silent for a few moments. "Yes, and Magic, too," he finally agreed, but his voice was low, and Julian looked around the room as though he was afraid of being overheard. However, except for the three of them, the room was empty as most of the others were. There had been no librarians at any of the desks they went by, and Viola understood that without patrons, there was no need for each room to be staffed. There were guards in the front of the library, but after that there were none in any of the rooms Julian, Viola, and Wren walked through. Apparently, Cinnial was confident that no interlopers would get past the front guards.

Viola thought, *Good to know*. And a red ladder nearby seemed to kick in agreement.

"Blasted ladders," Julian muttered as he started walking, and Viola wondered if the ladders might be allies at some point. The red ladder kicked again just before they left the room.

After a lot more walking they came to the room with Linea Carvella's books. The room was simply labeled *Bellefour, 4,500 to 5,000*. The room was not light, not dark, but somewhere in-between. In the middle, there were plenty of comfortable chairs with round tables beside them for stacking books. As Julian brought them over to the section with Linea Carvella's books, Viola saw that the ladders were definitely twitching.

"Behave!" Julian's voice was sharp, and for the first time Viola got a sense of the dangerous man he had once been and could still be. *Kip was right to warn us about Julian*, Viola thought.

Rebuked, the ladders only twitched a little.

"Are they alive?" Wren asked in amazement.

"Yes," Julian answered. "In a way. Oh, I don't know. But they can kick as hard as a horse, so be careful." Then he muttered,

"There is so much magic here. And we've been away so long..." Eyeing the ladders, Julian stopped and continued in a louder voice, "Anyway, the ladders are temperamental, and they try to get away with as much as they can. Back in the day, the librarians used to keep them in line." Julian shook his finger at one of the green ladders that had been the last to settle down. "And soon there will be librarians again, so watch your step. And if any of you get too boisterous, you know what Cinnial will do to offending ladders."

Wren glanced nervously at the ladders, and so did Viola. As Viola passed a blue ladder to get closer to the shelves, she accidentally brushed against one of its sides, and she felt a warm hum in response.

To Viola's astonishment, the blue ladder communicated with her. Not with actual words, but with a feeling that went from the ladder directly to Viola, and she learned that like the Great Library, the ladders were waiting for the right moment to spring into action.

Until then, they were biding their time.

Not wanting Julian to know what had just happened, Viola quickly moved away from the blue ladder. But Julian wasn't paying attention to Viola and the ladders. Instead, he was staring at the collection of Linea Carvella's books, which took up six long shelves.

"Wow." Wren reached up to put her hand against some of the spines.

"So many," Viola murmured.

"Right?" Julian said. His sharp side had disappeared to be replaced by his teacherly side, and he explained how the Great Library had many copies of each book so that they could be read and discussed in classes the apprentices were obliged to take.

Knowing how much Julian enjoyed leading book discussions, Viola said, "Too bad we're only going to be here for a little while." She sighed. "It would be so great to be able to read one of Linea's books and then talk about it."

Julian's expression was wistful. "Book talk is one of the best kinds of talk, isn't it?"

"Oh, yes," Wren said, taking Viola's cue. "It's my favorite part of reading class."

Julian's hand rested on some books with a purple cover and the title *At Sea*. "How long are you going to be here picking potatoes?"

"A couple of weeks," Viola answered. "Then it's back to school."

Julian said, "Enough time to read and discuss a book, don't you think? Maybe read a few chapters each night and discuss them over lunch? That way, I wouldn't be taking you away from the harvest."

Wren's smile was radiant. "Sounds perfect."

Viola smiled, too. "Sure does."

Julian pulled three books from the shelves. "Well, then. Let's do it. Do you think any of the other gardeners might be interested in a lunch-time discussion?"

Viola didn't want to speak for the others, but she didn't want to exclude them, either. "Maybe."

"Let's bring enough for everyone." Julian set more copies of *At Sea* on a nearby table. "Just in case."

"Great idea," Wren replied, sounding sincere. "Can't wait!"

Again, Viola was struck by the oddness of the situation, how in coming here to trap Cinnial, they had met Julian, who was eager to lead a book discussion, and, as a result, the gardeners were all going to read *At Sea* and discuss it over lunch while the horses rested.

Well, Viola thought, *we are at a library where there are lots and lots of books*. How this would lead to Cinnial's capture, Viola did not know, but she sensed they were on the right track.

Wren gave the briefest of nods, and Viola could tell she felt the same way.

21: CINNIAL'S WEAKNESS

That night, over dinner at Kip and Isik's home, there was a lot to talk about. Around the two tables, food was passed—some kind of roasted poultry, gravy, and vegetables. Bread and butter. The promised cookies were being saved for lunches for the next day, but for dessert there were berry bars made by Isik to go with the night's dinner.

Jay ate the bread and vegetables but not the meat. Lexie, on the other hand, ate everything.

"Jay, are you a vegetarian?" Isik asked.

"Yes." Jay shrugged. "When we were in Elferterre, we saw—really saw—how all things are connected. It's stayed with me."

Lexie made a face. "Me, I'm not ready. Maybe someday, but not now."

Isik nodded. "I see. We'll make sure to have plenty of vegetables with every meal. And none of our soups need to have meat. There are lots of meat substitutes we can use."

Mémère said, "And now that we know, we can plan for that." Then reaching into her pocket, Mémère pulled out a roll of brightly colored cash and put it on the table. Kip and Isik stared in astonishment at it.

"Where did that come from?" Kip asked.

"From Astrid," Mémère answered. "She thought you might need extra money to help feed us. And maybe for other things."

"No," Kip protested. "We're not doing this for money. We're doing it to get the Great Library back."

Mémère pursed her lips. "I know, I know. If it was me, I would feel the same way. But, Kip, you're a gardener, and Isik's a teacher. I don't know how it is here, but where I come from, most gardeners and teachers don't earn that much."

Ever the practical teacher, Isik said in a firm voice, "Kip, we should take the money." He turned to Mémère. "You're right. We're not rich. But we do all right. We have enough, more than enough. However, that money will come in handy. Not just for food, but to buy flutes, whistles, staves, and other instruments for the choir. We're finding that while our voices are strong, when instruments guide our voices, it makes them even stronger. I want everyone to have some kind of instrument. But there are hundreds of us, and there is only so much I can scrounge. Even I have my limits."

Jay said, "Kip, Isik is right. What I saw today was amazing, but we'll need all the help we can get when we go up against Cinnial's forces."

Kip murmured, "Captain Braylon will encourage the guards to fight to the bitter end. He's that kind of guy."

Glancing at Kip, Mémère pushed the money toward Isik. "And keep in mind that what we're doing here doesn't just affect your planet. It affects all the planets. Even little Earth, which is far, far from the center of things."

Kip sighed. "Okay, then. Take the money, Isik. But all of it goes for food and instruments. None for us personally."

Isik leaned over and kissed Kip. "Of course not, you silly thing."

Grinning a little, Kip shook his head, and everyone laughed.

As Isik took the money and set it by his plate, Jay said, "Today was quite the day for us. There Lexie and I were, in front of hundreds of people, helping Isik direct their voices, which came together as a solid force. I've seen a lot of things since I left New York, but this one goes somewhere near the top. I come from a family of musicians, and I always knew that music was powerful, but I never saw it work this directly. Not even in Elferterre."

"It was something else," Mémère agreed. "My voice is not the best, but when it joined with the others, I could feel how strong we all were."

Even Lexie was impressed. "All those voices coming together. It was amazing."

Isik asked Kip, "And how did your day go?"

"It was different," Kip answered.

Isik frowned. "Good or bad?"

"Good," Kip replied. "But weird."

"First the good," Mémère insisted.

Kip took a sip of wine and then another. "We got past the guard at the gate and Captain Braylon with no problems. I thought we would, but it was a relief when we did. Then there was Robbie." Kip stared in admiration at the blond boy, who blushed. "He saved the day. Believe it or not, at the Great Library they have horses and old-fashioned equipment to work in the fields. And Robbie knew just what to do. Because of him, we're more or less on schedule with harvesting the potatoes."

"Well," Robbie said as everyone cheered and clapped, "it's nothing special. I've worked with horses since I was young. That's how harvesting is done in the Forest of Arden."

"Let me tell you," Kip replied. "It was special to us. I don't know how we would have handled those horses without you."

Pleased, Robbie smiled, but he didn't say anything more.

"Okay, then," Isik said. "That's the good. What's the weird?"

"Julian came over to join us during our lunch break, the way he often does," Kip answered.

"And Julian wasn't carrying his Book in his back pocket," Viola said.

"Good!" everyone replied, more or less together.

Kip continued, "Isik, thanks to you, Viola and Wren were ready with their comments about Bellefour's writers, and Julian fell for it. He even brought Viola and Wren into the Great Library."

Jay pushed his dark hair away from his face. "Whoa! On your first day?"

"Yeah," Viola said. "How lucky was that?"

Wren shivered. "It was incredible. Everything that I had ever dreamed of. Room after room of books. I could be at the library for a hundred years, and I still wouldn't know every room."

Lexie asked, "But Julian knew about the Bellefour section?"

"He did," Wren answered. "Isik was right when he told us that all the apprentices at the Great Library have to study Bellefour's history. Even though Julian hasn't been a student for a long time, he remembered some of the books and knew just where to take us."

"The early years always make an impression," Isik said.

Mémère glanced at Kip and then Viola. "So what's the weird part?"

Viola grinned a little. "We're going to read a book called *At Sea*, a few chapters each night, and discuss it during our lunch break."

"We?" Lexie asked.

Viola pointed to Wren and Robbie. "Us three. And the other gardeners."

Kip raised his hand. "Even me! After all, how can you say no to Julian?"

"That is unexpected," Mémère said. "But how is that going to lead you to Cinnial?"

Viola replied, "We don't know. But encouraging Julian seemed like the right thing to do. I'm not sure how it will get us to Cinnial, but I have a feeling it will. And besides, I feel sorry for Julian."

Jay stared in astonishment at Viola. "Really? How come?"

Viola answered slowly, "I know Julian's done a lot of bad things. He captured Maya and brought her to the Great Library."

"Crotte de chien," Mémère muttered.

"Yeah." Viola sighed. "But I can feel and see how sad Julian is, how much he loves books, how much he'd like to be a teacher."

"Me, too," Wren put in.

"So why didn't he become a teacher?" Mémère asked, her voice sharp and angry. "Why did he have to join forces with méchant Cinnial and spread misery throughout the universe? Why did he have to kidnap Maya? Did anyone force him to do this?"

Viola said, "I don't know."

As Mémère regarded Viola, her gaze softened. "Of course you don't. You're twelve years old. Maudit, you shouldn't even be here."

Kip ran his spoon back and forth across his plate. "None of us may ever know why Julian did the things he did. But if Viola and Wren think a book discussion at lunch is a good idea, then we'll have a book discussion at lunch."

"We do," Viola and Wren said together.

Later that night, up in the attic bedroom, Jay and Robbie joined Lexie and Wren to sit on their cots, and Viola asked Earth's Book of Everything, "Was it a good idea to encourage Julian to lead a book discussion?"

217

"Yes," Earth's Book answered. "I can't see where this will all lead." The Book's voice was rueful. "I've told you how it is with us now that we Books have been exiled from the Great Library. But I know that connecting with Julian is the right thing for you to do. He is your way into the Great Library. Without him, it's unlikely you'd gain entrance."

Viola told Wren and Robbie what Earth's Book had said.

"But be careful," Alani's red Book warned. "Despite Julian's love of books, he's still dangerous."

"He's Cinnial's right-hand man," Alexander's black Book said.

"It's amazing that he's even taking time to read books with us," Wren marveled.

Robbie ran his hand over Wren's brown quilt. "Maybe Julian needs a break from running the Great Library. One look at his face, and you can tell what a toll it's taking."

"Oh, cry me a river," Lexie snorted, and nobody argued with her.

But because she'd had her eyes peeled and because she had actually met Julian, Viola tried to imagine what it was like for him to work so closely with Cinnial when his heart really wasn't in taking over the Great Library.

Wren glanced at Lexie. "Julian is pulled between what he really wants to do and his loyalty to Cinnial."

"Whatever," Lexie said. "But it's clear what you should do. Be good students. Read carefully. Ask a lot of questions."

"But don't push it too hard," Jay added. "Don't suck up to Julian. Good teachers always know when someone is doing that."

"Just be your eager selves," Earth's Book said. "That will be enough. As a rule, most teachers like bright students, and Julian is no exception."

"Then there's me." Robbie sighed. "Someone who doesn't like to read that much. I probably won't even know what to say about the book."

Alexander's Book said, "At heart, Julian is a natural teacher, despite all that he's done. Julian wants everyone to do well. It is unfortunate that he decided to follow Cinnial."

"How did that even happen?" Robbie asked after Jay related what the Book had said.

"When they were apprentices, Julian and Cinnial became fast friends," Alexander's Book answered sadly. "Where Cinnial led, Julian followed."

Lexie made a face. "Julian's weak."

"Lexie, you have never met Cinnial," Alani's red Book reprimanded sharply. "You have never felt the strong sway of his personality, how he pulls people to him."

"Have you ever met him?" Lexie asked, clearly offended by the red Book's tone.

"No," the red Book admitted. "But I have access to all the memories of all the Books of Everything. Those memories tell me a lot about Cinnial."

"And there are lots of memories to tell the story of Cinnial," Earth's Book said. "Even before he left in a rage because his Apprentice Book wasn't accepted, Cinnial was well known at the Great Library. Really, from the first day he came, Cinnial made an impression."

The black Book's voice was low. "The Great Library's Book didn't want Cinnial to be accepted as an apprentice. But Sydda overruled the Book."

"You shouldn't have told them that!" the red Book replied. "That's not common knowledge."

There was a long silence after Viola told Robbie and Wren about what Sydda had done. Shaken that Sydda had made such a big mistake, Viola pulled at her blue quilt. If Sydda was capable of that kind of misstep, then what chance did a group of kids have in trapping Cinnial, overcoming his forces, and setting the universe back on track? Viola's charm hummed warmly, comforting her, and she gratefully put her hand on the necklace. On the other cots, Wren, Robbie, Lexie, and Jay were doing the same thing with their charms.

Earth's Book said quietly but firmly, "This information about Cinnial is something the kids should know."

"It makes Sydda and the Great Library look bad," the red Book retorted.

"It is the truth," Earth's Book replied. "And we Books are dedicated to the truth. The kids must know what they're going up against if they're to have any chance of succeeding. Cinnial is a formidable opponent, and there is no mercy in him."

"You are right." The red Book's voice was uncharacteristically humble. "My apologies."

"No apologies are necessary," Earth's Book said. "We Books are facing a situation we have never had to face in all the long history of the Great Library. For the first time, our guidance is very limited, and we must rely on our own judgment. There are bound to be disagreements between us Books. Now perhaps Viola, Wren, and Robbie should settle in bed with their reading assignments. And read carefully. Julian will know if you skim."

After Viola recounted the Book's message, Robbie's expression was glum as he stood. "Aye, that he will. And I bet even though I'm the one who will study the hardest, it won't seem like it."

But Robbie was wrong. Somehow, the story of Skye Mousseron, who came from inland Bellefour but longed to travel the seas, appealed to Robbie's sense of adventure. He was moved by Skye's conflict of whether to stay home with family or go out into the world and find her own way.

Therefore, the next day, after lunch at the Great Library, under the shade of the evergreens by the edge of the potato fields, when Julian asked what the gardeners thought about Skye Mousseron, Robbie was the first to raise his hand.

Julian smiled. "Robbie, you don't have to raise your hand. This is a book discussion, not a classroom."

Robbie leaned forward eagerly. "Yes, sir."

"Well, go on. Tell us what you think."

Robbie launched into his take. "That Skye Mousseron is quite the girl. Her family doesn't want her to leave, and they do everything possible to hold her back. Her sister steals Skye's pouch of money. Skye's mother keeps telling her that maybe next year she can become a sailor but that this year they need her on the farm. Her father doesn't even think that girls should go off on their own. But Skye prevails, and away she goes."

Julian agreed. "She does indeed. Like many heroes and heroines, Skye is plucky and brave."

"*At Sea* is set in the past when things were just beginning to change," Kip said. "Bellefour is not like that now. Nowadays, most fathers encourage girls to go off on their own."

"Thank goodness," replied Billen, a lean and tall man.

"Things have improved," Julian acknowledged. "In *At Sea*, Linea Carvella is exploring how the changing times affect the various characters in the book. Not only Skye but her family as well."

Addea, a slight woman, frowned. "Even so, how rude and self-ish Skye is. Clearly, her parents need her help, and all Skye can do is think about having adventures at sea. She hardly cares about her parents at all."

Julian tilted his head as he considered Addea. "Do you think Skye should have sacrificed her own happiness to stay on the farm with her parents?"

"Yes," Addea answered. "That was her duty. By leaving, she put her parents in a terrible situation. Without Skye, they could barely manage the farm, and they didn't have enough money to hire help."

"No," Robbie argued. "Skye had a right to choose her own course. After all, her parents can't have her forever, and they needed to learn to manage without her. Sooner or later, Skye was going to leave, even if it was to start a family. It was time for her parents to let go."

And back and forth the conversation went, with some on Robbie's side and others on Addea's. With a light but sure touch, Julian guided the discussion, never letting it get too heated but allowing it to stay lively. Neither Viola nor Wren had much of a chance to share what they thought of *At Sea* and Skye Mousseron.

That's some impression we're making, Viola thought a little glumly. *Julian's probably going to forget all about Wren and me.*

But Julian did not forget about Viola and Wren. "You two have been quiet. What do you think?"

"I can see both sides," Viola said, not wanting to reveal too much about herself but wanting to give a heartfelt response. "It can be hard choosing between what your family wants and what you want to do. Skye was brave to make that decision."

Julian considered Viola. "Have you ever had to choose between what your family wants and what you want?"

Careful, careful, Viola thought as Julian stared intently at her. Viola knew she needed to tell some of the truth but not all of it. "I have," she admitted. "My parents want me to study law when I go to university. The way they did. But I already know I don't want to do that. Somehow I can feel that it isn't right for me."

"Have you told them yet?" Julian asked, and Viola could feel his sympathy for her. After all, Julian knew a thing or two about making the wrong decision.

"No, but I will," Viola answered in a firm voice.

Julian looked at Wren. "What about you?"

Wren rubbed her face. "I can see both sides, too. But how will Skye feel if she goes off and something bad happens to her parents? Won't she feel guilty?"

Julian's voice was gentle. "That remains to be seen, doesn't it?"

"Aye," Robbie said. "Still, I think Skye is right to go. When I left the Forest of…" Robbie stopped, putting his hand on his chest, and he had a pained expression as though he had gotten a sharp jab.

From his charm, Viola thought. She sat very still, knowing what a dangerous moment this was. Beside her, Wren was doing the same thing, waiting for Robbie to make a terrible slip. Sitting still, Kip stared at the potato fields.

But Julian was relaxed, not on guard. "The Forest of what?" he asked curiously but without suspicion.

However, before Robbie had to come up with some fictional forest on the Outer Islands, they all felt a presence. Everyone turned, and a man, darkly beautiful, was coming their way. He was trailed by two guards, and the ground seemed to tip in the man's direction.

Cinnial, Viola thought, and as she felt the weight of his charisma, it seemed as though she could hardly breathe. Viola was grateful for the charm's warm steadying presence, invisible to everyone but her.

All the gardeners, including Viola, Wren, and Robbie, leaped to their feet. Even Julian stood, but he didn't scramble the way the others did.

Cinnial took everything in—the gardeners, the books, the barrels of potatoes by the edge of the field, and finally, Julian, where his gaze stayed the longest.

"So here you are, Julian," Cinnial said, his voice smooth yet compelling. "I came down to the dining room to have lunch with you, and where do I find you? With the gardeners, having a book discussion."

Julian grinned a little. "You know how I am."

To Viola's amazement, Cinnial actually grinned back. "I do know how you are. What are you all reading?"

Julian held up the purple book. "*At Sea* by Linea Carvella."

"I remember that book," Cinnial said. "A girl defies her parents and goes to sea."

"That's the one," Julian replied.

Cinnial shrugged. "An exciting but silly story."

Julian patted the book. "There's more to it than you might think."

Cinnial shrugged again, but Viola could tell that Cinnial was not upset with Julian.

"Are you done with your discussion for the day?" Cinnial asked.

"We are," Julian answered, tucking the book under his arm. He asked the gardeners, "Three more chapters for tomorrow?"

Too afraid to speak, everyone just nodded.

"Good." Julian joined Cinnial. "If the weather allows, see you all tomorrow."

Leaning toward each other, Cinnial and Julian walked back to the Great Library, and behind them, the guards followed. In Cinnial's back pocket was the outline of a book, but Julian's back pocket was flat.

As Viola watched them go, she finally understood Cinnial's weakness—it was his affection for Julian. Because of this affection, Cinnial cut Julian more slack than he did with anyone else.

Beside her, Wren nodded, and Viola knew that she had come to the same conclusion.

Now the great trick was how to work it to their advantage.

22: MIXED FEELINGS

That night at dinner, Viola and Wren told everyone what they had concluded about Julian and Cinnial.

Kip said ruefully, "I should have figured that out before now."

"How?" Isik asked. "Have you ever seen the two of them together?"

Kip shook his head. "Not really. Only once or twice from a distance. I never got to see them interact up close."

Wren sat still and straight. "It was quite the thing to see Cinnial in person. Everything and everyone just bends toward him."

"I bet I wouldn't," Lexie retorted, and the blonde girl looked so imperious and beautiful that Viola could picture her not being swayed by Cinnial.

"Nay, Lexie," Robbie said. "Don't think that. Not many are like Cinnial. I bet not even that elf Lillian that you told us about."

With her finger, Lexie traced the edge of her plate. "Well, with any luck, I'll never get a chance to find out. While you're trapping Cinnial, I'll be with the choir, using my voice as a weapon to stop the guards."

"What about Cinnial's and Julian's Books?" Isik asked.

"Cinnial had his, but Julian didn't," Viola answered.

"Good," Isik said, clearly relieved. "The Books still haven't noticed you. Let's hope it stays that way."

Kip took Isik's hand. "We're just the gardeners. Hardly anyone thinks of us. Cinnial has bigger fish to fry."

Isik smiled. "Quite the metaphor."

As soon as the appreciation for Kip's wordplay died down, Mémère asked, "How are we going to coordinate all of this? We need to be ready with our voices as soon as Viola traps Cinnial with the lock."

"And we only have until the end of next week, when potato recess ends," Kip said. "After that, Viola, Wren, and Robbie won't be going to the Great Library anymore. Will the choir be ready?"

"It will have to be," Isik replied. "We're practicing a lot every day, and we're all improving. I have a better sense about how to direct the voices, and they can go quite a ways now. We've practiced moving objects, then each other."

"That was weird," Lexie said. "I've never been lifted by a voice."

Jay laughed. "You should have heard her squeal."

Lexie turned to Jay. "You squealed louder."

"I don't think so. I'm surprised you didn't break the sound barrier."

Giving Jay and Lexie a stern look, Isik cleared his throat. "Some people are bringing in their own hand instruments. I've ordered a lot with the money that Astrid gave us. By the middle of next week, everyone should have an instrument."

"Then we need to plan for the end of next week," Viola said. "Kip, do you know if Julian and Cinnial meet on a regular schedule sometime in the day?"

"Every morning in Cinnial's office," Kip answered. "When I first started working at the Great Library, I spent time in the atrium just so I could keep an eye on things. Each day at around 10:00, Cinnial and a couple of guards would come out of the elevator that's across from the atrium, march past, and head down the hall. After an hour or so, Cinnial and his guards would march by the atrium back to the elevator. I suspected he was meeting with Julian. One day, to check it out, I asked to have a meeting with Julian at 10:30, but the guards at the front desk told me Julian was unavailable. When I tried again the next day, I was told the same thing. I didn't ask again because I didn't want the guards to get suspicious."

"Sounds like it's a regular meeting," Mémère said.

"It does," Viola agreed. "Now how do we get into the Great Library right before Cinnial meets with Julian?"

"We'll come with a book," Wren replied. "At 9:30 on the last day of potato harvest, you, me, and Robbie will bring a gift to

Julian—a book—to thank him for leading the book discussion." Wren's expression was wistful. "Actually, it's been pretty fun. Julian is a good teacher and deserves a present."

"Great idea," Viola said. "And this week, we can ask Julian to give us permission to go to the reading room by ourselves to look at books. I bet he'll agree. If he does, then the guards will let us come and go on our own. That way, when we bring Julian his present, the guards will be used to seeing us there."

Mémère tapped the table. "And then what? How will you trap Cinnial without anyone noticing?"

Kip thought for a moment. "The elevator across from the atrium is in a hallway off the grand foyer. While Cinnial has his own guards, I've never seen other guards in that hallway, which is out of sight from the main reading room, where guards are posted at the desk."

"And what about Cinnial's guards?" Mémère asked. "They're not just going to stand by while Viola points the lock at Cinnial."

"Yeah," Jay agreed. "They'll think it's weird and go after her."

Robbie said, "I'll take care of the guards. After Humphrey sent his men to Greendale, the adults in the Forest of Arden decided we all needed to learn how to defend ourselves. Just in case. So from the time we're ten or so, we're trained in defense. It's an actual class in school now."

Wren raised her hand. "Me, too. At school, we take classes in self-defense so that if we ever leave the safety of our country, we can protect ourselves. I'll help Robbie with the guards." Wren smiled shyly. "I was at the top of my self-defense class. I even beat Isold. Had him pinned right to the ground."

Viola stared in admiration at Wren. "Another reason why I'm glad I picked you."

Mémère sighed. "Bon. Well, not really. Will the three of them just be able to wait in the hallway for Cinnial until he comes out of the elevator? Won't that look suspicious if someone does happen to walk by and look down the hall?"

Kip frowned. "It would." There was a long silence as everyone thought about this. Finally Kip said, "I'll leave my favorite clippers in the atrium. After Viola, Wren, and Robbie have given Julian his book, they can tell the guards at the desk that they have to go to the atrium to get my clippers, and they can wait there. In the atrium there's a door that leads right to the hallway with the elevator."

Robbie nodded. "Perfect! While Viola traps Cinnial, Wren and I can take care of the guards and stow them in the atrium. Kip, you'll leave some rope for us, too?" Kip nodded. "Good. Then we'll make our getaway with no one being the wiser."

"Well," Isik replied, "it seems like we have a plan."

"A lot has to go right," Mémère said slowly. "For this plan to work."

"Yeah," Kip agreed. "And on top of everything else, we also have to hope that the weather holds. It can be unpredictable this time of year."

The weather did hold. Day after day the sun shined, warm but not too hot. After the first week, Captain Braylon decided he no longer had to meet the gardeners outside the Great Library, and they could head right to the gardens without stopping. Potatoes were picked, and by the beginning of the second week, Viola and Wren found their rhythm. While they were tired each night, their bodies were not as sore. Still, they were grateful for their lunch-time break and their book discussion of *At Sea*. The gardeners continued to have mixed feelings about Skye and whether she should have stayed home to help her struggling family who had more bad luck than any family Viola had ever known. Julian encouraged the gardeners to express themselves freely, and gradually everyone became less guarded with him.

"Skye's family sure makes a lot of stupid choices," a wiry man named Breard said. "Skye's father never should have invested in more cows when he could barely take care of the ones he had."

Anner, a tall thin woman, protested, "If there had been some kind of social safety net, then Skye's family wouldn't have fallen so low."

"Do you think that's the point?" Julian asked.

"Maybe," Anner replied. "At least partly."

"I agree," Julian said. "Still, it seems to me that Carvella is suggesting that individual choices matter, too." Staring at the fields, he was silent for a few moments. "That's how it is with good books. There's no definitive take. We, as readers, have our own experiences and that shapes our reactions to the story."

Everyone agreed, and the group felt so close and comfortable that Viola decided now was the time to ask about taking afternoon breaks in the Great Library.

Julian was silent as he considered the request.

"Just in the front," Viola added hastily. "Not in the back where you took us to see Linea Carvella's books. There are plenty of books in the front reading room." She looked down at her dusty overalls. "And we'll only sit on wooden chairs so we won't get anything dirty."

Wren smiled pleadingly at Julian. "It would be such a treat for us. Next week, we'll be back at school, and who knows when we'll get a chance to come back to the Great Library."

"Why not?" he finally said. "The foyer and the front reading room are well guarded." With a slight twinkle in his eyes, Julian regarded the two girls. "But you'll have to promise me you won't try to steal any books."

Wren's expression was luminous. "Oh, thank you! And of course we won't steal any books."

"No, we won't," Viola said. "Thank you so much." Viola hesitated then asked. "Nobody will mind?" Even though Viola was being vague, both Wren and Julian knew she was referring to Cinnial.

Julian shook his head. "No," he answered in a low voice. "He spends most of his time in the lab and leaves everything else up to me. If I say it's okay for you to spend some time in the front reading room, then it's okay. The guards know that, too, and I'll have a word with them."

"Thank you, thank you," Viola and Wren said again.

Julian was true to his word. The next afternoon, when the bright fall day was at its hottest, Viola and Wren entered the library from the front, where the guards could see them. Trying not to gape, Viola and Wren walked through the grand foyer with its mosaic ceiling, and the guards standing by the entrance nodded at them. At the desk in the front reading room, the guards also nodded and left Viola and Wren alone to look at books. If the gravity of their plans hadn't been so great, Viola and Wren would have enjoyed their afternoon breaks as they browsed through the books in the reading room. They even stayed a little longer than they should, knowing Kip wouldn't mind.

Every so often, as they gathered a few books and settled on wooden chairs, Viola and Wren would become immersed in their reading and forget about the guards. But then a cough or a scraping of a chair would remind them why they were there. Startled, the girls would look up at the guards and then glance at each other.

When Viola mentioned this at dinner one night, Isik said, "Never forget why you are in the reading room at the Great Library. One slip, and it could be over for all of us."

Robbie sadly shook his head. "Aye, do you remember how once during book group I almost said I was from the Forest of Arden, which Julian knows about because of the time he spent in Caxton?"

"I remember," Kip answered, his voice grim.

Robbie said, "If Cinnial hadn't come just then, the cat would have been out of the bag, and then who knows what would have happened."

"Whoever would have thought that Cinnial would bring us some luck?" Isik asked.

Shivering, Viola knew Isik was right, and Mémère, who was sitting beside her, patted Viola on the shoulder.

Then there was the matter of the book, the thank-you gift to give to Julian. There were two bookshops within walking distance of Kip and Isik's home, and on several nights they were open late enough for Viola, Wren, and Robbie to visit when they came back from working in the fields. But none of the books in the two stores seemed quite right for Julian, and with only one day to go before the end of potato recess, they still hadn't found what they were looking for.

"It has to be special," Robbie said, and there was a note of sadness in his voice as they walked the narrow streets back to Kip and Isik's home.

Viola and Wren were on either side of Robbie, and knowing how conflicted he felt, they both leaned against him. On the one hand, they all liked Julian and the way he respected everyone in the group, no matter the age. Without a doubt, Viola knew that if Julian taught at her school, he would be a favorite teacher, one all the students would clamor to have. On the other hand, Julian was Cinnial's assistant, the one who had helped take over the Great Library, the one who was responsible for the day-to-day running of the place. Owing to Julian's hard work in making sure that everything at the Great Library went smoothly, Cinnial and his Book could focus on defeating Time and Magic.

As they rounded the corner to Kip and Isik's house, Robbie shook his head. "Never knew I'd come to like Julian so much. It's going to be hard."

229

"Right?" Wren sighed. "We didn't expect that, did we?"

"No, we didn't." Viola thought about how complicated it all was. Her father, who always seemed good and confident, had done a terrible thing in the Forest of Arden.

Viola's thoughts turned back to Julian, who had done so many bad things that Earth's Book didn't even want to list them all for Viola when she had asked about them. Instead, there had been a vague explanation of how in his rage, Julian had murdered innocent people. But after spending time with Julian, Viola knew he was not only a killer. Julian was also a teacher who loved books and his students.

"Julian's such a good teacher. That has to count for something, doesn't it?" Viola asked.

"I don't know," Robbie replied.

"Me, neither," Wren said.

In silence, they walked the rest of the way home.

Isik, Kip, Mémère, Jay, and Lexie were sitting in the living room as they drank their evening mugs of tea. Guitars leaned against Jay's and Lexie's chairs, and it was clear to Viola that there had been music while they were gone and that there would probably be more music when tea was finished.

As Viola, Wren, and Robbie brought chairs from the dining room to the living room, Isik made tea for them, and they all settled in together.

"Any luck finding a book?" Isik asked.

Viola shook her head. "No, nothing seemed exactly right for him."

Mémère frowned. "You're taking an awful lot of time finding the right book. You like this Julian, don't you?"

"Yeah," Viola answered slowly.

"Me, too," added Wren.

"Same here," Robbie said.

"Julian kidnapped Maya," Mémère sternly reminded them.

"I know, I know," Viola said. "Mémère, we didn't plan to like Julian. It just kind of happened."

"I like him, too," Kip admitted, and Mémère and Isik stared in amazement at him. Kip shrugged. "You've never met Julian. If you did, you might like him, too."

"Never," Mémère protested fiercely. "That man made my Maya suffer."

"Mémère's right," Jay agreed. "Because Julian brought Maya to Cinnial, she was sent to the Office, where Bigly tortured her. If she hadn't escaped..." Jay didn't have to finish the sentence. Everyone had heard the story and knew what would have happened if Maya hadn't escaped.

Putting her hands over her eyes, Mémère turned her head, and Viola knew she was crying.

"I'm sorry, Mémère," Viola said in a small voice.

Mémère nodded but didn't say anything.

To everyone's surprise, it was Lexie who came to Julian's defense, but in a roundabout way. For once the brash girl's voice was tender. "Mémère, Maya would have forgiven him. I know she would have. I've never seen her hold a grudge. Even with me."

Mémère sniffed. "I know. Maya has a big heart. She always has. But, Lexie, why would Maya hold a grudge against you?"

Lexie's voice was low. "In Elferterre, I caused a lot of trouble."

"You were a pain," Jay said, and he wasn't smiling.

Lexie sighed. "I know. I didn't listen to Hanss when he told me not to leave his little clearing, which he had guarded with magic. There was a stream just beyond the clearing, and I wanted to wash up. I thought Hanss was just a stupid cat who didn't know much." Lexie shook her head. "I sure was wrong. At the stream, the ogres captured me, and I had to be rescued. That really pissed the ogres off, and they were waiting for us when we came back into the forest to go home. Because of me, the ogres were on high alert."

Nobody said anything, and Jay set his mug down on the table beside his chair. "Lexie is right. The ogres captured her and she had to be rescued and the ogres were a little irritated by this. Okay, a lot irritated. But Maya, when she was a dragonfly, might have buzzed Novok, one of the ogres who captured Lexie. And Maya might have stuck her tongue out at Novok when we left the forest, and he couldn't follow because he was trapped there by elf magic."

Even though Viola hadn't known Maya for very long, she could picture Maya buzzing an ogre. She thought about how Maya had boldly stolen Julian's Apprentice Book from Humphrey. As Viola remembered Maya's pluck and impishness, she laughed. She couldn't help it.

For a few moments, everyone just stared at Viola, who put a hand over her mouth to still her laughter.

Then Mémère grinned. "That's my Maya."

"She's something else," Lexie said, her eyes shining.

231

Isik smiled. "I've had students like her. Always memorable."

Wren, Robbie, and Kip also smiled but didn't say anything.

Jay put his hand on the guitar next to his chair. "And, Mémère, Lexie is right. Maya would have forgiven Julian."

Mémère sighed. "I know. But my heart's not as big as hers is. I can't forgive Julian. He's done too much."

Isik stood. "I understand. I'd feel the same way if I were in your shoes. But Viola, Wren, and Robbie have a point in wanting to pick just the right book for Julian. It will help throw him even more off guard. We can hope that Julian will be so pleased with the present that he'll never suspect that in Viola's pocket is a lock that will trap Cinnial. With any luck the three of them will be out of the Great Library with the lock before Julian knows anything has happened." Isik stared coolly at Robbie and Wren. "But a lot will depend on you two and how quickly and quietly you can take care of the guards."

"You can count on us," Robbie said in a brisk voice. "We'll take care of the guards. A hard hand chop to the neck should take them down quickly and quietly. Wren, do you know how to do that?"

Wren grinned. "I do. Then after we tie them up, we'll just breeze out and make our way back to the gardens."

Kip muttered, "Let's hope so."

Isik went to a little bookshelf with glass doors. "The choir will be on the beach by the bay. A little past 10:00, some of the choir will start singing and immobilize the guard at the gate and folks in the village. The rest of the choir will head over to the Great Library, where they'll take care of the guards and the staff. I'm not sure how long we'll be able to hold them. You gardeners will have to spring into action right away."

"We'll be ready," Kip replied. "There's plenty of rope in the shed, and we'll bring some of our own. We can disarm the guards and tie up as much of the staff as we can."

"Earth's Book of Everything will let Astrid know when the choir has released their voices," Viola said. "Then she and the other librarians will come back to help take over the Great Library."

Wren clapped her hands. "And that will be that."

"We can only hope," Mémère murmured.

Isik opened one of the glass doors and took a book from the shelf. "We've planned as well as we can. With any luck, Chance will be on our side." Somewhat reluctantly, Isik handed a purple-covered book to Viola.

Viola stared at the book. "*At Sea*? But there are plenty of copies of that at the Great Library."

"Look inside," Isik said.

Wren and Robbie crowded around Viola as she opened the book. Inside, on the first page, there was an inscription in a flowing script. Viola read, "*From the private library of Linea Carvella. To Bettina Messun, one of my dearest friends. Without your encouragement, I wouldn't be the writer I am today.*" Viola looked at Isik. "Who was Bettina Messun?"

"My great-grandmother," Isik answered. "And this was her house. I hate giving away this special edition of *At Sea*. But Julian sure will be impressed. This book is worth a lot of money."

"And how would three kids be able to afford this special edition?" Viola asked.

Isik sat down. "Tell him you got it at a rummage sale in town. Stuff like that happens all the time around here. Folks pick up something for a song and then find out it's worth a lot of money. There's even a show that features people and their finds."

Viola laughed. "We have a show like that on Earth. My mother and I watch it all the time."

"Okay, then." Isik smiled. "You know how it works."

"I do," Viola replied. "Thank you, Isik. This is the perfect present for Julian. It will mean a lot to him."

"He'll get to enjoy it for a few minutes before all hell breaks loose," Jay said.

"Yeah," Viola replied softly.

Mémère's voice was firm. "Just remember what he did to Maya and to other people."

Viola sighed. "I will."

But she knew it still wouldn't be easy.

23: ON THE TOWN

Port Isleros was both like every port city Maya had ever been to and different from any port city she had ever seen. Its large harbor had docks and boats from all corners of Elferterre, and there were the usual bars, restaurants, and hotels to cater to the crowds that came to the port. But most of the buildings gleamed white, the streets were clean, and there was a sense of order that at the same time was balanced with a feeling of freedom.

Port Isleros was an island nation with its own laws and leaders. As Finneas had once told Maya, because Port Isleros was independent, it was a place where folks and creatures of all classes and types could mingle together. Ancient grudges, while not forgotten, were usually pushed to one side, a place where Clarin and Rhye, from two opposing houses, could meet and fall in love and make a life together.

Maya thought of this as she walked beside Braird on a street that had grenogs, elves, humans, castors, and other creatures of all shapes and colors. At an outdoor café, there were even some imps seated around two tables pushed together. Remembering Brosk, the imp who had stabbed her, Maya shivered as she looked at them, but the imps did not pay any attention to her. They were unconcerned about a small human on the town with an elf, a grenog, two castors, and a corbeau. Instead, they were focused on their steaming plates of food and each other.

When they had passed the imps, Braird said, "Watch out for those guys. They might look relaxed right now, but they can turn in a flash."

"Mostly they behave themselves in Port Isleros," Larz added. "But you never know."

Alie shuddered. "I don't trust them one bit."

"Neither do I," Maya said.

"Let's not talk about imps." Larz turned to the group. "To Lilywater's?"

"Yes," came the answer.

As Larz sped down the street, and they all followed, Maya asked Braird, "Ali's cousin Gustone owns Lilywater's?"

Braird took her hand. "He does. It's a place that has good food, a good vibe, and good music."

Maya smiled at Braird. "Sounds like a fun place."

"It is." Then he hesitated. "Just don't drink too much tonight."

Annoyed, Maya pulled her hand away. "I only did that once."

Braird grinned. "True, but it was memorable."

"And you've never had too much to drink?"

Braird's grin became broader. "Oh, I might have. Once or twice."

Larz, whose hearing was keen, called over his shoulder, "More than once or twice, buddy. Do you remember when I had to carry you home from that place in Dalvron?"

"I do. And I also remember when you fell down the stairs in Omri," Braird retorted.

Laughing loudly, Larz stopped. "That was a time, wasn't it? Took all four of you to help me up."

"You big oaf," Braird replied, but his tone was not sharp, and Maya could see how much affection there was between the outgoing elf and the reserved corbeau even though they squabbled from time to time.

Alie put her hand on Maya's arm. "At times, we've all had too much to drink. But we've learned our limits, and we stick with them. You're small, and our drinks are strong. One or two is probably enough for you."

Maya nodded seriously. "Right." There was no way she wanted to feel the way she did after that first night on the upper deck of *The Resolute*.

Within walking distance of the captain's house, Lilywater's was on a street with many bars and restaurants. They passed a place called It Figures, and when Maya looked in, she saw the room was filled with wooden figureheads who had left their ships and were out for a night on the town. Chantay sat at a table with three other figureheads, and she waved to Maya and the crew as they walked by. Maya and the crew waved back.

Three bars down from It Figures, they came to a bar that had a big sign with a pale pink waterlily shimmering in an expanse of blue. The floating water lily seemed to call to her, inviting her in.

"Beautiful," Maya murmured.

Alie flushed with pleasure. "It's a special place."

"Lilywater's really fills up at night," Takis replied.

Proko said, "That's why we came here early. So there would be a big table for all of us."

Both castors were dressed in baggy trousers instead of their usual overalls—red for Proko and blue for Takis, and they wore lacy tunics with them. To Maya, they looked utterly charming.

Braird regarded Maya. "You don't look so bad yourself."

"Thanks." Maya smoothed her new blue tunic with stars and moons, provided by a big chest at the captain's house, where she was staying. Maya hadn't asked for anything specifically. But she was delighted when the chest gave her a tunic and skirt that reminded her of the witch Myranda who had peeled Will's, Jay's, and Lexie's eyes, who had tempted Maya with the offer of becoming an apprentice, an offer that Maya had reluctantly turned down.

The captain had given Maya two silver barrettes, a moon and a star, to go with her tunic, and they gleamed in her blonde curls. "But you don't have to worry," he had assured her. "They are not relics."

"Good," Maya had replied, thinking of the three relics—Eloise, Aiken, and Orlaith—who were going to stay home with Finneas while she went out with her friends. For this night, Maya didn't want to have the three little guardians monitoring her behavior.

However, of them all, Alie was the one who was the most elegant. She wore a simple black dress and a freshwater pearl necklace, and when they walked into Lilywater's, a voice called out, "Alie, look at you! Are you finally going to sing here?"

A tall grenog, also dressed in black, came over to greet them, and Alie smiled at him. "I am."

He put a hand on her shoulder. "Finally! After all these years. What changed your mind?"

For a moment, nobody said anything as they thought back to all that had happened during the past week. Alie squeezed Gustone's arm. "Somehow, I found my courage."

Looking around, Gustone said in a low voice, "News of what happened on board *The Resolute* has spread all through Port Isleros. It's not every day that an elf goes on trial. Not even here."

"We've had quite a time," Alie said.

Gustone patted her shoulder. "Some morning over tea and algae toast, you can tell me about it. But for now, come in. Glad you're early. There's a big table in the corner, and we can get you something to eat and drink before the place fills up."

Maya pulled a small pouch of coins from her pocket and handed it to Gustone. "Tonight is on the captain as a thank you for all that we've done for him. The captain said that if this doesn't cover it, let him know."

Gustone smiled broadly. "That was good of him. So order what you want. Captain Blythewood is paying."

Gustone left, and they made their way to the table. "That was very generous of the captain," Larz said as they sat down.

"He is reunited with his daughter," Alie replied. "And that means everything to him."

With a pang, Maya thought of her own father, so far away from her even when she was home in New York City. He loved her, Maya was sure of it, but she also knew that her father would always put himself first. That's the way he was, and she had to accept the fact that he was not going to change, not even for his only child.

Braird said in a soft voice, "Try not to think about him tonight. Let's just eat and drink and listen to music. And dance."

Maya took his hand. "All right."

Food was ordered, and plates with food were soon heaped on the table. Maya had a few bites of everything, including crispy fried vegetables and a tangy dipping sauce; flat bread with some kind of smooth spread to go with it; and noodles in a brown sauce. Bottles of the same clear drink Maya had had on *The Resolute* were brought to the table, and following Alie's advice, Maya paced herself, making one drink last a long time.

As they ate, talked, and laughed, Lilywater's filled up. Despite its cool soothing tones, the restaurant was large enough for many tables, a dance floor, and a stage for musicians and singers. Midevening, three musicians—a piano player, a guitar player, and a drummer—went onto the stage, and Gustone beckoned to Alie. Without hesitating, the grenog joined the musicians on stage, and Larz whistled and clapped so loudly that Maya laughed, clapping along with him and the others.

Alie conferred with the musicians, and the music began, pulling at everyone in the restaurant. Soon the dance floor was full. Maya, Braird, Larz, Proko, and Takis started out dancing in a group, but it wasn't long before Maya was dancing only with Braird, and nobody else in the crowded room seemed to matter at all. Maya felt as though she were surrounded by feathers, tender and soft, and she leaned into them. But when she looked at Braird, he was not in bird form, and he held her with hands, not wings.

When the music became slow and a little sad, Braird leaned down and kissed her. Sighing, Maya felt the music swirl around them as Braird kissed her again and again.

Then a voice called out sharply. "Maya!"

Maya knew that voice, but it wasn't one she expected to hear in Lilywater's. Pulling away from Braird, Maya looked frantically around the dance floor, and on the edge, staring at her with hurt astonishment, was Will. A tall elf was with him, and he was shaking his head.

"Will," Maya whispered. "Oh, no!"

"The boy from Earth who came with you to Elferterre?" Braird asked.

"Yes," Maya said, looking from Braird to Will.

Jaw clenched, Will bolted from Lilywater's, and the tall elf ran after him.

"I have to talk to Will," Maya told Braird.

"I know," came the resigned answer.

Dodging the dancers, Maya ran as fast as she could outside. Will and the elf, whom Maya now recognized as Thirret from The Other Green Door, were standing on the sidewalk not far away, and Hanss was sitting next to them. Will had his arm across his face, and Thirret, with a hand on Will's shoulder, leaned toward him, speaking earnestly. Maya had a horrible sick feeling in her stomach, made stronger by the waves of sorrow that were coming from Will.

"Will!" Maya called. "Will!"

Lowering his arm, Will gave Maya a betrayed, reproachful look, which made her feel even worse. What could she say? Out of sight, out of mind as her mémère often noted tartly about Maya's father? Maya knew that in many ways she was like her father. Was she like him in this way, too, unfaithful to the ones she loved? Swallowing, Maya's chest felt tight as she considered this.

Thirret sighed, and Maya could tell he wished he were not in the middle of this teenage love triangle. Maya couldn't blame him. She wished she weren't in the middle of it either, even though it was her fault for creating it.

"Come here, Maya," Thirret said, and Maya walked over to them.

Hanss shook his head. "Well, at least Maya's in Port Isleros and not out to sea. I didn't relish chartering a boat and going after her. I hate being on water."

Will stared coolly at Maya. "She's here, all right."

Thirret glanced around. Not far from them was a café with an outside patio, and at the table closest to them, a group of grenogs jumped up and left as though they had suddenly remembered that they were supposed to be somewhere else.

"There," Thirret said with satisfaction. "Now we have some-place to sit and talk."

Somberly, they went to the table and sat down. Their server, a castor, took their order and brought back a huge carafe of elf wine, clear but with a slight shimmer. Thirret poured drinks for everyone but Hanss, who sat regally on a chair between the elf and Will.

As Thirret and Will took a long drink, Maya just sat and stared at hers.

She looked up. "Will, I'm sorry."

"Sorry that you got caught," Will replied, his voice bitter.

"Will," Thirret said, "that's only part of the truth. Maya's sorry she hurt you. I can feel it, and I bet you can, too."

Will took another sip of his wine. "Maybe."

"Thirret is right," Maya replied. "I didn't mean to hurt you, Will. What happened between me and Braird was...unexpected."

"Unexpected, huh?" Will asked roughly.

"Yes," Maya answered. "At first I didn't like Braird at all. He can be very rude." Then Maya blushed. "And sometimes I don't think before I act. This got on his nerves." Thirret covered his mouth with his hand, and Maya could see he was trying not to smile. She shrugged ruefully. "Well, it's true. I might as well admit it."

"Yeah, I remember." Will's tone was still cool.

"Right," Thirret said. "Well, here we are. In Port Isleros. In Elferterre. At a café drinking elven wine, which, by the way, tastes far better than anything I've drunk on Earth. In the meantime, in your universe, things are going to hell in a handbasket as you humans like to say. With Lexie's and Jay's help, Viola has gotten together a team to go to the Great Library to defeat Cinnial."

In shock, Maya stared at Thirret. "Viola? But she's only twelve. And she hasn't had her eyes peeled. Has she?"

"She has," Thirret answered. "I learned about it right before Will and I left Earth to come to Elferterre. And as for Viola being twelve, well, I've heard she's quite mature for her age."

Flushing, Maya realized Thirret's implication—even though Viola was younger than Maya, their maturity levels weren't all that different.

Maya was about to protest when Hanss came to her defense. "Thirret, you're not being fair. Maya went over the cliff with that ogre so that Will, Lexie, and Jay could bring the key and lock to the Other Side. And that key set you and your family free. I'm sure Maya thought she was going to be killed."

Thirret inclined his head toward Maya. "Hanss is right. I'm sorry. By the way, how did you survive? Hanss couldn't find either you or the ogre when he finally made it down the cliff to search for you. He figured the other ogres had hauled you both away. But Will was certain you had made it. And when we got to Elferterre with the tracker relic Father gave me, sure enough, we saw your blip."

"All the way out to sea," Hanss added gloomily. "Which is why we came to Port Isleros to charter a boat. But we got lucky. By the time we reached Port Isleros, you were here, too."

Maya told Will, Thirret, and Hanss all that had happened after she went over the cliff with the ogre. When she was done, Maya sat back, closing her eyes. "And tonight, we went out on the town for some fun before we go our separate ways."

"Out on the town for some fun," Will said, and he made it sound like an accusation.

Opening her eyes, Maya felt a spark of resentment rise up against his judgment of her. She tried to push it down, but she couldn't. "Why did you come here anyway?"

"For you, of course!" Will exclaimed. "I came for you."

"Well, you shouldn't have," Maya retorted. "You should have stayed behind to help Lexie and Jay. You can see better than either of them. Instead, you're letting a twelve-year-old girl face Cinnial, a man who killed Sydda and who wouldn't hesitate to kill Viola. What's the matter with you?" she ended in exasperation.

"Maya!" Thirret and Hanss said together.

Jumping up, Will knocked his chair over. "I wish I had never come here. I should have known you'd land on your feet and find somebody else. You always do, don't you? First Andy, then me, now Braird."

"Will!" Thirret and Hanss exclaimed.

Thirret added, "Will, when you finally let loose, you really let it fly."

Blinking rapidly, Maya gripped the table. Then grabbing her glass, she threw it to the ground. The wine splashed everywhere, but the glass didn't shatter and instead bounced back onto the table.

"What a waste of good wine," Thirret said.

"What's going on here?" a stern voice asked. Larz stood by the table, and Thirret gave him an appraising look. But the big elf's focus was on Maya and Will.

Maya stood quickly, and her lips quivered. "Please take me home, Larz."

Larz put an arm around Maya, who was crying. "Come with me. I'll take you home." With narrow eyes, he regarded Thirret, Will, and Hanss. "You three stay away from her. This little human is very special. She risked her life trying to find the captain's daughter, and I'll never forget that."

"No one could ever accuse Maya of being a coward," Thirret said with admiration.

Unmoved, Will glared at Larz. "Good! Take her away." Then to Maya. "I hope I never see you again."

Unable to think of a cutting response, all Maya could manage through her tears was "And I hope I never see you again, either."

Larz glowered at Will. "Watch it, human. You might not be as little as Maya, but I could take you down. No problem."

241

Shaking his head, Thirret stood, too. "Larz, Will and I came from Earth to find Maya and bring her back to her own dimension."

Will muttered, "We found her all right."

"Quiet," Thirret said to Will, who bit his lip and looked away. Then he turned to Larz. "I'm Thirret Greenwood, and it's been a long time since I was in Elferterre."

"Thirret Greenwood," Larz said slowly. "You're..."

"Yes."

"Ah." Larz inclined his head toward Thirret. "My apologies. It seemed as though you were all harassing Maya."

"I can see why it looked that way," Thirret replied. "Emotions were running...a little high. It's a good idea for you to take Maya home, wherever that is, but we need to come see her tomorrow and discuss what we're going to do next. There's a lot happening in her universe. So much that even Magic is involved, which hardly ever happens."

"Right," Larz agreed. "Maybe tempers will be cooler tomorrow." After telling Thirret where the captain lived, Larz said in a tender voice to Maya, "Let's go home."

With a shuddering sigh, Maya nodded, leaning against Larz, whose solid, warm bulk was comforting. Leaving Thirret, Will, and Hanss behind, Larz and Maya walked through the busy streets to the captain's house.

"Where are the others?" Maya asked.

"I figured it was better for them to stay behind. Especially Braird. But they were watching from a window in Gustone's office in case I needed help." Maya felt a rumble as Larz laughed. "Which I knew I wouldn't, no matter how it went down."

"Must be nice to be so strong that you hardly ever worry about getting hurt."

Larz gave her shoulders a squeeze. "Must be nice to be so cute and feisty that everyone just loves you."

"Not everyone," Maya said, thinking of Will.

Larz's voice was gentle. "Oh, Will loves you all right. Why do you think he's so hurt?"

Maya sniffed. "What am I going to do?"

"That I can't tell you," Larz answered.

"I said I was sorry, but he won't forgive me."

"Give him some time."

"Will takes things hard." Maya remembered what Will had said about his father, about how he still resented him because he valued his work more than he did his family. "Will doesn't forgive easily."

"The way you do."

Maya thought of Sir John and Andy. "Yeah, I guess so."

"Maya, what's done is done. And Will saw what he saw."

"Right?" Maya's tone was bitter. "I should have brought the relics with me. Then none of this would have happened."

"Sometimes we just have to let things take their course and then go from there."

"Do we?"

"Are you sorry you kissed Braird?" Larz asked shrewdly.

Maya was about to say that she was, but she couldn't bring herself to lie about this. "No, I had one of the most wonderful nights of my life. Until Will came."

"Okay, then."

"Okay, then," Maya repeated, remembering what the captain's daughter had said to her before leaving with Rhye on *The Cuttlefish*. Maya thought, *Clarin's right. I'm only sixteen. I don't have to choose. Not yet.* Maya thought back to when she had first met Will in Brooklyn, and her inner voice had told her that he was the one. Maya now understood that her intuition had told her this because Will's ability to see to the heart of things was nearly as strong as hers. This meant that Will was the best one to go with her to Elferterre to help with the mission. And that was that. Falling in love was secondary, Maya reflected sadly.

By then, they were at the captain's large house, light blue with dark blue trim and a cupola room at the top, which had been given to Maya for her stay in Port Isleros.

Larz stopped and gave Maya a hug. "We'll all be back tomorrow to say goodbye and to see you off."

Maya gratefully hugged him back. "I'll miss everyone so much."

"And we'll miss you," Larz replied, his normally bright face serious. "But you have a job to do. A big one."

"Yeah," Maya said, thinking of Viola going up against Cinnial. "I sure do."

Larz left, and the front door, a deep red, swung open for her. Maya slowly made her way up the four flights of stairs to the cupola room, which like her sleeping quarters on *The Resolute*, had once belonged to Clarin. Before pulling the curtains, Maya sat on a comfortable chair and stared out the many windows at the port's glittering lights, which twinkled in every direction. The relics were waiting for her on a table by the bed, and Maya was thankful there were no recriminations or "I told you so" from any of them.

Instead, as Maya turned off the lights and went to bed, there was silence, and she lay awake for a long time, thinking about her meeting with Will the next day. Maya knew what had to be said, but that didn't make it any easier. On the table, Eloise glowed softly, Aiken occasionally blew small puffs of smoke, and Orlaith settled into the curl of her own legs.

24: THE TEMPLE OF PORTALS

The next morning when Will, Thirret, and Hanss came to the captain's house, Maya was waiting in a small parlor off the large living room. Aiken, Orlaith, and Eloise were upstairs in the tower room. Maya had decided she needed to be by herself when she talked to Will. Finneas, his face wrinkled with sympathy, brought Will to the parlor, and Maya, who had been looking at a book, stood when Will came in. Before Finneas closed the door, he told Maya, "Thirret and Hanss are with the captain in his study. They'll be joining you later."

At first neither Maya nor Will spoke. Will looked around the sun-lit room, at the bookshelves lining the walls. Maya stared out the window at the gleaming white house next door. On a small round table in the middle of the parlor was a tray with tea things and cookies made by Bertaa, the captain's housekeeper and Finneas's sister.

"Sit down," Maya finally said, pointing to one of the chairs at the table. "Would you like some tea?"

Sitting down, Will shrugged. "All right."

After she sat down, Maya poured him some tea and passed him a cup. "Have a cookie."

Taking the cup, Will stared at his tea. "No thanks."

Maya sighed. It was no small thing for Will to refuse a cookie, and it illustrated just how tense he was. But Maya didn't need the cookies to let her know that Will was still upset with her. His unhappiness radiated from him in waves, washing over her, making her feel even more guilty.

"Will," Maya said in a soft voice.

He looked up. "What? What can we possibly say to each other that will make things better?"

"I don't know. But what are you going to do now? Go back to New York and pretend none of this ever happened? Go to parties with other rich people so that you can get ahead in the world?"

Will glared at her. "Is that how you see me?"

Maya shook her head. "No, Will. I think there's a lot more to you than that. You came to Elferterre with me. You had your eyes peeled. Without your help, I wouldn't have been able to steal the key and the lock."

"That's why you chose me, isn't it? Because I could help you."

Maya wanted to say no, but instead, "Yes."

Will took a deep breath. "All right. At least now I understand."

"But that wasn't the only reason. You must know that. I can't hide things from you."

Will took a sip of tea and then another. "Once you liked me," he acknowledged.

Maya stared evenly at Will. "I still do."

"But you like Braird, too."

"Yes, but Braird and I aren't as good a team as you and I are. We fight too much."

Will set his cup down with a clatter. "A good team! You hardly ever think of anything else but the mission, don't you?"

Maya did not look away. "Yeah, Will, that's mostly what I think about. And if you had seen the things I have, then that's what you'd be thinking about, too. I watched Chet murder Duke Owen. I've been to the Great Library. I've met Cinnial. I nearly died in the Office. I came back on my own to Earth, and saw myself when I was six. Then, to Elferterre where I went over a cliff with an ogre." Her lips trembled with anger as she considered Will, so self-absorbed that he couldn't see beyond his own feelings. "After all that, what am I supposed to think about?" Her voice rose. "You tell me, Will. What am I supposed to think about?"

There was silence in the parlor. Outside, a child called to her mother, a dog barked, and the wind rattled a branch against the parlor windows.

Finally Will said, "I couldn't go back to my old life even if I wanted to. When Jay, Lexie, and I took the key and the lock through the portal, we came back to Earth in your time. We've been gone for ten years in our time." Will made a sweeping motion with his hand. "As far as our families are concerned, we're dead."

Maya's anger snapped away. "And your disappearance is on the timeline, isn't it?"

"That's what Alani's and Alexander's Books said."

"Oh, Will." Maya reached across the table to squeeze one of his hands.

Will didn't pull away. "It's been especially hard for Jay. He's so close to his family."

"Still, it can't be easy for any of you."

"No, it's not. And I guess that means I'll be going with you to complete the mission. What other choice do I have?"

"You do have a choice," Maya told him. "You could go back to Brooklyn, where Alani and Alexander and the League of Librarians would help you. I know they would. You could make a new life there."

"I could do that." As Will considered his options, he sat up straighter. A variety of expressions moved across his mobile face, and Maya saw him reach a decision. "I'm coming with you. Because you're right. We make a good team. And I want to see this through, whatever happens." Will pulled his hand away from Maya. "After that, who knows?"

"Okay, then." Maya swirled the last of the tea in her cup.

"So where do we go from here?" Will asked.

With a pang, Maya realized the easiness that had once been between them was gone to be replaced by something more practical, more workmanlike. It was her fault and she knew it, but it still stung.

"To Tufrak, Cinnial's old planet, via the Temple of Portals," Maya answered. "I have to rescue my apprentice book, Ariel. Then to the Great Library to help Viola." Maya shivered. "I hope she's all right. She's so young."

"We're not exactly old."

"No, but we're not twelve."

Will said in a soft voice, "You're right. I should have gone with Lexie and Jay to help Viola. But I had to come back. Somehow, I knew you were alive. I just couldn't leave you here on your own."

"I understand." Maya's own voice was nearly a whisper. "Thank you. And Will? I didn't know if I'd ever see you again. Or if I did, how old you'd be. When I left Andy, he was seventeen. Now he's as old as my father, and he has a daughter who's nearly a teenager."

As Will nodded slowly, there was a knock on the door, and Thirret called, "Is it all right to come in?"

"Yes, come in," Maya said.

The door opened, and Thirret and Hanss walked into the parlor.

Hanss surveyed the room. "Well, at least there are no broken tea cups, which are no doubt more fragile than the wine glasses at the café last night. I don't think those delicate cups would bounce back to the table."

At this, Will even grinned a little. "No broken tea cups."

Hans considered Maya and Will then said to Thirret, "I believe they have come to a rapprochement."

"It looks that way," Thirret said.

"We have," Will replied.

"And?" Thirret asked.

"I'm going with Maya to help complete the mission," Will told him. "After that, I don't know what I'll do."

Sitting down, Thirret helped himself to tea and a cookie. "It's good to hear you're going with her."

Hanss jumped up on the last empty chair. "It certainly is."

"What about you two?" Maya asked Thirret and Hanss. "What are your plans?"

The cat's tail twitched. "I'm going back to Darkwood Forest to wait for Thirret and his parents when they return to Elferterre."

Thirret put his hand on Hanss's head. "Earth's universe is no place for you. Who knows how the diminished magic would affect you? All our abilities are dampened on the Other Side. You might not even be able to talk. Best for you to stay here."

Purring, Hanss rubbed his head against Thirret's hand. "You're right. But I wish I could go back with you."

"I know. I wish you could, too. But I'll be returning to Elferterre soon. With my family."

Will said, "Thirret, I'll miss you when you go back to Brooklyn."

Thirret grinned. "We had quite the adventures in Elferterre, didn't we? But I'm not going back to Brooklyn right off. First I'll be coming with you and Maya. Think I'd just let you two go off by yourselves to face Cinnial?"

Relieved, Maya said, "Great! But we wouldn't exactly be alone. Viola is there, and so are Lexie and Jay."

Thirret scratched his chin. "Oh, right. Thanks for the reminder. I guess you don't need me after all."

Will and Maya laughed, and a yowl that sounded like a laugh came from Hanss.

"Glad you're coming," Will finally said.

Maya smiled at Thirret. "Me, too."

Thirret winked at Maya, and she got an impression of his immense charm. "Well, that's a relief. Wouldn't want to push myself on you two." Then his expression became serious. "While I was with the captain, we sorted out a few things. He's received word that you have permission from the Portal Authority to use the Temple of Portals."

"Oh, that's good!" Maya said. "Just what I was hoping."

"Yes, that part is good," Thirret agreed.

"What part isn't good?" Will asked.

Thirret replied, "The Captain has a Big Book of Portals, and we found that Black Mountain has the nearest portal to Mortmain, the city where Ariel is being held."

"Black Mountain is where Tufrak's Book of Everything has been hidden," Maya said. "For years and years. In an underground bunker. By boat and car, it's about three days away from Mortmain." She frowned. "I was hoping the portal would be closer."

Thirret finished the last of his tea. "As usual, Chance is on your side. The captain was kind enough to give me six golden acorns. Three for when we go to Tufrak to rescue Ariel. The acorns will get us to Mortmain in no time. Then the other three will take us to the Great Library. I understand Cinnial's Books can block the Books of Everything from coming to the library."

Chagrined, Maya said, "I was thinking that there would be a portal close to Mortmain and that Ariel would take me and Will to the Great Library. I should have known better."

Thirret grinned. "Good thing you have me and the captain to think of things you might have overlooked. I have heard that you tend to act first and think later."

Will snorted, and Maya blushed.

Thirret patted Maya's hand. "No one's good at everything. And look how much you've accomplished. If you had taken too much time to think things over, you might not have come to Elferterre in the first place."

"Or gone over the cliff with an ogre," Hanss said.

Thirret gave Maya's hand another pat, and then he stood. "Will and Hanss, we'd best get going. Maya, we'll come get you this afternoon to go to the Temple of Portals."

"I'll be ready," Maya told the elf.

As Will stood, Hanss jumped down from his chair. Before leaving, Will looked back once as though he wanted to say something. But shrugging, he remained silent, following Thirret and Hanss from the parlor.

For a while, Maya sat at the table and crumbled one of Bertaa's excellent cookies into her plate. Reflecting on what she and Will had said to each other, Maya concluded that the conversation had gone as well as could be expected. While their old closeness might be gone, they had at least come to an understanding that would allow them to work together.

Maya thought philosophically, *It's not ideal, but it will be good enough.*

At noon, the crew of *The Resolute* came to wish her farewell. They had been invited for lunch, a buffet put together by Finneas and Bertaa, and Alie came early to help them. When everything was ready, the crew gathered in the captain's large dining room, which had a table long enough for everyone to sit around.

Before the meal started, the captain, at the head of the table, raised his glass. "To Maya and to the rest of the young crew who helped uncover Symi. If Symi hadn't sabotaged Maya and Braird and nearly gotten them killed, we might have forgiven the rest." He hesitated. "After all, we weren't blameless. I was at fault, too. Because of my prejudice, I jumped to the wrong conclusion about Rhye."

"So did I," Finneas said.

"Same," Hannie added, and Zeynip nodded.

Hawthorn shook her head. "We all jumped to the wrong conclusion." She glanced at Braird. "But that doesn't excuse what Symi did."

"No, it doesn't," the captain replied. Then he smiled. "But some good came of it. I am now reunited with Clarin. And for that I am so very thankful."

Finneas raised his glass. "Hear, hear. Cheers!"

"Cheers," Larz boomed. "And thanks to the ones who prepared this delicious lunch."

Everyone laughed, and the mood lightened as they ate and talked about what had happened and what was planned. But as lunch came to an end, and they went into the large living room across from the dining room to have tea, and the time for Maya's departure grew closer and closer, the mood became more somber.

Maya stood. Aiken, Orlaith, and Eloise were on her shoulders, their favorite spot. She looked around the room at the faces that had become so dear to her in such a short time. She gazed longest at Alie and Larz, then last at Braird, whom she knew she would always be attracted to even though they weren't exactly a perfect pair. When Braird nodded at her, Maya could tell he felt the same way.

As her eyes stung with tears, Maya cleared her throat. "I wish I could stay a little longer. I would like nothing better than to sail the seas of Elferterre and discover some of the beauties and dangers that live there. But I can't. My place is in my universe."

"In Elferterre, we refer to your dimension as the Other Side," the captain said. "But its official name is Autrevers."

"Autrevers," Maya murmured.

Coming over to her, the captain kissed her on both cheeks, which were wet, and gave her a hug.

Maya wiped her eyes. "I'll always remember you."

The captain smiled. "And I will never forget you." Then he handed her a small sealed envelope. "Give this to the guards at the Temple of Portals. This is permission from the Portal Authority for you to enter and use a portal."

Maya put the envelope in one of her pockets. "Thank you, Captain Blythewood."

"My pleasure."

One by one, the crew of *The Resolute* gave her a goodbye hug, even Hawthorn, who was less stiff than usual. But Maya had noticed that at lunch Hawthorn sat across the table from the captain, and there was an easiness between them that was new.

251

"You're a pain in the butt," Hawthorn murmured as she hugged Maya. "But you do get things moving."

"I don't mean to be a pain," Maya murmured back.

Hawthorn laughed. "Of course you don't." She squeezed Maya's shoulder. "But there it is."

Larz engulfed Maya in his large arms. "Goodbye, little human. I'll miss you."

"I'll miss you, too."

After giving Maya a hug, Proko and Takis each put a furry hand on her cheeks, "Good luck, good luck," they whispered, and Maya felt a small warm ripple spread from their hands to her cheeks.

Next to last was Alie, who wrapped her slender arms around Maya. "I'm glad you came aboard *The Resolute*. Your bravery, going out to sea with Braird, helped me to be brave."

By now Maya was crying, and when Braird enveloped her in a feathery embrace, she hugged him tightly. "Don't cry," he said, his sharp voice unusually tender. "I think we'll meet again someday when I come to the Other Side."

Feeling that Braird was right, Maya sniffed. "Okay." She smiled through her tears. "I'll be there." *Somewhere* came the unbidden thought.

Finneas, who was standing nearby, handed Maya a tissue. "My oh my, we're all going to miss you."

After blowing her nose, Maya said, "I'll miss you all, too."

Wiping her hands on her apron, Bertaa came into the room. "Maya, there are three waiting for you in the foyer."

As Maya waved a sad goodbye, the captain said, "Remember, you are always welcome here, either in Port Isleros or on *The Resolute*."

Afraid that she was going to start crying again, Maya just nodded and headed to the foyer, where Will and Thirret, wearing backpacks, were waiting for her. Hanss sat beside them. Will didn't say anything as he looked at her blotchy face and puffy eyes.

But Thirret smiled in sympathy. "Good-byes are never easy. Over the years, I've said more than my fair share of them."

Hanss sighed. "So have I."

Maya picked up a backpack that was waiting for her. "Does it get any easier?"

Thirret shook his head. "No, it does not."

"That's what I thought."

The red door swung open for them.

Maya took a deep breath. "Well, let's go."

And as they left, Maya felt a hand on her back and knew it was Will's.

The Temple of Portals was on top of a large hill overlooking the city. To get there, Maya, Will, Thirret, and Hanss rode a funicular up an incline so steep that Maya was relieved they didn't have to climb it on foot. The relics, who were still perched on her shoulders, gazed with interest out the window. When the funicular reached the top and everyone got out, the wind whistled as it blew. Before them was a large white building ringed with columns. Without saying anything, the relics made their way to the pockets in Maya's trousers.

"It really does look like a temple," Maya said in wonder, remembering the summer she had gone to Greece with her parents. "Except the Temple of Portals is not ruined."

Will whistled in appreciation. "Right?"

Thirret shook his head. "Never did understand why you humans allow buildings to fall into ruin, especially when so much effort and resources are put into them."

Shrugging, Maya and Will looked at each other. They had never thought about Greek temples that way, but they both conceded that Thirret had a point.

Despite being surrounded by columns, the temple was a building with walls and just one entrance, which could only be reached by a long set of steps. Two winged cats, one orange and one black and white, sat by two immense black doors, and the cats gave Maya, Thirret, and Will a considering look. They nodded in a more friendly way at Hanss, but it was clear they were not about to let just anyone stroll into the temple.

Thirret smiled his dimpled smile at the guard cats. "Greetings. We have permission to use the Temple of Portals."

"Do you now?" the black and white cat asked.

Maya stepped forward with the small envelope the captain had given her—*Portal Authority* was stamped on the front. A white paw opened it, and the two cats stared at what was inside.

"All right," the orange cat said with a twitch of the ears.

The black and white cat nodded. "You may enter. But no funny business. Remember, we're out here, and we can be inside in a flash if we have to."

Thirret shook his head. "There won't be any funny business, believe me."

Hanss said, "I can vouch for that."

The two cats regarded them with a friendlier look. "We believe you," the orange one said.

Hanss told the guard cats, "I won't be going through a portal with them. I'm just here to see them off."

"As you like it," the black and white cat replied. "Go ahead in."

Silently, the doors swung open, and a restless breeze rippled out, swirling around them, ruffling their hair and clothes as though it was checking them over.

"We don't have any weapons," Thirret said impatiently. "We're just traveling."

Relics, came the response.

"They'll help us on the Other Side as much as they can," Thirret replied.

The breeze gave a slight whistle and blew back inside.

Into the temple Maya, Thirret, Will, and Hanss went. The walls were lined with twenty shimmering portals, and in the middle was a large glass-domed machine on a wide pedestal with buttons, cranks, and slots. Inside the dome were wheels and pistons and rods and little troughs. On a narrow shelf that rimmed the dome's perimeter, gleaming balls perched by chutes. The balls vibrated slightly, and Maya got the impression they were ready to go.

Will asked, "Do you think any of the portals will even let us through and then take us to the right place? I remember the portal in the travel plaza. It sure was stubborn. It wouldn't open for me no matter how many times I asked."

Thirret said, "That machine will help us. I know it will."

As they went to the machine, they saw a small sign on the front that read *Determination Machine*.

Thirret smiled. "That's what I thought."

Maya ran her fingers over the dome, which felt warm to the touch. "What do we do?"

Will had gone to the other side. "There are instructions over here on the pedestal."

Maya, Thirret, and Hanss joined Will, and they all stared at a small plaque with directions for using the machine.

To Go from Here to There

1. Enter the name of the universe.
2. Enter the name of the planet.
3. Briefly describe where you want to go.
4. Enter the time. If you are not sure of the time, give
*   a short description of people or events in the desired*
*   time frame.*
5. Pull the enter lever.
6. Below the lever is a slot. If there is a portal in the
*   requested place, a punch card with instructions*
*   will appear in the slot by the keyboard. Take the punch*
*   card, and go to the nearest available portal.*
*   Insert the punch card in the slot to the right.*
7. If no punch card appears, then there is no portal
*   in the given location.*

On the pedestal beside the instructions sat a small keyboard on a built-in shelf that pulled out. Maya typed in the information and pulled the lever beside the keyboard. Inside the dome, the machinery sprang to life. Balls shot down the shoots and whizzed around the troughs; wheels spun in a blur; the pistons went up and down, up and down; and the whole internal mechanism whirled around at a dizzying pace.

"Wow!" Will yelled, looking happy for the first time since his encounter with Maya at Lilywater's.

Arching his back, Hanss hissed at the noise and commotion.

Laughing, Thirret put his hand on the cat's head. "I've heard of the Determination Machine, but I've never seen it in person. It's something else, isn't it?"

Maya couldn't look away from the speeding balls and the twirling gears. "Yeah, it's a wonder."

Hanss hissed again. "What a racket."

"It is indeed," Thirret said.

After what seemed like an age but was probably only a few minutes, the machinery chimed in triumph and a punch card shot out, landing on a small silver tray below the slot. Thirret picked up the card, and they all walked to the nearest portal. Bending over, he scratched Hanss's head.

"Goodbye, friend," Thirret murmured. "I'll be back soon with my parents and my cousins to retake Norlander from Tamick Ashglade."

Hanss rubbed his head against Thirret's hand. "I'll be waiting for you in Darkwood Forest."

Straightening, Thirret inserted the card in the slot, and the portal opened with a shimmer. Maya caught a glimpse of dark trees and heard a low rumble of power coming from Black Mountain.

"This is the place?" Thirret asked.

"This is the place," Maya said.

And they walked through the portal, which closed behind them, leaving behind Hanss, who sat and stared for a long while before turning to leave the temple.

25: TRAPPED

The final day of potato recess was the brightest, warmest day of them all. The last of the potatoes had been harvested, and there was a general clean up around the stable and shed. Robbie said goodbye to the horses. Viola and Wren helped sort potatoes. The previous afternoon, they had finished discussing *At Sea*, and there were still mixed feelings about the book. While Skye was out to sea, her mother had died because of too much work and worry.

"Skye's mother might have died anyway," Robbie pointed out.

But Wren shook her head. "Maybe, maybe not."

As Viola thought of the last discussion of *At Sea*, she was sorry they had to trick Julian. It was a betrayal, and although Viola knew it was necessary, it still felt bitter. The night before, Earth's Book of Everything had assured her that mixed feelings were perfectly normal, but this did not make Viola feel any better about what she, Wren, and Robbie were going to do.

A little before 9:00, after sorting potatoes, Viola washed her hands and gathered Julian's present, wrapped and with a bow, from their cart's basket. Wren and Robbie joined her, and they turned to Kip and the other gardeners, who were standing together nearby.

Kip nodded but didn't say anything. Neither did the other gardeners, who raised their hands in farewell. No words were necessary. The gardening shears and rope had been left in the atrium. In Watertown, the plan had been discussed many times, with the gardeners crowding Kip and Isik's small home for the past few mornings. Everyone knew what to do if Viola and the choir were successful, and the gardeners would be ready with their ropes. On the other hand, if either Viola or the choir was unsuccessful, nobody would be returning home that night to have supper with their families.

Taking a deep breath, Viola, with Wren and Robbie by her side, headed toward the Great Library. Blinking rapidly to keep back the tears, Viola wanted to look back, but she didn't, and the charm, soft and warm against her skin, helped steady her.

At the entrance to the Great Library, the guards, a man and a woman, regarded Viola, Wren, and Robbie. Just beyond the guards, Viola caught a glimpse of a slight dark-haired woman, who was there for a moment and then was gone.

For the first time, the guards smiled at the kids. The man, heavyset with sandy blond hair, asked, "A present? For me? You shouldn't have."

Grinning nervously, Viola shook her head. "It's for Julian. It's our last day of potato recess, and we wanted to give him something special to thank him for all that he's done."

"A-w-w-w, sweet," the woman, dark and trim, replied, and she sounded sincere. "Go in, then. But you'll have to make it quick. Julian always has an appointment midmorning, and a little before 10:00, you'll have to leave."

Nodding, Viola thought, *Yes, we will*. But she didn't say anything, and neither did Wren nor Robbie. The three of them trooped into the foyer. Glancing down the hallway toward the elevator, Viola was relieved to see that Kip had been right—there were no guards down there.

Viola, Wren, and Robbie stopped by the front desk, where there were two more guards, again a man and a woman, who would have to give them clearance to see Julian. The door to Cinnial's large office was closed, but right beside it was Julian's office, and his door was open. Viola saw that he was bent over his desk and that there was a stack of papers in front of him.

Viola thought, *His Book is not on the desk. Good. It won't be able to warn him when Cinnial's captured.*

The woman, who had smooth black hair pulled back into a bun, said, "You're here early today."

Viola held up the book. "We have a present for Julian. It's our last day on the island, and we might be leaving early."

The man, older with a wrinkled face, smiled. "That's really nice." He motioned to the office. "Julian's in his office. Go ahead over. But you can't stay too long. He has a meeting at 10:00."

"Okay, then," Viola replied.

As Viola, Robbie, and Wren walked over to Julian's office, he looked up and smiled, clearly glad to see them. Smiling back, Viola pushed away the terrible ache she felt, knowing that without the charm's help, she wouldn't have been able to do it.

"Come in, come in," Julian said when they hovered by the doorway, and Viola, Wren, and Robbie went into his office. "To what do I owe this honor?"

Wren answered shyly, "Potato recess is over, and the potatoes have all been picked. This is our last day on the island."

"And we came to thank you for all that you've done," Robbie said. "Because of you, I'll be going on to read other books." Robbie's voice was sincere, and Viola knew that if he survived this day, Robbie would indeed become a reader.

Viola put the book on Julian's desk. "This is for you, from the three of us."

Blinking, Julian unwrapped the book and ran his hand over the purple cover.

"Open it," Viola said.

Opening the book, Julian read the inscription. "Where did you get this?" he asked quietly, looking at the three of them.

"Last night at a rummage sale a few streets over from Kip's house," Robbie answered in a proud voice, as though they had actually found the book tucked away on a folding table in the back corner of a dimly-lit community center. "We were lucky the sale was open late. You never know what you're going to find at one of those sales."

In astonishment, Julian shook his head. "I guess not."

"You deserve it," Robbie said firmly. "You've made a reader out of someone who never liked to read."

"You helped us see the different sides of Skye and her family," Wren put in.

Viola said, "And how people are a mixture of bad and good. How circumstances can sometimes push them in a direction they don't want to go."

259

"I will treasure this book always." Julian looked affectionately at the three of them. "You know, things at the Great Library might not always be the way they are now."

Viola thought, *I sure hope not.*

Julian continued, "When things have settled down, I'm hoping the Great Library will be open to the public again. Then you three could come back when you have the time." Julian's expression became wistful. "There might even be classes where we read and discuss books. And people from the mainland would be welcome to join in."

Robbie's expression was bright and his voice sincere. "Aye, we'd like that. I'd sign up for one of your classes even if it was after school and not part of our regular studies."

Viola said, "Same."

"Me, too," Wren agreed.

Viola could almost imagine a scenario where after Astrid and the other librarians took over the Great Library, Julian was somehow allowed to stay and become one of its great teachers. She could picture class after class of rapt students listening to him as he guided them through works of literature. She wondered, *Could it happen?* And while a part of Viola was hopeful, another part of her realized just how unlikely this was.

They talked for a while longer, mostly about books, then Julian looked at his watch. "Much as I hate to end this conversation, you three will have to go. I have an appointment in about fifteen minutes, and I have to go over my daily report."

"That's all right," Wren replied. "We need to go back and help finish with the cleanup."

"Aye, they'll be needing us," Robbie said.

Viola smiled sadly. "Thank you again. We had a great time discussing *At Sea.*"

Julian's voice was soft. "So did I. Hope you kids can come back soon."

"So do we," Robbie replied cheerfully. "So do we."

Then Viola, Wren, and Robbie left. When they came to the desk with the guards, Viola said, "Kip left his favorite shears in the atrium and asked us to pick them up. Is that all right with you?"

The guards glanced into Julian's office, where he was looking at the book Viola, Wren, and Robbie had given him. The woman with the dark hair smiled at them. "Go ahead. We don't want the head gardener to be without his favorite shears."

"Nay, we don't," Robbie said. "That would be very bad. Along with the cook, you want to make sure the head gardener is happy. Between the two of them, that's where you get your food."

"True enough," the man said.

"Okay, then," Robbie replied.

Walking as casually as they could, the kids entered the atrium. For a moment, all they could do was stare as they stood in the glass-enclosed place that had the look and feel of a small woodland. There were rocks covered with moss and ferns that swayed in a gentle breeze that seemed to come from everywhere and yet nowhere. Small white flowers shaped like stars grew on the edges, where there were patches of sun, and in the middle, slender trees surrounded an Oak, which towered over everything. Not far from the Oak, a spring bubbled up, becoming a small stream that seemed to leap around the atrium, which, like the Great Library, appeared to be bigger on the inside than it was on the outside. And everywhere there was a tickling force, skipping from the trees to the moss to the water.

Robbie was the first to speak. "Whoa, the forest at home might be bigger, but this little patch is just as special."

"It's the magic," Wren whispered. "Can you feel it?"

"Aye," Robbie answered. "It's concentrated in this big glass room."

For a while, Viola, Wren, and Robbie were so absorbed with the little forest in the atrium that they nearly forgot why they were there. Kip's shears were on a bench by the Oak, and although Viola, Wren, and Robbie had no intentions of returning them, Kip had put the shears on the bench just in case any of the guards checked on them. Underneath the bench was some rope.

"Good," Robbie said. "After we knock out the guards, we'll bring them in here and tie them up."

But then Viola's charm buzzed softly against her chest as did Wren's and Robbie's. The tickling force became sharper, encouraging them to go to the edge of the atrium that overlooked the hall and the elevator.

"Cinnial's coming." Viola moved past the bench and the sheers.

Wren and Robbie followed her. By the atrium's door, a large clump of tall ferns grew, where the kids hid as they waited for the elevator to come to the ground floor. Above the elevator, a brass indicator kept track of the floors. In spans of twenty, the numbers on the indicator spun downward until finally it marked the last ten floors.

Viola's hand was on the door knob. "Ten, nine, eight," she whispered.

"Seven, six, five," Wren murmured.

"Four, three, two, one," Robbie finished, ready to spring.

But Viola held up her hand, and they all remained in place. The elevator door opened, and two guards walked out. Guns were in their holsters, but they weren't drawn. The guards were alert, but Viola could tell they weren't expecting anything unusual to happen on this bright fall morning. Behind the guards came Cinnial, shoulders back, head held high, confident that the Great Library was his rightful domain.

"Now," Viola said in a low, urgent voice.

Out the door they went, and Magic followed them, muffling their footsteps so that neither Cinnial nor the guards heard them. Viola put a hand in the pocket of her overalls, where the open lock was waiting. Her fingers closed around it, and she pulled her hand from her pocket. The lock made a slight humming sound, and Viola could feel its power. With Magic and the charm's help, Viola directed her thoughts toward the lock.

"Trap Cinnial, trap Cinnial, trap Cinnial," Viola thought in quick succession, and the lock thrummed in response, letting Viola know it was ready.

But as Viola began to open her hand, a blonde woman walked by the atrium and stopped, gazing down the hall at them. Cinnial glanced at the woman and then turned quickly to stare at Viola. With a triumphant smile, the woman left in a rush.

Cinnial's intense blue eyes held Viola in place, and neither the charm nor Magic could stop him from seeing her intent with the lock. His will was too strong. With a slight cry, Viola dropped the lock, breaking the connection she had with it, and on the floor it hummed neutrally. As the guards whirled around, they drew their guns and aimed them at the kids. Holding up a hand to stop the guards from firing, Cinnial looked from Viola to the lock. Without saying anything, he scooped up the lock and considered it.

"Come with me," he finally said, and the guards marched them to Cinnial's office.

At the front desk, the guards, the woman with the dark hair and the older man, started as they watched the kids go by, and Viola could feel their fear as they understood how they had mistakenly let Viola, Wren, and Robbie slip by them.

Julian's door was still open, and he was at his desk. Looking up, he smiled, but it quickly went away as he realized that Viola, Wren, and Robbie were Cinnial's prisoners. Standing quickly, he closed his eyes and put his hands on his desk.

"Julian," Cinnial called curtly, holding up the lock. "Come to my office."

Julian stared at the lock. "Yes, Cinnial."

"Shall we come in, too, sir?" one of the guards asked.

"No," Cinnial answered, his voice tight with anger. "I think I can handle three kids even if nobody else can."

"Yes, sir."

Into Cinnial's large office they all went. Viola didn't have to look at Julian to feel his anguish and disappointment. Viola had hoped she would never have to face Julian when he realized how he had been betrayed, that Astrid and the other librarians would somehow take care of him. But here they were, caught before Cinnial could be trapped, and Viola knew that she looked as guilty as Wren and Robbie did.

Cinnial slammed the lock on the desk. "Julian, look at what these kids had."

Julian sighed. "I don't even have to touch it to feel its power."

Reaching into his pocket, Cinnial took out his Book, and he put it beside the lock on the desk. The small Book grew in size until it was as big as a thick dictionary, reminding Viola of the one her father had, which traveled with him from office to office whenever they moved.

Cinnial sat down but did not open his Book. He motioned for Julian to sit down on a chair beside the desk, but it was clear that Viola, Wren, and Robbie were to remain standing.

At last, Viola did not have to pretend to be anything other than what she was, the daughter of two lawyers, a father who was the president of the United States and a mother who was his equal in every way. With her back straight, Viola held her head high and refused to show Cinnial that she was afraid. And while Wren and Robbie were not quite as collected as Viola was, her valor encouraged them to be brave, to stand tall in the face of the great danger they were in.

263

"Well," Cinnial said as he considered them, "not quite the humble kids that you seemed to be, content to go in the fields and pick potatoes to earn money for school clothes."

"No, we are not," Viola replied. "But I'm not telling you anything else no matter what you do."

"Right." Cinnial smirked. "That's what they all say. Julian, do you have anything to add to this?"

"Like what?" Julian asked bluntly. "That I was tricked by three kids and their seeming love of books?"

"Wren and I do love books," Viola protested. "That part was real."

"And I love books now, too," Robbie added, nodding toward Julian. "Thanks to you."

Wearily, Julian shook his head. "That's a relief to hear."

Cinnial looked at them one by one. "Unbelievable."

"Did your Book warn you about them?" Julian asked in a low voice.

"No," Cinnial admitted. "It seems that the kids eluded my Book's notice, too."

"Well, then."

Cinnial slapped the top of his desk, and the kids jumped. "Julian, did you even consult your Book? Never mind. I already know the answer. You haven't taken your Book off the shelf in your office since we got here."

Julian rubbed his face. "I can think more clearly without my Book always going on and on about everything."

Cinnial glared at Julian. "Maybe if you had consulted your Book, it would have recognized that these three kids are dangerous, and they wouldn't have nearly trapped me with this lock."

When Julian didn't respond, Cinnial held up the lock, and they all stared at it. "Now, where did this come from?"

Robbie asked, "How can you be sure it's not just a regular lock?"

Cinnial stared at Robbie until he looked away. "I am many things, but I'm not a complete fool. When you were all creeping behind me, I could feel the power in the lock. That's what made me turn and look. And even though I've never seen anything like it, I knew, without doubt, what the lock was for."

Viola thought, *The blonde woman had something to do with it, too. She helped warn Cinnial. I know she did.* But Viola didn't say anything, figuring she would just make things worse if she pointed out that Cinnial had needed some help, that without the blonde woman, Cinnial might be in the lock instead of on the other side of the desk.

"Another minute, and the lock would have had you," Julian said, and Viola couldn't tell whether he would have been relieved or sorry.

"That's right." Cinnial considered Viola, Wren, and Robbie. "I think there's only one place for you, a place where we can get some answers."

Julian shook his head. "The Office."

Viola took a deep breath. The Office. Where Maya had been imprisoned and had nearly died.

Cinnial smiled. "Yes, the Office. Bigly is there, and he will take care of these three the same way he did with the girl you brought with you from Caxton."

"Her name is Maya," Julian said.

Cinnial shrugged impatiently. "Whatever. I guess Bigly didn't get too much from her, or I would have heard by now."

Viola, Wren, and Robbie kept their expressions and their thoughts neutral, and to Viola's amazement, she could tell that Julian was doing the same thing. But it was clear that Cinnial wasn't concerned about Maya. He was too preoccupied with beating back Time and Magic, and a small girl from a distant planet wasn't worth his attention.

Before Cinnial could say anything else, there was a knock on the door, and a guard, the woman with the dark hair, called, "Sir, there are two people here to see you."

"Send them away," Cinnial replied curtly. "Right now I'm busy."

There was a brief hesitation before the woman said, "They have traveled across the universe with one of your Books, and they say they have important information for you."

Cinnial frowned. "With one of my Books? Send them in, then."

The door opened, and in walked a woman with white hair and bright red lipstick. Beside her was a bald man with a pale, smooth face and wire-frame glasses. The man was dressed in chinos and a red-checked shirt.

Although the man was wearing different clothes from when they had last seen him, Robbie and Viola recognized him, and they stared in astonishment.

265

"Chet," Robbie blurted out, and to steady herself, Viola grabbed the blond boy's arm.

Chet sneered at them. "Surprised to see me? Thought I wouldn't catch on to your plans if you moved far enough away from me, didn't you? But I knew where your plotting would lead." He looked around, and the sneer left his face to be replaced with an amazed expression. "Right here to the Great Library."

"Who are you two?" Cinnial asked. "Clearly, you know these kids."

Wren shook her head. "I've never seen this man."

Cinnial gave Wren a look that suggested she shouldn't speak unless spoken to, and Wren stared down at her feet.

The woman's voice was brisk. "My name is Lillian Rourke, and I come from Earth, a very small planet on the edge of the Milky Way Galaxy. This is Chet Addington, and he also comes from Earth. We're with an organization called APO, and we've worked long and hard to protect one of your Books."

"APO," Cinnial said. "I've heard of it and all that you've done. Have a seat."

Chet and Lillian sat down while the kids remained standing. Chet nodded at Julian, who wearily nodded back.

"You two know each other?" Cinnial asked.

"We met briefly in Caxton," Julian answered.

Cinnial shook his head. "Another planet that's on the edge of things. Odd how small places can have an outsize effect."

Chet's lips curled in disgust. "The same is true of people. Thanks to one small girl—Maya—I was imprisoned in Caxton for years, and only by the strangest circumstances was I set free."

"Maya," Cinnial repeated.

"Maya," Chet said. "Do not underestimate her, sir."

Opening his Book, Cinnial asked, "What is happening with Maya? Is Bigly done with her?"

The Book answered in a tone that in a person would have been described as sheepish. "No, Cinnial. Maya escaped before Bigly could get any information from her."

"You might have told me," Cinnial snapped. Then in a softer voice. "Bigly should have told me."

"I was not paying attention to Maya," came the Book's stiff response. "We were focusing on other more important things."

Chet pointed to Viola. "And here's another girl you should be concerned about. Even though her hair is a different color, I recognize her. She came with Maya to Caxton and has been foiling me in a way that's also at odds with her size."

Julian made a sound that was something between a cough and a laugh.

Cinnial glared at him. "Do you think this is funny?"

"A little," Julian admitted. "But of course you don't. And I understand why. But still..."

Turning away from Julian in disgust, Cinnial held up the lock for Chet and Lillian to look at. "Have either of you ever seen this?"

"No," Chet said.

"Neither have I," Lillian answered. "But I know what it is, and I know where it came from. Hell, I can even guess who made it."

Cinnial frowned. "So tell me."

Lillian replied, "The lock comes from a dimension called Elferterre. I expect you've heard of it, seeing as how you were educated at the Great Library." Both Cinnial and Julian nodded. "Locks like this are rare and are used to imprison folks and creatures. And unless I'm very much mistaken, an elf named Galli made this lock."

"How do you know all this?" Cinnial asked.

"Because I'm an elf, too, and I originally came from Elferterre." Lillian waved her hands over her ears. There was a slight shimmer, and her pointed ears were revealed.

Chet pointed at Viola. "Did she bring the lock here to trap you?"

"So it seems," Cinnial answered in a low voice as he considered Viola. "Did you get this lock in Elferterre?"

Viola stared evenly at Cinnial. "Remember what I said? I'm not telling you anything."

Before Cinnial could respond, Lillian rapped out a sharp command. "Look at me, child."

Against her better judgment, Viola turned from Cinnial and gazed into Lillian's eyes.

Lillian's voice was smooth but insistent. "Tell me where you got that lock."

If it hadn't been for the charm, Viola might have answered Lillian's question. But the charm was there, steadying her, shielding Viola from the elf's power.

"No," Viola said.

Lillian's eyes were narrow. "Something is protecting the girl."

"Like what?" Cinnial asked, clearly astonished that he had been caught off-guard yet again.

"Some kind of relic," Lillian answered. "Child, pull down the neck of your shirt."

"No," Viola repeated.

Lillian leaned forward. "Either you do it, or I will."

Reluctantly, Viola pulled down the neck of her shirt to reveal the glimmer of the charm and its chain.

Chet squinted at it. "I can barely see anything there. Is that a necklace?"

Lillian stood. "There's something there all right. A protection charm. A relic, in fact. Made with some kind of magic. But where did that kind of magic come from in this universe?"

Cinnial's Book said, "The ashes from the Ancient One."

"That blew over Watertown," Julian murmured, studying Viola, Wren, and Robbie. "You all have one, don't you?"

But before the kids could answer, a mighty sound—a song made of many voices—swirled around the Great Library, and deep inside, where there were no guards, came a great clatter, as ladders left their shelves, grouping to attack Cinnial's troops and staff.

26: BIGLY IS WATCHING

Maya shook her head as she looked around. It felt odd to be back on Black Mountain. So many adventures had happened since she had left that it seemed like years since she had been there. But as though it remembered her, Black Mountain rumbled in what felt like a greeting.

As the relics cautiously climbed out of Maya's pockets and made their way to her shoulders, Thirret said in relief, "The mountain's welcoming you." There were two more rumbles. "And me and Will, too." Thirret was still for a moment. "Something else is hidden there, too, besides Tufrak's Book of Everything. I can feel it. An oak with golden acorns."

"Makes sense," Maya said. "We could communicate with thoughts here. That only happens in my universe when there's a source of magic nearby, doesn't it?"

"That's right." Thirret looked around in admiration. "And the mountain has its own energy. When you combine that with the oak's, well, that's a lot of power. Anyway, as much as I'd like to explore Black Mountain and visit the compound, we'd better get going." He reached into one of his pockets, and out came his hand with three sparkling acorns nestled in his palm.

Maya said to the relics, "Better go back into my pockets. Traveling with an acorn is rough. I know we're not going very far, but I wouldn't want any of you to fall."

Eloise nodded. "Good idea. And who knows how our magic will work when we're away from the mountain?"

"Your magic will still work," Thirret replied. "But it won't be as strong as it was in Elferterre. You'll have to pace yourselves here."

"Right," Eloise said, and the relics made their way back into Maya's pockets.

Thirret passed an acorn to Maya and Will. "Ready?"

"Ready," they answered.

"Take us to Mortmain," Thirret instructed the acorns. "To where Maya's Apprentice Book is being held."

With a whoosh and a snap, the three were hurtled along a glittering route from Black Mountain to the sea, where they skimmed over the water, and finally back to land. In a blur, Maya saw ports and boats and people and trolls and big factories and cars and trucks. Nobody looked up as they streaked by, and Maya guessed that the magic shielded them from anyone's notice. There was one exception. As they passed a semitruck, a blue-skinned woman on the passenger's side glanced up, and with a start, Maya realized the woman was Arless, second-in-command at the Black Mountain Compound. With a slight smile, Arless looked at Maya and even gave a little salute.

Arless can see me, Maya thought in surprise. *But where is she going?* Then: *Arless and the resistance are going to try to take back Mortmain.* In a flash, Maya sensed that at the Great Library, Viola was confronting Cinnial, and the time for everyone to move was now, now, now while he was distracted.

"Hurry!" Maya cried aloud, and in her pockets the relics stirred in sympathy.

Soon after seeing Arless, they approached the imposing city of Mortmain, all gleaming angles and tall buildings unsoftened by any green spaces. They were whisked into the Office, the second tallest building in Mortmain, and Maya felt a shudder of fear as she remembered the devices Bigly had used on her in a basement room, devices that had drilled into her brain as they tried to dig out information, devices that had nearly killed her.

But to Maya's relief, the acorns did not take them to the basement. Instead, midway up the Office, they went to a large open room filled with long tables and chairs. Although the room was mostly empty, wires, cords, and odd parts were scattered on tables and on shelves against the walls. As Maya gripped the side of a table to steady herself from the short but intense trip with the acorn, she could hear faint ghostly sounds of the whirring of machines, and she knew exactly what this room had been used for.

Will, too, was gripping a table. "Where are we?"

"This is the Office," Maya told him. "And this room is where Cinnial's Books were created. It's where they broke the green Book so that Cinnial could find his way to the Great Library."

Thirret murmured, "A lot of misery was created here."

Maya felt the weight of Cinnial's Books. "Yeah, it's like everything is coated with it."

Will shuddered. "It hangs over the entire room. How could anyone even stand to be here?"

"Cinnial's followers don't see it that way," Thirret shifted uncomfortably, and Maya realized even his elven nature couldn't shield him from the room's oppressive vibes. "To them, this is the way to shift things in their direction, to control, to make everyone follow along."

"But why?" Maya asked. She had been puzzling over this question ever since the librarians in East Vassalboro had told her about Cinnial and his Books.

Thirret shrugged. "I don't know. But we have the same problem in Elferterre. That's why my family was exiled to Earth. But let's find Ariel and get out of here. Later we can have a longer discussion about why folks follow tyrants."

Maya looked around the room. On a bookcase at the far end, she saw a familiar blue Book on the top shelf. "Ariel!" she cried, moving across the room as fast as her shaky legs would allow. With trembling hands, Maya opened the Book.

"Maya!" Ariel called. "You came back for me. But be careful. There are cameras everywhere in this room. Bigly is watching."

Before anyone could respond, a deep voice behind them said in triumph, "I knew you'd come back for your precious little blue Book. That's why I didn't have it destroyed along with the green Book."

Maya, Will, and Thirret whirled around to see a short squat troll with a huge wedge-shaped head with thin strands of brown hair that looked as though they had been glued in place. Maya studied the pock-marked face, the small pale blue eyes. "Bigly," she said, her voice flat. "I should have guessed you'd be nearby."

271

The troll's eyes glittered. "For the past few weeks, I've been waiting and watching in the room next door." The troll was holding a gun, and he pointed it at Maya. "Don't move." With his head, he motioned to Will and Thirret. "And the same goes for you. I could shoot you one, two, three, and you'd be down before you even knew what happened. The bullets in this gun go very fast."

"Could you?" Thirret stared intently at Bigly as he directed the full force of his charisma toward the troll. "But why would you want to?" Thirret smiled. "Why not just let us go? We'll take the blue Book, and you'll never have to see us again."

Bigly laughed, a rasping noise that gave Maya the impression that this was a sound the troll seldom made. "That might work on humans. Or on other elves. Because that's what you are, isn't it? An elf. I've heard of your kind and Elferterre. But your bad tricks won't work on me. I can tell by your attitude that you think you're one of the loveliest creatures who ever came to Mortmain. Far better than us ugly trolls." He stared at Maya and Will, and his eyes gleamed with hate. "You two think the same way as the elf. But to me, you are all so hideous that I can hardly stand looking at your faces, and nothing would make me happier than to kill the three of you right here and now. So don't push your luck."

As Thirret continued to stare at Bigly, Maya trembled but made herself ask, "If you think elves and humans are so hideous, then why do you serve Cinnial?"

"Looks have nothing to do with why I follow Sir," Bigly replied in a voice choked with intensity. "I follow him because he's Sir, and he's above all creatures."

Thirret shook his head. "Nobody is above all creatures."

"Sir is," Bigly rapped out.

Will stared intently at Bigly. "And does Sir know that Maya escaped? I bet he doesn't. I bet you've kept that little fact from him."

Grimacing, Bigly pointed the gun at Will's head. "I should just kill you. Nobody would miss you."

Will said coolly, "But you're not going to do that because you want information, and you're going to take us to the basement."

Bigly smiled a terrible smile. "Correct. And you'll be in chains all the time, even when you're in your cells. There will be no escaping." Bigly glared at Maya. "How did you do it? You might as well tell me. I'll get it out of you one way or another."

Maya felt the relics stir as they slowly made their way to the edge of her pockets—the tickle of Orlaith's legs, the scrape of Aiken's claws, and Eloise's prickly slide. Maya thought, *I've got to keep him talking*. Aloud she said, "You're so smart. You guess. How did I do it?"

"Don't play games with me. I could shoot your leg. It wouldn't kill you. Matter of fact I could shoot each one of you in the leg."

"But if you did that, then we probably wouldn't be in the mood to tell you very much," Maya said. "We'd be in too much pain."

"That you might." Bigly pursed his lips. "But if I shot the elf, then I'd still have you two to work on. In fact, I think I will. That way you'll know I'm not just kidding around. I'm tired of his ugly smirk, and I probably wouldn't get that much out of him anyway. After all, he is an elf," Bigly conceded grudgingly.

There was no more talk. Bigly aimed the gun at Thirret's leg and pulled the trigger. With frightening speed and a high-pitched whine, a bullet flew from the gun. Murmuring and holding up his hand, Thirret tried to stop the bullet, but it hit his leg before the spell was finished. The elf, with a cry, fell to the floor, and blood gushed from the wound.

"Thirret!" Maya and Will exclaimed together, moving toward the elf.

"Stay right where you are," Bigly rapped out. "Or I'll shoot his other leg."

Maya and Will stopped, but in the uproar, the relics had crawled out of Maya's pockets. They had made their way up her back and were perched on her shoulders.

"Ready?" Eloise asked.

"Ready," Aiken and Orlaith replied.

As Bigly stared in surprise at the three relics, Eloise directed her light at the troll, wrapping it in coils around him and holding him in place. Orlaith climbed onto Aiken's back and the dragon flew to Bigly. So fast she was almost a blur, Orlaith dropped onto the troll's shoulder, and with a flash of tiny fangs, she bit him. As the gun clattered to the floor, Bigly screamed in pain and might have fallen if he hadn't been held in place by Eloise's rope of light.

With Bigly immobilized but still conscious, Maya and Will hurried over to Thirret. Sliding out of her backpack, Maya unzipped

273

it and found a shirt, which she wrapped in a tight band around Thirret's leg. Will helped her with the knot so that it was tight enough to staunch most of the bleeding.

"Maya!" Orlaith called. "Shall I bite the troll again? It would knock him out for a long time."

"That would be good," Aiken said.

Maya looked up from Thirret, whose face was pale with pain. Her hands and sleeves were bloody, and so were Will's. As Maya considered Bigly, she thought about Arless and the resistance just outside Mortmain. If Bigly, sharp and smart, were knocked out, then that would be one less problem for Arless to face when she attacked the city.

"Yes," Maya told Orlaith. "Bite him and knock him out for a long time."

The spider bit Bigly again, and the troll shrieked in pain and anger. "You haven't won," he said through clenched teeth. "You might be able to beat us back, but you can't destroy us. Cinnial's Books are everywhere across the universe." Then he choked, unable to say any more.

Orlaith jumped onto Aiken's back, and they flew to Maya, landing on her shoulder.

Eloise released Bigly from her light, and the troll fell with a thud. His legs and arms twitched violently, making a thump, thump, thumping sound on the floor. Bigly gasped a few times, and then he was still, his fierce face frozen into a grimace. But Bigly was not unconscious. Bigly was dead.

Maya blinked rapidly. "Oh, Will! I didn't mean for Bigly to die." Will didn't say anything. Instead, he put an arm around Maya's shoulders and held her close.

"I thought his system could handle one more bite," Orlaith said. "He seemed so tough. Like an imp."

Will shrugged. "Who knows what a troll's body can take? Anyway, Bigly is gone, and he won't be bothering anybody ever again."

In shock, Maya nodded slowly, and they turned to Thirret, who was sitting up and gripping his leg. Over and over, he chanted words that Maya couldn't understand. Finally Thirret stopped, regarding them with a weary look.

"I stopped the bleeding," he said. "But the bullet won't come out." Thirret shrugged. "Healing isn't my specialty, but it is my mother's."

"Use your acorn to go back to New York," Maya told him.

"I hate to leave you alone," Thirret muttered.

Maya replied, "We won't be alone. Don't forget, we have the relics. And there will be others waiting for us at the Great Library."

"All right. I'm certainly not much use to you right now." Reaching into his pocket, Thirret withdrew three acorns. He gave one to Maya and one to Will. Gripping the last acorn, Thirret gazed at Maya, Will, and the relics. "Best of luck to you all. We'll be waiting for you at The Other Green Door."

Will patted Thirret on the shoulder, and Maya gave the elf a gentle hug. She said, "We'll trap Cinnial in the lock and bring him to The Other Green Door. Now go back to Earth so your mother can heal your leg."

Thirret kissed them on both cheeks. "May Magic be with you." Then he said to the acorn. "Take me to Earth, to The Other Green Door."

With a pop, Thirret was gone, leaving Maya and Will with blood on their hands and sleeves, a dark stain on the floor, and a dead troll not far from them.

Will shook his head. "What a mess."

"Yeah," Maya agreed, looking around the room. She saw a closed door on the wall across from them. "Maybe that's a restroom?"

Will considered the door. "Maybe."

"I know we need to get out of here before anyone comes looking for Bigly..."

"But let's get cleaned up first," Will finished.

Maya smiled wanly. "Before the next mess."

Behind the door there was indeed a restroom with a row of stalls and two sinks. The relics perched on top of the paper towel holder closest to Maya's sink, and Ariel, as small as a pocket address book, was beside them and open. Without saying much to each other, Maya and Will took off their tunics and washed the blood from their hands. As Maya, wearing only a bra, glanced at herself in the mirror, she saw that Will was looking at her. He grinned sheepishly, and she grinned back, feeling that maybe, just maybe, Will was beginning to thaw. At least a little. They took clean tunics from their backpacks and put them on. Rolling their dirty tunics into a ball, they stuffed them into their packs.

"To the Great Library with the golden acorns?" Ariel asked, and the Book's tone was mixed with equal measures of dread and acceptance. Maya understood that things were in so much flux that Ariel didn't even have a glimpse of the various possibilities. The Book was afraid their mission would fail.

"Yes," Maya answered.

To make matters worse, Eloise said, "Thirret was right about our power being diminished in this universe. We'll do what we can but..."

"It might not be as much as it should be," Aiken added. "That battle with the troll drained us. I can't fly far in this universe."

Orlaith's legs trembled. "I'm not sure I even have one more bite left in me until I rest and recharge."

Maya nodded as she held up a hand for the relics to crawl into. "I understand. Do what you can."

After putting the relics into her side pockets and Ariel into a back pocket, Maya looked at Will, and she knew what he was thinking—instead of asking the acorns to take them to the Great Library, they would ask to be taken far, far away across the universe to a planet that didn't have one of Cinnial's Books. There they would make a life together, doing what they could to help whatever society they landed in. They would become partners, have children, and grow old together, dying a peaceful death when that time came.

A tear slid down Maya's cheek, and Will wiped it away with one of his fingers.

Removing the acorns from their back pockets, they nodded at each other.

"Take us to Viola in the Great Library," Maya said.

27: HIS FEARFUL POWER

From the Great Library came sounds Julian had been anticipating and dreading. The ladders were on the move, and he could hear screams as they attacked Cinnial's staff and troops. There were gunshots and responding screams, almost too high-pitched to hear, and Julian knew this sound came from ladders being blown to bits by Cinnial's troops. Julian sat still as he thought about how there were so many ladders on floors that never seemed to end. However, Cinnial's force was large. He had brought the bulk of his troops with him when he came to the Great Library and had left only a skeleton crew in Mortmain. Cinnial hadn't felt safe without a large force to protect him from an expected attack from Watertown. For weeks and weeks, they had waited. Nothing. The citizens of Watertown had been strangely passive, something that had puzzled both Julian and Cinnial.

As Julian listened to the mighty song that was swirling around the library, he realized the citizens of Watertown hadn't been passive at all. Instead, using the magic given to them by the Ancient Oak, they had been preparing for an attack using a weapon that Cinnial and Julian had least expected—their voices.

"What the hell is going on?" Chet asked, jumping to his feet.

Lillian remained seated. "Nothing good." She stared from Cinnial to Julian. "You are under attack. From within and without." There were more loud cracks and screams, and the volume of the song began to increase. "Chet and I came here to warn you that the exiled librarians were plotting against you." She considered Viola, Wren, and Robbie. "And that they would be using kids to do their dirty work. However, it seems we're too late. I had hoped to come sooner, but there other matters I had to attend to first." Getting up, Lillian went to the door and made circular motions with her hands. The air around the door shimmered as the magic took hold and created a barrier. Lillian went to the windows and did the same thing. "There," Lillian said to Cinnial and Julian. "That should hold the ladders and the voices off for a while. Not indefinitely. In this universe, my magic is not strong enough to hold for very long, even on this island where there's so much magic. But it will give you some time."

"Time for what?" Cinnial asked incredulously.

"To plan what you're going to do next," Lillian said with a flicker of impatience as though she expected Cinnial to be a more nimble thinker.

But Julian knew from long experience that Cinnial was not a nimble thinker. Instead, he operated at a slow burn, counting on his charisma and force of personality to power his way through any obstacles he might encounter on the way to his one shining goal—taking over the Great Library. So far, this tactic had worked all too well for Cinnial, but Julian saw with a piercing clarity that what had once been a good strategy was not going to be effective against the many forces mounted against him at the Great Library.

Shaking her head in disgust, Lillian got up and stood beside Chet. "You two should plan where you're going to go next and then get out of here." Speechless, Cinnial glowered at her. Pursing her lips, Lillian regarded him the way she might a stubborn child. "Your moods have no effect on me. Don't forget, I'm from Elferterre. I've lived a long, long time, and I've encountered many like you."

Julian watched in amazement as Lillian shook her finger at Cinnial. He couldn't remember the last time anyone had done that. Probably when they were students together at the Great Library, and a professor had given Cinnial a dressing-down for being late with an assignment. Even Chet looked shocked, but his expression indicated that he respected Lillian for her refusal to be cowed by Cinnial.

Lillian continued, "Really, it always comes down to the same thing. Humans like you are long on bluster and bravado and short on planning. My boss has had her doubts about you for a long time. We might use your Book. Why wouldn't we? It has its own crazy power, and we have been able to work it to our advantage. But we have seen your weakness right from the start. We hoped things wouldn't end this way, but there you are." She tilted her head as she regarded Cinnial. "Still, we thought you'd hold out a little longer."

"Shouldn't have burned down the Ancient One," Julian said in a soft voice.

"Right." Leaning forward, Lillian rapped her red nails on Cinnial's desk. "A big mistake. One of many."

In fury, Cinnial tried to open the drawer where he kept his gun, but he only managed to open it a crack before Lillian used her magic to slam it shut. "Oh, please," she said in disdain. "You were going to shoot me? Really? My magic might not be as strong here as it is in Elferterre, but I can certainly use it to lock a drawer."

Refusing to be intimidated by Lillian, Cinnial sat up straight and gathered his glittering pride, holding it close. For this, Julian admired Cinnial. The refusal to be unbowed, no matter the circumstance, had drawn Julian to Cinnial right from the start, when they were both apprentices and had first met at the Great Library. When their Books had been declined, Julian had felt a searing rejection that had nearly paralyzed him. Cinnial, on the other hand, had been energized and had forged ahead without looking back, stealing his Apprentice Book, convincing Julian to do the same thing, and then escaping to a planet with so many failing states that taking over one of them and setting up headquarters had been ridiculously easy.

"Are you finished?" Cinnial asked in a low enraged voice.

"Almost," Lillian conceded.

During this exchange, Viola, Wren, and Robbie had watched with a fascination that rocked between awe and terror. Wisely, they decided not to add anything to the conversation and instead let the adults thrash it out.

But Lillian hadn't forgotten them, and she turned her attention to Viola, Wren, and Robbie. "Then there are you three. I don't suppose you would consider coming to Earth and joining up with APO, would you? You got much further ahead than any of us could expect." She addressed Julian. "Am I right?"

Julian sighed. Viola, Wren, and Robbie's betrayal had cut deep. "Yes," he answered, his voice sad. "I never suspected them. Not once."

Lillian's lips quirked into an approving grin. "Young but devious. I like that. What do you say?"

With Lillian's attention focused on the kids, Cinnial tried the drawer again, but it wouldn't budge.

Lillian regarded Cinnial with exasperation. "You don't listen, do you?"

Here Julian actually laughed. "No, he never has."

With narrow eyes, Cinnial gave Julian a hard look, but he didn't say anything.

Ignoring Cinnial, Lillian studied Viola, Wren, and Robbie. "What do you say?"

Vehemently, Viola shook her head. "Of course we're not going to join you."

"No way," Wren added.

"Never in a million years," Robbie said.

"That's what I thought," Lillian replied. "But it never hurts to ask. You're as stubborn as Cinnial, but even at your young age, you're better planners than he is. If you make it out alive, no doubt we will meet again. But I wouldn't put money on your survival." She turned to Chet. "And what about you? Are you coming with me?"

"Yeah," Chet answered after staring at everyone in the room.

Lillian said, "Good choice." The windows rattled with all the voices pressed against them, but the elf's magic held, and the glass didn't break. Lillian glanced at the windows. "It's not going to end well here." She withdrew a blue Book from her back pocket.

Shocked, Julian noticed that small pieces had been cut from the cover.

Noting Julian's astonished expression, Lillian shrugged. "We used bits of the cover to make devices to shield our agents from Earth's Book of Everything. After all, needs must." To Chet: "Hold my arm." To Cinnial: "Goodbye. Sorry it turned out this way. I really am. We had such hopes for you." To the drawer: "You may open as soon as I'm gone." To the Book: "Take us back to APO's headquarters."

Then Chet and Lillian were gone, leaving behind an empty space where they had once been. Lunging for the drawer, Cinnial pulled hard, and it flew open, knocking him back in his chair. He swore and removed a gun, sleek and silver.

Getting up, Cinnial pointed the gun at Viola. "Now, then."

Cinnial was back in charge. But Lillian had left the lock on the desk, and in Cinnial's ensuing struggle with the drawer, the lock had somehow gotten pushed to one side and was partially hidden under some papers. Julian wondered why Lillian hadn't taken the relic with her. After all, it was from Elferterre. Did she leave it on the desk on purpose, her puckish way of handing Cinnial's fate to Chance or Nemesis? Or did she forget? Julian decided it was unlikely that Lillian had forgotten about the lock. He opened his mouth to call Cinnial's attention to the lock, but he didn't say anything. With that decision, Julian finally swerved from the path he had taken all those long years ago.

Cinnial told the kids, "I should kill you three right now. I don't need any more information. Lillian told me plenty, and that's enough."

Shivering, the kids held hands, but they didn't say anything.

Julian stood. "What would that accomplish?" He knew that changing Cinnial's mind was a long shot, but he had to try.

"You're not getting soft, are you?" Cinnial asked Julian. But his gaze and the gun were still trained on Viola.

There didn't seem to be any point in lying. "Maybe I am," Julian replied. "And maybe it's about time. Long past time."

Cinnial stood perfectly still. "What are you saying?"

"Let's leave this place. Let's take your Book and go far, far away. We can start over."

Cinnial's open Book had been silent, but now it spoke, "Julian has a point. The Elf's magic won't hold the doors and windows much longer. Your troops and staff are being routed by the voices, the ladders, and, odd as this sounds, by the gardeners, who have turned out to be fierce fighters. The Great Library is going to fall, and there's nothing we can do about it. It's time to leave."

"No." Cinnial's voice was hoarse with emotion. "I'll never leave. No matter what. This is my place. This is where I've always wanted to be. All the time we were in exile in Mortmain, it was the thought of taking the Great Library that kept me going." Cinnial's face was flushed, and his jaw was a hard line. "Sydda was wrong to reject our Books. He left us with no choice. All that has happened since is his fault. His death, all the other deaths are on him." Cinnial repeated, "He left us with no choice."

Julian put his hand on Cinnial's trembling arm. "We've always had a choice. You know that. But we made the wrong ones, and this is where they've brought us."

281

Outside, voices shook the windows, and there were loud crashes as ladders threw themselves against the office door.

With a tremor of fear, Cinnial's Book said, "Astrid and the Great Library's Book are here. She used a golden acorn to travel. I stopped them from coming directly into this office, but it's drained me, and I have just enough energy to take you and Julian someplace else. With the Great Library's Book hammering away at me, I won't even have that for long."

"Hold the Great Library's Book off as long as you can," Cinnial told his Book.

"Will do," came the resigned answer.

Turning to the kids, Cinnial said, "If I go down, then you'll go down, too." The gun was still pointed at Viola, and Cinnial's arm was no longer shaking.

Viola, Wren, and Robbie closed their eyes and waited for Cinnial to pull the trigger. But Julian grabbed Cinnial's arm, and when the gun went off, the bullet hit a vase at the far end of the room. In a burst, the vase shattered, sending shards of glass harmlessly to the floor.

"Julian!" Cinnial's face was twisted with disbelief, anger, and hurt.

Julian had a tight grip on Cinnial's arm. "The kids are going to make it out of here alive."

"I trusted you."

Julian closed his eyes and then opened them. "I know." He took a deep breath. "But this is how things will end. We're going to let the kids go, and then we're either going to leave this place or surrender."

Julian and Cinnial stared at each other. Neither man blinked. Neither man would back down.

Horrified and fascinated, Viola watched the confrontation between Julian and Cinnial. Their focus was on each other and no one else. To them, Viola, Wren, and Robbie didn't exist anymore. There was a tap on the window, and Viola heard a voice she recognized. It was Mémère's voice: "Viola, get the lock on the desk! Get it now!" Then Lexie's and Jay's: "Hurry while you have the chance."

"Go," Wren urged in a whisper.

"Now's the time." Robbie's voice was also a whisper.

Lunging toward the desk, Viola reached for the lock, but there was a tap on the window that made her look up. A blonde woman stared at Viola. Startled, Viola tripped over a metal wastebasket, which made a loud clatter as it went over. With great resolve, the voices outside joined together to push away the blonde woman.

The clatter of the wastebasket broke Cinnial's concentration, and he whirled around to see Viola sprawled over the desk. He raised the gun, aiming it at Viola, but as he did, Mémère's voice came through loud and clear: "Cinnial, if you harm that girl, I will break through this glass and strangle you with my own voice."

Blinking at the window and the voice, which was joined by a slight dark-haired woman, Cinnial hesitated for a brief moment, and as he did, Julian grabbed for the gun. Startled, Cinnial pulled the trigger and shot Julian in the chest. Crumpling, Julian fell to the floor. Cinnial let go of the gun, which hit the floor with a clang and skittered under the desk. Crying out in anguish, Cinnial dropped down to cradle Julian, who lay dying.

Screaming, Viola scrambled off the desk.

Wren cried, "Oh, no!"

Robbie called, "Julian!"

For a moment, everything was still—the voices outside the window; the ladders throwing themselves against the door; the people in the room. The dark-haired woman had vanished.

Cinnial touched Julian's face. "Don't leave me."

Julian sighed and sighed again. Then he was dead.

Crying, Viola held the lock in one of her hands. "You killed Julian!"

Wren was crying, too. "How could you?"

Robbie said, "He was the only one who really cared about you."

Cinnial looked from the kids to Julian and then back to the kids again. His voice was thin and brittle. "If you hadn't come, none of this would have happened. Julian would still be alive."

As her face flushed, Viola felt a rage she had never felt before. "No, Cinnial. This is on you. You shot Julian. You two could have taken your Book and gone off somewhere. But you didn't. You pushed and pushed to the very end, and this is what happened. Wherever you go, you destroy. And the pathetic thing is that you can't help it. You don't know how to do anything else."

Cinnial stood in a rush, and his rage matched Viola's. "You're just a half-cocked kid. The librarians are such cowards. They didn't dare face me. So they sent you." He scowled at Wren and Robbie. "And you and you."

There was a knock on the door, and a firm voice said, "Cinnial, it's Astrid. It's over out here. Open the door and let me in. The magic on this door and windows won't hold for very much longer. And neither will your Book."

Cinnial laughed, a wild unhinged sound that was as scary as anything Viola had ever heard. "No, Astrid. Not now. Not ever. Because it's not over in here, not by a damned long shot."

"Leave the kids alone," came Astrid's command.

Mémère's voice, along with Jay's and Lexie's, hurled against the window, and small cracks formed in some of the panes.

Cinnial's expression was as wild as his voice had been. "Don't worry, Astrid. I'm going to give the kids exactly what they want. A chance to trap me in the lock." Standing straight and tall, he faced Viola, Wren, and Robbie. "Go ahead," he goaded, gathering up his will into a tight coil. "Trap me!"

Viola pointed the lock at Cinnial, but her will was no match for his, and she felt him hammer away at her, pushing the lock's magic back toward her until Viola wondered if she was the one who was going to be sucked inside. In despair, Viola realized that it had been one thing to creep up on Cinnial and trap him unawares and quite another to face Cinnial head on, when his anger and fearful power were at their peak.

"Help me!" Viola cried. As Wren grabbed her hand, Robbie grabbed Wren's hand, and the three joined their wills together, directing the lock's energy to trap Cinnial.

But Cinnial's will held fast. While it didn't move the lock's energy, his will held the kids in place. And there they were, at an impasse: Cinnial against Viola, Wren, and Robbie with the twitching lock between them.

With a pop, the acorns brought Maya and Will to Cinnial's office in the Great Library. As voices smashed at the windows, and thuds and screams came from behind the closed door, the office felt like the eye of a strange wild hurricane.

Maya and Will dropped the blackened acorns onto the floor, and a glad voice called, "Maya! Oh, Maya!"

"Mémère?" Puzzled and in a daze from traveling with an acorn, Maya looked around, but all she could see were Cinnial, Viola, and two teenagers she didn't recognize, although the boy with the blond hair looked familiar. Cinnial and the teenagers were so absorbed with each other that they didn't notice Maya and Will.

"Over here." Mémère's voice rapped against the window. Another crack appeared, and then another.

"We're here, too," Lexie and Jay chimed together.

Maya and Will stared at the window behind Cinnial's desk. There were tiny shimmering forces battering away at the glass, which looked as though it wouldn't hold for much longer.

"Mémère, is that your voice?" Maya asked in amazement, shaking her head to clear it. "But where's your body?"

"A long story," Mémère replied. "Later, I'll tell you all about it. But right now you have to help Viola, Wren, and Robbie. Cinnial's too strong for them."

"Go, Maya!" Jay urged.

"You've been working toward this moment for a long time," Lexie said.

Maya stared at Cinnial. His face was red and scrunched into furrows as he tried to use the lock's power to trap the kids, whose faces were as red as Cinnial's. They were holding him off, but they weren't strong enough to bring him into the lock. Relentlessly, his will battered at Viola, Wren, and Robbie, slowly chipping away at them, directing the lock to trap them.

Eloise had climbed to Maya's shoulder as had Aiken and Orlaith. "I don't have much left after Bigly, but I'll use my light to help however much it can."

"Orlaith and I are in even worse shape," Aiken said. "But whatever power we have, we'll transfer to you and Will. Put me on his shoulder."

"Okay," Maya whispered, setting Aiken on Will's shoulder. She felt a tingle of power from Orlaith and saw Will straighten up as the dragon gave him the last of what he had. Maya's head felt clearer, and she could tell Will felt better, too.

He said, "Go get the lock from Viola."

"Right. But I need you, Will. I need everyone. I can't do this by myself."

Will took her hand. "I'll be right beside you." He gave her a quick kiss on the cheek. "Let's go."

285

Maya and Will went to Viola's side. Maya placed her hand on the exhausted girl's shoulder, and the contest of wills faltered. Cinnial, Viola, Wren, and Robbie looked away from each other to stare at Maya and Will.

"Maya!" Viola said in relief.

Panting, Cinnial managed to say, "Well here you finally are."

"Here I am," Maya replied as Viola slid the lock into her hand.

Cinnial sneered. "You think the five of you can take me down?"

Maya glared at Cinnial. "Yes." Her voice rang firm and clear. "We're going to trap you in this lock and never hear from you again. Any last words?"

With a mighty roar, Cinnial gathered himself and flung everything he had at the teenagers. In one hand, Maya grasped the lock, and she held it high. Will clasped her other hand. Viola took Will's free hand. Next came Wren then Robbie, and the five made a half-circle around the desk, directing their energy toward Cinnial.

Eloise's light, a little dim, shined on Cinnial, and while it didn't stop him, the way it had with Bigly, the light slowed him down. At the same time, the kids' energy pushed harder and harder, directing the lock's power away from them toward Cinnial.

Maya: "Give up! You're no match for all of us."

Will: "Get in that lock, you asshole."

Viola: "Come on, come on!"

Wren: "Just a little more."

Robbie: "Almost there."

And, finally, Cinnial: "No, no, no!"

A wild force surrounded Cinnial. It was Chaos, giving Cinnial a boost, and the chain of hands trembled.

The window by the desk crashed, and voices poured into the office. Mémère, Jay, and Lexie rushed around and around Cinnial, but still he held fast, bolstered by Chaos. Then two more forces—Time and Magic—swept into the room. They knocked Cinnial and Chaos off balance, and that last push was what it took to overcome Cinnial. With a scream of anguish and terror, Cinnial was sucked into the lock, which snapped shut with a horrible finality. Roaring, Chaos fled out the broken window.

A cry of victory rose from Will, Viola, Wren, Robbie, and the voices that filled the room.

Shuddering, Maya squeezed her hand around the lock. She couldn't help but imagine what it must be like to be trapped inside with no way out. Despite all the harm Cinnial had caused, directly and indirectly, Maya felt a measure of sympathy for him.

Mémère's voice gave Maya a tight hug. "Oh, Maya! Don't feel bad. Méchant Cinnial deserves it. You know he does."

"I know." Maya sighed. "But still."

The door burst open with a crash, and in walked Astrid, Elspeth, and a few other librarians. Behind them a phalanx of ladders twitched in anticipation, but Astrid waved them back.

Astrid surveyed the room—the shattered window, the swirling voices, the smashed vase, Julian's dead body, which, with a gasp, Maya noticed for the first time.

The office became quiet.

"Julian saved us," Viola finally said.

Wren rubbed her face. "If it hadn't been for Julian, Cinnial would have killed me, Viola, and Robbie."

"With the silver thing that shot little balls." Robbie's eyes were wide. "It blew that vase to smithereens. I can only imagine what it would have done to us."

"And Cinnial is in the lock?" Astrid asked in a hopeful voice.

Maya showed her the closed lock. "Yes."

The old librarian's wrinkled face creased even more as she smiled. "Good. Very, very good."

Winking, Elspeth said, "Very good is right."

More silence. Then Robbie whooped in delight, and soon everybody was cheering. The glad noise spread throughout the library, from its basement to its highest floors. Maya felt Time's deep chime of satisfaction and the wild swirl of Magic as the two forces left the room and circled the Great Library in a dance of triumph.

At the edge of the island, a slight dark-haired woman stood next to a tall blonde-haired woman.

"Well," said Nemesis, the blonde-haired woman, "your side won."

Chance sighed. "A close call, as always."

"Nah," said Nemesis. "There were too many forces arrayed against Cinnial. We were outnumbered. And somehow everyone on your side managed to work together."

287

"Everyone did work together." Chance smiled. "And numbers don't lie, do they?"

Nemesis sniffed. "No, but they can be manipulated. This isn't over, you know."

"I do know," Chance replied. She nodded at Nemesis. "Until next time."

Nemesis nodded back. "Until next time."

And the two disappeared.

28: LIBRARY REGAINED

Not long after the office was hurriedly cleaned up, and Astrid was installed as the new director, an exhausted Maya brought the lock to Pawel at The Other Green Door. Elspeth had offered to go instead, but Maya had refused.

"No," she'd said. "I want to see this through."

So Ariel took Maya to the diner in Brooklyn, where Pawel and Khirra were waiting. Thirret, who was pale but obviously healing, was there, too, and beside him sat his cousins Jace and Dagan. They were in the green room, taking a break after closing the café for the day. Ariel had timed it just right.

"You got him," Pawel said in triumph, taking the lock from Maya.

"Yeah," Maya said, then added frankly, "but I had lots of help. I couldn't have done it on my own. Cinnial is powerful." She shivered, remembering. "Very powerful."

"That's how Cinnial got so far," Pawel replied. "And it didn't hurt that he had Chaos to help him. However, Cinnial's loss will be a big blow to Chaos. All over the universe, Cinnial's Books will regroup now that he is gone. But because Cinnial is trapped, their power will be greatly reduced. Also, you should know that APO has moved from Brooklyn. To where, we do not know. But they still have Cinnial's Book. I felt its presence before they moved."

"Unfortunately, APO is run by elves," Khirra told Maya. "I think we mentioned it before, but you might have forgotten, with all that's going on."

"I didn't forget," Maya said. "And when I was in Elferterre, I heard about an elf named Lillian Pineglade. I think she might have something to do with APO."

Khirra nodded. "Lillian is the second-in-command. On Earth she's called Lillian Rourke, and she's sharp, smart, and dangerous."

Pawel said, "When we go back to Norlander and take our rightful places on the council, we will do what we can about Lillian and her boss, Jammisin. In the meantime…"

"Here they are," Maya finished. "Somewhere on Earth."

Pawel replied, "Probably not that far away. But I don't know. I can't feel them nearby. But no doubt they are near a portal."

Grinning, Thirret put his hand on Maya's shoulder. "Wherever they are, they'll have you to reckon with."

Shrugging, Maya didn't say anything, and Jace, Thirret's cousin, gave her a quizzical look. But Maya didn't elaborate. Instead, she gave each elf a hug. "Good luck," she said. "And be careful." Maya thought about Symi, the cook, who had seemed so warm and friendly but who was actually working for Tamick Ashglade. "There are enemies everywhere in Elferterre, and sometimes they're hiding in plain sight."

Pawel's expression was grave. "Thanks for the warning. We will be very careful. And thank you, thank you for all that you've done. Without you, we'd still be trapped on Earth."

"Will, Jay, and Lexie helped, too," Maya reminded him.

"Yes, Will, Jay, and Lexie," Pawel agreed. "They brought us the key."

Thirret cleared his throat. "What are they going to do?"

"I don't think they know yet," Maya answered.

"They have plenty of time to decide." Thirret's lips quirked into a grin. "And what about you and Will?"

Maya shook her head.

Khirra said, "You are a very young human. No need to rush things."

Maya sighed. "Clarin, the captain's daughter, told me the same thing."

"They're both right," Jace said, her voice serious, and Maya got a flash that after helping Pawel, Jace would return to Earth. But Maya didn't mention this, either.

Instead, she looked around at the dark beautiful elves. "Well, it really is time for me to go." Maya took Ariel out of one of the pockets in her trousers. "Goodbye. And good luck to you all."

"Same to you," came the chiming elven chorus.

"Take me back to the Great Library," Maya said to Ariel, and they returned to the lovely white castle with its towers and turrets.

For over two weeks, everyone stayed together at the Great Library. They each had their own bright rooms on the second floor, with Mémère acting as a sort of housemother. But very little chaperoning was necessary. Going against Cinnial had been a sobering experience, and the kids were all emotionally exhausted, going to bed early, sleeping late, and taking long walks by the ocean when they weren't gathering together for meals and snacks. Astrid and Elspeth, busy with putting the Great Library back together, left them alone to think things through. What remained of Cinnial's crew and force had been returned to Mortmain for Arless, now first-in-command, to deal with. The Great Library and the island seemed to sigh in relief when the last of them were gone.

Robbie, even more buoyant than Jay, was the first to recover. Only a few days had gone by before he was out helping Kip—planting cover crops and getting the gardens ready for winter. Over dinner one night, while Robbie explained to everyone the importance of cover crops, Wren gazed tenderly at him.

Next was Jay, who borrowing an electric cart from the Great Library, started going to Watertown to help Isik with his music classes at school, and it wasn't long before Lexie went with him. At night, full of music, they returned to the Great Library, where they played and sang in a packed lounge off the dining room. On the edge, Astrid and Elspeth watched and waited.

Viola, Wren, and Mémère spent happy mornings wandering through the Great Library's stacks. After gathering books, they settled into comfortable chairs to review what they had chosen. Feeling like a ghost, Maya followed them, brushing her fingers along the spines of the books, picking one or two to look at, but not really reading them when she sat with the others.

Without conferring with each other, Viola and Wren avoided the room with Linea Carvella's books.

"I just can't read anything that reminds me of Julian," Viola said sadly one day at lunch.

"Me, neither," Wren replied with tears in her eyes.

Mémère had softened, at least a little. "I'll never forgive Julian for what he did to Maya. But he did save your lives and that counts for something."

Maya didn't say anything, wondering about what really counted in the end. Will glanced at her, but when she looked at him, he turned away. Since the defeat of Cinnial, Will had grown distant, sitting next to Jay when they ate and hardly talking to her at all. Maya understood that Will was still hurt by what had happened in Elferterre between her and Braird. When they had faced Bigly and Cinnial, Will had been able to push the hurt away, but now that he had plenty of time to think, the hurt had come back, and he couldn't let go of it. Maya also knew that like her, Will was grappling with what to do next. Nevertheless, Maya was stung by his coolness, especially now when she was so bone-tired that it was all she could do to get out of bed and join the others for breakfast, lunch, and dinner.

The week following Cinnial's defeat, Maya took a long nap every afternoon after lunch. The first two days, Mémère had poked her head into Maya's room and asked, "Do you want to go for a walk?"

Maya put her hand over her eyes. "I can't. I'm just too tired."

On the second day, sitting on the edge of the bed, Mémère stroked Maya's cheek. "You're just plain worn out. After all you've been through, why wouldn't you be?" Maya pressed her hand against Mémère's hand. "How about if I read a little to you each day before your afternoon nap?"

Blinking away tears, Maya said, "That would be great, Mémère."

The next day Mémère came with a green book tucked under her arm. "Guess what one of the librarians found for me?"

Maya, already snuggled in for her nap, asked, "What?"

"*The Hobbit*! Whoever thought *The Hobbit* would be at the Great Library?"

Maya smiled, and for the first time since the defeat of Cinnial, she felt a slight lifting of her spirits. "Mémère, I think they have everything here."

Mémère laughed. "Of course they do. This is the Great Library. Anyway, I remember how much you loved this book when you were younger. Thought it might bring back good memories."

Turning on her side, Maya faced her grandmother. "*The Hobbit* is perfect."

Sitting down on a chair beside the bed, Mémère opened the book and read:

In a hole in the ground there lived a hobbit. Not a nasty, dirty, wet hole, filled with the ends of worms and an oozy smell, nor yet a dry, bare, sandy hole with nothing in it to sit down on or to eat: it was a hobbit-hole, and that means comfort.

Hearing Mémère's voice, Viola and Wren poked their heads in the doorway. "Is it all right if we listen, too?"

Maya sat up. "Come join us." There was just enough room for three on the bed. Smiling, Maya patted the space on either side of her, and kicking off their shoes, Viola and Wren settled next to Maya. When Mémère was done with the day's reading, three girls were sleeping, and she tiptoed out of the room.

By the time Bilbo Baggins confronted Smaug the dragon, the naps had grown shorter and shorter until none of the girls fell asleep anymore and instead listened avidly as Mémère read the last few chapters.

When the story ended, Wren said, "That Bilbo might be small, but he sure is clever. And he's fast on his feet."

"Bilbo is quite the hobbit," Mémère agreed.

Viola's voice was soft. "My father loves this book."

Maya said, "So does mine."

Mémère ran her hand across the book. "Bilbo had his adventures. And we've had ours." Looking at Maya then at Wren and Viola, she might have noted that life goes on. But she didn't. Instead, Mémère asked Maya, "A walk tomorrow?"

Finally ready for a walk, Maya said, "Sounds good, Mémère."

The next day, after breakfast, when Maya returned to her room, she opened Ariel, who had been allowed to stay with her. The relics were perched on the stand by the bed.

The Book said, "I've got some good news and some bad news for you. I've been waiting until you weren't so tired to tell you."

"Thanks, Ariel. Tell me the good news first. Please."

"In all likelihood, the Vassalboro Public Library is going to open again."

Maya smiled, thinking of the little library not far from her grandparents' farmhouse in Maine. "That is good news. What happened?"

Ariel answered, "Your grandfather had a bad feeling about the town manager. When he looked into the town's finances, he found out that the town manager had been skimming plenty from the budget. For himself."

"Skunk," Maya said in a fierce voice.

"Well, that skunk has been fired. There will be an emergency town meeting, and unless something goes very wrong, the library's budget will be restored."

"Oh, that's wonderful!" Then she frowned. "What's the bad news?"

"Sir John is dead," Ariel said.

Maya took a deep breath. "How?"

"He was killed in a fight with Humphrey."

"And Humphrey?"

"Dead, too."

Even though she had never wanted Humphrey to die, Maya couldn't feel too sorry that he was gone. Now Rosalind and Sebastian could return to Caxton, where they belonged.

"What about Simon?" she asked.

"Wounded but not badly."

Good, Maya thought. So much tragedy in Caxton, but finally things seemed to be going the right way. She was sorry about Sir John, but like Julian, he had come through in the end. *What they did does matter*, Maya thought, thinking of Rosalind and Sebastian and then the Great Library.

Ariel said, "Also, Earth's Book would like a word with you as soon as you feel up to it."

Maya held her head high. "I feel up to it now. Where is the Book?"

"In Elspeth's office, next to Astrid's. Elspeth is the temporary assistant director."

"Is Elspeth in her office?"

"She is. And she's not with anyone right now."

"Shall we come with you?" Eloise asked.

"No," Maya answered. "I need to talk to them by myself."

Elspeth's door was open, and when she saw Maya standing in the entrance, she said, "Come in." She pointed to a chair across from her. "Please have a seat." Maya sat down.

Earth's Book, open, was waiting on the desk. "Hello, Maya. You seem to be feeling much better."

Maya was still. "I am. Lately, I've been so tired."

Elspeth said. "No wonder."

"No surprise at all," the Book agreed.

Thinking back to how it all started, Maya murmured, "It seems so long ago since Mary slipped you into my bag on that train from New York to Boston."

"A lot has happened," the Book said. "And although we've had some rough patches, it all ended far better than I could have possibly imagined. You did well, Maya. Very well. Mary made the right decision to give me to you."

"Thank you." Feeling tears in her eyes but not wanting to cry, Maya looked down at her hands.

Elspeth's voice was gentle. "It's all right, Maya. You've been through a lot."

Not saying anything, Maya brushed away the tears.

Earth's Book said, "I'll soon be returning to Earth, and I called you here to say goodbye. APO is in hiding, and their Book will be able to help them even though Cinnial is gone. Viola told me how pieces have been gouged out of that Book and then used for devices." Earth's Book made what sounded like a clucking noise. "If APO goes too far, then the Book will be damaged beyond repair. I suppose that would be good for us, but I hate to see any Book disfigured like that, even one of Cinnial's."

Shuddering, Maya imagined that the cover was similar to a turtle's shell. "Terrible." Then came the question, "What happened to Cinnial's own Book? And Julian's?"

Elspeth answered, "We have put them in a lockbox that stops them from giving and receiving information." She sighed. "We are hoping someday they might be rehabilitated, but I don't have any great hope that will happen. At least not in my lifetime."

As Maya shook her head, Earth's Book asked, "Have you decided what you're going to do?"

"I have." And Maya told Elspeth and the Book what she had planned.

"Yes," Elspeth said when Maya was done.

"Excellent," the Book agreed.

In the afternoon, as she had promised, Maya went for a walk with Mémère. Again the relics wanted to come, and again, Maya left them behind. "I have a lot to talk about with Mémère. It needs to be just the two of us. I'll be leaving Ariel behind as well."

The relics did not argue, and Ariel, open on the desk by Maya's bed, made no comment.

For most of the walk, Maya and Mémère were quiet as they took in the loveliness of the shimmering water. Maya noticed that Mémère was wearing her pink sandals, the ones she had worn when she had first gone across the universe with Maya.

Finally, Maya delivered Ariel's news about the Vassalboro Library and the role Pépère had played.

"That's my Roland!" Mémère said happily. "I hope that ratty town manager goes to jail."

"Me, too."

They had finished their walk and were sitting on the rocks. From their vantage point, they could see Watertown across the bay and then by only shifting a little, the Great Library and the little village below that sat slantwise on the hill.

Mémère put her hand on Maya's arm. "I'm guessing no place in the universe is more beautiful than it is here at the Great Library. But I miss my home. I miss Roland and Lily." Mémère smiled a little. "No matter how far I travel, home is best, and I'm ready to go back to Vassalboro. What about you, sweetheart?" Shaking her head, Maya began to cry, and Mémère drew her close. "I know. I know. But I was hoping it would be otherwise." Maya cried, leaning against her grandmother, who wiped away her own tears. "You'll at least be coming home for a little while to tell your mother what you're going to do, won't you?"

"Yes," Maya managed to say.

Mémère had tissues in her pocket—somehow she always did—and she handed some to Maya, who stopped crying, wiped her face, and blew her nose. "What about the others?" Mémère asked.

"I don't know. Somehow, I just haven't been able to talk about it with them."

"Understandable," came Mémère's brisk reply. "But it's time."

Maya knew Mémère was right. It was time. Squeezing her arm and kissing her on the cheek, Mémère left, but Maya stayed where she was, watching the tide come in, lapping against the causeway but not covering it.

After a while, Will joined her. "Is it all right if I sit down?"

"Of course it is."

He settled beside Maya. "Lately it seems as though you've wanted to be alone. You haven't been your usual chatty self."

"I know. And you've been pretty quiet, too."

Will looked out to sea. Then he turned to Maya, and she caught how alone and lost he felt. "I've been thinking about what to do next."

Maya smiled a little. "The universe is your oyster."

"But I don't know the universe. I know New York City ten years ago. A little bit about Elferterre." There was a pause. "And the Great Library."

Lexie and Jay came next. There was no school that day, and they had stayed at the Great Library. Lexie sat beside Maya and Jay next to Will.

Jay tilted his head as he looked at Maya and Will. "Looks like there's a serious discussion going on here."

"Yeah," Maya replied.

Lexie came right to the point. "What is Will going to do now that his family thinks he's dead? What are Jay and I going to do? We can't just waltz back and tell everyone what happened. They'd think we were nuts."

"They sure would," Will said.

Maya asked, "What would you like to do?"

Jay ran his hand over the nubbled rock he sat on. "I would like to stay in Watertown and become an assistant music teacher at Isik's school. The magic from the Ancient Oak makes everything wild. I love it. Then, eventually, have my own class."

"Same," Lexie said. "But we're a little young to be assistant teachers. Besides, would the school want us full-time along with Isik? Most schools have limited budgets."

Maya replied, "I bet Astrid or Elspeth could arrange something and help with your salaries. After all..."

"We saved their butts," Lexie finished.

"We saved their butts," Maya agreed, smiling a little, and Will actually laughed.

Jay clapped Will on the shoulder. "What about you?"

Will looked at the Great Library. "I'd like to stay here and become an apprentice. If my Book is accepted, then I'll go on to make other Books. If not, well, then I'll find something else to do. There are plenty of jobs here at the library." His face became still. "If my book isn't chosen, I'm certainly not going to go full-on Cinnial against the Great Library."

"Not your style," Lexie told Will.

Maya said, "Thank goodness."

Will stared at Maya. "And what about you?"

Maya didn't look away. "I want to stay at the Great Library and become an apprentice. Just like you."

Will was quiet.

Jay laughed nervously. "Well, I'm sure you've both passed the audition."

Lexie squinted at Maya and Will. "What's up? There's been a problem between you two ever since Cinnial was trapped in that lock. Will, you wouldn't tell me or Jay what was wrong, no matter how many times we asked. And Maya, until this afternoon, you weren't saying much to anyone. We figured it was better to leave you alone. But now it's time to spill it."

Maya gazed out to sea, and Will studied the Great Library.

"Maya found someone she liked in Elferterre, didn't she?" Lexie asked shrewdly.

Will sighed. "Yeah."

Maya faced her three friends. "I was alone in Elferterre. I didn't know if I'd ever see any of you again or how old you'd all be."

Nobody said anything, not even Lexie. The ocean splashed against the rocks, and gulls cried as they flew overhead.

"You three mean everything to me," Maya said fiercely, and her voice caught at the end. "I don't want to be apart from any of you ever again." She ran one of her hands through her blonde curls with their dark roots. "Don't you see? I can't just go back to my old school and pretend none of this ever happened. I don't belong there anymore." She looked at Jay and Lexie and finally at Will. "I want to be here. With you three."

With a serious expression, Will considered Maya, and she waited nervously for his response. Then nodding, he smiled.

As Jay laughed in relief, Lexie hugged Maya and then Will. "You two are such freaks." She wiped tears from her eyes. "But I'm so glad you'll both be at the Great Library just across from Watertown, where we'll be staying. Probably with Kip and Isik. At least at first." She gave Jay a look. "I get the guest bedroom. You can sleep in the attic."

"Always thinking of others," Jay replied, but there was a sparkle in his eyes, and he grinned.

"What's going on here?" Robbie's voice called. He, Viola, and Wren were making their way to the rocks where Maya, Will, Jay, and Lexie were sitting.

"Did Mémère send you?" Maya asked.

"Aye," Robbie answered. "She sent us all, didn't she? Good thing I was in a field by the library, and it wasn't hard for her to find me." Although his face and hands were clean, Robbie's overalls were covered with dirt. Viola and Wren, in white shirts and black pants, were cleaner and more composed.

"So what have you all decided?" Robbie asked.

Maya told him, Viola, and Wren what their plans were.

Viola said, "Good. I was hoping that's what you'd do. You all belong here."

"What about you?" Maya asked Viola.

"With Earth's Book of Everything, I'm going back to Aarde, to pick up my father and Diana. Astrid will let us borrow an Apprentice Book for Diana. After that to Bar Harbor, to Mom." Viola grimaced. "She needs to know what's happened."

"And then?"

Viola looked at the sea and then at the Great Library. "This place is fantastic. But I'm not ready to leave my parents yet. I belong on Earth with them."

"I understand," Maya said in a soft voice. With a pang, she realized how much she was going to miss Andy's daughter.

"Wren?" Will asked.

"I'm staying here." Wren shrugged. "My parents are dead. And my aunt, well, she has her own life." With bright eyes, she gazed at the Great Library. "I just want to be at a place with so many books that they can hardly be counted. I'm not even sure I want to work on an Apprentice Book." Her voice rang loud and clear. "What I want is to be a librarian."

Laughing, Lexie patted Wren's back. "Well, Wren, you are in exactly the right place for that."

Last was Robbie. "I'm going to stay here for a while and work in the gardens. I'll probably bunk with Jay in the attic room at Kip and Isik's home," he said comfortably, and Maya got the impression the blond boy would feel at home no matter where he was. "Kip and the other gardeners have so much to teach me." He winked. "And I know a thing or two about horses. Then after that? Who knows? But I'll go back to the Forest of Arden from time to time to see my parents and the rest of my family. Elspeth said there are plenty of Apprentice Books to borrow for a quick trip and back."

They talked for a while and then the lunch bell rang. Robbie stood up and patted his stomach. "Don't want to miss my meal. There's still plenty to do in the gardens."

Wren and Viola stood, too, and followed him to the Great Library. Viola looked back once, and Maya could tell she would miss everyone at the Great Library. Especially Maya.

Lexie nudged Jay. "You must be ready for lunch."

"Always am," Jay replied with a laugh, and they left Maya and Will.

"Are you coming in for lunch?" Will asked.

"No, I'm not hungry."

Will got up. "I understand. For me, it's easier to stay. I can't go back to my family."

"I'm so sorry, Will."

"Yeah, well, my family was never as close as yours is."

Maya frowned. "My father's no picnic."

Will put his hand on her shoulder. "No family is perfect, is it?"

"I suppose not."

He turned to leave but stopped. "Maya?"

"Yes?"

"I'm glad you're staying. It wouldn't be right here without you." Then Will left quickly, not looking back.

Smiling, Maya hugged her knees as she stared out to sea. The autumn sun was low in the sky, but somehow it felt as warm as a summer's day. Her stomach rumbled, and Maya realized that she wanted lunch after all. Standing quickly, Maya felt a little dizzy, and she needed a few moments to regain her balance.

Relieved to see that Will was still in earshot, Maya called, "Will, wait for me!"

And stopping, Will waited.

CAST OF CHARACTERS

From Planet Earth

Maya Hammond: The girl from New York who sets the story in motion when on a train to Maine, she gains possession of Earth's Book of Everything.

Will Henley: The boy Maya meets at the Little Bard Theater in Brooklyn when she goes back in time ten years into her past. They fall in love, and Will becomes one of her companions when they travel to Elferterre.

Jay Valdez: Also from the Little Bard Theater. Will's friend and a talented musician. He, too, goes to Elferterre.

Lexie (Alexis) Norton: From the Little Bard Theater. Initially, Lexie is Maya's rival for Will's affections, but eventually they become friends, and she also goes to Elferterre.

Drew (Andrew) Murphy: President of the United States, but Maya first met Drew when he was a poor boy in Waterville, Maine. In *Maya and the Book of Everything*, he went with her across the universe to the duchy of Caxton on the planet Ilyria.

Viola Murphy: Drew Murphy's daughter who becomes Maya's friend and then gets involved with the battle between Time and Chaos. In *Library Lost*, she traveled with Maya to Caxton.

Diana Wagner: A former CIA agent who helps President Murphy.

Mémère (Celine Turcotte): Maya's grandmother. In *Library Lost,* she traveled with Maya to Caxton and subdued Chet Addington by clunking him on the head with a small log.

Jeff Perry: A librarian from Waterville, Maine, whose greed impels him to get involved with APO, the shadowy organization that works against Earth's Book of Everything.

Chet Addington: A tracker from APO. A remorseless killer, Chet's obsession is to steal Earth's Book of Everything. At the end of *Maya and the Book of Everything*, Maya brought him to Caxton, where he was imprisoned and then eventually escaped.

From Elferterre

Pawel Greenwood: An elf from Elferterre who has been exiled to Earth. He and his family own The Other Green Door, a café in Brooklyn, New York. Pawel set Maya and her friends on their mission to Elferterre, to steal a key—to unlock his chains—and a lock to trap Cinnial.

Khirra Greenwood: Pawel's wife, also in exile.

Thirret Greenwood: Pawel's son, also in exile.

Hanss: A cat in Elferterre. He is Thirret's friend, and he helps Maya, Will, Jay, and Lexie when they cross over from Earth to Elferterre.

Jace (Jacinda) Willowdale: Pawel and Khirra's niece who came with them from Elferterre to Brooklyn.

Dagan Willowdale: Pawel and Khirra's nephew. Jace's brother. He, too, came from Elferterre to Brooklyn.

Lillian (Pineglade) Rourke: An elf living in Brooklyn. She works for APO.

Orlaith: A spider relic from Elferterre.

Aiken: A dragon relic from Elferterre.

Eloise: A lioness relic from Elferterre.

Captain Christophe Blythewood: Commander of the ship *The Resolute*.

Clarin Blythewood: Captain Blythewood's daughter.

Cali: A sea beast who's devoted to Captain Blythewood.

Chantay: The figurehead on Captain Blythewood's ship *The Resolute*.

Azal Hawthorn: An elf and *The Resolute*'s first mate.

Braird Hawthorn: Azal's son and a corbeau—part bird, part elf.

Hannie Snowrunner: An elf from the cold lands. Chief Magic Engineer on *The Resolute*.

Larz Snowrunner: *The Resolute*'s Assistant Magic Engineer and Hannie's nephew.

Zeynip Lakewood: A castor and the bosun on *The Resolute*.

Proko Branch: A castor and bosun mate.

Takis Branch: A castor and bosun mate.

Symi Larchgrove: An elf and cook on *The Resolute*.

Ali Lilywater: A grenog and assistant cook on *The Resolute*.

Finneas Watermoss: A grenog and Captain Blythewood's personal assistant.

Rhye Ashglade: An elf and captain of the submarine *The Cuttlefish*. Tamick Ashglade's nephew.

Tamick Ashglade: The elf who plotted against Pawel Greenwood and his family and sent them into exile.

From the Great Library

Ariel: The Assistant Book from the Great Library who becomes Maya's devoted companion.

Sydda Guptel: Director of the Great Library and murdered by Cinnial in *Library Lost*.

Astrid Guptel: Sydda's wife, Assistant Director of the Great Library who becomes the leader of the exiled librarians.

Elspeth Jortensen: Roving ambassador for the Great Library. In exile with Astrid.

Alani and Alexander: Two librarians who helped Maya in Brooklyn in *Out of Time*.

From Caxton

Owen Warwick: Duke of Caxton who was murdered by Chet in *Library Lost*.

Rosalind & Sebastian Warwick: Owen's children who are in hiding in the Forest of Arden.

Humphrey Warwick: Owen's brother. Humphrey staged a coup and took over the Duchy of Caxton from Owen.

Sir John Oldcastle: A knight who serves Owen and has a complicated history with him.

Simon Forster: A boy from the village of Greendale who helped Rosalind & Sebastian escape their murderous Uncle Humphrey in *Library Lost*.

Elwyn & Sophie Brooks: Stewards of the lodge in the Forest of Arden.

Robbie Herbert: A boy from the forest of Arden who befriends Viola.

From Planet Tufrak

Cinnial: Former Apprentice at the Great Library. When his Book was rejected, he fled the Great Library. He set up headquarters in the city of Mortmain on Tufrak, where he plotted to take over the Great Library.

Julian Jortensen: Cinnial's devoted friend who fled with him to Tufrak.

Bigly: A troll and Cinnial's personal assistant. Bigly captured and tortured Maya in *Library Lost*.

From Planet Aarde

Wren (Elowren) Joss: An orphan who becomes Viola's companion.

Ensante Madeleine: Headmistress of Chêne Grove Academy.

From Planet Bellefour (The Great Library's Planet)

Kip (Christopher) Tamarant: Gardener at the Great Library.

Isik Messun: Music teacher in a school in Watertown, a small city across the bay from the Great Library.

AUTHOR'S NOTE

Blending Fantasy with Reality and Reality with Fantasy

Most books, no matter how realistic, contain elements of fantasy. Stories that deal with everyday life might not have magic or wizards or witches, but they certainly fit one of *Merriam-Webster*'s definitions of fantasy: "[T]he free play of creative imagination." Whatever the genre, characters are created, dialogue is invented, and settings are conceived. The better the creative imagination, the more vivid the story and the characters.

The reverse is also true. No matter how fantastical a book might be, there are usually elements of realism to ground the story, to balance the unfamiliar with the familiar. In *The Hobbit* and *The Lord of the Rings*, the Shire was a direct reflection of the English countryside, with Bilbo and Frodo Baggins being country squires. Both the Shire and the hobbits are solid representations in a world filled with magic, elves, and orcs.

All of my novels, from *Maya and the Book of Everything* to *Of Time and Magic*, blend fantasy with reality and reality with fantasy.

Here is one example from *Of Time and Magic* where I combine magic with realism: There is a scene at the Great Library—the mystical place at the center of our universe—that involves a potato harvest. To uncover potatoes, horses pull a digger in the fields. Area schools give students a potato recess of two weeks so that they can help with the harvest at the Great Library and in the surrounding countryside across the bay from the library. It's a big deal for the students as it lets them earn money for clothes and treats. Picking potatoes is also essential to my plot. It allows three of my teenage characters—Viola, Wren, and Robbie—to be at the Great Library without arousing the suspicions of Cinnial's staff.

Where did I come up with this idea? Did it come to me from out of the blue when I was taking a shower? It did not. My great-grandparents were potato farmers in northern Maine, and in their early days of farming, they must have used equipment very similar to what I describe in *Of Time and Magic*. (Eventually, tractors would replace horses in Maine.) In addition, I have friends from northern Maine who picked potatoes during potato recess. It was hard, dirty work, but my friends certainly appreciated making the extra money. Because I am from Maine, potatoes are a big part of my culture, even though I didn't grow up in an area that gave students a two-week potato recess. Therefore, it seemed perfectly natural to include a potato harvest in *Out of Time* even though it's a fantasy novel.

Now for blending realism with magic. In *Of Time and Magic's* first chapter, I have three teenage characters—Will, Jay, and Lexie—go through a portal in Elferterre and find themselves in a janitor's closet at the service plaza in Kennebunk, Maine. While the plaza actually exists, readers will not be surprised to learn it does not have a magical portal. (At least I think it doesn't.) I also took liberties with where the bathrooms were and their relationship to the janitor's closet. However, most of what I describe, right down to the food court, matches what is actually at the plaza.

For me, mixing fantasy with reality and reality with fantasy is a great pleasure. The fantasy gives my stories a symbolic zing, and the realism gives them an earthy tone that most people can relate to.